Welles-Turner Memorial Library
Glastonbury, Connecticut 06033

Cornelia H. Nearing
Memorial Collection

Cornelia H. Nearing (1871-1959) was a fine artist
and a great citizen of Glastonbury. She loved and
used our library and was a great believer in
sharing resources. The citizens of Glastonbury
continue to enjoy the benefits of her generosity
through an endowment she established for the
library. It is from those resources that this book
has been purchased for your use and enjoyment.

Welles ➤ Turner
MEMORIAL LIBRARY

THE GIRL FROM BERLIN

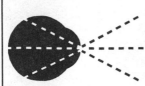

This Large Print Book carries the
Seal of Approval of N.A.V.H.

THE GIRL FROM BERLIN

RONALD H. BALSON

THORNDIKE PRESS
A part of Gale, a Cengage Company

Farmington Hills, Mich • San Francisco • New York • Waterville, Maine
Meriden, Conn • Mason, Ohio • Chicago

Copyright © 2018 by Ronald H. Balson.
Thorndike Press, a part of Gale, a Cengage Company.

ALL RIGHTS RESERVED
This is a work of fiction. All of the characters, organizations, and events portrayed in this novel are either products of the author's imagination or are used fictitiously.
Thorndike Press® Large Print Basic.
The text of this Large Print edition is unabridged.
Other aspects of the book may vary from the original edition.
Set in 16 pt. Plantin.

**LIBRARY OF CONGRESS CIP DATA ON FILE.
CATALOGUING IN PUBLICATION FOR THIS BOOK
IS AVAILABLE FROM THE LIBRARY OF CONGRESS**

ISBN-13: 978-1-4328-5913-8 (hardcover)

Published in 2019 by arrangement with Macmillan Publishing Group, LLC/St. Martin's Press

Printed in the United States of America
1 2 3 4 5 6 7 23 22 21 20 19

In loving memory of Sara Titlebaum, a gifted concert pianist and teacher, who soloed with the Detroit Symphony Orchestra, and from whom I inherited my love of opera.

And to my wife, Monica, for more reasons than I can count.

ACKNOWLEDGMENTS

The Girl from Berlin is a work of historical fiction. The principal characters portrayed herein are imaginary and do not refer to any actual person, living or dead. Ada, her family, her friends and acquaintances are fictitious. Individual players in the orchestras, judges, lawyers and city officials are fictional representations. The Berlin Junior Orchestra and conductor Dr. Kritzer are also fictitious, but symbolic of youth orchestras in Germany during the era.

The Bologna State Opera is widely recognized as a magnificent and accomplished opera company, though I have chosen to create a fictional music director, Stefano Vittorio, to more easily suit the story. The Berlin Philharmonic Orchestra is and has been one of the world's finest symphony orchestras. Wilhelm Furtwängler was its principal conductor from 1922 to 1945, and from 1952 until his death in 1954. His reputation and his accomplishments during the time in question are portrayed as accurately as possible. He did indeed stand up to Hitler and Goebbels. The public quotes attributed to him in which he criticized Hitler and the Nazi regime are true. The episodes regarding the Mannheim Concert, the Hindemith Case, his negotiations with the New York Philharmonic and his interactions and compromises with Goebbels are true. He was sympathetic and was deeply affected by the events of *Kristallnacht.* He did his best to protect his Jewish members and sought to keep the music of Jewish composers alive at the Philharmonie during a time when the Nazi government declared them to be degenerate. He was treated unfairly after the war by those who thought he should have left Germany and turned his back on his orchestra.

Sister Maria Alicia and her Christmas concert series is fictitious, but the Italian operatic stars were real. Beniamino Gigli, *Caruso Secondo,* was one of the finest Italian tenors who ever lived. The plaza in front of the Rome Opera House, Teatro dell'Opera di Roma, is named for him, Piazza Beniamino Gigli. Bernardino Molinari was the conductor of the Rome orchestra, l'Orchestra dell'Accademia Nazionale di Santa Cecilia, between 1912 and 1944.

Rafael Schächter was a Czechoslovak composer and a true hero. He was sent to the Theresienstadt Concentration Camp where

8

he organized and trained fellow prisoners as singers and musicians. They practiced in the basement under brutal conditions and performed the difficult Verdi *Requiem* for the International Red Cross when the camp was inspected in 1944. In the fall of 1944, he was sent to Auschwitz as set out in the narration. He died while on the Auschwitz death march in 1945.

Brigadeführer Reinhard Heydrich, one of history's most malevolent men, was second only to Heinrich Himmler in the SS. It was Heydrich who ordered the arrests of thirty thousand Jewish men during *Kristallnacht.* Heydrich also convened the Wannsee Conference in 1942 in order to implement the Final Solution to kill Europe's Jews. As noted in the story, he was in fact an accomplished violinist and a lover of music. His father was a composer. Heydrich was ambushed by Czech freedom fighters on May 27, 1942, and died of his wounds days later.

Commandant Karl Rahm and Waffen-SS Colonel Hollman were actual persons. Herbert Kleiner was fictitious, but his character was in large part based upon SS-Sturmbannführer Herbert Kappler, one o the most brutal Nazi killers. It was Kapp who operated out of the Via Tasso as hea security forces in Rome. He imposed th of 110 pounds of gold upon the Rom ish community and personally super roundup of Roman Jews in October 1943. He was also responsible and personally participated in the massacre of 335 Jews who were marched into the caves of Ardeatine with their hands tied behind their backs and shot to death, most times with a single bullet to the head. After the war, he was tried, convicted and sentenced to life imprisonment by an Italian court. Dying of cancer, he escaped from a military hospital in 1976 and died of his illness soon thereafter.

The system for land recordation in Italy is somewhat confusing in comparison to the American system. I have tried to simplify it in order to tell the story. Beginning in the 1990s Italy's land registry system began the conversion to computerization and was at various times thereafter searchable online. Beginning in 2012, deeds were filed online in a digital format, so that VinCo's deed in 2015 would likely have been filed online. The project to convert all handwritten paper archives to digital format is ongoing. For the purposes of this story, I have assumed that the paper archives covering the Villa Vincenzo property had not yet been digitized, were not searchable online and that the only practical way to determine land ownership was by reference to the handwritten registry books. Further, though the handwritten entries of a transaction may be contained in more registry book, I have often referred to them in a single book for simplicity's sake.

I have received wonderful help and encouragement during the research and writing of this book. I have had access to a wealth of information and material from several institutions and I am grateful for the assistance of their staffs: the Jewish Museum Berlin, the German Historical Museum, the Philharmonie, the Teatro Comunale di Bologna, the Illinois Holocaust Museum and Educational Center and in particular, Yad Vashem, whose archives hold thousands of personal histories, including those of Italian Jewish survivors. I am also indebted to those historians who spent time with us and took us from site to site, providing first-hand knowledge. Isabel Bahiana Wotzasek was a well-spring of historical information and insight about Berlin and Germany. She dauntlessly guided us to historical sites throughout the city despite the persistence of a driving rainstorm. In Bologna, we were lucky to meet Micol Mazzeo and tap into her knowledge of the Ghetto Ebraico and the history of the Portico City. Finally, it is astonishing to me how much information is available on YouTube. I have watched Maestro Furtwängler conduct Beethoven, Maestro Molinari conduct Paganini, Beniamino Gigli sing Bizet arias, and I have sat in virtual attendance at several master violin classes taught by Jascha Heifetz.

11

Once again, thanks to my supportive group at St. Martin's Press: my editor, Jennifer Weis, my publicist, Staci Burt, Brant Janeway and Sylvan Creekmore. Thanks to Martha Cameron, for her talented and insightful copyediting.

As always, my heartfelt thanks to my cadre of readers and their invaluable advice: Rose McGowan, Cindy Pogrund, David Pogrund, Linda Waldman, Richard Templer, Katie Lang Lawrence and Benjamin Balson. And my deepest gratitude to my patient and tireless wife, Monica, who read each of the pages as they were written. She must have read and edited the story a thousand times and always stayed upbeat, positive and encouraging.

ONE

Pienza, Italy, July 2017
The silver Alfa Romeo kicked up a tail of dust as it traveled the road between Montalcino and Montepulciano. The brilliant afternoon sun baked the rolling landscape of the Tuscan hills and forced Lorenzo to squint. It had been hot and dry for the past ten days, and in the struggle for Lorenzo's comfort, the Alfa's air conditioning was inadequate.

He stopped briefly in the little town of Pienza for a cold soda before heading south into the countryside. To be frank, the weather wasn't the only unpleasant aspect to this day's assignment. On the passenger seat, in his attaché case, lay a court order. Lorenzo Lenzini, *Avvocato,* was headed to the Villa Vincenzo to serve an eviction.

It wasn't that he minded dispossessing a resident, goodness knows he'd done that a thousand times. And it wasn't that she was elderly and in failing health, for Lorenzo had no feelings for her one way or another. It was the universal support that this perverse woman had somehow managed to rally from the local populace that unsettled him. His obligations to his client had backed him into a corner. Now he was forced to play the role of a heartless villain, and while it didn't bother him personally, he felt sure it would affect him professionally in the province of Siena.

The old stone villa was perched on a pleasant hill above groves of olive trees and rows of grapevines heavily laden with the season's crop. Well-tended flower gardens lined the perimeter of the structure. The villa was typical of Tuscan architecture — oatmeal-colored stone exterior, seasoned oak beams beneath a roof of overlapping terracotta half-pipes, flower boxes under the windows — all in the Etruscan fashion. To Lorenzo's way of thinking, nothing exceptional. Seen one, you've seen them all.

The lawyer parked his car, grabbed his attaché case, placed his Borselino panama hat squarely on his head, straightened the lapels of his cream-colored suit, puffed his chest out and strode purposefully up the stairs of the veranda and directly to the villa's front door, there to confront the intransigent Signora Vincenzo. Before knocking, he paused to take in the surrounding landscape, the green and cappuccino pastels of the richest vineyards in the world. In all directions, as far as he could see, the land was owned by his client, VinCo S.p.A., one of Italy's largest wine producers. In all directions, that is, except for the land he was standing on.

Villa Vincenzo was a rogue island in the sea of VinCo's vineyards. A trespasser. Lorenzo, on behalf of his client, had tried for months to persuade Signora Vincenzo to sell. It was an inconvenience for his client to farm around this obtrusive appendage. Villa Vincenzo was an aberration in the midst of VinCo's perfectly contiguous rows of Sangiovese, merlot and cabernet. It was a break in symmetry. It had to go.

Lorenzo had conveyed VinCo's offers to Signora Vincenzo on a dozen occasions, and they were more than fair — a cost-free relocation to a lovely rental home in the village and a cash bonus. She was foolish to turn them down. In truth, VinCo didn't have to offer a damn thing. VinCo owned the land.

It seemed to Lorenzo that Signora Vincenzo had some unnatural and unreasonable attachment to the property. How could this commonplace parcel of property have such a strong hold on such a sick old lady? She wouldn't take the offer, so now she'd forced his hand. The legal steps had all been taken, the court order had been issued, and the obstinate Signora Vincenzo would have sixty days to vacate. Sorry, but that's the way it goes.

Lorenzo gritted his teeth and knocked on the door. A young woman, whom Lorenzo knew to be Signora Vincenzo's equally obstinate nurse, answered. "What is it this time, Mr. Lenzini?"

"Please summon Signora Vincenzo to the door. I have a document to hand to her."

"I'll do no such thing. She has told you and your soulless client that she will never sell. This is her land. She has lived here for years. Now be gone."

Lorenzo rattled the eviction order in the face of the young woman. "Not so fast, *Signorina,*" he barked, sternly and loudly. "This is a court order. Now it is *you* who will be gone. Signora Vincenzo must surrender possession within sixty days, or I will have the pleasure of watching the *polizia* toss the two of you out."

From inside the house, a raspy voice cried out, "Va via! Va via!" Gabriella Vincenzo, on unsteady legs, made her way to the front door. Age had bowed her back as though her head had become too heavy. Despite the pains she suffered in every joint, she waved her cane as menacingly as she could. "Get out. Get out! Get off my land!"

Lorenzo took a step back. With a shaking hand, he held the eviction order front and center. "You have sixty days, Signora Vincenzo. Sixty days and no more." Then he threw the order on the floor and beat a hasty retreat to his car. As he left, the young nurse consoled her *patrona,* who wept on her shoulder.

Two

Chicago, July 2017

"Tell me again why we're having dinner at Café Sorrento tonight," Catherine said.

Liam parked alongside the curb and handed his keys to the valet. "Because we love the food."

Catherine raised a single eyebrow. "We do. But an urgent afternoon phone call asking me to get a babysitter at the last minute on a Thursday night means something more than 'I'm dying for a plate of Tony's veal parmesan.' Fess up. What's going on?"

Liam smiled at his perceptive wife. "Tony called me this afternoon. He sounded troubled. He asked if we could come over and be his guests for dinner tonight. *Pleaded* would be more like it."

"Troubled? That's all he said?"

"Well, he didn't *say* troubled. That's how he sounded. What he said was, 'I have a small legal matter to discuss.' "

Catherine groaned. "Liam, you should have

18

told him to make an appointment at the office, where it's quiet, confidential and uninterrupted. This packed restaurant is no place to conduct a client interview."

"He said it was a small matter. What if it's just a parking ticket or some simple licensing issue? Maybe the city's hassling him. You know, he practically lives in this restaurant. He's here fifteen hours a day. It's hard for him to come to your office."

Café Sorrento was indeed packed. There was a line at the hostess stand and several patrons were standing at the bar and in the entryway waiting to be seated. No sooner had Catherine and Liam squeezed their way through the door, then the stocky restauranteur in his three-piece suit hurried over to greet them. He warmly kissed Catherine on each cheek and vigorously shook Liam's hand.

"*Buonasera, buonasera, miei cari amici,*" Tony Vincenzo said. "*Grazie per la venuta.* Thank you so much for coming." He opened his palm and gestured toward a booth in the corner. "*Prego,*" he said, walking briskly through his restaurant. A small bouquet and an open bottle of wine were already on the table. A server promptly appeared with menus, but Tony waved her away. "No menus tonight. These are my dear friends and I have planned a very special dinner."

Midway through the meal, Catherine leaned

over and quietly said, "Liam, this dinner is over the top. We've had bruschetta, minestrone, gnocchi with veal ragout and Lord knows what he's bringing for the main course. It makes me feel that this 'small legal matter' might not be so small after all. If there's any equivalency, we're likely headed for complex litigation."

It was almost ten o'clock, after servings of grilled branzino, pecan gelato and a tray of cookies with coffee, and after the restaurant had nearly emptied, when Tony reappeared at the table carrying a briefcase. He slid into the booth and said, "Did you get enough to eat?"

"I can't move," Liam said.

"It was wonderful," Catherine said.

Tony opened his case, took out a stack of papers and laid them on the table. He looked at Catherine. "Did Liam tell you that I have a very serious legal matter?"

She gave Liam a quick evil eye and then nodded. "Yes, he did, but he used a different adjective."

Tony leaned back in the booth and spoke expressively, using his hands and arms for emphasis. "I have an aunt Gabi back in Italy. Such a sweet lady. A widow. Heart of gold. But, sorry to say, not too healthy these days. Everyone loves her. You talk to anybody, they love her."

Liam spread his hands. "And?"

Tony leaned forward. "So, some rotten bastard is trying to throw her out of her house. Can you imagine that? A seventy-eight-year-old woman, never hurt a single person, and she's not well. She can hardly walk." Tony dabbed at his eyes. "And now this *stronzo,* this asshole, wants to throw her out of the house that she's lived in for as long as I can remember. He's given her sixty days."

"How does this man claim rights to her property?" Catherine said.

"It's not just this man. If it was just him, I'd take care of it. Believe me, I wouldn't need a lawyer and a private detective. No, he's an attorney and he represents a big company, VinCo. Big-deal wine producer. They say VinCo holds the deed to her property."

"Did Aunt Gabi sign a deed? Did she transfer her rights?"

"Never. My aunt Gabi may be physically disabled, but mentally she's sharp as a tack. She tells me she has good title to her land. If she says it, it's so."

Tony had the dishes cleared and then rolled out a survey. "Here's her land. She calls it Villa Vincenzo. Such a sweetheart." In the middle of the survey he drew a circle with his finger. "This part, these seventy acres, are hers. She has olive trees, vineyards and vegetables. The best vegetables. Zucchini like you've never seen. I wish I could get 'em in

21

Chicago." Then Tony circled his finger around the rest of the survey. "All the rest of this land surrounding Aunt Gabi's little piece, it all belongs to VinCo. That's why they hate her. She's a pimple on their ass. They can't stand that they don't own her little piece. They've been pestering her for months to buy her out. But she's been firm, God bless her. And now they have some slimy lawyer trying to figure out a way to steal it from her."

"Has she hired a lawyer?"

Tony nodded. "Two of them. One in her little town of Pienza and one from Siena. Cost me plenty."

"Can't they help her?"

Tony shook his head. "They say that VinCo has better title than Aunt Gabi."

"How can that be?" Liam said.

Tony shrugged. He gestured to the stack of documents. "They sent me these papers."

Catherine thumbed through the documents. "They're all in Italian. What do they say?"

"A lot of words that don't mean much to me. I can't make any sense out of this. But you, Catherine, you're the best lawyer in Chicago. Maybe the whole country."

Catherine smiled. "I appreciate your confidence, but I don't practice in Italy. I'm not familiar with Italian law, I'm not licensed to practice there and I don't even speak the language. You need an Italian lawyer."

"I told you, I've hired two of them. They both say the same thing — VinCo is the legal title holder and Aunt Gabi has to move. You want my opinion? VinCo paid them off."

"I can't read these papers, Tony."

"I'll get them translated for you. Would you go over there and straighten this out? You could talk to these lawyers. Italian, English, it doesn't matter. You all speak legalese. Would you go help my aunt? You'd love her."

Catherine sighed. "Have the documents translated and delivered to my office. I'll review them and try to give you my opinion. No promises."

Tony leaned over, cupped Catherine's face and kissed her. "*Grazie, grazie.* And then you'll go over there and stop them from evicting Aunt Gabi?"

"I didn't say that. First things first, Tony. Let me read through the papers, try to figure out what's going on and then we'll talk."

"*Fantastico.*" He turned to his bartender. "Franco, three glasses of limoncello."

Catherine Lockhart's law office was situated in a storefront building on Clark Street in Chicago's Lincoln Park neighborhood. Catherine had been a solo practitioner in that location for five years, enjoying a comfortable neighborhood practice, in contrast to the pressured life she had previously endured as an associate lawyer with the downtown firm of Jenkins and Fairchild. It was during the case of *Solomon v. Rosenzweig* that Walter Jenkins had given her an ultimatum — drop Ben Solomon as a client or leave the firm. She chose the latter and has never looked back.

Tony Vincenzo entered her office early Tuesday morning and was greeted by Catherine's receptionist. She walked him back to the conference room where Catherine and Liam were waiting.

"I hope you have good news for me," Tony said.

Catherine shook her head. "The records are not as complete as I would like, but from what I can see, it looks like the Italian lawyers were right. VinCo purchased the Villa Vincenzo property, all seventy acres of it, from a decedent's estate in 2015. The deed was accepted by the province of Siena and recorded."

"What estate? My aunt is alive. How could there be a decedent's estate? Whose estate?"

"The deed came from the administrator of the estate of Gerda Fruman, a German citizen. She was the sole owner of Quercia Company, the corporation that owned the land. I have a copy of the administrator's deed. It was filed online."

"This has got to be a mistake. I never heard of Gerda Fruman. Or Quercia. I've been to Pienza many times, I've stayed at my aunt's villa for weeks at a time, and take my word for it, there's never been any Gerda Fruman. You gotta clear this up for me."

Catherine reached into the stack of papers and withdrew a court order. "This order, the one Attorney Lenzini dropped at Gabi's house, grants possession to VinCo on September 10. It was issued by a judge after a hearing. The order recites that neither your aunt nor her lawyer came to court. They didn't show up."

"Okay, that's the reason then. She probably fired the last lawyer. He told her she didn't have a good case. My aunt can be stubborn."

Catherine shook her head. "The judge ruled that your aunt's title to the land was not valid. It was outside the chain."

"The chain? What chain? What does that mean?"

"The chain of title, Tony. How the property passes from one owner to another. When you look at the history of the property in the official records, it shows each time it was deeded from one person to another. The judge ruled that your aunt got a deed from someone who didn't own the property."

"When was this? Who did she buy the property from who supposedly didn't own it?"

"In 1995, Carlo Vanucci deeded the property to Gabriella Vincenzo and it was recorded."

"Well, okay then, it was recorded before 2015 when VinCo got a deed."

Catherine shrugged. "I know, but the court ruled that Vanucci didn't own the property. If Italy is like the U.S., the registrar's office will accept anything you give them to record, as long as it correctly identifies the land. It's not the registrar's job to determine if a deed is valid — he just records it as a document. If someone claims it's invalid, it is up to a court to decide. From what I see here, a judge examined the chain of title and came to the conclusion that Gabriella's deed was *not* valid and that the deed from Fruman's estate to VinCo *was* valid."

Tony stood. He paced the room. "Something's wrong. This is a fraud. My aunt has lived there for years. I've been going there for fifty years, since I was a boy. There's no such person as Gerda Fruman. I never heard of no company named Quercia whatever. Can't you see? VinCo's paying off everyone. They made up this Fruman estate. Holy Mother of God, this is going to kill my aunt Gabi. She can't be evicted from her home. You gotta help me. You gotta go there and stop this."

"I don't know what we can do in Italy," Liam said. "You heard her, Catherine's not an Italian lawyer. If you're going to attack this order, you need to do it through a lawyer who practices in the province of Siena."

"I've had two of them. They both sided with VinCo."

"Maybe they're right, Tony. Maybe Aunt Gabi's title is defective."

"I don't buy it. Liam, I know you for years and you can trust me when I tell you this — it stinks like a dead fish. Please, go there and see if there's something you can do for my aunt. Catherine may not be licensed in Italy, but she has a sharp mind. She can figure things out. And you, you can find out who the hell this Quercia is. I'll pay all the costs, I'll pay Catherine's attorney's fees and you two can stay at the villa. Worst comes to worst, you got a couple weeks in Tuscany. Is that so bad?"

"It's very tempting," Catherine said, "but I'm pretty sure you'd be wasting your money."

"It's my money. So let me waste it a little and try to help my aunt."

Catherine and Liam looked at each other. They shrugged. They tilted their heads. They pursed their lips. "Give us a minute," she said. Once outside the room she whispered to Liam, "Do you really want to do this? It's a wild goose chase."

He nodded. "I do. I want to give it a shot. Tony and I go back a long way. I feel like we might dig something up. This could be a scam. And like he says, we'd have a couple of weeks in Tuscany. That's not so hard to take."

"What about the baby?"

"What about him? We'll take him. He loves Italian food."

"No. That's a terrible idea. Let me talk to Sarah and see if she can stay."

"You'll go?"

"I feel like I'm being selfish here. You and I haven't been away since Belfast, and that was hardly a vacation. Like Tony says, 'couple of weeks in Tuscany — is that so bad?' I would go, but I don't have a lot of faith in our ability to resolve this problem."

Tony was waiting at the table, drumming his fingers, when they returned. "So?"

"With the understanding that I may be entirely ineffective," Catherine said, "we'll go. I have some matters that need my attention first and I'll have to juggle my schedule, but we can go in two weeks."

With tears in his eyes, Tony gave them each a hug. "*Grazie.* God bless you. I'll let my aunt know you're coming. That'll lift her spirits for sure."

THREE

Pienza, Italy, July 2017
The Piazza Pio II was alive with the sounds, colors and aromas of its weekly outdoor market. Townsfolk, tourists and the plainly curious arrived from all directions. The brick clock tower of the Palazzo Piccolomini anchored the piazza and threw a long shadow onto the plaza's wide brick expanse. Commissioned and built over five hundred years ago by Pienza's founder, Enea Silvio Piccolomini, the man who would later become Pope Pius II, the piazza overlooked the fertile Tuscan valley, known as the Val d'Orcia. On the left edge of the piazza sat the building that Pope Pius II gave to Cardinal Rodrigo Borgia, who would later become Pope Alexander VI. On the right sat the Duomo. Between the buildings, dozens of portable canopies and folding tables were set up by vendors who trucked in their fruits, vegetables, charcuterie, cheeses, pastries and crafts to sell at the Sunday market.

Gabriella Vincenzo, guided by her nurse, Floria, slowly made her way through the market, sampling a piece of fruit here and there as she bid *buongiorno* to the kiosk owners she had known for so many years. Gabriella was no longer able to navigate the town's stone passageways on her own. Floria guided her wheelchair.

"We'll take one pint of strawberries and a small sack of apricots," she said to a vendor.

He smiled, nodded, bagged up her order and said, "And here's a pint of cherries, Gabi, the end of the season. Sweet, just like you." He handed the bag to Floria. Leaning over his counter, he whispered, "How's that nasty matter with Lenzini working out? Is he going to leave you alone?"

"He should roast in everlasting hell," Gabi answered loudly, clenching her fist. "Would you believe that last week, Lenzini threw a court paper at me, Piero? It orders me to vacate my own house in sixty days."

"How awful for you. I am so sorry. I want you to know that you and Floria have a room at my house whenever you want it. You know there isn't a soul in Pienza who wouldn't make the same offer. And we'd all love to throw Lenzini into the goat pen where he belongs."

"That's very nice of you. I am lucky to have friends. But my nephew Tony in America says he might be able to help. He's friendly with a very sharp lawyer. And she's coming here next week."

Piero smiled. "Is she *Italiana*?"

Gabi shook her head and winked. "No, and that's a good thing. VinCo and Lenzini can't buy her off. Tony says she looked at the papers and figured out the reasons that the judge ruled against me."

"Why was that?"

Gabi shrugged. "She says the judge found my title to be 'outside the chain' or something like that."

Piero nodded his understanding. "When did you get your title to the property?"

"Twenty-two years ago, way before VinCo. What does that have to do with a chain?"

"It means that the judge thinks that when you got your deed, it didn't come from the owner."

"It most certainly did, and I know that for a fact."

Piero shrugged. "Well, your American lawyer's going to have to convince the judge. Sometimes these title issues are hard to figure out. May God's graces fall upon that *avvocata*. She's going to need a lot of help."

Gabi raised her eyes to the heavens and nodded. Then, turning to Floria, she said, "I have an idea. You know those papers I keep in the leather portfolio? The one locked in the cabinet by my bed?"

Floria nodded. "Ada's story?"

31

"Right. Take it to Mr. Campagna in Siena and have it translated from German to English. I want to ship it to my nephew right away."

Floria wrinkled her forehead. "But, signora, it is a very long story, written many years ago. I know Tony. He's not the reading type."

"It's not for Tony, it's for the woman lawyer."

Floria smiled. "Very wise, signora."

FOUR

Chicago, July 2017

Liam stood in the foyer of his Lincoln Park townhome and scratched his head. Three suitcases and a large briefcase with Catherine's computer and working papers lay on the floor. "How are we supposed to get all this to the airport?" he said.

"I ordered a large car," Catherine called from the second floor. "Do you know where my passport is? I can't find it."

"I have it. You asked me to hold it for you ten minutes ago. Did you also reserve a large car in Italy?"

"Of course."

"And a muscular porter to carry all this stuff?"

"That would be you."

The doorbell rang, and Liam made his way around the baggage to answer the door. Tony was standing on the stoop with a leather binder in his hand and a paper bag. He looked at the floor of the foyer and started laughing.

"This is all your fault, you know," Liam said.

"You're on a humanitarian mission. You should feel honored I gave you the opportunity," he said between chuckles. "I have something for Catherine and something for you."

"That's what we need, more stuff to take on the trip."

Tony held the binder out. "My aunt Gabi sent this to me and told me to 'hand it directly to the woman lawyer.'"

Liam started to take the binder, but Tony pulled it away. "You ain't the woman lawyer. I got clear instructions."

"I believe that I am the woman lawyer," Catherine said, coming down the stairs.

Tony greeted her with a kiss and a warm hug. "Aunt Gabi asked that I deliver this to you and only you. It's a binder full of papers. I got it yesterday."

"They're not in Italian, are they?"

Tony shook his head. "Nah. It's all in English. I think it's like a book."

Catherine opened the binder. There were easily two hundred pages. The title page just said *My Meditation: A Work for Solo Violin*.

"It looks like a manuscript. What's this all about, Tony?"

He shrugged his shoulders. "I didn't read it and Aunt Gabi didn't say."

"Why does Aunt Gabi want me to read it?"

Again, he shook his head. "She didn't say, but she spent good money on overnight delivery service to make sure I'd get it to you before you left."

Catherine nodded. "What's in the paper bag?"

Tony smiled broadly. "That's for my buddy, Liam. Italian deli sandwiches. You can't eat that airplane crap."

FIVE

En Route — Somewhere over the North Atlantic Ocean,
2:00 a.m.

The cabin lights had dimmed, and Liam was asleep. Catherine opened Aunt Gabi's binder and took out the manuscript.

My Meditation
A Work for Solo Violin

My name is Ada Baumgarten. In the time that has been allotted to me, I will recall and write as much of my life's story as I am able, all for a very special person. I am fortunate that my memories are so vivid and detailed. I can see the people, I can hear their voices and I can recall the conversations word for word, as though it were playing out before me.

Despite my present circumstances, I have no regrets. I have led a rich and fortunate life. From an early age, my father told me that I was kissed by the muses, and in truth, I offer no other explanation for my gifts. I have stepped onto celestial stages, I have soared through barriers and I have loved and been loved truly and deeply. Whatever God has in store for me, I will accept with grace. He has given me more than my share.

Berlin, 1918

I was born in Berlin, Germany, on November 11, 1918, the very day the Armistice was signed ending the Great World War. I was the first and only child of Jacob and Friede Baumgarten. My father was a musician, and not just any musician. He held the first chair in the first violin section of the world's greatest orchestra — the Berlin Philharmonic Orchestra. He was the orchestra's concertmaster.

On the day I was born, the orchestra's principal conductor was Arthur Nikisch. On the day I was born, Jacob Baumgarten was a no-show. He was at the hospital, pacing in the father's waiting room with a box of cigars. He was expecting a boy. I disappointed him, but only momentarily. The box of cigars was meant for his friends, but they never made it out of the hospital. He was so overcome with joy, that he handed a cigar to everyone he saw on the fifth floor of Berlin General. He was a proud papa.

My father was a sweet and gentle man who had but two preoccupations: his music and his family. All else he relinquished to the governance of my mother. He deferred to her on all matters concerning the home, our finances, our social circles and, most significantly, the ground rules for my upbringing. Whatever she decided was accepted with an affectionate smile.

My mother was a very beautiful woman. She had dark eyes and long, luxurious hair that she would brush more times than I could count. Our home was her domain and every piece had its place. She managed our household efficiently, cooked the dinners, policed my activities, supervised the household staff and created a proper and inviting Jewish home. To that end, she sought to mirror her own upbringing. My maternal grandparents, while not wealthy, were quite comfortable. They were *Ostjuden,* having immigrated from Eastern Europe.

My grandfather owned a jewelry store on Oranienburger Strasse in Berlin's Hackescher Markt area. He was small in stature but tall in character. And he loved me deeply. On my tenth birthday, he gave me a cameo locket, and it became my most treasured possession. He said it was a magic locket and I believed him. In his business, Grandpa was keen and sharp, but in his home, he was kind and easygoing. He didn't like to make waves. Like my father, he left that to the women. Mama and Grandma were two peas in a pod; efficient, organized women, not necessarily the warm and nurturing type. They left that to the men.

Though Mama never considered herself a socialite (she thought the moniker demeaning), she moved easily and gracefully in the grandeur of interwar Berlin, and she loved to entertain. Always in control, she could host a fashionable dinner party, a garden luncheon or a child's birthday party, all with equal elegance. Because of Papa's celebrity as the Philharmonic's concertmaster, she was called upon to host a number of dinners with local and visiting musicians. She understood social politics — who sat where, who to invite and who to exclude. She would later explain to me that some couples were oil and some were water and we would try not to mix them.

I grew up during the time of the Weimar Republic. Berlin was the epicenter of the era's frenetic explosion of art, music, philosophy and intellectual spirit they called the Weimar Culture. Those years were also pinnacle years for German and Berlin Jewry. At least initially, we never felt displaced or excluded. Jews held positions of high esteem, and we were an integral part of the burgeoning cultural scene. Max Liebermann painted striking impressionistic paintings,

Otto Klemperer and Bruno Walter often led the Philharmonic, Erich Fromm was a noted psychiatrist, Arnold Schoenberg and Kurt Weill were composing music and in 1921, Albert Einstein won the Nobel Prize in physics. And they all had dinner at our home, except for Professor Einstein, even though my mother invited him several times.

We lived six blocks from the Tiergarten, five hundred acres of winding trails, forests, gardens, roads, sculptures and bridle paths, all for me to explore. I spent whatever time I could romping through the gardens and forests of the Tiergarten, most times with my poodle, Mitzi. Many an evening, when I'd stayed out too long, I'd return home to face my mother's stern reprimand, her arms folded across her chest. Do I know what time it is? Why do I want to put her through such worry? Couldn't I be just a little more considerate? Still, a sunny day would come along and off I'd go to my enchanted woods.

While my mother took on the responsibilities of ushering me through my childhood to the woman she expected me to be, it was my father who introduced me to my first and enduring love — my violin. There was never a question about which musical instrument I would play, or who would be my mentor. It was only a matter of when I would take it up. Papa told me my fingers needed to mature before I could begin serious studies.

I was five when he gave me my first violin.

Naturally, the occasion was a dinner party. The guests included Wilhelm Furtwängler, the principal conductor of the Philharmonic. Arthur Nikisch had died suddenly of a heart attack and Uncle Wilhelm, as I had come to call him, was hired as principal conductor and music director. Uncle Wilhelm and Papa — the maestro and his concertmaster — had formed a very close friendship. Since Papa let me tag along whenever he could, I came to know and love Uncle Wilhelm.

It was during coffee service that Papa brought out a package, placed it on the table and called me over. I squealed when I saw it was a violin. Considerably smaller than my father's, it was beautiful — light, delicate and richly polished. It was a bench-made violin, crafted by a single master violin maker in Stuttgart to my father's strict specifications. Papa held it to my chin, placed the bow in my right hand and my fingers on the fingerboard, and from then on, my fate was sealed. I drew the bow across the strings and, from the sound, you would think someone had stepped on the cat's tail. Papa clapped and Uncle Wilhelm nodded his approval. "That's a beautiful violin, Ada. Given time, the instrument will open nicely," Uncle Wilhelm said.

When Uncle Wilhelm had left, Papa lifted me upon his knee, placed my violin in a ready position, adjusted my hand, told me to keep my thumb curled and my fingers flexible and helped me draw the bow so that it actually sounded like a violin. "We'll work together every day, Ada, and soon you and your violin will be best friends."

From then on, unless the Philharmonic was on tour, Papa and I spent an hour a day on my lessons. And Papa was right. We became best friends.

Berlin, November 1929

Winter had come early to the Tiergarten. There was a covering of November snow and the forest was sugar-frosted. Mitzi and I were out and about early to make fresh tracks. Later in the day, I was scheduled to try out for the prestigious Berlin Junior Orchestra. And I was excited. Normally the cutoff was twelve and although I was only eleven, Papa convinced the director that I was proficient and should get a chance. After all, Nathan Milstein was accepted at the St. Petersburg conservatory at age eleven. Yehudi Menuhin was seven when he played with the San Francisco Symphony and thirteen when he played with the Berlin Philharmonic.

"She's a natural," Papa said to Dr. Kritzer, director and conductor of the Junior Orchestra. "A prodigy." Proud papa or not, he was the Philharmonic's concertmaster, and his praise carried a lot of weight. Dr. Kritzer allowed me to participate in the auditions with the understanding that I would probably need a few more years of seasoning. Both Papa and I thought I was seasoned enough.

It had been six years since Papa gave me my violin, and thanks to his daily instruction, my skills had increased dramatically. Although my parents supplemented my instruction with sessions at the Stern Academy, Papa was the best of all my teachers. He made learning fun. He never ended a session without positive feedback. Teaching technique or not, negative criticism would not have been in his nature. He was as kind and gentle a man as God ever created. I practiced as hard as I could and as often as I could and not just because Papa demanded it. Quite the contrary. He often told me to put down the instrument and go out and play. But my violin beckoned to me and I was constantly energized by my progress. I took to my scales and my études like Mitzi took to her dinners. We devoured them. "Wolfed them down," as my mother would say.

The Junior Orchestra evaluations were held at the Philharmonie, the magnificent home of the Berlin Philharmonic. I had been a frequent visitor since I was old enough to walk. It was like a second home. Not so for the other candidates, who were visibly intimidated by the prodigious venue. They were wide-eyed and skittish. There were perhaps twenty-five to thirty of us trying out. We were sorted into sections — brass, strings, woodwinds, percussion — and taken into separate rehearsal rooms. Nine of us were candidates for the string section.

The Junior Orchestra was open to both boys and girls. It was gender-neutral, unlike the Philharmonic, which did not have a single woman musician. I raised that subject with my father off and on. "Why aren't there any women in your orchestra? Women are just as good as men. Surely some are better."

"I have no justifiable explanation," he said. "There are no women members of any major orchestra in the world. And it's not because they're not good enough. It's just been that way for as long as anyone can remember. Women play in string quartets, in ensembles, in chamber orchestras and in a few of the smaller orchestras and opera companies. And goodness knows, women soloists have played in major music venues all over the world. Clara Schumann played with every major orchestra in Europe fifty years ago. Myra Hess recently played with Thomas Beecham at the New Symphony Orchestra in London."

"But they were soloists playing concertos, not permanent members of an orchestra," I said. "I want to be a full-fledged member."

"You're right, and someday that will change. I predict you will play for one of the world's great orchestras."

"I will. I will play for the Berlin Philharmonic alongside my Papa. Just watch. I will be the first. A pioneer."

At the audition, a sixteen-year-old cellist was the first to be called. I could see that her hands were sweaty, and she had to start over twice. She had tears in her eyes when she left the stage. A tall girl with a string bass was next. She also made a number of technical errors. Later in the afternoon, midway through the tryouts, we took a break. The boy sitting next to me struck up a conversation. He was a violinist too.

"What are you going to play for them?" he asked me. He wore large glasses and his blond hair could have used a brushing. His arms were long and thin, as though they were growing faster than the rest of his body, but his face was pleasing in a kind and innocent way. His voice was changing; it wandered between octaves. He seemed apprehensive every time they were about to call the name of the next candidate.

"I'm going to play a Paganini caprice," I said, and he gasped.

"Are you kidding? Number 24? You? Are you some kind of wizard? That's an impossibly hard piece. It has parallel octaves, double and triple stops, even a left-hand pizzicato, and you have the nerve to play that at your audition?"

I laughed. "I'm not doing Caprice no. 24, that's over my head. I'm playing the one in E major. Number 9. It's not all that hard."

"Well, I could practice Paganini till my fingers bled and I couldn't play any of them well enough to bring them to a tryout," he said. "I'm playing a Mozart sonata, an easy one. I've been working on it for a long time. I understand you are Concertmaster Baumgarten's daughter."

I nodded. "And I'm not twelve. I guess that's cheating."

"It's not cheating if you have the skills. I'm almost fourteen. My name is Kurt Koenig."

"I'm Ada. Is your father a musician too?" I asked.

"Oh no. He's a soldier. Or he *was* a soldier. My whole family — father, grand-father, uncles — they've all been military. That would be my future as well if Germany wasn't demilitarized. Now my father works in a hardware store. He's not really happy about that."

When we reconvened, it was my turn. I stepped up to the stage and announced that I was playing Paganini Caprice no. 9. It raised the eyebrows of the judges. One of them said, "Very good, Miss Baumgarten. Go ahead whenever you're ready. Don't be

46

nervous."

That made me smile. With my violin under my chin, I was never nervous; I was totally at ease. And as for the Paganini, I knew the piece. I loved the little melody, and the way it imitated flutes on the upper two strings and horns on the lower strings. Paganini called it "The Hunt." My fingers flew and before I knew it the three-minute étude was finished. I bowed and my audition was over. I saw the judges nod to each other.

The news that I had passed my tryout and been selected for the Junior Orchestra was delivered to me by my father at dinner. "You wowed them," he said.

I was giddy. I shouted with glee and danced around the room. My mother laughed.

"Do you know if Kurt made it?" I asked. "Kurt Koenig? He was very good too."

My father shook his head. "I don't know. I heard that one other violinist was chosen, but I don't know the name."

My mother had made a special dinner to celebrate and, of course, we had a guest. This time it was a banker, Alfred Gross. My audition was the subject of conversation for the first hour. After that, it was the economy. There had been a stock market crash in the United States. How would that affect Germany? Since the Armistice eleven years ago, the German economy had been struggling, but now it seemed that the Western world was in for a depression, or so Mr. Gross predicted. Hard economic times meant less support for the orchestra, or so my father said.

Six

En Route — Somewhere over the North Atlantic Ocean,
3:15 a.m.

Liam stirred and stretched his arms. "What are you reading? Why aren't you sleeping?"

"I can't sleep on a plane, you know that. I'm reading the manuscript, the one Gabi sent."

"Does it unravel the mystery of who owns the villa?"

"Not so far. It's the story of a girl named Ada Baumgarten. Apparently, she was a child prodigy in prewar Berlin."

"Why would Gabi give you that to read? Is Ada really Gabriella Vincenzo? Is that the reason?"

"I don't think so. Ada Baumgarten was born in 1918. She'd be ninety-nine if she were still alive. Tony said Gabi was seventy-eight."

"Maybe she's Gabi's mother."

Catherine shrugged. "So far she's only

eleven years old and playing her violin in the Berlin Junior Orchestra."

"So why do you think it was so important for Gabi to overnight that book to you?"

"I have an idea. I'll let you know later if I'm right." She shifted in her seat and arched her back. "You know, Liam, I'm feeling really guilty about this trip. We shouldn't have taken Tony's offer. The chances of helping his aunt are pretty slim. I reviewed the records and they don't look good."

"This is a fine time to have second thoughts."

"That's not fair. I expressed my concern to both of you last week. Now Tony's spent a lot of money and I feel bad."

"We can repay him for the airfare. Staying at the villa is free."

"It's not just the money. We took the assignment on the premise that we could provide a service, maybe assist in preventing the eviction. We gave them hope. I'm thinking that was pretty reckless and irresponsible on our part."

"They had nowhere else to turn, Cat. We did give them hope, but there were no promises and they understood that. Maybe you can negotiate a resolution. And who knows, you might find something to turn the tables. You're a damn good lawyer."

Catherine shook her head. "But not a magician."

Liam grabbed his little pillow and gave Catherine a kiss. "This plane is not going to turn around, so we might as well finish going to Italy and see what we can do."

Catherine returned to her reading.

Berlin, November 1931

Mr. Gross' prediction was correct. The crash in the United States and the subsequent worldwide depression had a devastating impact in Germany. Within months, millions of people lost their jobs and several banks were forced to close. Mr. Gross came over to say his good-byes at our dinner table. His bank had shut its doors the previous April and been vandalized by angry depositors. Mr. Gross was on his way to Philadelphia to live with relatives.

"Jacob," he said, "if you're smart, you and Friede will get out of Germany now. I see no improvement on the horizon and the orchestra is bound to lose its funding. Why don't you seek out a position in an American orchestra — New York or Philadelphia or Boston or Chicago."

My father shook his head. "We still have patrons. We don't fill the seats like we used to, but things can turn around."

"I'm not just talking about the economy, Jacob. The political climate is changing. Oppressive times like this are ripe for exclusionary right-wing populists. You can see it growing. Extremist parties are gaining followers. You saw it in the 1930 election. President Hindenburg was forced to issue emergency measures. Now I hear that Adolf Hitler is going to run against Hindenburg in the 1932 elections. He's that ranting maniac with the National Socialist German Workers' Party — the Nazi Party."

My father shrugged it off. Politics didn't concern him. "Alfred, I'm truly sorry for your circumstances, you know I am, and I wish you weren't leaving, but the Nazis are a minority fringe group. In last year's Reichstag election, they got less than twenty percent."

"Up from two percent, Jacob. They went from two percent in 1928 to eighteen percent in 1930. What does that tell you? Times are bad, and people want answers. The Nazis have support from the industrialists whose hands have been tied since the Armistice. Even more worrisome to people like you and me is the fact that Hitler preaches anti-Semitism. He wrote about it in his book, which is now a bestseller. He's a hateful man. You should explore options in the U.S."

I listened to the men talking and I hoped that my father didn't want to move to the United States. I had just turned thirteen, I liked my house, I liked my school, I liked my Tiergarten and I especially liked the friends

I had made in the Junior Orchestra. We were working on our winter concert: Haydn's Symphony no. 82 and Mendelssohn's *Italian.* I had moved up and was now playing in the first violin section, fourth chair. To make it all the more exciting, I sat directly in front of Kurt. He was in the second section and doing well. We had become good friends. I would meet him in the canteen a half hour before practice began, and we'd share a soft drink and talk. He was funny. Sometimes in practice he would poke me in the back. I'd turn around and he'd say, "It wasn't me," and I'd try to put on my angry face, but most times I laughed.

In late November, Kurt told me that things were rough at his house. His father had lost his job and was talking about selling the family car. If that happened, he would probably have to leave Junior. Like most of us, he took the bus straight to orchestra practice after school, but he needed a ride home at night after practice. I told him not to worry; I would ask my father if we could drive him home.

That night I raised the subject. Could we drive Kurt home from practice if his father lost his car? Papa hesitated. Kurt's neighborhood was on the other side of the city. "Pleeease," I begged. "If he doesn't have a ride, he'll have to quit and he's a really good player. And he's my friend."

My father smiled. "How do I let you talk me into these things? Okay, if Mr. Koenig sells his car, we'll offer to drive Kurt home." I was overjoyed.

A few weeks later, Kurt's father did sell his car and I extended the offer. Surprisingly, we got a little pushback from Kurt's father. Mr. Koenig was not a particularly friendly man, and I felt he was resentful of us — we hadn't suffered as much as he had in the struggling economy. Initially he said no, he couldn't pay his share for the rides. My father said he didn't expect any money, he was happy to help out.

"We are not a charity," Kurt's father said. "Our situation is temporary. Work is scarce. Maybe not for a concertmaster, but for the average German workingman." Then he hung his head. "But I will support my son, so Kurt may ride with you. Thank you."

"Oh, it's nothing," my father said. "No trouble at all."

Mr. Koenig added, "But just until things get better. Then I will drive Kurt myself."

"Of course," my father said, and from then on, we drove Kurt home.

Our rides after practice were a lot of fun. Sitting next to each other in the backseat, we laughed a lot. We talked about music, we talked about technique and we gossiped about the other kids in the orchestra. I really enjoyed Kurt's company. Soon we were furtively interlocking little fingers in the backseat. I thought my father hadn't noticed, but he took me aside one night and reminded me that I was only thirteen.

In January 1932, Kurt told me that his father had found a job with the Sturmabteilung as a security guard for the upcoming political elections. The SA, as they were called, had been providing protection for the Nazi Party at its rallies and assemblies. They wore brown shirts and were organized like a military branch with squads and group commanders, ultimately responsible to Hitler as head of the Nazi Party. That job suited his father perfectly. He was a military man at heart.

As the 1932 election day approached, the Brownshirts became more visible. The Nazis were promising to increase jobs, to dismantle the aristocratic estates, and to make Germany great again. The Brownshirts, now numbering almost half a million, were ubiquitous and frequently seen marching in formation through the streets of German cities. Though they were frightening in number, my father, like most of his friends, showed little concern. Hitler was a blowhard. Hindenburg would crush him in the election. This whole SA thing would go away.

I took Mitzi for her walk in the Tiergarten in February and while we were on the footpath, a group of Brownshirts came marching by. They were chanting their theme song, "Raise high the flag! Stand rank on rank together. Storm Troopers march with steady, quiet tread." Mitzi barked at them as they passed and one of them suddenly turned and feigned a lunge at her. Mitzi squealed, the man laughed and marched on. I told my father about it and he told me to stay away from the Brownshirts. "They're a nasty bunch. I hear that after Hitler and his party loses, they will be outlawed," he said.

That night Papa took Mama and me to the Philharmonie. Oskar Fried was the guest conductor and Sergei Prokofiev was the soloist, playing his Piano Concerto no. 3. The Philharmonic never sounded better but attendance was down. Still, Prokofiev was brilliant and the orchestra handled the difficult third movement with grace. Papa brought me backstage to introduce me after the concert.

"So, this is the next Milstein?" Prokofiev said with a smile. "I've heard about you, young lady, and your prodigious exploits with the Berlin youth. When will you come play with me in Russia?"

Papa winked at me. I blushed. What could I say?

SEVEN

Berlin, January 1933

Although Hitler had come in second in the April 1932 elections, throughout the summer and fall Hindenburg had been unable to form a majority government in the Reichstag. The eighty-four-year-old president bowed to pressure from his wealthy industrialist backers and appointed Hitler as chancellor. For the first time in my memory, my father was upset by politics.

Uncle Wilhelm also detested Hitler. Last year he called Hitler a "hissing street peddler." Uncle Wilhelm felt that Hitler and all his cronies were nothing more than street-gang racists. "They will not stay in power long," he said one evening at dinner. "And I'll tell you this: if Hitler ever interferes in any way with the Philharmonic or its members, I will resign immediately and leave Germany. I've made that known to Hitler's spokesman, Dr. Goebbels."

Despite the talk of the disturbing political

climate, life went on and I was once again treated to a concert, this time with the most famous violinist in the world, Jascha Heifetz. Papa had been raving about this concert for weeks. "The last time Heifetz played with the Philharmonic, it was 1912 and he was only eleven years old!" Papa said. "He played the Tchaikovsky concerto so brilliantly there was a spontaneous standing ovation from the entire orchestra led by Maestro Nikisch himself. After hearing him play, Fritz Kreisler said, 'We might as well take our fiddles and smash them across our knees.' Wait until you hear him, Ada."

I sat in awe that January evening as Heifetz played the Brahms Violin Concerto. My father, and indeed the entire string section, was mesmerized. His technique, his passion and his command of the stage were inspiring. Once again, he received a standing ovation. Though I was only fourteen, I was allowed to attend the champagne reception after the concert.

Maestro Heifetz shook my hand. His hands were smooth and soft. His smile was warm. He asked me about my studies. How often did I practice? Which composers were my favorites? How often did I practice my scales?

"I play them every day," I said, but my answer did not please him.

"Nothing is more important than your mastery of scales, Ada. Do not take them as a necessary appetizer before you can eat your dinner. Play them in all different keys, in arpeggios, in double stops, in octaves. Play the difficult scales, like G-flat major. Never be satisfied. Push yourself."

"Yes, sir," I said, though in truth I had never placed such emphasis on my scales.

"You and I have so much in common," he said, winking at Papa. "I was taught by my father as well."

After a while, he took Papa aside. "You have a delightful daughter. You are doing well, but one would have to be blind not to see things are very unsettled here in Germany. This Hitler, he is dangerous, and he is no friend to the Jews. He made that very clear as far back as 1920 at the Munich beer hall when he proposed that Jews should be denied citizenship."

My father shrugged. "Germany won't follow him. Jascha, these are troubled times everywhere in the world. It will get better."

"Consider America," he said. "I have been a citizen for almost eight years now. I was only sixteen when I debuted at Carnegie Hall, but I knew right then and there, I was going to live in America. I can tell you there are opportunities not only for you but for Ada. We just elected Franklin Roosevelt and things will improve. You should think about

Ada, Jacob."

"Well, maybe someday for Ada, but I am a Berliner. I'm loyal to Wilhelm and to my orchestra. Jews are still doing just fine here. Things will change in Germany too."

"That's what I'm afraid of. But I understand your loyalty, my friend. I will see you next time."

Two months later, I arrived at Junior for our daily practice. I went directly to the lunch-room where Kurt and I usually met before practice, but Kurt wasn't there. When we all assembled, Kurt was still missing. Then I noticed that a new girl had been added to the second section and everyone had moved up a chair. Another boy was seated in Kurt's chair. I asked Dr. Kritzer what had happened, and he told me that Kurt had resigned. It had happened quite suddenly and Dr. Kritzer didn't know the reason. He was disappointed, as he was sure I would be too.

Disappointed didn't begin to describe my reaction. I was devastated. I had lost my best friend. My stomach felt uneasy and I asked to take a break. When I returned, I resumed playing, but my heart wasn't in it and my attention was unfocused. I made several mistakes, including failing to turn a page. Dr. Kritzer shook his head, but he understood.

When my father picked me up, I was crying. "There must be some mistake," I said. "Kurt would never quit Junior. He loved the orchestra. And he wouldn't leave me without talking to me. I'm sure his mean father put him up to this. You met him, he's a horrible man. You have to go talk to him. Tell him to let Kurt stay in Junior."

Papa shook his head. "It's not my place. If that was his father's decision, I cannot interfere. Maybe the family is moving. There could be any number of reasons."

I couldn't stop weeping and I kept begging my father. Finally, he said, "All right, Ada. We'll drive out to Kurt's. We'll ask, *politely,* if there's anything we can do. But I don't want you to argue with his father."

There was a big sigh of relief and a big hug from me for the world's best father. If anyone could right the ship, it was my papa.

We knocked on the door and Kurt's father answered. He was wearing his SA uniform and black boots. "Kurt is no longer in the children's orchestra," he said brusquely. "I am sorry I did not tell you, but I do not have a telephone. So, Kurt will not need any more rides. Thank you for what you have done."

I was still in a state of shock. "Why?" I said. "He is such a good player. What about his future? Why would you do this to him?"

My father looked at me angrily. "Ada, I told you not to argue." Mr. Koenig's face became

61

stern. "His future will be just fine. That is not your worry. Good-bye." He turned and shut the door. Two weeks later, I learned the reasons for Kurt's resignation.

I found a letter in our mailbox. It was posted at Stuttgart.

Dear Ada,
Please forgive me. I am sorry I didn't tell you myself and that you found out the way you did. As you may have noticed, my father has become very involved in the SA. He was appointed a Sturm commander and he is hoping to be transferred to headquarters in Stuttgart. (That is where I am today.) He used to be a sergeant in the Reichswehr, but after the war, the army was limited to 100,000 soldiers, and they kicked my father out, leaving him without a job. Now he tells me that the SA is the "People's Army" and it will be over a million strong by the end of the year.

He says he wants me to follow in the footsteps of my forefathers and be a military man. My family have always been soldiers. Two weeks ago, he enrolled me in the Hitlerjugend, the Hitler Youth. I have to wear a brown shirt, a black neckerchief tucked under my collar and black shorts. (I look very silly. You would laugh.) My father raves about what I'll learn in the HJ. He tells me how much fun I'll have camping, hiking and weapons training. (Bluch!) There are activities planned every day in the HJ and that is why I had to drop Junior. Believe me, I'd much rather be at Junior with you.

I still practice every day, though most times it is late at night after my father goes to bed. I really miss Junior, but most of all, I miss you. Do you think we could see each other socially? Would your father permit it? Could you ask him?

Friends forever,

Kurt

"Exactly what does young Kurt mean by *socially*?" my father asked.

"Papa, I'm almost fifteen. Kurt is sixteen. Most of my girlfriends have boyfriends. They socialize in groups, sometimes at a dance, sometimes at the movies. And you know Kurt, he's a nice boy."

"Yes, he is. But he is now a member of the Hitler Youth and they are indoctrinated with Nazi ideology. You are a Jewish girl. I am surprised that his father would permit Kurt to socialize with you. I always had the feeling that Mr. Koenig didn't like Kurt riding with us, and maybe it was because we are Jewish."

"I'm not going to date his father."

"Who said anything about *date*? You're fourteen."

"Okay, socialize, not date."

My father thought for minute and then said, "In groups, Ada. Only in groups."

It never really mattered to me that I was Jewish and Kurt was something else — Lutheran, I think. I suppose I had been insulated from racial prejudice to the extent it existed in the Weimar Republic. I had attended Jewish schools since kindergarten. We walked a few blocks to attend one of Berlin's seventeen synagogues. I attended the Stern Music Academy with several young Jewish musicians (until my father decided that I had progressed beyond their curriculum).

We knew that some stores were owned by Jews, but I never heard my mother tell me that she was shopping at a Jewish store or a non-Jewish store. She shopped at a store that carried what she wanted to buy. As far as I knew, so did all the Berliners. All that changed in 1933. Ever since January, when Hitler came to power, the Nazis were claiming that German Jews and foreign Jews were spreading false stories in the foreign press in an effort to damage the German reputation. As a reprisal, the Nazis declared a one-day national boycott of Jewish-owned stores on April 1, 1933. Signs were posted all over Germany that read, GERMANS DEFEND YOURSELVES. DO NOT BUY FROM JEWS.

Of all the people I knew, and all the outrage I heard expressed in our community, my grandfather was the most upset. "They're going to boycott my jewelry store where they've been buying their wedding rings and necklaces for fifty years? Where are they going to go? Are the Nazis going to sell jewelry now? All these years, I have been scrupulously honest with my customers. Many times, I extended credit to young people who could not afford their wedding rings. I let them pay in installments whenever they could. I trusted them, and they trusted me. And now I am to be boycotted? Screw the bastards!"

On April 1, my friends and I decided to boycott the boycott. We were told to stay away, but we were teenagers and when did teenagers ever listen? Rachel wanted to buy a purse and we all went shopping with her. We walked straight to the Tietz Department Store, the biggest one in Berlin, on a busy commercial street. We knew Tietz was owned by a Jewish family. Brown-shirts were standing boldly in front of the store, holding a boycott sign that read: GERMANS, DEFEND YOURSELVES AGAINST THE JEWISH ATROCITY PROPAGANDA, BUY ONLY AT GERMAN SHOPS!

Rachel made a face at the Brownshirt and said, "In case you didn't know, Tietz is a *German* shop!" We all laughed.

It made us proud that many people were ignoring the SA and going in and out of the store anyway. The Brownshirts didn't physically prevent us from entering, but they insulted us as we passed. We laughed, we giggled and we walked right past them. As far as we could tell, the boycott was a flop.

I was proud of our little rebellion and I told my father what happened, but he was furious. Stories were circulating about the SA and physical abuses. "You confronted the SA? They push people down, they beat people right on the street and the police do nothing. Do not ever confront one of those Brownshirts again!" my father warned.

"Papa," I replied, "they weren't doing anything; they were just standing in front of Tietz saying stupid things and no one cared. Everyone went into the store anyway. It was just a silly one-day boycott."

But my father knew better. "If only it were just a single day," he said sadly.

Surprisingly, my mother stuck up for me. "Good for you, Ada. We won't let those Nazis bully us. Your grandpa wasn't afraid. He stood up to them. He hung a sign on his jewelry store window that read, ICH BIN JUDE. ARIER BETRETEN MEIN GESCHÄFT AUF EIGENE GEFAHR. I AM A JEW. ARYANS ENTER

THE STORE AT YOUR OWN RISK."

My father was shocked. "Is Mordecai crazy? Does he want those Storm Troopers to destroy his store? Does he have a death wish? Ada, no matter what Grandpa does, you are to stay away from the SA," he said firmly. "Do you understand?" For the first time ever, I saw real fear in his eyes. It was no joke to him. The most mild-mannered man I knew was firmly issuing an order. His muscles quivered from the tension and his face was red. "Do you understand?" he repeated loudly. I nodded.

Two days later, we realized that my father was right. Grandpa's store was vandalized. The front window was broken, the glass display cases were smashed and the interior was set on fire. The store was boarded up, but Grandpa vowed to reopen as soon as he could get it repaired. No Nazis were going to shut him down. I was proud but frightened for him.

Berlin was changing quickly. Less than one week later, a law was passed excluding all Jews and political opponents of the Nazi Party from all civil service positions. Thousands were immediately thrown out of work. At the end of April, the Reichstag passed the Law Against Overcrowding in Schools and Universities. Of course, there was no overcrowding. It was a pretense. The law only applied to Jews and restricted the number of Jews who could attend public schools.

My friend Eva was forced to leave her public high school. She was transferring to the Jewish high school on Hamburgerstrasse that my friends and I attended. So, naturally, she decided to throw a party. What better way to meet her new classmates? I asked my father if it would be all right to invite Kurt. He wavered. After assuring him that Eva's parents would be chaperoning and would be home all night, he consented. I wrote to Kurt, gave him the address and told him to meet me there.

The party began at seven and for two hours I watched and waited for Kurt. Finally, I gave up. It was not meant to be. Then, at nine thirty, Kurt showed up. Thankfully, he was not wearing his Hitler Youth uniform. He looked so good. I was so happy to see him. We had a lot to talk about. There was food, soft drinks, popular music on the Victrola and dancing. After some cajoling, I got Kurt off the couch and onto the dance floor. He was a little clumsy and unsure of himself, but I think we were making pretty good progress — that is, until his father showed up.

Mr. Koenig stood in the doorway with two other Brownshirts. He had a scowl on his face and he scolded Kurt in front of all of us. "Is this the camping meeting you told me about?" he yelled. "Where are your other friends from the HJ? You lied to me, Kurt." Then he glared straight at me. "That's Ada Baumgarten! Didn't I tell you that you couldn't go out with her? What did I tell you about socializing with Jews? That's an infraction of the HJ rules. Do you want to get expelled from the HJ?" He roughly grabbed Kurt by the arm, slapped him on the back of his head so hard it knocked his glasses off and proceeded to pull him toward the door. As he was being yanked out of the room, Kurt turned to me and mouthed, "I'm sorry. I'm so sorry."

Although the party was to last until eleven, my father arrived early and told me we had to leave. I started to protest, but I could tell something was terribly wrong. When I got into the car, he said, "We have to go to the hospital, Ada. Mother and Grandma are already there." I felt chills. "Grandpa was attacked at his store. He was badly beaten and is fighting for his life."

"Who attacked him?"

My father shook his head. "There were no witnesses, at least none that will speak. And what difference would it make if they did? Who will discipline the SA?"

Mama and Grandma were seated by Grandpa's bed. Grandma held his hand and wailed. My poor grandfather, a delicate man in his seventies, had been beaten and kicked by several Storm Troopers. His bones were broken. He lay unconscious while a nurse took his vitals and shook her head. "I don't know," she said. "He is so badly injured."

No one gave him a chance at recovery, but they didn't know my grandpa like I did. Every day I would come to visit. I always wore my locket. After a few days, he opened his eyes and smiled at me. He saw my locket and winked. "The magic locket," he said. "You see, it works!" They kept him at the hospital for three weeks and gave him strong drugs. When he was finally discharged, he needed a wheelchair. He would never walk again.

The sudden and violent attack on my grandfather had a numbing effect on us all, but nowhere did it resonate more deeply than with my mother. Her attitude toward the Nazis had previously been dismissive, like shooing a fly. Now she was frightened. She did not want to go out alone. It was a profound shift in her spirit, one that would never change.

EIGHT

Berlin, July 1933

I had overheard discussions, off and on, that the Philharmonic was having financial problems. Attendance was down. The Wolff family, the Jewish owners of the Philharmonie and chief benefactors of the orchestra, were financially wounded by the depression and by the campaign against Jewish businesses. They were struggling to fund the operations, and their call for backers was falling on deaf ears. My father said it was only a matter of time until the Reich would take over the Philharmonic.

Both Uncle Wilhelm and my father feared that if the Nazis nationalized the Philharmonic, they'd impose their racial restrictions and seek to expel the Jewish members. So-called Jewish quotas were becoming commonplace in other industries and professions, and pressure was being exerted to dismiss Jewish performers from all the arts. Uncle Wilhelm decided to be proactive and, at considerable risk to himself, wrote a letter of protest to Goebbels.

"Ultimately, there is only one dividing line I recognize: that between good and bad art. If the campaign is directed at truly great artists, then it ceases to be in the interests of Germany's cultural life. It must therefore be stated that men such as Walter, Klemperer, Reinhardt, etc. must be allowed to exercise their talents in Germany in the future as well, in exactly the same way as Kreisler, Huberman, Schnabel and other great instrumentalists of the Jewish race."

Not only did Uncle Wilhelm write that provocative letter, but he sent a copy directly to the newspapers. All of us were shocked by his open defiance, and we feared he would suffer reprisals. But Uncle Wilhelm felt he was untouchable. Hitler considered him the centerpiece of German culture, a fine-arts deity, and Goebbels was left with the task of trying to manage him.

After his letter was published, Uncle Wilhelm and three other leading members of the orchestra came to the house for dinner to discuss the Philharmonic's future. I sat in the living room not far from the group, trying to listen. Just a fly on the wall. Theodore Goldberg, a trumpet player who had been with the Philharmonic since the 1890s, asked, "When Goebbels and Hitler nationalize the orchestra, what will that mean for us?"

"It's hard to say," Uncle Wilhelm said. "There's talk about nazification; bringing arts and culture in line with the Nazis' so-called values and policies. In that case, God help us. Dr. Goebbels called me yesterday after my letter appeared in the paper. Needless to say, he was furious, but restrained. He demanded a meeting. I told him I'd try to work it in, but with our Mannheim concert scheduled for next week, we were very busy. I know he's going to pressure me to publicly apologize, but it won't work."

"When are you going to meet?"

"We scheduled it for next Thursday, after the Mannheim concert. I hope he'll tell me what the mighty führer has in store for us. If I find out, I'll let you know, but let's face it, we should all take stock of what lies ahead. Times are changing. If you think it's time for you to go, believe me, I will not hold it against you or any of our members. In fact, I'll use all my resources to assist you in placement elsewhere if you choose to resign. But please know this; I will not stand for the dismissal of any member because he is Jewish. I'm counting on Hitler's vanity. He boasts we are Germany's treasure, the world's greatest orchestra. At least for now, it's hands off my orchestra."

"Why did we agree to play a joint concert

in Mannheim?" Goldberg asked. "They are a small, local orchestra, nowhere near our proficiency. Besides, they are strong Nazi supporters. They play beneath a giant swastika flag, they give the Hitler salute and they begin their concerts with the 'Horst Wessel Lied,' the Nazi anthem. Are we now going to be Nazi supporters?"

Uncle Wilhelm brushed it off. "We agreed to go to Mannheim at the request of their director to celebrate the fiftieth anniversary of Richard Wagner's death," he said calmly. "It's a necessary fund-raiser for them and a big boost to their prestige at a time when all orchestras are in trouble. I will tell them to tone down the politics. No Nazi propaganda." He smiled. "Don't worry, Theo, we're not going to be Nazi supporters. No flags. No salutes."

"I admire your strength, Wilhelm, but Hitler and Goebbels can be relentless in pursuing their so-called nazification," my father said. "Just last month, Bruno Walter gave up. He left his post as principal conductor of Leipzig. For years, Hitler had been ridiculing him, calling him names, stating how there are far too many Jewish conductors. Whenever Hitler mentioned Bruno's name, he mocked him. He called him, 'Bruno Walter, alias Schlesinger.' "

Uncle Wilhelm nodded. "Well, I've made my position clear, Jacob; if Hitler and Goebbels seek to interfere in any way with our artistic autonomy, they will not have Furtwängler as a conductor."

"Then we will lose another fine conductor," Goldberg said. "I hear that Otto Klemperer is moving to America as well."

"He's a Catholic," my father said. "Why should he worry?"

"He has Jewish parents," Goldberg replied. "But it's not only Jews, all of Germany should be worried. We have a power-grabbing lunatic in charge of our country. Maybe going to America is the answer. You should think about it as well, Jacob." Then turning to my mother, he added, "Friede, talk to him. You have a gifted child. She should grow up in a society where she can flourish." (I blushed and slid down in my chair.)

My mother smiled politely. "That is a decision for my husband."

"I'll be firm at the meeting," Uncle Wilhelm said, as he stood to leave. "I intend to stand strong. If I'm right and they value our Philharmonic and our reputation, then I will do everything I can to insulate us from their racist policies. I promise you, we will not be Hitler's house band."

Uncle Wilhelm was true to his word and that was demonstrated when the orchestra traveled to Mannheim. The president of the Mannheim Orchestra Committee approached Uncle Wilhelm and insisted that Papa be replaced as concertmaster for the evening. "It's just for one night," he said. "There will be several dignitaries and benefactors in attendance, and after all, your concertmaster, Jacob Baumgarten, is a Jew. In such times as these, doesn't one need to be sensitive to national policies? Let my man be concertmaster."

The great Furtwängler turned to his assistant music director and said, "Put the instruments back on the bus, Philip. We're not staying."

The Mannheim president turned white and apologized. He begged Uncle Wilhelm not to leave. "Let me make it clear," Maestro Furtwängler said, "there will be no Nazi flags, no Nazi anthem, and no one in either orchestra will flash a Hitler salute. This is an artistic endeavor to honor a German composer, not to provide propaganda footage for a newsreel. *In such times as these.*"

Of course, the committee yielded, the concert went on as scheduled and Uncle Wilhelm had his way, as he usually did. The concert concluded with a rousing *Ride of the Valkyries* in honor of Wagner. Ironically, we were all unaware at the time that the piece would later be adopted as background music to play at Nazi political rallies.

There was a gala banquet scheduled following the concert. Since there was no longer a risk of cancellation, the committee's president decided to take a swipe at Maestro Furtwängler. As the dinner was beginning, senior members of the Mannheim committee stood and stated what a shame it was that the Philharmonic exhibited such a "lack of national sentiment." Furtwängler stood, faced the dignitaries, took my father by the elbow and said, "Let's go, Jacob, I have lost my appetite for the dishes they serve."

News of the Mannheim controversy quickly reached Goebbels, who insisted on moving up his meeting with Uncle Wilhelm. My father feared this might be the end of Furtwängler, but like so many others, he underestimated the maestro's unparalleled prestige. As my father would later explain, "The meeting went smoothly. First, Dr. Goebbels said that both he and Hitler cherish the Berlin Philharmonic as the world's premier orchestra and the pride of Germany, and they intend to keep it that way. 'As you know, our führer is a classical music devotee,' said Goebbels. 'He has attended several Philharmonic concerts and plans to come more often in the future.' Apparently, Hitler is also a fan of Maestro Furtwängler. Goebbels promised not to disturb the wonderful working camaraderie of the Berlin Philharmonic."

Shortly after the Mannheim concert, I received a letter, post-marked Mannheim, Germany.

My friend Ada:
I had the privilege of being in the HJ honor guard at the Wagner Memorial concert last night. I saw your father, but I did not have a chance to speak with him. The orchestra sounded marvelous and I only think to myself, some day you will sit in that orchestra and you will be concertmistress. Of that, I am sure.

I hope you understand how ashamed I was when my father insulted you at Eva's house. He was quite harsh with me that night, and I still have a bruise or two to remind me. He has forbidden me to play my violin, and he took it away from me. But I would do it all again if it meant I could see you. I miss you terribly.

My father has moved us all to Stuttgart. He is rising quickly in the SA ranks and is pushing me farther along in the Hitler Youth. I am now a group leader. My father plans to send me to a training academy in the fall. I don't know when I'll ever be able to see you again, but I think of you often.

Your friend,
Kurt

P.S. Do not write back to me. I am sure you understand.

I understood all too well. And I cried.

NINE

En Route — High Above the Swiss Alps, July 2017

The cabin lights were turned on and breakfast service commenced in advance of the plane's approach to Rome.

"That sounds like a very interesting story," Liam said, "but what does it have to do with a vineyard in Tuscany? Why did Aunt Gabi send it to you? Do you think that Ada is really Gerda Fruman, the woman who VinCo alleges held legal title to the villa?"

"No, I do not think that Ada is Gerda Fruman."

"Why not?"

"Because Gabi said she never heard of Gerda Fruman. Because Ada is Ada Baumgarten, a Jewish violinist in Nazi Germany. Why that's important, I don't know yet. The manuscript is autobiographical and unpublished. Ada wrote it, and in her introduction, she intimated that her time was short and that something terrible was about to happen to her. How does Gabi come to have this manuscript? I don't know that either. But I'm only partway through the book. These are mysteries yet to be revealed. I'm sure that I'll find out sooner or later."

"Maybe there's a simpler answer," Liam said. "It's a World War II story and Ada is a Jewish girl in Berlin. Tony might have told Gabi that we've worked on a couple of Holocaust cases. Maybe she knows about Ben Solomon or Lena Scheinman. Maybe she just wants to share a World War II story with you. Could it be as simple as that?"

Catherine scrunched her nose and shook her head. "No. There's something about Ada's life that Gabi wants me to know. Something that will impact the fight for her property. This is all background. Maybe there's a relationship. Maybe there's a purpose. Embedded in this story is information that will assist us in this case, I'm sure of it."

"I have another thought," Liam said. "Gabi instructed Tony to give the manuscript directly to the woman lawyer. Only the *woman lawyer.* From what you tell me, Ada is a strong young woman who dreams of breaking gender barriers in the music world under the most difficult of circumstances. Maybe Gabi sees a correlation between Ada Baumgarten and America's most brilliant woman lawyer. You know, maybe the story is meant to be inspirational."

Catherine turned in her seat with a look of pleasant surprise. "Liam, that's a very nice thing to say. I'm flattered."

"I don't know how I should take that. Are you surprised that insensitive Liam could have a sensitive thought?"

Catherine smiled. "I plead the Fifth."

"Here's another paradox," Liam said, pointing down the aisle. "There's nothing more unappetizing than airplane food, yet look — everyone watches the cart moving slowly down the aisle, willing it to hurry up so they can get their tray of faux eggs and mystery meat."

"But not you?"

"Nope." Liam unwrapped Tony's Italian sub sandwich. "Not me."

TEN

Berlin, December 15, 1933

The Philharmonie was all aglow for the Berlin Junior Orchestra's annual winter concert. Its stone columns, archways and neoclassical façade were brilliantly lit with torches and spotlights. Fir trees dressed for Christmas lined the Tiergartenstrasse with twinkling lights. Guests arrived in black limousines, festively dressed for the occasion — furs and long gowns, top hats and tails. Doormen in long wool coats held the massive doors open.

It is such an exciting time for me. Six weeks ago, I was elevated to first chair. As such, I am the Junior's concertmaster for the winter concert. Even more exciting, I am to be the featured soloist! Mozart's Violin Concerto no. 3. My father and I have been practicing nonstop for weeks. The piece runs twenty-five minutes and I am to stand stage center the entire time.

As the hall was filling up, I stood in the

wings behind the curtain and watched. The deep red of the Philharmonie's velvet seats was fading under a tide of black tuxedos and colorful evening gowns. My heart beat as I watched the concertgoers file in — the patricians, the dignitaries, the socialites, the parents, the music lovers and, of course, the uniformed Nazi Party members. At long last the hall was full — every main-floor seat, every balcony seat and every box.

The chimes rang and the lights dimmed. The orchestra filed in to enthusiastic applause. As concertmaster, I entered last. I mirrored what I had seen my father do as concertmaster on countless occasions. I bowed slightly to the audience, acknowledging the applause for the orchestra. I smiled and nodded to Martin, our oboist, as a cue for him to play a sustained A as the note to tune the orchestra. As I stood in the presence of the full auditorium, it was comforting to focus on protocol. It took my mind off the fact that I would soon be standing alone, soloing Mozart. Finally, Dr. Kritzer entered, shook my hand, bowed to the audience, tapped his baton on the music stand and raised his arms. The winter concert was under way.

Our first two short pieces went well, and the audience was engaged and loudly appreciative. Then it was my turn. Mozart's Violin Concerto no. 3 in G major. I walked up next to Dr. Kritzer and smiled. Like a sprinter before the gun, I felt as if two dozen butterflies were darting around in my stomach. I was anxious but not frightened. I was confident. I knew the piece. We'd practiced well and the only thing I really worried about was how I looked. My mother had my hair styled back in a bun. I had a new floor-length sleeveless gown. If I was to be judged on my appearance, as so many women artists are, we had done the best we could.

Dr. Kritzer looked at me, I nodded, he raised his hands and the orchestra struck the opening chords of the concerto's first movement. In the classic style, the orchestra set the opening melody and tempo in the first several measures while I waited. Dr. Kritzer then turned to me and I began my solo. The first notes, light and lively, sprang into the air. The concerto's first movement is an allegro with rapid fingering and great fun to play. I was totally caught up in the music and my fingers did exactly what they were trained to do.

Behind me, enveloping me, supporting me and sounding heavenly, were all my friends. My peers. The Berlin Junior. Kids who came from all directions and all walks of life to practice together every day. They were boys, they were girls, they were fourteen, they were sixteen, they were eighteen, they were Jewish, they were Christian, they were masterful, and tonight, they were one and they had my back. I never felt prouder to be a Junior member than at that moment.

The concerto's second movement is slow and sweet, adagio, one in which I mimic the orchestra. The flutes and I have a conversation. Back and forth. It is soft and passionate. At the end of the movement, Mozart inserted a cadenza. It was a door the composer left open for me, a few measures for a solo passage in which I could express my own creativity. Papa and I worked on it for weeks. This night I gave it my all and it went off perfectly. Though it is not customary to clap between movements, the audience gave me a hearty round of applause that made me blush. Dr. Kritzer smiled and tapped his baton.

The concerto's final movement is a spirited rondo. I danced through that movement with joy. I felt like I could stand there and play all night. Before I knew it, the horns and flutes sounded the final seven notes and the concerto was finished. I took a deep breath and bowed. When I looked up, the entire hall was standing. I was in tears. Dr. Kritzer stepped down from the podium and hugged me tightly. I turned around to acknowledge my orchestra and bowed to them. The clapping continued. It was the best night of my life. How could it possibly get any better?

After the concert, we were all backstage celebrating with our parents and friends when Dr. Kritzer walked up and said, "Did you notice the blond gentleman in the second box, stage right?"

I nodded. "The one in the black uniform. He was with a younger man and two women."

"That is Brigadeführer Reinhard Heydrich," Dr. Kritzer said. "He is the chief of the Sicherheitsdienst, the SD, the intelligence arm of the SS. He is one of the most powerful men in Germany. But he's also an accomplished violinist. His father was a composer. He loved your performance. He said it brought tears to his eyes. He wants to present you with his compliments."

I was impressed. I looked at my father. "He's a Nazi officer, is this all right?"

Papa shrugged and nodded. "Who is the young man with him?" my father asked.

"Herbert Kleiner, an overly aggressive corporal with the SS. His father is very influential in the party and has him fast-tracked under Heydrich. He also has a cousin in the orchestra. A month ago, his father asked me to give Herbert four tickets for the concert. Herbert is a nasty fellow and I don't like him. He's hanging onto Heydrich's coattails, trying to climb the Nazi ladder."

I followed Dr. Kritzer out to the front of the stage where Heydrich was waiting. His blond hair was slicked back. He stood tall and looked striking in his uniform. He was very handsome, but his steel eyes sent chills up my spine. He took my hand, bowed slightly and kissed it. "I have never heard the concerto played more elegantly," he said. "And to think, it was so masterfully played by a fifteen-year-old girl. Young lady, you have a starlit career waiting for you, and I, for one, will be delighted to watch it rise."

I was humbled. I didn't know what to say other than, "Thank you, sir."

"I would love to hear more of your music," he said. "Please let me know whenever you are scheduled to solo again."

While Heydrich was talking to me, Kleiner stood by his side, eyeing me up and down. He had a snarky smile on his face. Then he leaned over to whisper in Heydrich's ear. Although he cupped his mouth, I could still hear. "General, I'm sorry, but you obviously didn't know that this girl is a *Jew.* She should be barred from performing in this building, not praised. My cousin plays the trombone in this orchestra, and he's the one who told me she's a Jew. I wouldn't be so quick to shower this Jewess with praise."

Heydrich took a step back. He was clearly put off by Kleiner's impertinent interruption.

"Do you now suppose it is your prerogative to tell me who I should praise?" Heydrich said. "Is that what corporals do these days? Did you hear this girl play? Was she brilliant?"

Kleiner shrugged, nodded and then shrugged again. "I don't know if she's brilliant," Kleiner said. "I know she's a Jew."

Heydrich was furious. "Well, *I* am telling you that this girl is brilliant, you ignorant idiot. I am praising her artistry because it is well deserved. Can a simpleminded asshole like you understand that?"

Kleiner swallowed hard and stuttered, "B-but sir, J-Jews are being removed from orchestras all over Germany. It's the law. How could she possibly have a starlit career?"

Heydrich pushed Kleiner away from him like he was a stray cat. "Do not presume to correct me ever, Corporal. You're way out of line. You have the manners of an uncultured boor. I am sorry I accepted those tickets from your father, and I regret I am in your company tonight. I assure you that I will not make that mistake again. Now, get out of my sight." Then to me, he said, "I apologize for this man's disrespect. You played beautifully tonight."

As Kleiner was leaving the stage, he stopped. He looked like a beaten dog. His jaw was quivering, and he stared at me with cold, hate-filled eyes. Though I had neither said nor done anything to offend him, I was sure I had made a mortal enemy.

Eleven

Berlin, December 1934

A year had passed, and as well as my career had progressed, as comfortable as I had become with my music and my education, I was distressed to see how Berlin was changing. Like all of Germany, it was becoming intolerant, irritable, mean and, from my point of view, frightening. Goebbels, through his propaganda ministry, had seized control of all artistic disciplines. In September, he formed the Reich Culture Chamber, which controlled music, theater, literature, fine arts and the radio.

Goebbels used his position to infuse Nazi policies and ideology into the arts. He called it *Gleichschaltung* — synchronizing — but to me, it meant that the bull was in charge of the china shop. Goebbels fancied himself a writer and had tried for years to get published. Failing at that, he wrote two plays that remained unsold. As the self-proclaimed "culture minister," he set about implementing Nazi principles, burning books, banning composers and excising from the arts Jews and other "undesirables."

As was bound to happen, in late 1934 Goebbels finally locked horns with Uncle Wilhelm. Paul Hindemith's compositions were scheduled to be performed by the Philharmonic. Hindemith's music was a bit avant-garde, racy and sexually charged. His new composition, *Mathis der Maler* (Matthias the Painter), concerned the plight of artists in a politically oppressed environment. The public loved Hindemith. Uncle Wilhelm appreciated the work's artistic value. He was also a friend of Hindemith.

The Reich Culture Chamber proclaimed Hindemith's music to be "degenerate" and banned the Philharmonic from playing any of his compositions. Although not articulated, there was also a Jewish issue. Hindemith wasn't a Jew, but he was married to one. Refusing to be bullied, on November 25, 1934, Uncle Wilhelm wrote a letter to the newspaper arguing the Philharmonic's right to play Hindemith's composition, *Mathis der Maler.*

A nasty dispute arose over artistic autonomy. Uncle Wilhelm called Hitler an "enemy of the human race" and described the general state of politics in Germany as a "pigsty." The acrimony increased and on December 5, Uncle Wilhelm abruptly resigned from the Philharmonic.

The resignation was sudden and the consequences were harsh. Goebbels immediately seized the opportunity to Aryanize the Philharmonic and turn it into the Reichsorchester. All the Jewish players were immediately suspended, including my father. Goebbels set strict rules for composers and musicians — which compositions and which musicians were banned. Jewish composers, including Meyerbeer and Mendelssohn, were banned. Mendelssohn's *A Midsummer Night's Dream,* one of Uncle Wilhelm's favorites and a yearly offering of the Philharmonic, was declared to be "degenerate."

Hitler and Goebbels sorely underestimated the great Furtwängler's popularity. When he resigned, more than 30 percent of the subscribers canceled their season tickets in protest. University music students collected signatures calling for his immediato reinstatement. It was a public embarrassment for the Reich, and Hitler did not like embarrassments.

Uncle Wilhelm, much in demand all over the world, was offered the post of permanent conductor of the Vienna Philharmonic, and he accepted! We were all dismayed. Now our hopes that he would patch things up and return to the Berlin Philharmonic had vanished. Papa told us that we should consider moving to Vienna as well. Papa felt sure that Uncle Wilhelm would always find a place for him. Austria did not have religious restrictions or intolerant culture ministers.

The Junior's winter concert was set for December 18, 1934, and I was once again to be featured as a soloist, though this time not in a concerto. I was to play Massenet's "Meditation," the symphonic intermezzo from his opera *Thaïs*. I loved that piece and it gave me the opportunity to play with emotion. Initially, I resisted the offer to solo. I told my father I didn't feel that it was appropriate for me to play in light of the fact that he had lost his job and Jewish musicians were being dismissed from orchestras all over Germany. I thought it was disloyal.

My father would hear none of that. "You will solo as requested. That is an honor. We will not let the Nazis silence your music. So far, the Junior Orchestra has been exempt from nazification. If a Jewish girl is given the opportunity to shine like the sun in the face of the Nazis, we must grab on to it proudly. You will play for those of us who can't."

Once again, the Philharmonie was glamorously decked out for the seasonal event. Once again, there was not a single vacant seat in the hall, and though we were just a youth orchestra, our concert was a jewel in

Berlin's winter social calendar, coming the week before Christmas. My solo was next to the last number.

As I walked from my seat to the front of the stage, Dr. Kritzer turned to the audience. "I am sure all of you remember Ada Baumgarten from her brilliant performance last year in the Mozart no. 3. Tonight, she will grace us with Massenet's 'Meditation.' " He nodded, tapped his baton and lifted his arms.

After two measures of quiet string introduction, my solo began. Unlike the burst of rapid allegro fingering that initiates the Mozart, the "Meditation" was soft, slow and emotive with continuous vibrato. Massenet wrote it to be played *poco a poco appassionato* — little by little with much emotion. The piece runs just over six minutes, but it is so lovely, it can literally bring tears to the eyes of a listener. Once again, I was proud to be standing in front of my orchestra. This night especially, for I was a symbol. I was all the Jewish musicians who had lost their jobs and were banned from standing on this stage. I thought to myself, who knows how long before I will be banned as well?

I gave the "Meditation" my all and it went very well. While I was taking my bows, I saw Brigadeführer Heydrich in a box off to the right. He was standing, and I believe I saw him wipe a tear with his fingertips. I nodded to him and smiled. He was a Nazi and a notoriously coldhearted official. But this night, I was an artist and he was a devotee and together we shared the emotion of the "Meditation." That was a bond I cannot explain nor justify.

Afterward, he came backstage to pay his respects. I knew by then that as head of the SS he had opened a prison at Dachau outside of Munich. Communists, socialists, professionals and so-called dissidents were being detained and tortured. Jews had been snatched off the streets under the aegis of the Reich, if not by its direct order. This night, Heydrich was fashionably dressed in his uniform, elegant in his bearing — Lucifer in formal attire. He walked backstage, a smile on his face. He had come to connect with a musician whose performance had moved him to tears. I was flattered in a manner that made me ashamed. I did not extend my hand to him.

Heydrich bowed slightly and told me that he had never heard the "Meditation" played with such feeling. I thought Heydrich was giving me false praise because Yehudi Menuhin had performed it here three years ago, but I accepted the compliment. He asked what was next on my schedule, and the question hit me like a splash of cold water. I thought immediately of my father and the other Jewish orchestra members.

What was next on their schedule? I answered curtly, "I suppose that depends on what the Reich allows me to do, Brigadeführer. My father, concertmaster of the Berlin Philharmonic, has lost his position because he is a Jew. And I am a Jew, just like him."

My father was stunned. One cannot talk to Reinhard Heydrich that way. He could shoot you on the spot. "Oh, Brigadeführer, please let me apologize for her," my father said. "She is young and does not . . ." The smile never left Heydrich's face and he held his hand up like a stop sign. He wagged his index finger back and forth like a windshield wiper.

"She needs no assistance, Herr Baumgarten," he said. "She plays what she feels and she says what she feels. I respect her for that. But she is right. Her professional career will not blossom here in the Reich. You would be well advised to pursue her magnificent future outside of Germany. As soon as possible. I'm sure you understand."

He bowed and left. Because I was sixteen, and because I was passing through the innocence of a young woman's development, I accepted his praise and his defense of my honor. I felt proud, but badly conflicted. I was a teenager. What should I have thought and felt? In many ways, I look back now and realize that those years, my teenage years, should have been years of carefree innocence. But for me and young women of my age, our innocence was stolen from us by the Nazis.

TWELVE

Berlin, February 1935

After two months of sitting around the house, my father went back to work. He returned to the Philharmonic! Not because national policies changed, but solely because Uncle Wilhelm resumed his post. He and Goebbels reached an accord. The great Furtwängler was promised artistic autonomy. "Within reason." In exchange, Uncle Wilhelm promised to be "nonpolitical." He would not write public letters to the newspapers, he would not call Hitler an enemy or Germany a pigsty, but he reserved the right to object to authoritarian regulations that ran contrary to his artistic values. There would be no swastika flag hanging behind his orchestra, no "Horst Wessel" anthem before or after the program and no Hitler salutes. Uncle Wilhelm would have the right to invite Jewish artists as guest soloists and to keep his Jewish members. To all intents and purposes, it seemed as though Hitler and Goebbels had totally capitulated, but that was naïve. Hitler achieved his goal. He always did. He retained his famous Reich orchestra and Europe's most celebrated conductor, and he could showboat them to the world. It was all about outward appearances, and the Olympic Games were coming to Germany in less than a year.

The first thing Uncle Wilhelm did was reinstate my father and four other Jewish members. My father was once again appointed concertmaster. Uncle Wilhelm did not relinquish his position as permanent conductor of the Vienna Philharmonic, but he would not be in residence in Vienna very often. He would do the majority of his conducting duties in Berlin.

I was overjoyed, but Papa was sad. Only five of the Jewish members were rehired. Four had already left Germany, as had many of our friends. They had officially resigned with Furtwängler's blessings.

For Joshua Berne, the Philharmonic's leading string bass player, his fate was tragically sealed last month. Joshua was about to enter the Freundliche Bäckerei on Beusselstrasse with his little daughter when a parade of Brownshirts passed by. As they marched, they scanned the sidewalks with the eyes of coiled snakes, scanning pedestrians and daring defiance. They shot their arms out in Hitler salutes, a command to bystanders that they had better do the same. It was common knowledge that a person foolish enough to ignore the command risked a brutal retaliation, a physical assault or detainment in one of the SA detention centers. Unfortunately, Joshua Berne did not return the salute. To Joshua, the Hitler salute was an abomination, an anathema. He casually turned the other way, looking in the window, pretending not to see. But the Brownshirts saw. An over-zealous, muscle-bound Brownshirt jumped out of line, grabbed Joshua and carried him away.

Joshua's daughter screamed and ran into the bakery. They sent for her mother and called the police, but as usual, the police were ineffectual. They would try to help when they found out where Joshua was taken. In truth, they did not know. Joshua had in fact been thrown into a detention center on Petersburgerstrasse, one of many such makeshift detention centers in Berlin.

A week later, Joshua was released and made his way home, malnourished and badly injured. My father told us that Joshua had been interrogated and beaten. They accused him of being anti-Nazi, anti-Hitler and anti-Germany. Not only had he refused to salute, he had turned his back on the SA and everything they stood for. And he was a

Jew. When his captors learned that he was a member of the orchestra and that Goebbels had barred Jews from performing in the arts, one of them suggested that they make sure Joshua could not violate the order. They stretched his fingers out on a board and smashed them with a hammer. It would be months before his hands were out of bandages, and my father doubted that Joshua would ever play again professionally. Uncle Wilhelm even told my father that he was worried about Joshua's mental state. The suicide rate had been rising among Jews and displaced professionals.

When he finished telling us about Joshua, Papa turned to me and clasped my hands. "Ada, I want you to promise me that you will never confront the SA. When they walk by, you will return their salutes, yell 'Heil Hitler' at the top of your lungs, jump up and down, do whatever they expect. If you are walking Mitzi, and if you see them, make sure you stand tall and salute. You don't have to believe, you just have to stay alive." I could see that his warning scared my mother half to death. Still in shock from her father's ordeal, she cried and went to her room.

THIRTEEN

Pienza, Italy, July 2017

"I think we were supposed to turn there," Catherine said, looking at her map. "We were supposed to take the second right at the roundabout."

"We did take the second right, the first right was a driveway."

"We should go around again; we're on the wrong road."

"No, I'm sure we're on the right road," Liam answered in an unconvincing tone.

"I'm looking at the map, Liam."

"Let's try going down this road a little farther."

"What is the point of having GPS if you don't use it?"

"I have a great sense of direction."

"Not likely. Wait. There's the turnoff. Strada provinciale. I'm sure that's it. Turn right. She lives south of Pienza on SP18."

The narrow road wandered over gentle hills and down through verdant valleys, around olive groves and alongside mirrored lakes, until at last it came to a turnoff. There, at the end of a long dirt-and-gravel driveway, perched on a sunny hilltop, was Villa Vincenzo. Liam maneuvered the Audi into a small parking area in front of a raised veranda. A slender woman with shoulder-length brown hair and an apron tied around her blue cotton dress hustled out to greet them. *"Buongiorno, buongiorno,"* she said. "Welcome to Villa Vincenzo. I am Floria."

Floria waved them up to the stone veranda where a table was set with plates of cheese, charcuterie and bread and a cold pitcher of lemonade. *"Prego,"* she said. "Come and sit. It is a long drive from Roma. Franco will tend to your bags."

"This is lovely," Catherine said. "Is Gabriella at home?"

"The signora is sleeping. She suffers from time to time with chronic maladies. Regretfully, she is not as active as she once was. But" — Floria raised her eyebrows and smiled — "do not lower your guard."

Catherine stood at the edge of the veranda and took in the view. Nothing but an impressionist landscape as far as the eye could see. A warm southerly breeze tousled her hair. "How much of this belongs to Gabriella?"

"Well, I suppose that is the question of the day, isn't it?" Floria answered. "I would say all of it. Mr. Lenzini would say none of it."

"VinCo's lawyer?"

Floria nodded and twisted her lips into a sour expression. "A weasel of a man. He comes out here all the time to harass the signora. He takes great pleasure in the suffering of others."

"And now he has a court order."

Floria nodded. "We have forty-six more days before we must leave, but the signora will not prepare. She is in denial. Perhaps she thinks you will work a miracle and save her farm."

"But you do not?" Liam said.

Floria shrugged. "I am a realist. We have been through two lawyers and both of them examined the papers, both of them fought with Mr. Lenzini and, in the end, both of them told us that we must leave. I mean no disrespect, but I don't know how you can do what these other two lawyers failed to do."

"I don't know that we can," Catherine said. "I told that to Tony, but he insisted that we come and look into it. I examined the papers he gave me in Chicago. When I did, I was bewildered. It occurred to me that there were several loose pieces. Unanswered questions. For one, Gabriella has lived here for many years without anyone challenging her title. If the land really belonged to someone else, Gerda Fruman or the Quercia Company, why wouldn't they have come forward long before this? For another, why would VinCo, such a large conglomerate, be so covetous of Gabriella's seventy acres? Can it be worth that much to them to go through the expense and effort of opening an estate in Germany and enforcing it here through the Italian courts? Besides, it's bad public relations. For yet another, why was Gabriella's deed, which predated VinCo's by twenty years, determined to be invalid? Why would she take a deed from someone outside the chain? Finally, how is it that Gabriella has never heard of the supposed title holder, Gerda Fruman, or her corporation, the Quercia Company? In many ways, it looks like a setup to me, and as Tony would say, it stinks like a dead fish. And that is why I think there might be a chance."

Floria smiled. "I think I like you."

"I'd love to get a tour of the property," Liam said. "Any chance we could do that today?"

"Signora is very proud of her land, and she'd scold me if I preempted her. She would insist on introducing you to Villa Vincenzo herself. She'll be up and about in an hour or so. In the meantime, I'll take you to your room."

Inside the villa, it was pleasantly cool. The windows were designed to funnel the breezes. The floors were tiled, the ceilings were high and blades from the hanging fans slowly moved the air around. Catherine and Liam were shown to a back bedroom. The arched windows overlooked the slopes of the western vineyard and the lush green Tuscan hills beyond.

"You two make yourselves at home. Feel free to use the kitchen and help yourself to anything you find. The cupboards are well stocked, and you'll usually find a nice pinot in the wine cooler. Franco goes into town every other day, so if you need something, he'll be happy to pick it up for you."

After Floria left, Catherine started to unpack her suitcase and Liam stretched out on the four-poster bed. "Pretty sweet, isn't it, Cat," he said. "Not sorry you came now, are you?"

"It's beautiful. I'm not sorry I'm here, I just hope we haven't created any false expectations."

"I think you made yourself clear. We gave no promises. How are you coming with the manuscript?"

"Ada's story? It reads more like a memoir, not with daily entries but at set periods in Ada's life. And it is extraordinarily detailed with descriptions and dialogue. I get the feeling that Ada wrote the manuscript at a much later time, maybe to preserve her memories."

"For whom?"

"I don't know. It's well written. It's very introspective. It's extremely informative. You need to read it as well."

"That's all right. I'll let you read it and give

me the cliff notes. Have you come across any connection with Gabriella or her property?"

Catherine shook her head. "So far it's all about Ada Baumgarten's life in Berlin. I'll ask Gabriella when I see her."

"It's Gabi," said a raspy voice from the doorway. "Or Aunt Gabi, if you like. Either one will suffice." Gabriella, a smile on her face, tottered into the bedroom with the assistance of her cane. "Welcome to my Villa Vincenzo."

She greeted Catherine and Liam with a warm hug each and a kiss on the cheek. "Has Floria settled you in? Are you comfortable? Do you need anything?"

"It's all very lovely," Catherine said. "The view is marvelous."

Gabi walked to the window. "The windows open outward, like this. There are shutters that you may close for warmth or to sleep a little longer. Floria said you would like to see my farm. Are you up for a brisk walk?"

Catherine looked at Gabi. It took effort for her to cross the room. She hesitatingly said, "We'd love to, Gabi, but we don't want you to strain yourself on our account and . . ."

Gabi smiled. "I get to ride. We have a golf cart. I'll meet you out front in ten minutes."

Gabi, Floria, Catherine and Liam walked from the steps of the villa a few dozen yards to a small stone building where farm equipment, tools and the golf cart were stored. A man with a broad-brimmed, weather-beaten hat and a thin moustache over a large smile came out to meet them. Gabi said something in Italian and he thrust out his hand to greet Liam. He dipped his cap to Catherine. "Signora."

Gabi said, "This is Franco, who has been with this property for all of his sixty years. He was born here, and his family was here for many years before that. And their family before them. They were *contadini.* All of this land, all of Tuscany for that matter, once belonged to the church or the dukes. The vineyards were independent little serfdoms. The *contadini* worked and cared for the land. My house and the other little homes in the area were *poderi,* housing for the *contadini,* who were basically sharecroppers. Franco does not speak English, but he's very wise and often communicates well without words. If you want to interview him or talk to him about the property, either Floria or I will translate for you."

They strolled from the villa toward the vineyards, down walkways bordered by Italian cypresses, tall evergreens that resembled dark green tapers. They passed groves of fruit trees and olive trees and entered the vineyards, stopping here and there for an explanation of the development of the vine, the variety of the fruit, the cultivation techniques or the mechanics of harvesting. It was easy to see how deeply and lovingly Gabriella was connected to her land. Eventually they came to a smaller section on a gentle slope.

"This is my best, the finest vineyard in Tuscany," Gabi said proudly. "All of my sections produce elegant fruit, but they are not all the same. The fruit can vary from hectare to hectare. It has to do with the sun and the breeze and the drainage and the minerals. They vary a little from here to there. But this section, the vines that grow right here, are the best in all of Italy, and I have awards to prove it."

She waved her arm. "Look around. The fruit grows on a southwest-facing vineyard at an elevation of over four hundred meters. Beneath the vines is Tuscany's famous limestone-rich *galestro* soil. The vines dig deep here and create a wine of incomparable depth, concentration, elegance and balance."

Gabi picked a few deep purple grapes, seemingly ready to burst through their skin, and handed them to Liam and Catherine. They squirted when Catherine bit them. She wiped her chin and said, "Very sweet. The skin is thick and different from table grapes." She looked out to the horizon. "This is all very beautiful. I can understand why you fight for this land."

Gabi turned serious. "I will die before I let Lenzini take my farm. I will stand here with my shotgun. He will not have my land.

Especially these vines."

Franco nodded. He didn't know English, but he knew what she was saying. *"Le viti di Ada,"* he said. *"Questo é il vigneto di Ada."*

Catherine quickly glanced at Gabi. "What did he say?"

"He said these are Ada's vines. This is Ada's vineyard."

Catherine bit her bottom lip and nodded. "Ada lived here? She planted these vines? You know I've been reading Ada's story."

Gabi smiled and raised her eyebrows.

"Who was she, Gabi? Was she your mother, your sister, your aunt?"

"How far have you come in the story?"

"February 1935. When Ada's father warned her about the Brownshirts, Ada's mother was frightened."

Gabi nodded. "For now, I will let the story talk for me."

"Why did you send her story to me, Gabi? Why do you want me to know about Ada? Tell me."

She shook her head. "Finish reading. Then you will understand, and maybe then we will talk. Not now."

"Just answer one question. Who is Ada?"

Gabi turned her golf cart. "It's time to return to the villa. I'm tired. Read Ada's story. Please. You will find lots of answers."

On the walk back to the house, Liam smiled. "Frustrated by the signora?"

"You bet. I wish she'd give me a hint, but did you see her face when we asked about it? Her eyes opened wide and her facial muscles twitched."

"I'm sure you'll find out soon enough. Maybe tomorrow. Aren't we going into town?"

"Yes. We have a meeting with Gabriella's first attorney, Paulo Giangiorgi. He said he'd share his file with me."

Liam turned to Floria. "Would you please ask Franco if he knew Gerda Fruman or if he ever heard of the Quercia Company? He's been here sixty years."

Floria posed the question and Franco shook his head.

"Odd," said Liam. "Would you ask him if he knew Carlo Vanucci?"

Again, Franco shook his head and answered in Italian.

"He says he is sorry, but he does not know any of those people," Floria said.

Franco added, *"Non sono mai stati in proprietà."*

"They have never been to the property, as far as he knows," Floria translated. "And I would say the same thing, but I have only been here for ten years."

"Thank you," Liam said, and then he yawned. "Sorry. Jet lag. If we have a few hours before dinner, I'm going to take a nap. Want to join me, Cat?"

Catherine shook her head. "I'm not tired. I'm going to sit on the veranda, drink a lemonade and read. The curiosity is killing me."

FOURTEEN

Berlin, November 1935

It was barely a month until our winter concert and our rehearsals were running late every day. On Sunday, our practice started at 9:00 a.m. and did not finish until 2:00 p.m. I was exhausted and hungry, and I rushed to get home. When I opened the door, what should I see but Kurt Koenig sitting on the couch in our front room. It had been nearly two years. He had grown tall and filled out. All teenage vestiges of gangliness had given way to square shoulders and a powerful posture. He looked strong and handsome in his uniform. I rushed over and gave him a hug.

"What are you doing here?" I said.

"My unit is in Berlin and we have the afternoon free. I couldn't imagine coming to the city and not seeing you."

His voice had deepened, his smile was gorgeous and I wanted nothing more than to be alone with him. But my parents were in the house. "Do you want to take a walk?" I said. "Let's get some hot chocolate in the Tiergarten."

The late November sky was clear and bright, but a cold wind was blowing from the north, a hint of what winter had in store for us. We walked the footpaths, my hand in his.

"When did you join the Wehrmacht?" I said.

"I enlisted six months ago. I would have been drafted if I hadn't volunteered, and enlisting made my father very happy. But let's talk about you. I have heard wonderful things, Ada. I even read an article in the paper about the night you played the 'Meditation.' I always knew you would be a star. Didn't I tell you that?"

I blushed. "Yes, you did."

"And you will be the first woman concertmaster of the Berlin Philharmonic. No doubt."

I laughed. "I would have to be a member of the orchestra first and they don't let women in."

"That will change," Kurt said. "The world is changing, and it will be women like you who change it."

"Wow, pretty suave, Mr. Koenig. Are you trying to charm me?"

"Yes, I am, but it is the truth."

"Well, it worked, so you better give me a

kiss." He didn't need to be asked twice. He stepped over and took me in his arms. Perhaps it was that moment, that very moment, when a kiss conveys more than playful banter. It was full of promise and hope, and it touched me deeply. It was a kiss to build upon. I returned it in kind.

"I miss you. I wish you were still with the Junior," I said. "I wish I could see you every day, just like before."

"So do I. But my life is on a different track. I am a career military man, just like my father."

What a waste, I thought.

We bought hot chocolate and cookies at the refreshment cart and sat on a bench.

"Our concert is set for December 15. Can you come?"

Kurt shook his head. "We're stationed in Frankfurt and we'll be on maneuvers all of December. I don't know when I will be in Berlin next. In February, we'll be stationed in Garmisch-Partenkirchen for the Winter Olympics."

I pouted. "Can't you get away for a little while? A weekend pass?"

Kurt laughed. "No such thing. Besides, my squad commander is a real jerk. Mean and tough. Very hard on us." Kurt stood and pretended to salute. "Yes, sir, Corporal Kleiner. No, sir, Corporal Kleiner."

I was shocked. "Did you say Kleiner? Her-

116

bert Kleiner? Short red hair?"

"Yes, do you know of him?"

I nodded. "I saw him put in his place by Reinhard Heydrich. He was scolded like a child."

Kurt turned very serious. "It was *you*? You were the violinist? You were on the stage?" He slapped his forehead. "Of course, I should have known. The Jewish violinist."

"What?"

"Kleiner. He blames you for the collapse of his career. He says he was on track to be Heydrich's right-hand man, a top officer in the SS, until some Jewish bitch side-swiped him and embarrassed him in front of the general."

I laughed. "Ha. I'm glad. He was a snarky, evil rat who told Heydrich that I should be banned from the stage. He embarrassed himself by publicly contradicting the general. I really didn't do anything."

"Well, Kleiner thinks you did. He thinks you ruined his career. If I were you, I'd steer clear of Corporal Kleiner."

Just then, a group of Brownshirts came marching by. We stood and saluted. Kurt looked at me with caring eyes and said, "You've learned to be careful. Bad times are coming, Ada, and we need to be smart. We need to survive. There will be a place for us when the madness is over."

I squeezed the locket that I wore every

day, the one that Grandpa gave me, my magic locket, and I made a wish. "There will be, I'm certain," I said. "How can we continue to see each other?"

He shook his head and shrugged. "I'll be here whenever I get the chance, I promise," he said, and kissed me again. "You'll come home one day and I'll be sitting in your living room. I have to go now."

He walked away, and I thought to myself, "Magic locket, you better do your job."

A group of teenagers walked by, smiled and gave me a Hitler salute.

Oddly, by 1935, the Hitler salute was not solely a political pledge or military statement. It was a greeting. It had become as commonplace as a handshake. You'd see a person enter a restaurant, approach a table and give a Hitler salute. Everyone would chuckle. It was jocular. Then it worked its way into daily exchanges. Greet a friend on the street and flash a Hitler salute. It was nationalistic. It was very German. It was second nature. But not for Jews.

In many ways, Hitler's tirades and rantings were energizing the German people. He loudly condemned the onerous conditions that the world had imposed on Germany in the Treaty of Versailles, and his condemnations resonated with the populace. He promised to make Germany great again. In 1931, before the Nazis took over, five million Germans were unemployed, one out of every eight. Now, the German economy was rebounding. After years of shame and guilt, people were starting to feel proud to be German. Once again, that did not include the Jews.

If a salute was given in my social circle, there would be an apology. Sorry, they would say. It was just a reflex. Only an expression of enthusiasm for Germany, not an endorsement of racial policies. No one wanted to openly admit they condoned nazification. In general, even among adults, Hitler's hateful rhetoric was discounted as bluster, as if to say, "I don't believe in all that Nazi ideology, but you must admit, Germany's doing much better economically."

Of course, "much better" was not a perception held by Jews. With every passing day, our world became darker. Last September, at the annual Nazi party rally, Hitler introduced the Nuremburg Laws, which were unanimously adopted by the Reichstag. First was the Reich Citizenship Law, which defined a citizen as a person of "German blood." Next was the Law for the Protection of German Blood and Honor, which forbade marriages or extramarital relations between Jews and persons of German blood. Two months later, "German

119

blood" was defined to exclude Jews. Thus, on November 14, 1935, Jews were no longer citizens, could not vote, could not hold even the most insignificant public office, and we were barred from relationships with 90 percent of the country.

The subject of our family leaving Germany was always playing in the background. My mother recounted how many of her friends had already sold their houses, taken what money they could and left Germany. Grandma and Grandpa had made arrangements to move to New York and they were leaving soon. Mama's social circle had dwindled down to just a few people. From a life of glamorous entertaining, my mother now felt isolated. The law required her to dismiss her household help — a Jew could not employ a person of German blood — and so my mother was forced to discharge Krista, a woman who had been with us for twelve years. She cleaned, she cooked, she cared for me and now she was gone. It was like another member of the family had moved away. As far as Mama was concerned, it was time to leave.

As for seventeen-year-old me, I was strongly and vocally opposed to moving. My father still had a job and a prestigious position. I loved my high school. I had a starring role with the Junior Orchestra and our winter concert was less than a month away.

Once again, I was scheduled to be featured as a soloist, this time playing Pablo de Sarasate's *Carmen Fantasy:* five movements based on themes from Bizet's opera. Every day was exciting for me and I couldn't conceive of life away from my orchestra and my friends. Someday this ship would right, and Kurt and I had made promises to each other.

"It's not fair, Papa," I said. "I don't want to leave Berlin. I don't care about being a citizen. I don't care if I can't vote. Even if I could, Hitler would win anyway. I don't want to work in a civil service job. I'm still with my orchestra and so are you. We're both doing what we love. All my friends are here. Germany is my home. It's not always perfect, but it has been very good for us."

My father looked at me with sadness in his eyes. "There are things that you should see. Tomorrow we will take a ride, Ada."

We packed a lunch and left early in the day. I did not know where we were going and my father did not say. We drove south out of Berlin and into the countryside. Miles and miles of farms, pastures, forests and lakes.

"This is also Germany, Ada. Over half a million Jews live in Germany, though I concede, it's probably fewer now. Many have left. But it is our land and it should belong to us just as much as it belongs to any other German. We helped build this land, we taught its children and we fought in its wars. But Germany doesn't want us anymore."

"That's just the Nazis, Papa."

"This is 1935 and the Nazis *are* Germany. The Nuremburg Laws make that clear. Sadly, that's a reality most Jews don't want to face. Hitler and his followers want a country that is bereft of Jews. Like crumbs, we are to be swept away and out the door. It's right before your eyes. How much more evidence do you need? You have seen Jewish stores close. You have seen laws passed stripping Jews of their professional licenses. You have seen signs on restaurants telling us we are not welcome. We are less than nonentities — we have no rights."

"Papa, you are the concertmaster of the world's best orchestra."

"Only so long as Furtwängler is conductor. And what will happen when the frenetic führer tires of him, or Furtwängler decides to move on? Even though Wilhelm protects us, most of our Jewish members are resigning and emigrating."

After driving for a couple of hours, a small road branched off toward a village and Papa stopped the car. Above us, a banner had been stretched across the road. It read, JUDEN SIND HIER UNERWÜNSCHT — Jews not welcome here.

"You see, Ada, we are not even welcome to drive into this town. And if I took you from small town to small town you would see similar signs. We are not Germans anymore. We are Jews. And the signs tell us we are not welcome."

Of course, I had seen similar signs in Berlin. Some in café windows, some in salons. JUDEN WERDEN HIER NICHT BEDIENT — Jews not served here. JUDEN SIND IN UNSEREM ORT NICHT ERWÜNSCHT — Jews are not desired in our place. JUDEN UND HUNDE VERBOTEN — Jews and dogs prohibited. To me and my friends, these were foolish, ignorant businessmen who were excluding a significant portion of the economy. Who would want to eat there, anyway? We could choose to eat elsewhere. Still, the lesson was not lost on me, the walls were closing in on us, and there was no ignoring what had happened to my grandfather.

He turned the car around and headed back toward Berlin. Halfway back, he stopped the car again. "Look, Ada. There, in the middle of that wheat field. What do you see?"

"It looks like they're building an airplane hangar. Those paths could become paved runways."

"Tell me, Ada, why would Hitler want to build a hangar out here in the middle of nowhere?"

I shrugged. We passed other farms where we saw more new construction — large manufacturing buildings and long buildings that resembled barracks. We saw armaments, tanks and other military equipment sitting in the fields or beside buildings. There seemed to be no effort to conceal what was going on.

"I thought the Treaty of Versailles prohibited Germany from rearming," I said. "How is Hitler getting away with this military buildup in plain sight?"

My father shook his head. "Who is stopping him? Last March, Hitler reinstituted the draft. He has now conscripted almost half a million men into the Wehrmacht. He did it in flagrant violation of the treaty. He even told the world he was going to do it, and he watched as the rest of the world did nothing. Make no mistake, Ada. He has military ambitions, he has designs, he has plans. Did you hear him ranting on the radio last week about the *Sudetendeutsche*?"

I shook my head. I knew my father listened to the broadcasts, but at seventeen, I had better things to do than listen to Hitler scream. "I don't know," I said. "Who are the *Sudetendeutsche*?"

"They are German-speaking people who live in the Sudeten mountains in northern Czechoslovakia. At the end of the Great War, those people became residents of the new country of Czechoslovakia. The borders for Czechoslovakia and Poland were dictated by the Treaty of Versailles and imposed upon Germany as the price of losing the war. Hitler says they have split the German people and he's probably right. There are Germans in the Sudetenland; there are also Germans in Polish Danzig. He vows to protect and reunite all the German people in defiance of the rest of the world. It doesn't take much imagination to connect Hitler's rantings with his military buildup. This is yet another reason for us to consider leaving Germany before all hell breaks loose."

"Where would we go?"

"I don't know."

"When would we go?"

"I don't know that either."

FIFTEEN

Berlin, December 15, 1935

Ten days before Christmas, and there was a buzz of excitement running through the Junior Orchestra. Not only was it the night of our winter concert at the Philharmonie, but we had just learned that in six weeks we would be performing at the opening ceremonies of the Winter Olympics in Garmisch-Partenkirchen in the Bavarian mountains. And of course, Kurt told me he would be there as well!

There were two soloists the night of the winter concert. Cecilia, a harpist, who played selections from Gluck's *Orfeo ed Euridice,* and me. I was scheduled to perform the *Carmen Fantasy.* Dr. Kritzer mentioned that there was a good possibility we would repeat the performance in concert before international dignitaries at the Olympic Stadium.

This had been a rough season for the Junior. We had major personnel turnovers.

Some of our Jewish players had moved. Some of our seventeen- and eighteen-year-old boys had been conscripted. Except for the brass and percussion sections, the Junior had become predominantly female. How strikingly different from the Philharmonic, which didn't have a single woman member.

I noticed that the evening's audience had a different appearance as well. Several of the men were now in uniform, not tuxedos. Tickets, as usual, had been at a premium, but distribution to Jews had been strictly controlled. The normal channels for ticket purchases were monitored by the Culture Chamber. Thus, Jewish attendance was limited, even though Jewish participation in the arts had always been disproportionately high.

I did not see Heydrich and I was glad. I did not want him coming backstage to kiss my hand and flatter me with his compliments. He was one of the leaders of Hitler's tyrannical regime. He was building concentration camps to imprison Jews. He was a monster. It gave me the creeps that he had played upon my vanity.

My parents, as usual, sat fifth row center with proud smiles on their faces. Right next to them sat Uncle Wilhelm. The great Furtwängler had come to hear me play. As before, my solo would be the second-to-last number.

I don't know why Dr. Kritzer chose the *Carmen Fantasy,* but from the very beginning, I was drawn to Carmen's character. I wanted to feel like her — sassy and bold. I wanted to tantalize soldiers like Don José, reel them in and throw them away. In playing the piece, I imagined myself as that irascible, devil-may-care woman. Now, on stage in front of uniformed Nazis, at that very moment, Carmen suited me just fine.

The *Carmen Fantasy* begins with a strong orchestral introduction, a bold flamenco, unmistakably Carmen, which quiets after a few bars and gives way to my solo. The first movement recalls the scene outside the bullfighting arena. The second movement is an expressive jaunt through several variations of the famous habanera. The third recalls Carmen's teasing of Zuniga and to demonstrate it, there are teasing little grace notes. As I played the fourth movement, I could hear sultry Carmen in my mind, flirtatiously singing the words "Lillas Pastia" and "Manzanilla" as she twirled her skirt and brazenly danced the seguidilla with its flamenco rhythms. The final movement ended in a rapid, energized flourish. I bowed to appreciative applause, and to my conductor and my orchestra. Once again, I felt triumphant. The orchestra played "Joy to the World," and just like that, the winter concert was over. It was to be my last.

Garmisch-Partenkirchen, Germany, February 4, 1936

The Winter Olympics was just two days away and the Junior was scheduled to play at the opening ceremonies. We boarded the train with our instruments in Berlin and arrived the next morning at the Kainzenbad Station in Garmisch. The Junior had a railroad car all to itself, but it wasn't as much fun as you'd imagine: there were six parents assigned to chaperone us. My parents were not among them, nor were any Jewish parents. Dr. Kritzer explained to my father that credentials for chaperones had to be issued by Dr. Karl Ritter von Halt, the head of the Olympic Organizing Committee. Dr. von Halt had given Dr. Kritzer strict instructions on chaperones. He said that Garmisch was not a Jew-friendly region, and while he was no friend of the Jews himself, it was his job to protect the Jewish players and make sure there were no incidents at the Olympics.

My father could read between the lines and took me aside to explain what was going on. "The U.S. Olympic Committee has been considering whether to boycott the winter and summer games. They can see what's going on here in Germany; they read the newspapers and they get the reports. There is strong pressure from the American press to boycott the games. If the United States were to withdraw, other countries would surely follow suit. It would be a devastating humiliation for Hitler and Germany. German officials have been meeting with the U.S. committee and have made several promises. Finally, just last December, the United States agreed to participate.

"Hitler cannot afford to let the world see his racist policies during these winter games. If there are incidents, and if they reach the newspapers, the U.S. and its friends will pull out of the summer games. That is why the anti-Jewish signs have all been taken down. That is why there have been no new race laws. And that's why Dr. von Halt cannot risk an incident with a Jewish chaperone. Do you remember when we took our ride through the country and saw the signs and the banners — Jews not welcome here?"

I nodded.

"In southern Germany, there aren't many Jews and there is strong anti-Jewish sentiment. There had been a sign at the entrance to the Garmisch ski area that said NO JEWS ALLOWED. You can be sure it's no longer there. I'm also sure that if you walk through the town, you won't see a single anti-Jewish sign in any restaurant or shop. You could even go to the movies if you wanted to. But be careful."

My father was right. There were no anti-Jewish signs in Garmisch-Partenkirchen. Hitler, Goebbels and von Halt had done their work. They had painted the country with brotherhood. Look at us, they said, Germany is a warm, welcoming and inclusive country. Even the newspapers stopped running their incessant stories insulting Jews and Jewish businesses.

The Olympics brought energy to Garmisch-Partenkirchen and the sidewalks were packed. There were people everywhere. Half a million visitors had come to Bavaria to watch the games. There were a thousand athletes walking around in their colorful team jackets and hats. There were reporters and photographers. Bright-red swastika banners and flags were draped on the sides of buildings, attached to the streetlamps and hanging at the train station. The ski stadium and the ice-skating stadium were ablaze in red. And of course, there were uniformed Nazis everywhere.

Garmisch-Partenkirchen was the archetypal Alpine village. A picture postcard. Our hotel was on the main street. Before us lay the magnificent Alpine range and Germany's highest mountain, Zugspitze. When we arrived, we learned it had not snowed in the past week and the weather was unseasonably warm. Though there were glaciers on the mountaintops, the ski runs were slushy and everyone was talking about the danger of running the ski events. How could this possibly be Hitler's perfect Winter Olympics with no skiing?

Other than at set rehearsal times, we were allowed to wander through the village. Mindful of my father's warnings, I was careful, but I was also keeping my eyes open for Kurt. I stood on the sidewalk, sometimes through two or three cups of tea, watching the uniformed soldiers walk by, hoping I would see him. We were only staying for three days. We were set to play in the opening ceremony and again in a concert that same evening. Since we were in the hometown of Richard Strauss, and he was a Hitler favorite, we were going to play *Also Sprach Zarathustra* to commence the parade of the athletes, and selections from *An Alpine Symphony* would be added to our evening performance.

February 6, 1936, The IV Winter Olympics Begin
Hitler arrived by special government train, just as a fresh layer of snow fell — a good eight inches. I guess the Nazis even intimidate the weather gods. The streets were lined with people from all over the world, and they shouted "Heil!" and "Seig Heil!" as

he drove by. They gleefully thrusted their arms in the Hitler salute, even athletes from other countries, which I didn't understand at all. Didn't they have a clue what he stood for?

For ten days, this Bavarian town would look like the world's most friendly snow globe. It was a make-believe world of young athletes, friendship and festive partying. It was hard to believe we were in Nazi Germany. That seemed so far removed.

The Junior was scheduled to play on opening day and leave on the eight o'clock train the next morning. For two days, I stood outside in the cold and snow, but sadly, I had not seen Kurt.

The opening ceremony began at noon. Hitler stood on the terrace of the Olympiahaus wearing a heavy winter coat and peaked cap. His first deputy, Rudolf Hess, stood beside him. The Junior assembled at ground level in the corner of the stadium. We shivered while we waited for the ceremonies to begin. Finally, the march of the athletes commenced. It was cold and foggy, and it was hard to play our frozen instruments, but we were the Berlin Junior Orchestra and we could shine without the sun. When the athletes all reached the stadium center, Dr. von Halt welcomed them and declared the Winter Games open.

Thankfully, our evening performance was

indoors. Hitler, Eva Braun, Hess, von Halt and several dignitaries were present. I played my *Meditation* to an appreciative audience. When the performance was finished, they stood, politely clapped, turned and hurried out. The chancellor's party did not come to compliment us after the performance. I had mixed emotions. On the one hand, I was peeved. We deserved compliments! On the other hand, I was relieved. I would not have to smile and pretend to be flattered by such evil people.

After the evening concert, we returned to our hotel for a gala dinner. Everyone was bursting with joy. I shared in the exuberance, but I was disappointed that I hadn't met up with Kurt. I told myself that was foolish. He was on duty and I had been performing. Still, I wished I had seen him and had the chance to talk to him. Our chaperones had planned a celebration party. There was to be general socializing, music and some dancing, all under the watchful eyes of the chaperones, of course.

In the midst of the party, I spotted him. He poked his head in the doorway and I was shocked. Unable to control my excitement, I rushed over to meet him. He was in full uniform with a long winter coat.

"How did you know where to find me?"

He smiled and put his finger over his lips to mimic a Hitler moustache. "Ve haf shpies everyvere!"

We talked for a minute, and I saw Mrs. Linder, one of the chaperones, walk over. I knew she was a sourpuss and would tell Kurt to leave. After all, this was a private party.

He whispered, "Can you get away?"

I smiled. "I think so. Where can I meet you?"

He said, "Outside in front of the hotel at midnight." And he left.

I shared a hotel room with four other girls. I asked them if they'd cover for me. They nodded and giggled. My co-conspirators — they loved the intrigue. I stuffed pillows under my covers to make it look like I was sleeping, and at the stroke of midnight I was out the door.

Kurt was waiting under a streetlamp, just like in a movie. He grabbed my hand and we raced down the street.

"Where are we going?"

"There is a café-bar three blocks away. It's quiet and open late."

The Alpine Bierhaus was not as quiet as Kurt expected. With so many visitors in town, the bar was noisy and a little rowdy. Kurt bought us a couple of steins and we stood against the back wall. He was sorry he didn't get a chance to see the Junior. He told me again how he missed playing with

135

us. He was interested in who had left and who remained. I told him about the winter concert and that I hadn't seen Heydrich.

Quietly, he said, "You don't want to see Heydrich. He's a ruthless man. He's one of Hitler's inner circle. As head of the SS, he's developed a network of spies and informants. Himmler was so impressed that he made him second in command of the Gestapo. Two years ago, Heydrich, Himmler, Goebbels and Hitler carried out a purge known as the Night of the Long Knives. That night, Ernst Röhm and the SA leaders were executed, and the Brownshirts were absorbed into Heydrich's SS. Just the other day, I heard Kleiner talking. He's trying to get himself transferred from the Wehrmacht back to the SS." Kurt smiled. "But Kleiner is persona non grata with Heydrich."

"And he blames me for his misfortune?"

"Oh, without a doubt. You're the bitch that ruined his career."

I laughed. "Good riddance."

Kurt laughed too, but added, "Just be careful. Stay away from Kleiner. He's a scorpion."

We had another round of beer as the bar was emptying. "Do you have to get back now?" Kurt said.

It was one of those flip-a-coin moments. It was already 2:00 a.m. We were supposed to board the bus at 6:00 a.m. I said, "What do you have in mind?"

"Could we just take a walk?"

I was pushing my luck, but I had made my decision. "The bus leaves at six o'clock and our train leaves at eight. You have to get me back to my room by five."

We started walking through the town, hand in hand. At the corner, he stopped, took a deep breath, turned me around and passionately kissed me. There we were — me and a Nazi soldier in full uniform — kissing under a streetlamp. The wind was still, soft snowflakes were falling, the world was quiet and I was in love.

"You know, you're breaking the law," I said. "You just kissed a Jew and we're holding hands. The kissing police are going to arrest you."

"I'll gladly take the punishment, it was worth it. You want to talk about breaking the law? I'm in love with a Jewish girl. How am I supposed to deal with that?"

That was just what I wanted to hear. He felt the same way I did, but he was taking a much bigger risk. Not only did Nazi Party rules prohibit contact with Jews, but the 1935 racial laws forbade marital or *extramarital* relations between Jews and people of German blood. And Kurt was in the military.

There were other people out walking, but the streets were clearing. And it was cold.

Kurt could see I was shivering and he put his arm around me. We were near the temporary quarters that had been constructed for some of the athletes. Kurt stopped in a bar, picked up a couple of lidded beer steins and we ducked into the hall of a temporary residence.

Time was short, but the hours were sweet. We found a corner and some privacy. It was a chance for intimate conversation and talk of hopeful days to come. Kurt was so easy to be with. He had always been that way, but it seemed as though there were always forces trying to pull us apart.

Kurt told me that he hated the army. He had no desire to make a career of it like his father, but Hitler was quickly building the world's largest army and there was no choice. All able-bodied young men were being conscripted. The army was continually getting new equipment. Soldiers were being trained on heavy artillery. There was talk about remilitarizing the Rhineland or marching into the Sudeten mountains. Kurt was sure that war was on the horizon.

We were interrupted by the sound of men talking outside the building. I checked my watch. It was already 5:15. Where had the time gone? I started to panic. "I'm late! We have to go."

"Just a minute," he said quietly and put his finger to his lips. "One of those voices

— it's Kleiner. Believe me, he'll recognize you. If he catches us, we're done for. We can't let that happen."

"I can't stay here. I've got to get back."

"We have to wait."

We waited for thirty minutes, but from the tenor of their conversations, it didn't seem like the men were leaving any time soon. There were three, maybe four of them and they were joking around, passing a bottle and smoking cigarettes.

"Kurt, we have to make a run for it."

He nodded and took off his coat. "Wrap yourself up in this coat and make sure to cover your face. Let's hope they've been up all night and they're hammered. If Kleiner thinks I just picked up a town girl and brought her in here, he'll scold me, but he'll do it with a wink. I don't think he'll chase us."

I put my hands on my hips. "A town girl? Is that what I am? How many town girls have you picked up?"

I wrapped Kurt's coat around my shoulders and pulled it down over my head. I couldn't see very well. "Don't let me fall, Kurt."

"We clasped hands, opened the door and bolted out of the hallway. We practically knocked Kleiner over.

"Halt!" one of the soldiers shouted. "Halt!"

"Keep running," Kurt whispered. "It's our

only chance."

"Halt!"

"Nein, nein," Kurt yelled. *"Ich bin Kurt Koenig."* And we kept running.

I heard Kleiner laughing. "Let them go," he said. "He's one of mine, out to get some action. I hope she's worth it, Koenig."

"Jawohl," Kurt yelled over his shoulder. "She is."

I made it back to the hotel just as the instruments were being loaded into the truck. Mrs. Linder pulled me aside. "Where have you been, Miss Baumgarten?"

"Out for a walk. I got lost."

"I'm ashamed of you," she said. "Even though you asked them to lie for you, your roommates finally confessed that you left at midnight. I have reported this to Dr. Kritzer, and I will make sure your father is informed."

Papa met me at the train station in Berlin. Before he could even kiss me hello, Mrs. Linder pushed past me and cornered him. She went on for a good five minutes about how I had stayed out all night. About how she had seen me talking to a German soldier at the reception — a grown man, no less. About how shameless and embarrassing my conduct was. And of course, all about my loose morals. Finally, she said, "Well, what are you going to do about it?"

"First, I'm going to say hello to my daughter, tell her that I'm happy to see her and ask her if she had a good time. Then I'm going to inquire about the performances, and then I'll take her home. Good day, Mrs. Linder."

Mrs. Linder huffed her indignation and stormed away. I was sure I hadn't heard the last of this.

In the car, my father turned to me. "Was it Kurt?"

I nodded.

"Well, you picked a fine time for your indiscretion, Ada."

"We didn't do anything, Papa. We had a few beers and sat in a hallway talking. I'm sorry. It isn't like I get to see him very often. I may never see him again."

"You know Mrs. Linder is a busybody. You can be assured that her gossip will spread far and wide. Staying out all night compromised the chaperones. They were responsible for you."

"I didn't think they would find out. I lost track of time."

"Well, how is young Kurt?"

"He's wonderful. Thanks, Papa."

Then my father laughed. "I'm afraid we're in a heap of trouble here at the Junior. I hope you're prepared to eat some humble pie."

I nodded. "I understand. It was worth it."

Sixteen

Pienza, Italy, July 2017

Catherine closed her eyes and smiled in the warm morning sun. "Breakfast on a veranda in Tuscany. Fresh strawberries, warm bread. Can I use the cliché 'I could get used to this,' even if I mean it?" She took a deep breath. "Even the air is sweet."

"Nothing wrong with Chicago air," Liam said, and then he sang, "That's where the lake breezes blow. It's always fair weather, when we get together in C-H-I-C-A-G-O." He took a bow. "Thank you, thank you, I'm here all week."

Catherine shook her head and muttered, "And I married this guy." She reached into her purse and took out her cell phone.

"Who are you calling?" Liam said.

"Well, first I'm texting Sarah to remind her of the baby's medicine, and then I'm calling Attorney Giangiorgi."

"Cat, you've called Sarah four times since we arrived. She knows about Ben's medicine.

Ben is just fine. It's three in the morning in Chicago. Your text will beep and wake her up."

Catherine nodded. "You're right. I just miss him. We've never left him before."

"He has Sarah and your sister Carol looking after him. He's fine."

Catherine dialed the attorney, confirmed the appointment for 11:00 a.m. and wrote down the directions. "Mr. Giangiorgi is located on the Via del Giglio, just off the Corso Il Rossellino, a few steps from the Piazza Pio," she said, letting the Italian names roll off her tongue. "He said that if Gabi wasn't coming, we should bring a signed authorization allowing him to speak to us. I'll write one out for Floria to translate."

"Doesn't Gabi want to go with us?"

Catherine shook her head. "Floria said it would be too exhausting for her, but I think she means emotionally, not physically."

The town of Pienza was a postage stamp on the provincial envelope called Siena. If you stretched your arms in opposite directions, you could touch the city limits. Catherine gushed her adoration for the picturesque countryside, oohing and ahhing during the entire fifteen-minute drive from Villa Vincenzo.

"Look at this, Liam. Are you looking at these hills? I expect that any minute I will see the ducal army on horseback, or maybe Caesar's legions marching toward Rome. I could live here, Liam, I really could."

"And what would you do with yourself?"

"I'd eat strawberries on the veranda and take Ben for long walks in the Tuscan sun."

"I mean how would you support yourself — you can't practice law here."

"Lord almighty, do you always have to trample on my daydreams? Can't you just say, 'Yes, and I would sit in the shade and drink the finest Sangiovese'?"

"But how could I afford to buy the finest Sangiovese?"

"Ach. You're too Irish to enjoy a Tuscan dream."

"*Northern* Irish. We dream of castles and kings."

The office of Paulo Giangiorgi, *avvocato,* was on the first floor of a small commercial building on the Via del Giglio. His office was not unlike Catherine's, with file jackets, books and papers strewn over his desk. Paulo appeared to be in his midforties, his light blue shirt was open at the collar and his sleeves were rolled up to his forearms. His smile was warm.

"How can I help?" he said.

"You represented Gabriella Vincenzo in the case where VinCo is trying to evict her?"

"*Si.*"

"We'd like to get some idea why Gabriella Vincenzo is being evicted from the property she has lived on for so many years," Catherine said.

Paulo shrugged. "Yes, it is sad, but the answer is simple. She does not own the property. It is owned by another."

"She believes she owns the property. I've seen the deed. It was signed by Carlo Vanucci. She bought it."

"No, no. You are mistaken. Gabriella did not buy the property; she was given a deed as a gift. No money changed hands. I know that because there were no taxes paid on the transaction, which are required for a sale."

"Why would that matter? Isn't the gift of property valid in Italy? Wasn't the deed recorded?"

"I only point out that it was not a sale. Yes, it was recorded, but so what? The registrar will record whatever you give him, even an invalid document. The act of recording doesn't make a document legally valid. It is just a public notification. Its legality can always be challenged in court. Isn't that true in the U.S. as well?"

"Yes, it is. The company that is challenging Gabriella's title, is that VinCo?"

Paulo smiled. "Oh yes, and there you have your problem. VinCo is a well-respected company. A very wealthy company. It employs hundreds of people in this province and pays lots of taxes. A very good company."

"But VinCo did not get a deed until 2015, is that right?"

Paulo shrugged again and opened his hands. "*Si.* But VinCo's deed was good, and Gabriella's was no good."

"Why was Gabriella's deed no good?"

"Again, the answer is simple. It came from a man named Carlo Vanucci, but Signor Vanucci did not have ownership of the property. So he had no authority to give Gabriella a deed. The Italian judge made the determination that the owner of the property in 2015 was the Quercia Company. The German court determined that Gerda Fruman was the sole owner of the Quercia Company and her estate had the right to transfer title. The administrator of her estate deeded the property to VinCo."

Catherine exhaled through her nose, a sign of frustration that Liam was all too familiar with. "Mr. Giangiorgi," she said, "who owned the property *in 1995,* when Vanucci deeded it to Gabriella? That would seem to be our foundational question?"

"Paulo. Just Paulo, please. Not Mr. Giangiorgi. Just Paulo. And you are so right. That is the foundational question. In 1995, it was owned by Quercia Company. It's right in the registry book. That is why Vanucci's deed is worthless."

"Did you look at the registry book yourself?

Did you see for yourself that Quercia Company was listed in 1995?"

Giangiorgi was becoming irritated. He was looking for a way to end this conversation. "Of course, I did. Now, if you'll please excuse me . . ."

But Catherine was neither dissuaded nor put off her mark. "Fine. You saw Quercia in title in 1995. Then please tell me how and when Quercia bought the property."

Paulo shrugged. "I do not know when Quercia bought the property."

"Really? You said you looked at the registry book."

"The book only goes back to 1980. Quercia Company was in title all the way since 1980, the whole time."

"Before 1980. What do the books say then? Who sold the property to Quercia?"

Giangiorgi shrugged. "I don't know? It was many years ago. The current registry book doesn't say. But the registrar is very careful going from one book to the next. He would not make a mistake."

"I would like to see the books. Where are the registry books kept?"

"At the registrar's office in the government house in Siena. The current book, the one from 1980, is there. It shows that as of the beginning of the book in 1980, Quercia Company owned the property, and then in 2015, VinCo owns it."

"Where is the prior book, the one before 1980?"

Paulo chuckled and shrugged. "I don't know. This is Italy. In storage, someplace."

"And you never asked to see the old book?"

"No. It was entirely unnecessary. The court has ruled. The case is over. I am sorry, but I am busy with a most important appointment now. I must bid you good-bye. Let me know if I can help you further."

Back in the car, Catherine turned to Liam and said, "Stinks like a dead fish."

SEVENTEEN

Berlin, April 1936

Uncle Wilhelm was coming over for dinner, and my mother was hard at work preparing a special meal. She said that Papa and Uncle Wilhelm had a surprise for me. I had no idea what she was talking about and I couldn't coax it from her. But I knew that the past few months had been rocky for me and also for the great Maestro Furtwängler.

I had been through my share of ups and downs since the Winter Olympics. Mostly downs. When we returned to Berlin, Dr. Kritzer severely reprimanded me and placed me on probation for violating curfew. While I was sorry to have put him in that awkward position, I could have lived with his written and oral reprimand. But Mrs. Linder, that nasty woman, insisted that Dr. Kritzer demote me from first chair and from the title of concertmistress for impugning the reputation of the Junior by my blatantly immoral conduct. Dr. Kritzer responded by telling her that I had received a reprimand and that was sufficient. People make mistakes. Teenagers are certainly known to have lapses in good judgment.

But that wasn't enough for Mrs. Linder. She went on a hate campaign and rallied some of the wealthier parents. They threatened to withhold financial support from the Junior if I was not removed from my position. They insisted that second chair Lisel Preston replace me. Without the donors' financial support, the Junior would fold. That left Dr. Kritzer with no choice. He told me I would have to be demoted.

I immediately tendered my resignation, but Dr. Kritzer wouldn't accept it. He called for a meeting with me and my father. He explained his dilemma. He didn't want to demote me, but the Junior could not survive the withdrawal of substantial contributions. Mrs. Linder was a powerful socialite. She and her friends controlled a lot of money and, indeed, the fate of the Junior Orchestra. Dr. Kritzer promised me that I would still be featured in solos. Even if I sat in the second chair, just one chair over, I would still be playing the same sheet music as the first chair. I would just be giving up the so-called prestige of first violinist and concertmistress.

"Exactly," I said. "And I won't do it. Mrs. Linder is a hateful woman who thinks she can get her way just because she's rich. She's a dictator. She's a perfect Nazi. I'm sorry I stayed out late and broke curfew. I was not immoral. I was nothing more than a teenage curfew violator, and I apologized. If that's not good enough, I resign."

Surprisingly, my father said, "I don't want you to resign. The Summer Olympics are coming up. There will be opportunities for you to solo in front of the international community. It's your last year with the Junior; you'll be eighteen in November. I urge you to stick it out until then."

"But Papa, it's so humiliating. I didn't do anything wrong. I'm seventeen. I had a beer with a boy and stayed out late. I returned before the bus left. For that, I am to be demoted and humiliated? You know what everyone is going to think. You know the rumors that Mrs. Linder is spreading. How can I go to practice every day and sit in the second chair and face my peers?"

"Because you are doing it for the good of the orchestra. In many ways, I face the same dilemma, Ada. There are many reasons for us to leave Germany, but I am loyal to my orchestra and my conductor. It's easy to quit. It takes courage to stay. Your peers won't condemn you. They'll know the demotion is not talent-based, that it's coming from intolerant adults. Ada, the decision is ultimately yours, but I would like you to stay.

151

I'm sure Dr. Kritzer would appreciate it."

Dr. Kritzer nodded. "Ada, you will always be first violin to me. You are the finest musician I have ever conducted. Please reconsider."

That night I sat in my bedroom and cried. After a while, my mother came in and shut the door. We hugged. I knew that for years she hadn't been keen on my friendship with Kurt, especially when he became involved in the Hitler Youth. She would always say, "Why can't you find a nice Jewish boy?" The truth is, I wasn't looking for a boy at all. Now I was sure that she was going to say, "I told you so." I waited for her to tell me that I stayed out all night, put myself in a compromising situation, and this was the result. But I was wrong. She was warm, forgiving and comforting.

"Papa wants me to stay with the orchestra," I said, "but I don't see the point. Next winter, when I turn eighteen, I have to leave anyway. What do I do then? There are no women in orchestras. My music career is over. I might as well end it now."

"You're a brilliant artist," she said. "You can't give up your music. You have to continue to play."

"Where, Mama? There are no positions for a woman violinist in any major orchestra in the world. Not Berlin, not Vienna, not New York, not Chicago. Should I play dinner music in some restaurant? I would like to continue my education, maybe become a music teacher, but the schools are all closed to Jews. Even the music academies." Just thinking about it was making me angry.

Mama smiled and patted my shoulder. "Maybe you'll join an ensemble or a string quartet. Or maybe something else will come up."

"Or maybe I could find a nice Jewish man and become a housewife, right?" I was immediately sorry I said that. There were tears in her eyes. Oh my God, how do I unring that bell?

"I didn't mean that, Mama, I'm just feeling sorry for myself. There's nothing wrong with being a wife and a mother. You've always been my role model. I'm just not ready for all that yet. I want a career. I want to be the world's best violinist."

"Then you should listen to your father. If it concerns a life in music, he knows best. When you're with the Junior Orchestra, there's a spotlight on you. You solo. You shine like a star. If you quit, that spotlight goes out."

"But it's only for another eight months."

"Lots of things can happen in eight months."

We hugged and smiled and ostensibly ended the conversation on a high note, but I had hurt her feelings.

When we reconvened at the next practice, I came early and sat in the second seat, the one usually occupied by my good friend Lisel Preston. Lisel saw me sitting there and said, "Oh no. I will not take Ada's chair. I'm a decent player, but I'm no Ada Baumgarten."

"It's not your decision," I said. "It's for the good of the orchestra."

From then on, I sat in the second chair. I intended to stay until I turned eighteen.

As for Uncle Wilhelm, he had a rocky time over the past few months as well, but he always landed on his feet. Last fall, one of the baritones from the Berlin State Opera betrayed him to the Gestapo. He testified that he overheard Uncle Wilhelm say, "Those in power should all be shot and things in Germany will not change until this is done." It was true, Uncle Wilhelm did say those words, and he did not deny it, but he said them in private. Hitler was furious and suspended him from the Philharmonic. It was only a three-week suspension, but it turned out to be an unwise move on Hitler's part. Uncle Wilhelm immediately started looking around, and because he was the world's greatest conductor, he didn't have far to look.

Arturo Toscanini, the famed conductor and music director of the New York Philharmonic, announced his retirement and said that Wilhelm Furtwängler was the only musician worthy of succeeding him. The New York board reached out to Uncle Wilhelm, and to their surprise, he told them he would accept their offer! But the Gestapo had been monitoring overseas conversations and quickly told Hitler. Göring and Goebbels immediately undertook to sabotage the deal. Uncle Wilhelm was in Vienna, and in his absence, Goebbels cleverly appointed Maestro Furtwängler as music director of both the Berlin Philharmonic and the Berlin State Opera. They also gave him the title of *Staatsrat,* state councilor. Uncle Wilhelm knew nothing about these appointments. Then Goebbels publicly announced the appointment and the news was carried by papers around the world.

When the New York newspapers saw the story, they assumed that Uncle Wilhelm had rejected the New York offer and was now a supporter of the Nazi Party. Uncle Wilhelm was never a member of the Nazi Party, and try as he might, he could not correct the erroneous impression. The mood in New York turned against him. People demonstrated and petitioned the board not to hire a Nazi sympathizer. Rather than take the post under those controversial circumstances, Uncle Wilhelm withdrew his acceptance and stayed in Germany.

When this evening started, my mother told me that Papa and Uncle Wilhelm had a surprise for me and it would be revealed at dinner. Uncle Wilhelm had brought his wife, Zitla, and when I greeted him, he wore a grin like the cat that ate the canary. So, I asked him, "What's the big surprise?"

"If I told you, it wouldn't be a surprise, now, would it?"

"How can I be surprised if no one will tell me?"

He laughed. "After dinner, we will tell you."

So all through dinner and dessert I was fidgeting, and my father and Uncle Wilhelm were getting the biggest kick out of teasing me. Finally, I said, "Okay, that's it. You've had enough fun. What's the big surprise?"

They laughed. "What are you doing from May 13 to May 21?" Uncle Wilhelm said.

"I don't know," I said. "That's almost a month away."

"Well, if you're not too busy, Miss Baumgarten, I'm conducting Massenet's *Thaïs* for the Berlin State Opera."

"Well, thank you very much. I'd love to go."

"Well, that's not exactly what I had in mind," he said.

"That's the surprise? I *don't* get to go?"

Uncle Wilhelm leaned forward. "No, Ada. I want you to sit in the pit, in the first violin section. I want you to play the whole score with the orchestra, and at the end of act two, scene one, I want *you* to play the intermezzo. I want *you* to solo the 'Meditation.' For five performances."

Oh my God. Knock me out. Playing solo with the Berlin State Opera! "But there are no women in the orchestra," I said.

"There will be between May 13 and May 21."

"Are you sure that's all right?"

"I am the newly appointed director of the Berlin State Opera, thank you very much, Dr. Goebbels. I can assure you, no one will object. You won't be a permanent member; you'll be a guest soloist. We've had women solo before."

"But I'd also get to play the entire opera with the orchestra?"

"Yes, you would. And that would be a first."

Eighteen

Berlin, May 13, 1936

I auditioned for the Junior when I was only eleven. I performed a Mozart concerto before a packed hall at the Philharmonie when I was fourteen. I soloed the "Meditation" when I was fifteen and the *Carmen Fantasy* when I was sixteen. And on none of those occasions was I frightened or even nervous. But tonight, oh my goodness. Operagoers tend to be discriminating listeners. They are demanding. They are critical. And there is nothing casual about attending Massenet's *Thaïs.* It is a long opera with many slow passages. My solo comes at a critical phase of the story in act two. Tonight, I am playing with the big boys. There is no place to hide. Tonight, I am nervous.

The theme of *Thaïs* is unsettling and, from my perspective, preposterous. Taking place in fourth-century Egypt, it portrays a clash between monastic austerity and wild debauchery. Thaïs is a courtesan, and a very pricey one at that. Athanaël is a Cenobite monk who travels to Alexandria with the impossible mission of converting Thaïs to Christianity and persuading her to leave her life of partying and enter a convent. In the end, Athanaël falls victim to his lust and Thaïs, purified, rises to the angels. Conversion complete. The "Meditation" is played while Thaïs is weighing the plusses and minuses of leaving her sumptuous, voluptuous life and entering the austere Egyptian convent. Really? This is a choice? Only in an opera. The story is goofy, but Massenet's music is gorgeous.

I had butterflies. I watched the audience file in and listened to the sounds of multiple conversations echoing off the walls and ceilings. Orchestra members were taking their seats, reviewing their music and warming up. I was seated next to an older man, Gustav. I met him in practice. He was nice. Some of the other orchestra members eyed me suspiciously. What is she doing here? A woman. She wouldn't be here if she wasn't Furtwängler's pet project.

The house lights dimmed. Uncle Wilhelm entered to applause, took his bow, mounted the podium, tapped his baton, raised his arms and off we went. Before this month, I had only seen Uncle Wilhelm conduct from behind, from the seats. Now he was facing us, directing us, setting the tempo, the flow, the mood. It was well known that Uncle Wilhelm was fitness-conscious. He skied, he swam, he hiked and he watched his weight. When he conducted, he was full of energy and animation. He bounced on his heels, his arms flew around, his head bobbed with intensity and the orchestra fed on it. And tonight, I was part of the whole. I was playing with consummate professionals in one of the finest opera orchestras in the world. My nerves calmed. I was in my music.

Act one ended and the orchestra used the break to get a drink of water or tea. Uncle Wilhelm winked at me. "Everything okay?" I nodded. He whispered, "I saw your friend, Reinhard Heydrich. He's with a group of high-level party members in a box on stage left." This gave me the chills. If it wasn't for my violin, he'd just as soon send me to a detention camp.

The orchestra assembled. Uncle Wilhelm once again took to the podium and the second act began. Soon the first scene would be coming to an end. Athanaël and Thaïs are arguing on the stage: he is begging her to give up her life of sin and she is equivocating. Finally, Athanaël says that he will wait for her: *"J'attendrai ta venue."* And Thaïs, in inner torment, declares she will not change: *"Je reste Thaïs, Thaïs la courtisane."* She laughs derisively and then begins to sob. The curtain falls — and it's

160

time for the intermezzo. My intermezzo.

I knew this piece so well, it just flowed. Uncle Wilhelm, his arms stretched regally over the orchestra, his head slowly nodding, his body lifting, felt the music just as I did. He drew the pathos out of me. I played it from my sitting position in the second section. The hall was totally silent but for my violin and the orchestra quietly supporting me like a pillow. In five minutes, I was finished. The applause was loud. I heard shouts of "Bravo." I saw my string section tipping their bows and smiling. And then it was on to scene two.

When the opera ended and we were packing our instruments, several of the members came over to congratulate me. They asked how I liked playing with the orchestra. I told them it was a dream come true. But some of the members avoided me. A small cadre confronted Uncle Wilhelm. There was arm gesticulation and raised voices. I heard the word "girl" several times. I saw Uncle Wilhelm shrug and shake his head. Then I heard the word "Jew."

Two SS officers in black uniforms and long leather coats came backstage. They went into a corner with Uncle Wilhelm and talked quietly, but the conversation was not friendly. I knew it was about me.

When everyone had left, I asked Uncle Wil-

161

helm what the conversation was about. At first, he tried to brush it away. I told him I heard some members say "girl" and "Jew." He nodded.

"First of all, Ada, you better get used to this backstabbing if you intend to pursue a career in music. Ever since we started rehearsals, I've been hearing grumbling from a few members who resent my giving a seat to a woman. They feel that the 'Meditation' was meant to be played by the first chair. By a man. I told them I made the decision on the basis of talent and I am the music director. That didn't make them happy, but they know it's true. Then, of course, they played the 'Jewish' card. Why did I invite a Jew to play with the orchestra when Goebbels removed six of the members last fall solely because they were Jewish?"

"That's a fair question," I said. "They're right to resent me."

Uncle Wilhelm grabbed me by the shoulders and looked at me sternly. "No, they're wrong. You are innocent, just as the six members were last fall. My players should resent the Reich for its racist policies, not you. You didn't displace anyone, Ada. That chair was empty. It was Chaim Rosenberg's chair and he was barred last October. The truth is we were short and needed another talented violinist and I filled it with the best

162

one I know. It was strictly a professional decision."

"Thank you," I said. "What did the two Nazis want? I saw them talk to you."

"Same thing. Someone sent word to Goebbels that you were sitting in the pit and playing a prominent piece. They ordered me to release you."

Now I felt terrible. Not only did members of the orchestra resent me, but Uncle Wilhelm was in trouble with the SS. "Please let me resign. I'm causing too much trouble. There's dissension among the members, and now you are in trouble with the SS."

"And what about tomorrow night's performance?" he said. "Shall I just hum the 'Meditation'?"

"Peter Strom can play it. He's first violin."

"Did you hear the applause tonight, Ada? Did you hear the shouts of 'Bravo'? Strom cannot deliver that performance. Look, I'm not afraid of the SS. I'm not afraid of Goebbels, Hitler, Göring or any of them. I am Furtwängler. I told those two SS officers that I will make the decisions on who plays and who doesn't. If they don't like it, then they can get another music director. Believe me, they're not going to do anything, especially six weeks before the Summer Olympics."

It was empowering to have the great Furtwängler standing in my corner. "Thank you," I said. "Thank you for everything you are doing for my career."

But Uncle Wilhelm sighed. "Ada, my dear Ada. There is only so much I can do. I cannot stem the tide in Germany. Right now, this summer, there is an artificial lull, like the eye of a hurricane. There is no overt persecution of Jews. There are no mass arrests, there are no hateful articles in the Nazi newspapers and there are no new laws designed to punish Jews. But after the Olympics, when Hitler will no longer care if the world is watching, the lull will end. You must make plans to leave."

"Where would I go? What about my parents?"

"I can protect your father, at least for a while. But mark my words, the day after the closing ceremony, you and the other Jews will be dismissed from the Junior Orchestra. We need to find you a place to play."

"He's right, Ada. Maybe it's time for all of us to leave Germany," my father said after we arrived at the house.

"It would be hard, this is my home," my mother said. "But I am afraid to walk the streets. When I think about Grandpa and what those monsters did to him, I have no love for the Germans."

"It's not the Germans, Mama," I said. "It's the Nazis. Maybe things will change. Right now, things are quiet."

"Only because of the Olympics," my father added.

"Are you prepared to leave Wilhelm, Jacob?" my mother asked. "I worry he will not have his concertmaster on the eve of the Philharmonic's fall season. Is that the right thing to do to a man who has been so good to us?"

"I'm torn, Friede. I don't want to leave Wilhelm short this season. I don't want to let my colleagues down. All my life I have cared nothing for politics, I've taken no sides, I've hurt no one. My life has been dedicated to my family and my music." He shook his head. "I cannot put you in danger any longer. I will talk to Wilhelm. Perhaps I'll stay one more season. But you and Ada should go."

"Where?"

"I don't know. We'll find a place."

"I'm not leaving without you," she said.

NINETEEN

Berlin, August 1, 1936

The XI Olympiad, the 1936 Berlin summer games, was staged as Hitler's showcase. The Hitler Games. Pomp and pageantry were the stars, and the superiority of his Aryan athletes was to be his exclamation point. Take notice world, Germany is back, powerful again, economically sound and prepared to accept its role as a world leader. And this, only a decade and a half after being vanquished in war and stripped of its pride by the Treaty of Versailles.

Berlin's avenues were lined with flowers, Nazi banners and Olympic flags. Thousands of young people dressed in white were everywhere, offering to help visitors in any way they could. Colorful posters emphasized the link between ancient Greece and Nazi Germany. Hitler even staged a relay of torchbearers who ran all the way from Athens to Berlin, a first in Olympic history. For two weeks in August, all signs of German racist policies were masked. To all appearances, Germany was a warm and welcoming society.

But we knew better. During the previous two years, Jewish athletes had been purged from the German sporting clubs. As the games approached, Germany had only two token Jews on the team: Helene Mayer, the world's greatest woman fencer, and Gretel Bergmann, a record-holder in the high jump. Two weeks before the games began, Gretel was removed from the team. It was rumored that Helene was acceptable to the Nazis because her mother was not Jewish.

Once again, the Junior was scheduled to play during the opening ceremonies and at a Sunday afternoon concert one week later. On August 1, we sat in the stands in the far end of the oval Olympic Stadium, a massive concrete structure built specifically for the games. Like the Roman emperors, Hitler and the elite party members sat in a specially built mezzanine section. A fanfare sounded, and Hitler and his entourage entered to 110,000 shouts of "Seig Heil" and 110,000 arms raised in Hitler salutes.

Germany had 348 athletes, the largest in the games. During the parade of athletes, the Americans insulted Hitler by giving an "eyes right" salute and not a Hitler salute, and by refusing to dip the flag as they passed Hitler's reviewing stand. I was proud of the brash Americans, that is, until the final days of the games when, for some undisclosed reason, they pulled their Jewish athletes from the 4 by 100 meter relay.

To start the festivities, the airship *Hindenburg* flew across the stadium pulling the Olympic flag, and the response was deafening. A welcoming speech was given by the head of the Olympic Organizing Committee. Hitler announced, "I proclaim the Games of Berlin, celebrating the eleventh Olympiad of the modern era, to be open." Richard Strauss then led the Berlin Philharmonic and the National Socialist Symphony Orchestra in the "Olympische Hymne," a four-minute piece he had composed.

Uncle Wilhelm did not conduct at the games at all. Everyone believed that it was due to an incident that happened a few weeks earlier at the Bayreuth Festival. I asked Papa what that was all about, and he said, "I recently learned about it from Friedelind Wagner. Do you remember her?"

I did. She'd been to our house for a social gathering. "She's Richard Wagner's granddaughter."

"Yes, and unlike her mother, she's no friend of the Nazis. She told me about a meeting she witnessed between Wilhelm and Hitler at her mother's house. Hitler told Wilhelm that the Olympics were coming, and he wanted to use Wilhelm for a Nazi

Party propaganda film. Wilhelm flatly refused. No propaganda for him. Hitler flew into a rage and said, 'In that case there will be a concentration camp ready for you.' As you might imagine, Wilhelm stuck out his chin and replied, 'In that case, Herr Reichskanzler, at least I will be in very good company.' Friedelind told me that Hitler was red-faced and stormed out of the room."

I told my father I was worried about Uncle Wilhelm. "Hitler is irrational and Uncle Wilhelm is arrogant. That's a bad combination. He might be sent to a concentration camp."

"The great Furtwängler seems to know his boundaries. He is no fool. He's confident that his prestige gives him a certain level of invulnerability. To tell you the truth, it's that arrogance that keeps me and the few Jewish orchestra members still working. Uncle Wilhelm takes no guff from the Nazi Party leaders. Even der führer."

Guff or no guff, the great Furtwängler did not conduct his orchestra at the games.

The Junior was scheduled to play the matinee on Sunday afternoon at the newly built Dietrich-Eckart Open Air Theater. I was to solo the "Meditation" as the next-to-last number. I was so excited. The world press would be there. And best of all, it was to be televised!

On Friday, Dr. Kritzer asked me to come into his office. "Ada, I am very sad to tell

169

you this. Believe me, it was not my choice. I am striking the 'Meditation' from the program."

My heart sank. "Why? What did I do?"

He shook his head. "You didn't do anything. Dr. Goebbels and Dr. von Halt came to me earlier today. They ordered me to have someone else play the 'Meditation.' Someone who wasn't Jewish. They said it didn't comport with the Olympic theme of German superiority."

"I am a German!" I said, clenching my fists.

Dr. Kritzer hung his head. "I'm sorry, there was nothing I could do. I pulled the selection from the program. I won't have anyone else play it."

I was boiling. "No one else *can* play it!"

All Dr. Kritzer could do was shake his head. Uncle Wilhelm would never have crumbled like that, but Dr. Kritzer was no Furtwängler.

"Then I'm not going to play at all Sunday," I said. "I'm not coming."

His head hung low and he wiped a tear from his eye. "I understand."

Although I hadn't yet decided about the fall season, I never played for the Junior again.

TWENTY

Pienza, July 2017

Liam rolled over, noticed that the other side of his bed was empty and sat up. Catherine was standing by the window.

"Cat, are you all right? It's three a.m."

"Sorry, I didn't mean to wake you."

"It's metaphysical. I can sense when you leave the bed. Why are you up?"

"Didn't you hear it?"

"Hear what?"

"The music."

"I was sleeping. What music?"

"I don't know. I don't hear it now. I know you'll think I'm crazy, but it sounded like someone playing the violin."

Liam walked over and embraced her from behind. "You were dreaming. Ada's story is putting thoughts into your head."

"No, Liam, I wasn't sleeping. I woke up an hour ago and I've been lying here listening to the music. Someone's playing the violin."

"What was the person playing?"

"I don't know, just some scales and a sweet melody."

"Don't you think it might have been the wind?"

Catherine turned and gave Liam a look. "I know the difference between the wind and a musical instrument."

"Maybe Aunt Gabi was playing the violin. Or maybe it was Floria."

Catherine nodded. "Could be."

"Or what? Ada's ghost? Would you come back to bed now, please? We have an appointment with the lawyer in Siena at nine o'clock."

Floria brought a fresh pot of coffee out to the veranda to where Catherine and Liam sat. "How are you two this morning?"

"Just fine," Liam said. "We're getting ready to drive to Siena. We have an appointment with Mr. Santi."

"Hmph," Floria responded. "The eloquent Mr. Santi. Very smooth, very expensive and very ineffective."

Catherine turned in her chair. "Floria, does Signora Gabriella play the violin?"

"Why do you ask?"

"I heard someone playing the violin last night."

Floria shrugged. "Sometimes the wind blows though the cedars and can make a whistling sound."

"That's what I thought," Liam said.
"It wasn't the wind," Catherine replied.

The ride from Pienza to Siena took almost an hour. With the windows rolled down, Catherine's eyes were glued to the landscape and her hair was tousled by the wind. The road meandered past vineyards, farms, cypress-covered mountains and several small hilltop villages, all too picturesque for Catherine to pass without recording the moment.

"Liam, pull over, I want to take a picture. Just look at that view. Have you ever seen anything like it?" She held her hands like a picture frame. "Wouldn't this look great on the den wall? My sister will be so jealous."

"Cat, we're supposed to be in Siena by nine o'clock and you heard Floria describe Mr. Santi. He bills by the minute."

"But look, Liam, look at that farm — the neat little rows of trees, there must be a thousand of them. Do you suppose they're olive trees? Stop, seriously, I need to get a picture."

Where Pienza is a sleepy little Tuscan village with barely two thousand people, Siena is a larger, more commercial city with over fifty thousand inhabitants. In addition to being the seat of government for the province, it is a major tourist hub. The center of the city, partially walled off from the twenty-first

173

century, is a fourteenth-century jewel, adhering as closely as commercially feasible to its medieval Tuscan lineage. Sylvio Santi's office was a short distance from the old city.

Santi greeted Liam and Catherine, warmly shaking both their hands. His blue designer suit, smartly tailored to his thin figure, his styled brown hair with touches of gray and his gold watch and cufflinks confirmed the image Floria had described. Santi led them to his conference room where his window overlooked the Duomo, the white-and-green marble Siena Cathedral, once the largest basilica in the world. He smoothly gestured for them to be seated.

"How is the lovely Signora Vincenzo?" he asked, and without waiting for an answer, he said, "You know, I negotiated a very favorable solution for the signora. She has no legal rights, none at all." He leaned forward in his chair, his manicured hands folded on the table. "But I appealed to Mr. Mastroviani, VinCo's senior vice president, who happens to be a very good friend of mine. I said, 'Riccardo, we must help this lovely widow. Think of the goodwill that would come to VinCo.' " Santi smiled and pointed to his head. "You see, I was playing on their sympathies and telling them that it would be good public relations for them to give Signora Vincenzo money and a place to live."

"Tell me, Mr. Santi, why doesn't she have

legal rights to the property?" Catherine asked.

Santi spread his hands. "Why does the sun come up in the morning? Because it is a fact. VinCo owns the land. Signora Vincenzo has been living there for many years but has never owned the land. The deed that she recorded in 1995 at the Registrar of Titles was a worthless piece of paper."

"What do you know about the Quercia Company?"

He pursed his lips and shook his head. "Not much. It was the prior owner of the property. An Italian corporation. Apparently inactive. Quercia never took any steps to operate the farm or harvest the grapes. So I guess that is why Signora Vincenzo took it on herself to do so. I suppose, in legal terms, she was a squatter. Eventually, VinCo took the initiative to investigate the company. They discovered it was owned by the late Gerda Fruman. Signora Vincenzo could have accomplished the same thing herself, had she come to me many years ago. Perhaps the signora could have made a similar offer."

"Why does VinCo care so much about Gabriella's property?"

"Simple. It is thirty hectares of tillable land sitting in the middle of VinCo's operation. It is currently a nuisance to them, but it could be usable. The signora tells me she plants vines, but I don't know. I know that commercially, VinCo can make much better use of the land than a sick, elderly woman."

"What is the market value of this nuisance?" Liam asked.

Santi shrugged. "A million euros, more or less."

"Tell me, how does VinCo allege to have obtained a valid deed?" Catherine said.

"Allege? VinCo followed the law. It found out that Gerda Fruman was the sole owner and that she died. VinCo opened an estate in Germany and got a deed from the public administrator. It was all very legal."

"How did Quercia Company become the owner?"

Santi smiled. "They are listed on the books as far back as it goes."

"You mean to 1980?"

Santi nodded. "They are shown as the owner in 1980."

"Who owned the property before 1980?"

Santi shrugged again. "Quercia, I'm sure."

"What makes you so sure?"

"When the Registrar of Titles makes a new book, as he did in 1980, he copies the last known owner from the previous book. So it had to be Quercia. Bear in mind, Miss Lockhart, that no one contested Quercia's title for almost forty years."

"Someone would have to know that Quercia was listed as the owner to contest it, though, wouldn't they?"

"Perhaps, but the book is a public record

for all to see. I do not undertand the importance of this discussion. The issue is closed."

"Mr. Santi, the fact that I am sitting at this desk should tell you that the issue is not closed."

"You are wasting your time and, frankly, mine as well."

"Truly sorry. May I ask one more question? Who sold the property to Quercia Company and when?"

Santi shook his head. "It would be in the older books and they are in storage."

"Why didn't you look at the older books to find out?" Catherine said.

Santi had an irritated look on his face. "I did order the book, but I didn't follow up on it. I was arguing with the signora, it would have been a waste of time and the amount of my fee was becoming an issue. I never went back to the registrar. Why would it matter who sold the property to Quercia? Maybe it was Piccolomini himself. What's the difference who?"

"Because maybe the 'who' never had good title to begin with, nor the right to transfer it to Quercia. Maybe Quercia's title was defective."

"And maybe the moon is made of green cheese. I'm sorry, Miss Lockhart, but the matter is closed. A judge has ruled, and I tell you, he has ruled correctly. But the good news is this: even though the signora has no legal rights, I believe I can still prevail upon VinCo to honor that wonderful arrangement I worked out. VinCo's lawyer, Mr. Lenzini, happens to be a very good personal friend of mine."

"Why did I know that?" Liam said under his breath.

Santi stood, signaling that the meeting was over.

"One more thing," Catherine said. "Did you contact Mr. Vanucci to learn why he would give a deed to Gabriella?"

Santi chuckled and shook his head. "Two reasons, Miss Lockhart, and then we must end this meeting. *Uno,* it would make no difference what he had to say, even if I could find him. The book is the best evidence. And *Due,* my rates are very expensive, and I do not recklessly charge my clients for chasing wild gooses."

"Thank you, Mr. Santi. Can you point us to the government office where the property records are kept?"

"But of course."

Catherine and Liam decided to have lunch before tackling the registrar's office. There were several restaurants lining the brick seashell-like plaza that was known as the Piazza del Campo. It seemed to be the thing to do in Siena. There were students, tourists and even businessmen in suits sitting on the

178

bricks of the Piazza del Campo. At the base of the piazza stood the brick-and-stone Palazzo Pubblico, with its crowned campanile, at one time the tallest tower in Italy. Catherine ordered a vegetable assortment while Liam opted for the pepperoni pizza, which he devoured without any help from Catherine.

Liam took a sip of beer, stared out at the Campo, the medieval gathering place still functioning so gracefully in modern-day Italy, smiled at Catherine and said, "Tell me again that we could live here."

"Oh, I could. I'd move tomorrow. Let's sell the Chicago house. I'll work in that store over there selling sunglasses while I learn Italian law. Then I'll open up an office right here in Siena. I certainly couldn't do any worse than Santi. Or Giangiorgi. Tony warned us about the lawyers he hired. He said they were all paid off. At the time, I took it with a grain of salt. But this guy, Santi, has a lot of *very good friends* that are all on the payroll of VinCo. I have no proof Santi was paid off, but he certainly didn't advocate very hard for Gabriella."

"What should he have done, sunglasses girl?"

"Well, to begin with, he never should have assumed that the listing of Quercia as owner in the 1980 registry book was correct. He should have confirmed the chain of title. Both

179

Santi and Giangiorgi should have examined the prior registry books, and that's exactly what we're going to do, Liam."

"Santi said he ordered the book but changed his mind."

"Right. Stinks like a dead fish." Catherine reached into her valise and took out Gabriella's deed. "Carlo Vanucci. If he's still alive, we need to find him. He'll know why he deeded the property to Gabriella in 1995."

"Find Vanucci? Is that my job?" asked Liam.

"Definitely your job."

At the Registrar of Titles, Catherine asked if there was an English-speaking person who could assist her. In a few minutes, an older man in blue slacks and a short-sleeve white shirt came out to the counter. His reading glasses hung from a chain around his neck. He had three pens in his shirt pocket.

"I can converse with you in English," he said with a smile and wagged his finger back and forth, "if you don't get too complicated."

Catherine handed Gabriella's deed to him. "We'd like to see the book where this deed is recorded and also the prior book."

The clerk returned in a few minutes with a large, heavy clothbound volume. He turned to a page and pointed to an entry. "Here is the notation for this deed. It was recorded in 1995. But as you can see, the owner of the property at that time is shown as Quercia

Company, not Vanucci. Apparently, your deed is out of the chain of title."

"May we see the older book, the one where Quercia Company became the owner."

"That volume is in storage in the archive building. It's a few kilometers from here. I can put in a request for the book, but it is normally done with an attorney."

"I am an attorney in America. All we want to do is look at the book."

He nodded. "There is a twenty-euro fee. Fill out this form, and I will order it for you, but it might take several days."

TWENTY-ONE

Berlin, November 1936

The relative tolerance that was exhibited during the months preceding the Olympics vanished after the rest of the world went home. The false congeniality that Hitler marketed to the world was replaced by a renewal of his venomous campaign against non-Aryans. *Der Stürmer,* Julius Streicher's tabloid newspaper, was so hateful, so incendiary, that it was banned from publication during the Olympics, but just a few weeks into the fall, there it was on the newsstands. Once again, the cover page depicted horrid cartoon caricatures of ugly Jewish monsters with grotesque noses, sexually abusing innocent German girls. *Der Stürmer* was the workingman's newspaper and it appealed mainly to the lower strata of German society, but it had a large circulation and was prominently displayed everywhere periodicals were sold.

The mainstream *Völkischer Beobachter,*

the Nazi Party's official newspaper, resumed running stories that accused the "scheming Jewish banking elite" and "Jewish dishonesty in business." It praised the efforts of the government to stop Jewish corruption. It lauded the removal of Jews from their positions in education and the arts.

Nazi Party members, now numbering in the millions, were forbidden from having contact with Jews, and that mandate was broader than mere social contact: it meant no commerce whatsoever. Thus, no party member could buy from a Jewish shop or hire a Jewish worker. An infraction could result in a trial by the Nazi Party court and removal from the party.

Almost daily, there were proclamations from Hitler or Goebbels designed to disparage Jews or isolate us economically. If it wasn't for the fact they were cumulatively toxic, some of the proclamations were downright laughable. For example, on September 19, all German churches were required to eliminate the word "hallelujah" from prayers because it was a Hebrew word.

We all saw the writing on the wall, but some were quicker to act than others. Many of my parents' Jewish friends were leaving or making plans to leave. "Do you have a bag packed?" was a question heard more and more frequently. Some were planning to move to Palestine, some even as far as

South America. It wasn't easy to move to another European country. Visa restrictions were complicated. It was even harder to emigrate to the United States, which had a Jewish quota of 27,000 for Germany and Austria combined. On top of that, Germany had imposed a severe emigration penalty called the *Reichsfluchtsteuer* — the Reich Flight Tax — equal to 25 percent of the value of one's assets, payable in cash before one could leave.

Despite the tax and the emigration hurdles, Jewish houses were flooding the market. My parents' friends who still owned stores were trying to sell them before they became Aryanized. Those who were licensed professionals had either lost their license to practice or been severely restricted, and they were searching for jobs in other countries.

Perhaps the most hurtful and inimical result of the campaign was the pervasive acceptance of Nazi policies by German society. While the law didn't require our non-Jewish friends to shun us, it became apparent that they would no longer stand up for us. Those who uttered hateful speech were sinful, but the greater sin was committed by those who did not speak at all. Some would sigh and turn the other way. It was painful when one of my friends stopped inviting me to her home or when she abruptly canceled a social engagement. Too often I would hear, "I'm sorry but so-and-so is coming, and you know how they feel." Polite avoidance became a social norm.

As for me, I did not rejoin the Junior after the Olympics. Both Uncle Wilhelm and Papa urged me to return to practice in September, and in truth, I was considering it, when on September 25, the Berlin Junior Orchestra became *Judenfrei.* No more Jews. The four other Jewish girls who were still in the Junior came to practice one Thursday and were told to go home. Dr. Kritzer was sorry. Everyone was always "sorry."

I still attended the Jewish high school, but I became conscious of dangers walking to and from the school. The Brownshirts, substantially reduced since the rise of the SS, still roved the streets, committing random abuse with abject autonomy. I stopped walking the dog in the Tiergarten, our favorite playground, for fear of running into Brownshirts. One afternoon while walking Mitzi on Behrenstrasse, I stopped at the Jewish grocery store. A few minutes later, five Brownshirts came into the store, laughing and talking very loudly. I knew party rules didn't allow them to shop there, so it was bound to be an abusive encounter. They went behind the counter, stuffed their pockets with packages of cigarettes and started to leave. One of them stopped,

185

stared at me and said, "What are you looking at? Do you have a problem with this vile shopkeeper voluntarily giving us cigarettes? Do you? Ask him if he's bothered."

I stood there frozen in fear. The Brownshirt stepped closer, inches away. "Go ahead," he commanded, "ask him. I said ask him if he's bothered."

I swallowed. "Are you bothered?" I said with a lump in my throat. The shopkeeper shook his head.

Then the Brownshirt pointed at me. "But *you're* bothered, aren't you? You think he should be paid, don't you?"

I don't know where I got the courage, or the foolhardiness, but I shrugged my shoulders and nodded my head. "Yes, I do."

"Good. Then pay him," he said. "Pay the shopkeeper for the cigarettes, you smartass little Jewess."

I took money out of my purse and put it on the counter. The Brownshirt laughed heartily, scooped up my money and walked out of the store.

Daily life in Berlin had become incomprehensible. How does one respond to something one cannot understand? Every day another edict. Every day another piece of life was torn away. In our house, as in other Jewish households, the subject of relocating was always on the table.

"I went by the Deutsche Bank today and while I was there I spoke with Don Probst," my father said. "He asked me how we were doing. He asked about you, Ada. And then he quietly said he wanted to give me a warning. He told me Deutsche Bank had just initiated severe lending guidelines for non-Aryan businesses, and they have started to call loans of non-Aryan borrowers if they felt they were in acute risk of default."

My mother slammed her palm on the table as if to say, "Enough is enough!" Deutsche Bank held the mortgage on our house. "Is that supposed to mean us? We've never missed a single payment," she said, "and we don't even owe that much. The mortgage balance is low and the market value is high. There is substantial equity in our house. How can the bank be at risk?"

"He wasn't talking about us, Friede. He didn't say the bank perceives *our* loan to be insecure. He was talking about loans to Jews in general. They're insecure because being a Jew is insecure. I'm a Jewish musician playing professionally in an orchestra that is supposed to be Aryan only. They see Furtwängler's rebellious protection of his Jewish musicians as temporary at best. 'As much as I'm against it,' Probst told me, 'the bank is going to request non-Aryan borrowers to pay off their loans. Sell their houses, if need be. Maybe that won't apply to you,

Jacob, but if your situation were to change at all, well, you understand, there wouldn't be much I could do.' "

"Do we have to sell our house?" I asked. "Where would we go?"

"There's no reason to panic, Ada. Mr. Probst said that for the moment we were okay. You're going to stay here and finish your senior year in high school. Then, as we've discussed, we're going to look for a college or a music academy."

"But Papa, they're all closed to Jews."

"Then we'll look outside of Germany. It's time to start sending out applications anyway. The Paris Conservatory has a wonderful program. There are also very good academies in Belgium and London."

My post–high school plans were once again brought to the surface three months later. My father brought Uncle Wilhelm over for dinner and both of them wore that I've-got-a-secret smile.

"Ada, you know how we've been talking about what you'll do next year?" my father said.

I knew. In January, I had sent applications to the Paris Conservatory, the Royal Academy of Music in London and the Royal Conservatory of Brussels. I had not heard back from any of them. The scary truth was that they were extremely selective, and I was a German and a Jew. Since I hadn't received an invitation to audition, I was not hopeful.

"Well, Uncle Wilhelm has some very good news."

Uncle Wilhelm smiled at me. "I've been watching you since you were a little baby. I have seen you blossom into one of the finest musicians in Europe. Now it's time we all think about what to do with Ada, the prodigy. Where does she go to continue her brilliant career? Unfortunately, we all know that you have no future here in Berlin. Even General Heydrich told you that."

I nodded. I was well aware. So far this did not sound like very good news.

The maestro continued. "I recently spoke to Stefano Vittorio, the director of the Bologna State Opera. He called me last week to ask if I could recommend an accomplished violinist. One of his violinists is about to go on sabbatical and won't be returning until after the season. He hasn't been able to fill the vacancy and he's looking for someone available in the fall, someone who will agree to a one-year appointment. He's very picky."

I'm listening to Uncle Wilhelm and my heart starts beating like a drum. Oh my God, he means me.

"I told him I had just the person. Ada Baumgarten. You can imagine the buildup I gave you. When I told him about your talents and your performances to standing ovations, well, he said he'd be honored to give you an audition. If he likes what he hears, you can come for rehearsals beginning in July and stay for the entire 1937–1938 season. And the pay is good. Ada, he's not opposed to having a woman sit in his orchestra. You wouldn't be a permanent member, just a guest for a year, but he told me he has no prejudices against women. Ada, I have no doubt you'll be sitting in the violin section of the Bologna State Opera when their season begins next September."

I was flustered. "When am I supposed to audition? What should I prepare?"

Uncle Wilhelm smiled. "The auditions are in May. And do I need to tell you what to play? Doesn't my little Ada have her signature piece?"

"The 'Meditation'?" I said softly.

He nodded. "And that's not all. Maestro Vittorio is also on the faculty of the University of Bologna, the oldest university in the Western world. They have a doctoral program in music."

I was overjoyed. "What do I need to do?"

Uncle Wilhelm smiled. "If it were me, I'd start learning Italian."

My father and I were delighted, but my mother did not smile. "Italy is a fascist state," she said. "Mussolini is a dictator.

How will Jews be treated in Italy? The same or worse than here? I don't want Ada to travel to Italy only to be persecuted."

"The fascist government does not persecute Jews," Uncle Wilhelm said. "There are no exclusionary signs, there are no limits on professional licenses, there is no prohibition on social contact and they do not interfere with Jewish musicians. Jews enjoy legal equality in Italy."

"But Mussolini is a friend of Hitler. Didn't they sign a treaty last November?"

"Friede, that was the Anti-Comintern Pact. It was signed by a dozen countries to oppose communism. It had nothing to do with Jews. This is a wonderful opportunity for Ada. Be happy for her."

Twenty-Two

Berlin, April 1937

Many of my high school classmates did not come to school today. It was Hitler's forty-eighth birthday and he was scheduled to review troops here in Berlin. There were thousands of German soldiers everywhere. They were on the Unter den Linden, they were in the Tiergarten, they were on the streets, in the cafés, in the parks and in our neighborhood. Many Jewish families chose to keep their children at home. On my way to school, I passed three separate formations of Wehrmacht soldiers. Naturally, I looked to see if Kurt was among them. I was not especially frightened by the Wehrmacht. They were soldiers, not Brownshirts, and I hadn't had any run-ins with them, although that was a distinction that was foolish. After all, Kleiner was a Wehrmacht corporal.

The papers announced the opening of the Adolf Hitler Schulen — the first of fifty planned schools that would train and edu-

cate the Hitler Youth. The papers also ran a story on how the Jews made their fortunes by lending money at usurious rates and fencing stolen goods. But most of the stories were about the various ways that Berliners were celebrating and wishing their führer a happy birthday.

There was a note in the mailbox for me when I came home from school: "Queen Louise at 6:30." My heart leapt. I recognized the handwriting. It was a note from Kurt telling me to meet him at the statue of Queen Louise in the Tiergarten. My mother cautioned me not to go. It was too dangerous; there were Brownshirts and soldiers marching through the Tiergarten. I told her I'd be careful.

I stood at the base of the statue, holding Mitzi on a leash. From time to time, groups of soldiers would pass. No one paid any attention to me. It was starting to get dark. Finally, I saw Kurt approaching in full uniform. He scanned the area and the footpaths, took me behind the statue and kissed me. With my arms around him, I could feel that the army was toughening him up. There were taut muscles in his neck and back that hadn't been there before. I hadn't seen him in a year and he had grown even more handsome.

"I can only stay a minute," he said. "I came to warn you."

"What? Warn me?"

"Kleiner. He has been swearing to get even with you and your family."

"Still? That concert was years ago."

"It's a deep wound, Ada. At the time, he was an adjutant to Reinhard Heydrich. He thought he had cemented a career with the general. According to his father, Kleiner's future was set. After all, Heydrich is now director of the Gestapo. To his father's way of thinking he should have been the deputy director, not merely a corporal in the army. Kleiner won't let that go."

"Then he should have kept his mouth shut. I didn't do anything other than play my violin. But why now?"

"Every so often, Kleiner puts in for a transfer. He'd like to be back with the SS. In his most recent application he cited his service, which included a stint as an adjutant to Heydrich. After contacting Heydrich, they denied his request for a transfer. Despite all of his father's influence, he still hasn't been transferred back. I don't know the stated reasons for the denials, but he says it's all your fault. Now he's in Berlin, he knows your name, I'm sure he knows your address and he's swearing to get even. Tell your father to take you and your mother out of the city for a few days. Our unit will be here until Friday."

A group of soldiers approached from the

east and Kurt said, "I have to leave. Those men are from my squad."

"Don't leave yet."

"Gotta go."

"Just one kiss?" I said.

He gave me a kiss that lifted me off my feet, smiled and disappeared into the woods.

My father rejected the suggestion that we get out of town. "We'll lock the doors. I have my father's hunting rifle. If someone is brash enough to break in, German law justifies me in protecting myself."

"Oh, I'm sure the criminal court judge would agree with you," my mother said. "It's always justifiable for a Jew to shoot a Wehrmacht corporal. Jacob, where is your head?"

"Where do you think we should go, Friede? If you took a ride with me like Ada did, you'd see the signs: 'Jews not welcome in this town.' There's nowhere for us to go."

"We could stay with friends. I'm sure Marcia Stein would put us up."

"Do you want to place the Steins in danger?"

"Then we should stay in the house and not leave until Friday. It's only two nights. I'm going to keep Ada in the house," my mother said. "I'll stay in as well."

Papa shook his head. "I have a concert tomorrow night. You two will have to come with me. I can't leave you home alone."

The short ride to the Philharmonie was uneventful. As always, the streets surrounding the Tiergarten and the Philharmonie were busy. Tonight's program included Brahms and the house was full. It was always a treat to watch Uncle Wilhelm conduct. His energy was infectious. I wished I was sitting in the orchestra and watching him from the front. At the start of the second half of the concert, the orchestra played "Happy Birthday Dear Führer." I looked around, but I didn't see him in the house.

After the concert, we gathered backstage. Uncle Wilhelm could sense that something was wrong. "We've received a threat," my father said. "It's that spiteful soldier I told you about, the one who blames Ada for his misfortunes. He says he intends to get even. We received word that he's in town for the birthday celebration. Given the current climate in Berlin, it's conceivable he could arrest and detain her or take her some place for interrogation."

"Good lord, Jacob. Have you reported this threat to the police?"

"Would that make a difference, Wilhelm?"

"Let me send someone to follow you home."

Papa shook his head. "We'll go straight home and lock our doors. He'll be gone by tomorrow. Maybe the threat was exaggerated."

"I think you should have someone protecting you. I wouldn't take the threat lightly."

My father shrugged, thanked him for his concern, and we left.

By the time we left the Philharmonie, the hall was empty and the streets were quiet. The ten-minute taxi ride was unremarkable. All of us kept a careful eye as we exited the cab and my father paid the driver. We started walking to the front door when Kleiner and two other men appeared out of nowhere.

"This is the time we settle our debts," he said.

My father grabbed me and put me behind him. "The police have been alerted," Papa said. "You'd better leave."

Kleiner had that sinister sneer on his face. "Let's see now, how does it go?" he said, then raising his voice. "Do you presume to tell me who to praise? Is it now your prerogative? Isn't that how it went?"

The three soldiers moved closer. I could see handcuffs in Kleiner's right hand. He stood inches from my father and said, "Do you remember the words? I remember every single word. They haunt me." Then in a mimicking tone: "Well, I am telling you that the girl is brilliant, you ignorant idiot. Simpleminded asshole. You have the manners of an undignified boor. I am ashamed to be in your company. I can assure you that it will not happen again." He pointed at me and said, "Do you know what those phrases have done to my career?"

"She didn't do anything," Papa said. "You brought it on yourself by trying to correct General Heydrich. You should have kept quiet."

Kleiner reached over, grabbed my father by the lapels of his coat and threw him to the ground. "The great concertmaster tells me to keep quiet. Is that now your prerogative, Herr Concertmaster, to tell a Wehrmacht officer to keep quiet? Isn't that how it goes, you simpleminded asshole? Those were the words that killed my career. How is *your* career, Herr Concertmaster? Is it intact? I wonder how well your career would fare if it was sabotaged by some smart-ass girl. Because that's what happened to me. How well would you play if someone broke your arms?" He turned to his companions. "Maybe we should find out. Which arm should we break? The right one pulls the bow. But the left one plays the notes. I can't decide. Should we flip a coin? Nah, let's break them both."

"Stop!" my mother yelled. "You're a monster. Someone help us!"

He laughed, and then he grabbed my

wrist. "We are all going to Sachsenhausen for a little chat."

"For what?"

He shrugged. "For intensive interrogation." Turning to his companions, he said, "Bring them all along. And let's make sure that the concertmaster suffers an unfortunate accident along the way."

One of the soldiers picked my father up off the ground. He held his arm straight out while the other soldier prepared to strike him with a nightstick.

I tried to pull away from Kleiner's grip. I was hysterical. "Don't you touch him!" I yelled. "He didn't do anything." With all my strength, I kicked Kleiner in his shin. My heel caught him square on the bone; he yelled and loosened his grip long enough for me to break free. I flew at the man with the nightstick, knocking him sideways.

"You little bitch," I heard Kleiner say, and he grabbed me from behind. He had me in a choke hold and I thought I would pass out, when suddenly we were flooded by the headlights of a black Mercedes that had pulled into the driveway. Kleiner and his men froze. The back door of the car opened, and a Wehrmacht colonel got out. The uniformed officer and his adjutant walked slowly up the driveway. "What's going on here, Corporal?"

Kleiner immediately snapped his heels

and saluted. His two companions stood at attention, released my father and gave an exaggerated Hitler salute. Kleiner responded as calmly as he could. "It is nothing for you to be concerned about, Herr Oberst. I have the matter under control."

"What matter is that?"

"These people are Jews, Herr Oberst. They have been denounced as enemies of the state. We are taking them to Sachsenhausen for questioning."

"To the concentration camp? Have they been assigned there? May I please see your orders?"

"I . . . I have no specific orders, other than the desire to protect my fatherland from the treachery of Jews. They have been denounced by a concerned citizen and they need to be interrogated and I . . . I thought Sachsenhausen would be appropriate for that. It is the designated detention area for political prisoners."

"The man whose arms you were about to break, what treachery has he committed?"

"Well, he has interfered with my questioning of his daughter, and he is a Jew who plays in the Philharmonic in violation of Dr. Goebbels' directives. I am sorry, Herr Oberst, I only live to serve the Reich. I am going to take them all in for questioning, and we will see what else we can learn about their treachery."

"The girl, what threats does she pose to the fatherland?"

Kleiner smiled. "Now there, Herr Oberst, I have direct knowledge. She flagrantly insulted me and General Heydrich and brought dishonor upon one of the highest officers in the realm. She continues to defy authority. She even assaulted me just before you arrived. She kicked me in the leg. I was trying to restrain her."

The colonel nodded. "I saw the restraint. The occasion at which she brought such dishonor, did that occur on the stage of the Berlin Junior Orchestra?"

Kleiner's face lost its color. This colonel hadn't just stumbled along. He obviously knew who the players were and what had happened. "Why, yes, Herr Oberst. That is s-so."

The colonel walked to my father and brushed the dirt off his coat. "Herr Baumgarten, my apologies to you and your family. Maestro Furtwängler sent me with his regards. He said you might need assistance, and indeed he was correct. Are you quite all right?"

My father nodded. "Yes, thank you, Colonel."

Then the colonel turned to me. "Fraulein Baumgarten, are you unharmed?"

I nodded.

"Sir, I was only doing what I've been

201

trained to do," Kleiner said weakly.

"Corporal, who is your commanding officer?"

"Oberstleutnant Martin."

"Are you telling me that he trains Wehrmacht soldiers to brutalize innocent people on the street?"

"No, sir, I was just . . ."

"Where is your unit?"

"Stationed at Barracks sixteen, Herr Oberst."

The colonel pointed to the end of the driveway. "Go! Return to your unit. I shall contact Oberstleutnant Martin and have this incident noted in your file."

Kleiner's jaw was quivering and his body was twitching. He turned and looked directly into my eyes. If looks could kill, I would have been slain on the spot. He spun around, saluted the colonel and walked away.

"Again, my apologies, Herr Baumgarten," the colonel said politely, "and may I say how much I enjoyed the Brahms this evening." The colonel bowed and left.

TWENTY-THREE

Pienza, July 2017

Catherine rolled over and nudged Liam. "Do you hear it?" The bedroom was dark, but for a sliver of moonlight sneaking in through the shutters.

"Hear what?"

"Listen. Just be quiet and listen."

He sat up. "Listen to what?"

"Shh. The music. The violin. Don't tell me you can't hear it."

"Okay."

"Then you *do* hear it?"

"No, but you told me not to tell you that." Liam furrowed his brow and held his breath. Then he shook his head. "I don't hear anything."

Catherine quietly rose from the bed and walked to the window. She slowly opened the shutters and leaned out. After a moment, she returned. "It's not coming from the outside. Someone in the house is playing the violin."

"It's the middle of the night, Cat. If someone wants to play a violin so softly that I can't even hear it, that's really their business, don't you think? Come back to bed."

She shook her head and put on her robe. "I'm going to see where that music is coming from."

She walked quietly toward the front of the house. A light shone under Gabi's bedroom door. Catherine stood outside the door and listened. A beautiful gypsy melody could be faintly heard. Every once in a while, Gabi would talk to someone. A few minutes later, the light went out and the music ceased. Catherine returned to bed.

"It came from Gabi's room. Someone was playing the violin in her room."

"Someone? It was Gabi, right?"

"The door was closed. I heard Gabi speak very quietly. In Italian. If I knew what she was saying, I'd tell you. If I were more schooled in the classics, I'd tell you what she was playing. You didn't hear any of it because you don't sleep, you hibernate. Something tells me that Ada was there."

"She'd be ninety-nine years old, Cat."

Catherine shrugged. "If that was her, I give her credit. She certainly has retained her talents."

"C'mon, Cat, there's no way that ninety-nine-year-old Ada's hiding in the house."

"Why do they keep it a secret? When I asked about the violin music the other day, everyone acted like I was nuts. Wind in the cedars!"

"There are lots of secrets here. Can we talk about it in the morning? I'd like to go back to my hibernation."

The hibernation didn't last long. Catherine and Liam were abruptly awakened by the sound of a woman screaming. *"Va via! Va via!"*

Liam jumped up. "That's Gabi." He slipped on his pants and dashed out of the room.

In the courtyard in front of the veranda, Gabriella was yelling at a portly man in a cream-colored suit. She was waving her cane all around; her face was red and she was shaking in anger. Floria was trying to calm her.

"What's going on here?" Liam asked.

"That's Mr. Lenzini, the lawyer who is trying to evict us," Floria said, pointing at the man who stood defiantly before them with his arms folded across his chest. "He came today with workers who want to dig in the vineyards."

"Does his court order give him the right to dig in the fields?"

"Absolutely not. It only provides a date for us to move. Until then, it's ours."

Liam nodded. "Okay, what's Italian for 'Get lost'?"

"*Va via* works."

Liam turned to the stubby attorney who

205

stood with his chin out, wearing a smug smile. "*Va via,* buddy. Take a hike. And take your diggers with you."

Lenzini curled his lip and stared at Liam as though he were a foul odor. "*Scusami.* Who are you?"

"A friend of Signora Vincenzo. Now just turn around, take your work crew and leave."

Catherine came rushing up, waving a paper. "This court order doesn't entitle you to exercise any rights of possession until September 10."

"And you, who are you?"

"I'm Signora Vincenzo's attorney."

"Another one? You're American."

"Yes, I am."

Lenzini reached in his suitcoat pocket, took out a business card and handed it to Catherine with a slight bow. "Well, I am Lorenzo Lenzini. *Avvocato.* My client is VinCo, the owner of this land." He waved his arm in circles. "All around you, it belongs to my client. VinCo only. Judge Riggioni of the provincial court declared my client to be the owner. Not Signora Vincenzo. Because he is gracious, he gave her sixty days to get herself and her belongings out of the villa. *Adesso basta!* Enough is enough." He punctuated the final remark with a sharp nod of his head.

"Show me in the order where it permits you to enter upon the premises in advance of the sixty days," Catherine said.

206

"There are no specific words, but they are not necessary. It is VinCo's land."

"Your client obtained that court order in Signora Vincenzo's absence," Catherine responded. "And I am giving you fair notice that we intend to contest Judge Riggioni's ruling. This time, you will not have a defendant in absentia. Possession is deferred until September, and maybe much longer. Now, please leave."

"Contest, contest all you wish, it will do you no good," he responded with a shrug and a smile. "Today we do not seek possession, we only take soil samples. VinCo wants to be ready to farm the day Signora leaves." Then he looked at Gabriella. "And she *will* leave. You can bet. On September 10 we say, *Arrivaderci, Signora.*"

Catherine shook her head. "That remains to be seen. Until then, you have no right to be here. Please take your men and leave."

Lenzini looked over at the two workers he had brought with him and back to Catherine. He laughed loudly. "You're an American. What do you think you can do in Italy?"

Liam stepped forward. "She can cause you more trouble than you can imagine."

"Please," Lenzini grunted. "No *Americn woman lawyer* is going to order Lenzini around in Italy. She has no power here. Zero. Now be a nice little girl and get out of my way."

"That's it," Liam said, taking two quick steps forward and thrusting his face into Lenzini's. "Miss Lockhart is a respected professional, not some *nice little girl.* Understand? She is also my wife. If you insult her again, I will take that straw hat off your head and stuff it down your throat. Now take your diggers, get in your car and *va via.*"

Lenzini held his ground and shook his head. "The signora may be an *avvocato* back in the United States, but here in Provincia Siena, she is nothing. She has no authority. No power. She cannot tell us to leave. She cannot do anything. She is nobody." He turned to his workers and motioned for them to commence their work. "She has *no power,*" he said again, flipping his hand at Catherine as though he were brushing away a fly.

"You must be dumber than you look," Liam said. "I've asked you twice politely and you continue to insult my wife. You want to talk about power? Now you're in my backyard." Liam held up his fists. "See these? Toonder and Lightning. Raw power, and I'm about to let them loose. Now I'm telling you for the last time, get the hell off this land."

Lenzini seemed to grasp the situation. He took a step backward, uttered some phrases under his breath and turned to his workers. "*Andiamo.* Let's go." He started for his car, then stopped and pointed at Liam. "Nobody threatens Lenzini," he yelled. "Not some female lawyer, not the stubborn signora and surely not some thug from America. I'll be back, Mr. Toonder, this time with the *polizia,* and then we'll see who has power."

When he had left, Catherine turned to Liam and smiled. "Nice work."

"Thug?" Liam said.

"Maybe a little," she said. "Just the right amount. And Toonder and Lightning? What was that all about?"

Liam laughed. "In 1959, Floyd Patterson was the undisputed heavyweight champion of the world and he fought a Swede named Ingemar Johansson. Patterson was heavily favored, but Johansson knocked him down seven times in the sixth round and won the fight. When they asked Ingemar how he did it, he held up his fists and said 'Toonder and Lightning.' I've been waiting all my life to use that phrase."

Catherine put her arm around Liam as they walked back to the veranda. "I'd kinda like to see a little toonder-storm sometime. Do you suppose that could be arranged?"

"Under the right circumstances, if the purse is sufficient."

Gabriella joined them on the veranda and Floria brought them breakfast. "*Grazie mille.* I knew my nephew was right about you two." She cupped her hands on Liam's face and gave him a big kiss.

Catherine smiled. "You're welcome, Aunt

Gabi, but I wouldn't be counting any chickens just yet. We have to stop this possession order."

"Aunt Gabi," Liam said, "can I ask you a few simple questions?"

Gabriella shrugged. "Sure."

"Does someone here play the violin?"

Gabriella raised an eyebrow. "Did you hear one?"

Liam shook his head. "Not me, but Catherine did. Can I ask: does Ada Baumgarten live here?"

Gabriella tightened her lips. She looked at Catherine and shook her head. "Not now, please. Have you finished Ada's story?"

"Not yet."

"We will talk when you finish reading her story."

"But, Aunt Gabi . . ."

"Ut." She held her finger up and wagged it back and forth. "When you finish." Gabi struggled to her feet and walked into the house.

"What was that all about?" Liam asked Floria. "Why doesn't she tell us about Ada now?"

Floria pressed her lips. "She does not because she cannot. You saw her face. Believe me, she cannot. When a person has been through trauma, sometimes they do not talk about it. It is like a psychological block. She cannot open the door to a discussion about Ada."

"What trauma?"

Floria shrugged. "I do not know the details or I would tell you. It is something in her childhood, maybe something to do with Ada, I don't know. I do know that she is most upset by the present situation, this legal matter. She's on the verge of losing her farm and I have never seen her so distraught. This farm means everything to her. That is why she wants you to read Ada's story. It will speak for the signora. It will tell you the things that she cannot. I am sorry, but at this time, it's the best we can do." Floria smiled, picked up dishes from the veranda and walked into the house.

Liam shook his head. "She needs to talk to us, no matter how difficult, Cat. We don't have enough information to save her farm."

Catherine exhaled and lowered her voice. "Floria's right, she can't. You saw how she tensed up. As I'm coming to realize, Gabi's life is entwined in Ada's story. From the preface, we infer that Ada's story is fraught with tragedies. I don't yet know how that affects Gabi, but I'm sure it does. Floria tells us that Gabi is blocked from talking and I'm sure she's right. You remember Lena Woodward? The story of Karolina's twins? For many years she couldn't talk about her life during the Holocaust. She couldn't even tell her husband about the twins. It was only after her husband died that she forced herself to

211

face her memories, and then only because she was desperate to find the twins.

"During Lena's case, we learned about what they call the 'survivor's syndrome' or 'concentration camp syndrome.' Often, people who have endured such horrors suppress the memories and push them to the back of their consciousness. They have to get on with their lives, so they do not allow those painful memories to surface. Children of survivors often talk about a psychological disconnect. Their parents don't discuss those years with the family. It's the elephant in the room, but the door stays closed."

"But Cat, Lena was in the Holocaust. That's why she had survivor's syndrome."

"Ada was a Jewish girl in wartime Germany. I haven't finished her story."

"I'm thinking that Gabi must be her daughter."

Catherine shrugged. "Daughter? Relative? Friend? Maybe it's the legal case and the farm is the focal point after all. Gabi said she's lived here all her life. Anyway, we're not going to get the story from Gabi. At least, not yet."

Liam nodded. "Then you'll have to dig it out of Ada's story."

"*We* will have to dig it out. I'm going to have a copy made. You have to start reading the story yourself, mister private investigator.

There are answers buried in that story. Don't leave the detective work to me."

Twenty-Four

Bologna, May 1937

It was midmorning when my father drove Mama and me to the station for my trip to Bologna. The train from Berlin Hauptbahnhof to Bologna Centrale would take almost twenty hours, with a change of trains in Munich. I had only vacationed outside Germany twice, both times with my family — once to Vienna and once to Paris — both times when the Philharmonic was on tour. Back then I was young, on summer vacation and a tag-a-long. Now I was headed to the Teatro Comunale di Bologna to audition for my future, and my mother was my travel companion.

Papa insisted that she accompany me to my audition. He felt that I would feel more secure, more confident. At least those were his expressed reasons. In truth, I think he had come to the realization that Mama needed to get out of Berlin for a while. Since the incident with Kleiner, her nerves were on edge. She was in a constant state of apprehension, waiting for the next shoe to fall.

In my early childhood memories, I see Mama as a vivacious woman going all over town, shopping for shoes, meeting her friends for lunch, ordering centerpieces from the florist for her next dinner party. As far as I was concerned, she owned Berlin. Now she didn't want to leave the house. The Nazis had terrorized her, they had brutalized her father and Kleiner was the last straw. He was around every corner, behind every tree. If it wasn't him, it was some other Brownshirt or Gestapo agent or SS officer.

"Besides," as she said, "if I did leave the house, where would I go? The signs in the shop windows and cafés tell me that Jews aren't welcome." On those rare occasions that she ventured out, she'd go to a friend's house, but only if my father drove her and picked her up. She had totally given up going to synagogue or to any of her women's organizations. But now, we were on our way to Italy, and I was hoping her spirits would rebound.

Mama and I had started Italian lessons last month, and we had been trying to speak Italian to each other as often as possible. In the event I passed my audition, I would need to know enough to follow instructions from my conductor and my section leader, and rehearsals were scheduled to begin in a couple of months. But all in all, it was pretty funny to see us walk around the house butchering Italian phrases.

My father and Uncle Wilhelm made all the arrangements for our stay in Bologna. Our hotel, the Baglioni, was on the Via Marsala, a block from the Piazza Maggiore in a lively section of Bologna, a ten-minute walk from the opera house. Papa had arranged for us to spend five days — two before the audition and two afterward.

Before we left, he pulled me aside. "Mama has been having a hard time," he said quietly. "I want the two of you to go on holiday like never before. Take her shopping. See the museums. Eat late dinners al fresco. Order a bottle of wine. See if you can get her shickered."

"Papa!"

"I'm serious. She needs a break, a vacation from stress. I'm worried about her."

I smiled. "Wining and dining and shopping, that's a tough assignment, but I'll try my best not to fail."

When we arrived in Bologna, we gathered our bags and hailed a taxi outside the train station. My mother got in and immediately said, *"Vogliamo mangiare l'hotel Baglioni."*

I doubled over. "Mother, you just told the cab driver that we wanted to eat the Baglioni Hotel."

The Baglioni sat in the old quarter of the magnificent city. I had only pictured cities like this in my imagination. Medieval architecture, red tile roofs, colonnades, archways, narrow walkways, covered bridges, basilica towers and domed churches. And the colors — so different from gray Berlin. The lovely renaissance buildings were covered with a dusting of cinnamon or nutmeg. Houses and churches were colored in shades of rose and orange. Bologna was known as the "portico city" because arched porticos covered most of the pedestrian walkways.

My father chose our hotel because it was a six-block walk from the Teatro Comunale and the University of Bologna, where I planned to apply. There were also several music conservatories within walking distance. Not to mention chocolate shops and fabulous restaurants. It didn't take long for me to realize that I was in a wonderland of music and food.

The Accademia Filarmonica di Bologna was steps away. Young Mozart went to school there to study composition in 1770. Rossini and Donizetti studied in the Conservatory of Music just around the corner. There were several ancient basilicas where choirs and ensembles performed all the time. And of course, there was the famous Bologna State Opera.

217

I told my mother that I wanted to check out the Teatro Comunale before my audition. I needed to see and hear where I would be playing. I brought my instrument to hear how it would sound in the two-hundred-year-old auditorium. Would there be echoes? Would the soft harmonics carry? The human ear hears the vibrated note in its highest pitch. Would the auditorium swallow that sound?

The door was open. We didn't see anyone, so we made our way into the darkened concert hall. It reminded me of the Philharmonie, but with an Italian flair. The seats in the great hall were empty and I knew that would affect the sound. Like a cavern, the music would reflect off the empty hall's walls and ceiling and would sound brighter. When the seats were full, they would dampen the sound.

Mama sat in the middle of the hall. I played a few warm-up scales and études. Then I played the concluding portion of the "Meditation." Although the hall was large, I played the notes as quietly as they deserved, stretching out the final note and letting it fade. Mama smiled and gave me a thumbs-up. The sound was clear to her.

Suddenly, I heard clapping. A chubby man with tufts of white hair above his ears walked into the hall from a side door. *"Dolce. Che bello."* He kissed his fingers like they had tomato sauce on them. *"Benvenuto, Signorina Baumgarten."*

I bowed. *"Grazie, Maestro Vittorio."*

He saw my mother and said, *"Buongiorno, Signora Baumgarten."* He took a seat in the third row. *"Ada,"* he called out, *"portei sentirti suonare una selezione vivace?"*

I grimaced. I didn't understand the words; he spoke them so quickly. I had a blank smile on my face, like a child.

"Vivace," he repeated. *"Capisco ti conoscere* La Carmen Fantasie. *Dammi il flamenco!"*

As limited as my Italian was, I understood he wanted something lively. He said he knew I played the *Carmen Fantasy.* He wanted flamenco!

"Okay," I thought, "here you go." I smiled and tore into my seguidilla and its sassy twelve-beat rhythm. I was on the stage of the Teatro Comunale in Bologna, Italy, auditioning in front of the Bologna State Opera's music director, and suddenly I felt like dancing. I wanted castanets. I wanted to tap-dance across the stage. I ended in a flourish and took a bow with a smile on my face.

"Brava, brava," Vittorio said, clapping enthusiastically. Then he let me know, in slow and simple Italian, that his concertmaster, his artistic director and some of his play-

ers were most anxious to meet me. He stood, gave me a short bow and said, *"A domani."* Until tomorrow.

"Well, he certainly seemed to like you," my mother said as we left the theater.

I nodded. "I'm a little concerned about the other orchestra members."

"I'm sure you'll do fine. You play beautifully. Why wouldn't they love you?"

"Why? Because I'm young? Because I'm a woman? Because I'm a Jew? Because I'm not Italian and I don't know what the hell they're saying half the time? I'm fighting all those prejudices. I'm not worried about whether I can play the instrument well enough — you know me, I'm confident. It's all those other reasons."

My mother smiled and patted my arm. "You saw Maestro Vittorio. He loved you. Let's get an ice cream."

"A gelato, Mama."

As it happened, Maestro Vittorio brought twelve people to my audition. I began with the Bach *Chaconne* and followed it with a Dvorak Slavonic dance. The stage lights were on and it was difficult to see the faces of the members as I played, but the applause after each number was proper. The third number was my calling card — Massenet's "Meditation." I heard a *"Ben fatta"* and a *"Abbastanza buono."* I knew those words. They were compliments. *"Forse . . . un po' di lettura a prima vista?"* Vittorio said.

That was more Italian than I knew. I had to shrug, smile and shake my head. *"Mi dispiace, non capisco,"* I said. I don't understand.

Vittorio's smile was kind, but it also conveyed a bit of annoyance with the language barrier. He pointed to his eyes and then the sheet music.

Oh, of course, he wants to know if it's possible for us to do a little sight-reading. I nodded. *"Si, si."* I worried he might ask for this because there was no way to prepare for it. But sight-reading was part of the business.

Eight of us assembled as a small group to play "Spring" from Vivaldi's *The Four Seasons.* I was familiar with the music, it was common enough, but I wasn't familiar with the score. The members who played with me were quite good and I wasn't sure I held up my end. I knew I came in too soon from a pause and underestimated the tempo of the last movement. Then Maestro Vittorio said in elementary Italian that the company was scheduled to perform Rossini's *Il Barbiere di Siviglia* next fall. Was I familiar with it?

I tilted my head from side to side as if to say, "somewhat." Then I added in my broken

Italian that I'd never seen the sheet music.

He smiled and nodded, so I must have communicated. He left for a minute and returned with sheet music for the overture to the *Barber of Seville* and four more musicians to join us. Now we were a little chamber orchestra. I was a little nervous at first, but it all went well, and I must say, playing with those men was a lot of fun. The violinist sitting next to me nodded and shook my hand. He went on and on in Italian and I nodded back, although the only words I caught were *sono impressionato* (he was impressed) and *è stato un piacere conoscerti* (he was happy to meet me).

When the piece was finished, Maestro Vittorio stepped down from the podium, came over to me and shook my hand. Then, taking great pains to use simple, short words, he thanked me for making the journey and for playing with his members. With the help of hand motions, he conveyed that he and the others would get together and have a discussion about my audition. They would let me know within a few weeks.

Once again, he shook my hand and said, *"Buona giornata a Bologna,"* which I understood to mean have a nice day in Bologna.

As we were leaving, he indicated he wanted to talk to my mother privately.

While they talked, I stood off to the side

thinking, "That's it? Thank you for making the journey? Enjoy your day in Bologna? We'll let you know in a few weeks? I played well. Better than well. I knocked it out. Didn't I deserve more than thanks for coming, have a nice day? And why does he want to talk to my mother? She doesn't speak Italian any better than I do."

When the two of them had finished talking, my mother and I left the Teatro. She could see the disappointment on my face.

"You played very nicely," she said.

"I could have played better."

"Stefano said you performed very nicely."

"Stefano, is it? Then why did he say have a nice day and send us on our way?"

"Oh, did you expect him to hand you a contract? Maybe he should have come off his podium with a written contract in his hand and begged you to sign it, without any input from his artistic director or any of the other players. Do you think that would that have been the diplomatic thing to do?"

"Well, what did he say in private?"

My mother looked at me a bit askance. She had that coy expression on her face. "He said you were truly a gifted artist. He said your Italian needs a lot of work. And then he asked if he could assist in finding you *an apartment in Bologna*!"

With that, we both shouted and jumped up and down.

We stayed one more day in Bologna. I hadn't seen my mother this cheerful in such a long time. The cloud that had settled over her in Berlin had evaporated in the Italian sun. We perused the shops for trinkets, bought new Italian handbags of the softest leather and ate sumptuous meals. Pasta bolognese, of course. Both of us developed a taste for Brunello di Montalcino and craft olive oil. "If I lived here," my mother said, "I would grow wine and olive oil."

I laughed. "I think the way it's done is that you grow the grapes. I didn't see any bottles on the trees."

"Oh, you're such a smarty. But I am serious. I would take viticulture classes, bottle the finest wine in Italy and drink it all myself," she said and then laughed. We both laughed. It was the perfect end to the perfect trip.

TWENTY-FIVE

Berlin, May 1937

As far as my mother was concerned, the train from Bologna to Berlin was a voyage from day into night. From heaven into hell. Nazi soldiers, SS guards and Brownshirts were everywhere within the noisy Hauptbahnhof Station and they scurried about like rats in a dumpster. Everything was in motion and every face was cast in stone. There was an unmistakable air of order and obedience. There were twenty suspicious eyes upon you as you disembarked and twenty more as you walked along the platform with your luggage.

The contrast was evident in my mother's mood as well. It seemed as though her depression had been patiently waiting to consume her upon her return from Bologna. I watched as a palpable fear engulfed her and plunged her back into a darkened state. She was now in enemy territory. Her head turned from side to side as she passed groups of Nazis. Was Kleiner here?

My father met us in the station, happy to see us and full of nonstop questions. "How was the audition? Did you do well? What did you think of Italy?" He loaded the bags into the car and headed home. I told him all about Bologna, Maestro Vittorio and the likelihood that I would be invited to join this summer. He took all that in stride, as if there had never been a doubt. He was clearly more interested in our extracurricular activities. Did we wine and dine? Did we shop? Was my mother happy? I assured him that I hadn't seen her so at ease in a long time.

My mother scoffed. "Stop analyzing me. I was on holiday, why wouldn't I have been at ease? But I have to say, Italy is a pleasant country and distinctly different from Nazi Germany. Germans could learn a thing or two, and maybe they wouldn't be so eager to 'Heil Hitler.'" She pointed out the window at the ubiquitous Nazi banners.

"I'm sure you're right," Papa said, "but things seemed to have stabilized. It's been weeks since there were any new restrictions. I have faith in the German people. They will soon tire of Hitler's bombast and tirades. In the meantime, we are making plans for a wonderful fall concert season. Sir Thomas Beecham has contracted to come and conduct us in the world's first recording of *The Magic Flute*, Mozart's *en-*

tire opera. It will be released on nineteen records, thirty-seven sides. Can you imagine? There has never been such a recording."

My mother smiled. "At least the music world is still sane."

My acceptance letter from Bologna came on June 10.

I am pleased to offer you a position as violinist for the 1937–1938 opera season. You are expected to appear for our first organizational meeting on July 3. We will commence rehearsals in our Bologna practice facility on July 5. I have taken the liberty to arrange for your temporary living quarters in the university dormitory until you decide on something more permanent.

With warmest regards,
Stefano Vittorio

Mama immediately made plans for a celebration dinner, inviting the Furtwänglers and two other couples. For the briefest of moments she was Friede Baumgarten, hostess extraordinaire of the Weimar Republic. Although she could not hire servers or household help, the house was made to shine, adorned with all her special treasures and decorations, with flowers on every table. Candles burned in all the windows. She wore a beautiful gown and was back in her comfort zone.

She greeted each of our guests as they arrived. Canapés were set on silver trays. Wine and champagne were served in her finest crystal. Her roast was warming in the oven. The conversation was bright, and though the party was thrown in my honor, my mother was truly the star. I will remember just that moment and keep it locked in my mind, for it immediately preceded the fall of the House of Baumgarten.

Before she could serve the dinner, we heard the squeal of tires and the voices of men in front of our house. We all looked at one another and shrugged. Then we heard shouts of *"Juden"* and *"Juden schweine."* Our male guests rushed outside the house only to see the intruders jump into their cars and speed away. On the brick walls on either side of our doorway, they had painted KILL THE JEWISH PIGS, and they had splashed a red swastika on our front door. My mother fainted on the doorstep.

My father called the police, but they did not come. The guests reassembled in the house and tried to reignite the celebration, but the moment had come and gone. "It's just hooligans, it's just paint," they said. "We'll remove it tomorrow."

But my mother said, "It was Kleiner."

My father put his arm around her and said, "Kleiner and his unit left a month ago." She shook her head slowly at first and then violently. "There are three million Kleiners!" she screamed. "They're all Kleiners!" She began to cry hysterically, and my father took her to the bedroom. I bid our guests good-bye and extended my apologies. They all expressed their sympathies as they left and offered to help Mama in any way they could.

For three days, my mother rested in her bedroom. Dr. Gruen came and gave her sedatives. My father and his friends from the orchestra removed the paint from the bricks, but the emotional damage was permanent. The security of our home had now been violated twice within a few months. My mother had seen Kleiner and his men prepared to break my father's arms and take us all to a concentration camp, only to be rescued at the last moment. If there were any hopes that the situation had been resolved or diffused, the desecration of our home at the dinner party had served to shatter them. All illusions that her home was a safe place dissolved that night.

Later that month, my father asked me to sit with him. I knew he was at his wits' end. "Ada," he said, "I'd like to send Mama to live with you when you move to Bologna. Her nerves are hanging by a thread. It's only a matter of time until something else goes wrong — another edict, another confrontation, another vandalism. Whether it happens at a store, on the street or at our home again, she won't be able to handle it. She's so fragile. Will you take her with you?"

"Of course. But will she go?"

"We'll talk to her."

"I know," I said. "I'll tell her that I need her, that I am afraid to move to Bologna by myself and I can't perform without her."

Papa smiled at me and kissed me on the forehead. "That would be lovely, but she'll know that's a fib. It's better we stick to the truth."

Two nights later, my father told Mama that he and I wanted to talk to her. She had been his wife for thirty years, so she knew something was up. "What do you two schemers have in mind?" she said.

"Friede, Ada is leaving in two weeks. I'd like you to go with her."

She nodded. "She really doesn't need me, she's quite independent. If you think I should travel with her to make sure she gets there safely, it's unnecessary, but I will go."

He shook his head. "No, that's not what I think. I think you should go to Bologna and live with Ada. I think you should leave Berlin. Permanently."

"I understand, but what about you?"

230

"I can't leave yet. You'll go with Ada."

Her voice was quivering. "No, Jacob, I can't go without you."

Papa put his arms around her. Tears were rolling down my mother's cheeks. Her world was disintegrating. "Why couldn't we go together?" she said. "We could all leave Berlin. It's time. The Schwartzes left, the Seligmans left, the Rothschilds left, the Bergers left. All our friends have left or they're leaving. We've been together for thirty years, Jacob; I can't live somewhere without you."

"I know. It's time for us all to move, but I can't leave Wilhelm and the orchestra without their concertmaster a month before the season starts. He promised me that if I stayed, I would continue to receive my salary no matter what laws are passed. But Friede, you and Ada need to be safe. You have to leave without me."

Mama was inconsolable. "I can't."

"It will only be temporary," he said. "Just until the end of the season. By then Wilhelm will have found a replacement for me. Look at the bright side: we'll have a steady income and you'll be there to support Ada in her career. We're much better off than many of our friends."

She shook her head and cried. "I can't do this without you, Jacob. Please don't send me away. I'll get better. I'll be stronger. You'll see, you won't have to worry about me."

He hugged her tightly. "Oh, Friede, my darling, don't cry. I'm not sending you away, I'm doing my best to protect you. I'm doing this for both of us. I would go if I could. Berlin is no place for Jews." He kissed her and ran his fingers gently through her hair. "You'll only be a train ride away and I will come and visit as often as I can. It will just be for a little while and before you know it, the season will be over. By then I will have found a position in another orchestra, maybe Vienna, maybe America, and we will make a new home, a sweet home wherever we land. Until then, you'll have Ada to help you. You can help each other."

She went into the bedroom and shut the door. My father followed her.

Over the ensuing days, my mother sank into a deep depression. She couldn't accept being separated from the man she had lived with and depended on for thirty years. She couldn't understand what was happening all around her. Her walls were crumbling. She cried all the time. She'd walk around her home, look at her things, spend time with her memories and sob. Nothing we said or did would cheer her up. But my father felt he had no other options. He had made the hard call, done what he had to do. My mother and I would leave in two weeks.

TWENTY-SIX

Pienza, August 2017

Catherine and Liam were once again alarmed by shouts of *"Va via."* Floria burst into the room and frantically let loose a long string of Italian, interspersed with an occasional English word — "Gabi," "Lenzini," "gun" and "police." Cat and Liam dashed out of the room and ran through the vineyards until they came to the patch that Gabi called "Ada's Vineyard."

Lenzini stood with his arms folded across his chest, smiling smugly. Beside him stood his two workers with shovels and farm implements. In front of Lenzini were two uniformed policemen. Gabi was standing in a cotton robe, loosely tied around her nightgown, holding a vintage shotgun by the barrel and screaming in Italian. Thankfully, her hand was nowhere near the trigger. Her face was red, her tears were flowing and her words came out in gasps. She was hysterical. A policeman was patiently asking her to hand over the gun.

"What's happening here, Officer?" Liam asked, as he gently took the gun from Gabi.

"I tell you what's happening, Mr. Tough-guy," Lenzini interjected. "The *polizia* are here to protect me from your assault. No fists today, Mr. Thug. No crazy old women with guns. VinCo will take soil samples and cuttings of the vines and no one will stop us."

"Aahh!" Gabi screamed and reached for the shotgun. "They will not touch Ada's vines! Please do not let them touch Ada's vines." She pulled on the policeman's arm. "Please. Those vines are precious to me."

Catherine waved a copy of the court order. "Lenzini has no right to be here. There is nothing in this order that allows VinCo to come upon this land before September 10. They have no right to take soil samples or cut vines. Those are possessory acts, and possession is deferred by court order."

The policeman took the order and started to read it when Lenzini stepped up and handed another paper to him. "Aah, but this is a *new* court order, Officer," Lenzini said. "It was entered yesterday by Judge Riggioni. It gives us the right to come onto the land at any time we choose to take samples. As many as I like. As often as I like. I could dig up this whole section if I want to. Here, read it."

The policeman read the order, shrugged and handed it to Catherine.

"Did you tell Gabriella that you were going back to court?" she asked Lenzini.

Lenzini just smiled.

"You didn't tell her, did you? You didn't tell her that you were going to present a motion to the judge to conduct testing on her property, did you?"

"Not her property," Lenzini said with his chin pushed out. "VinCo's property. Sadly, there have been rumors of mold in some Tuscan vineyards. We must make sure that these are clean. Besides, the old lady is not entitled to notification. She is in default."

"There is no mold here!" Gabriella yelled. "There has never been mold in my vineyards."

Lenzini smiled and shrugged. "We shall see. It will take many cuttings to make sure."

"I am sorry," the officer said. "But this is a court order. I can't stop him."

"Just give me two days," Catherine said. "Let me get the matter before Judge Riggioni. Lenzini snuck in behind her back. The judge didn't hear Gabriella's side. When he does, he may very well vacate this order. Just two days. There will be no harm in waiting two days."

The policeman shook his head. "I'm sorry."

"VinCo will not be harmed by waiting two days. Just one day then, please."

The policeman grimaced and shook his head again. "I can't."

Lenzini waved to his workers and they took large cutting instruments over to the vines.

"Stop! *Fermare!*" Gabi screamed. "Do not touch those vines!"

Lenzini laughed and motioned for his workers to proceed.

Floria stepped forward and spoke in desperate tones. "Don't you know that improper cuttings could kill the plants? These are irreplaceable. They are award-winning vines. Cutting these plants would be like cutting into the signora's veins. Please, let Miss Lockhart talk to the judge."

The policeman sadly shook his head. "I'm sorry. Truly I am, but my hands are tied."

The workers loudly snapped a branch of a large vine and put it into a cart. Gabriella shrieked and moved forward to stop the worker. Lenzini took a quick step and hip-checked her with enough force to knock her hard to the ground. "Oh, how clumsy of me," Lenzini said. "A thousand apologies."

In a flash, Liam was on Lenzini, throwing him to the ground, pinning his arms behind his back and pushing his face hard into the dirt. "How do you like it, you heartless son of a bitch?" Liam said through clenched teeth. "If you touch that woman again, I'll break every bone in your body." Just as quickly, the two policemen grabbed Liam and pulled him off.

"You had better come this way, Signore,"

an officer said, and led Liam down the path to the police car.

"Hoo, hoo, Mr. Big Toughguy," Lenzini called. "Welcome to Italy." Then he motioned for his workers to cut more vines. As the workers snapped another branch, Gabriella fainted.

"When you're done with these, cut those over there," Lenzini said loudly for all to hear.

Catherine and Floria helped Gabriella to her feet and then to the golf cart. She was inconsolable and barely cognizant. "There's nothing more we can do here," Catherine said. "I will try to reopen the case as soon as I can. Right now, I have to figure out how to get my husband out of custody."

Catherine returned to the house where the police car was parked in the driveway. "Are you charging my husband with an offense, Officer?"

The policeman, whose name tag read FORESTA, shook his head. "No charges. To my observation, the American detective was protecting his client. In America, I think they call it justifiable use of force in defense of another. I'm sure you understand, it was necessary for me to remove him from the scene. He can go now." Officer Foresta tipped his cap. "A word of caution. Lenzini is a despicable man, but he has friends. Powerful friends. You have made an enemy of a well-connected person."

Once out of the custody of the *polizia,* Liam said, "Cat, Lenzini won't stop until the court order is changed. Somehow you have to get into court."

"I agree. But I can't practice here. I'm going to have to hire local counsel to file a motion and I surely can't use any of Gabi's previous attorneys. Santi and Giangorgi may well be in Lenzini's pocket. In the meantime, we have to find Carlo Vanucci. He signed the deed that was supposed to transfer the property to Gabriella. I'm sure there had to be lawyers involved. They must have all believed that Vanucci had good title. In my professional opinion, finding Vanucci calls for the work of America's finest private investigator."

"At your service."

Back in the house, Catherine heard loud sobs coming from Gabi's bedroom. She poked her head in the doorway to ask if there was anything she could do. Gabi lay on the bed, Floria by her side trying to calm her, a sad and heartrending scene. Catherine brushed away a tear. "Liam and I will find someone who will help us get before the judge. I promise."

"It doesn't matter," Gabriella said. "He has won."

Twenty-Seven

Bologna, August 1937

Rehearsals began in July. Mama and I had settled into an apartment in a busy neighborhood near the Teatro Comunale. It was a four-room *appartamento* on the second floor of a rehabbed two-hundred-year-old stone building. Two bedrooms, a kitchen and a living room. And a tiny little bathroom. For me, it was my first apartment, and I was delighted. For my mother, moving from her gracious Berlin home, it was an uncomfortable little cracker box.

Our apartment was also close to the sprawling campus of the University of Bologna and its sixty-five thousand students. As such, the streets of Bologna's Old City were alive at all hours of the day. I thought it was magical having so much youthful energy right outside my door. Students were ubiquitous — in the cafés, on steps of the piazzas, under the porticos and clustered in groups. At first, the bustle was intoxicating to both of us, but as the days passed, it seemed to get on Mama's nerves. To be fair, my mother was not herself. She had been forced to separate from her husband and leave her home under the most frightening of circumstances. While she tried to keep a positive outlook, it was evident that her depression was gaining a foothold.

When we arrived, we were met at the train by Francesca Denardo, the promotion and marketing director of the opera company. Franny became our Bologna resource and my good friend. She was young, vivacious and always running in several directions at the same time. As they say in Bologna, she had many pots on the stove. She helped us furnish our apartment. She took us around the city, showed us where to shop, gave us valuable insight into life in Bologna and shuttled us through the intricacies of immigration.

Unlike the other European countries, Italy did not require visas for entry or immigration. Even a person with no passport, a stateless person, could be granted entry. Within three days of entry, Mama and I were required to register and submit a residence declaration at the nearest *questura,* or police headquarters. Mine was a little more complicated because I wanted permission to work. Franny went with us and helped us file our registration forms. It did not escape my attention that the forms asked for our religious preference, though there didn't seem to be any outward signs of discrimination against Jews. There were no Italian laws designed to isolate Jews. There were no anti-Semitic signs in the windows or pasted to the lampposts.

Professionally, Franny was my liaison to the company. She introduced me to the routines: when to arrive, where to change, what to wear, what to say and, most important, what not to say. As our friendship grew, she took me into her confidence and revealed her studied profiles of the company's personalities. This one is a pompous elitist. This one is a drinker. This one has roving hands. This one can be trusted. This one seems distant but is really just shy. And so on.

Most importantly, Franny was very social. She had a large circle of girlfriends in their twenties, and she brought me into the group. I went out with them quite often. One of the girls, Natalia Romitti, a doctoral student in political science, became a close friend. She was extremely intelligent and keenly aware of current world affairs. How she got her information I didn't know, but she was well-informed. She was particularly interested in my experiences in Berlin, and she spent hours asking me about nazification. I soon learned that Natalia was not merely curious; she was Jewish and fearful of what she called the dark clouds on the Italian horizon.

"But there are no laws against Jews here, are there? Isn't Italy a tolerant country?" I asked.

"We are a small minority, Ada. There are only fifty thousand Jews in all of Italy. We are vulnerable. As yet, the Fascist Party has not passed any legislation discriminating against us, and there are even Jewish members in the party. But Mussolini covets a friendship with Hitler. Ever since his failed war in Ethiopia, European leaders have scorned him, all except Hitler. I'm worried about what Mussolini would do to gain Hitler's favor. It's best we keep our eyes and ears open."

"Aren't Italian Jews well integrated into Italian society?"

"Weren't German Jews as well?"

I nodded. "Sadly, that's true."

"But Ada, here's a big difference — Italy doesn't have Joseph Goebbels and his propaganda machine. No one has taken over the public communication channels to tell us that Jews are evil. Italians will not be so easily manipulated."

The season's first opera was Verdi's *La Traviata* and practices were intense. We were also rehearsing *The Barber of Seville* and *Tosca,* the next two operas in the schedule. I sat in the middle of the second violin section and shared my music stand with an older gentleman who was very patient with my broken Italian. Our initial rehearsals were orchestra only. We did not rehearse with the singers. We started promptly at 8:30 a.m. and rehearsed until lunch. The singers practiced in the afternoon in an adjoining room with a rehearsal pianist and, of course, with Maestro Vittorio. The afternoon was practice time for me, learning the score, reading the libretto and studying my Italian. In the evening, I would dine with Mama and retire early. On the weekends, I would go out with Franny and Natalia and join in whatever social plans they had.

Maestro Vittorio was a dynamic conductor with expressive, exaggerated movements, more like Uncle Wilhelm and not at all like Dr. Kritzer. He expected excellence and would accept nothing less, but this was a professional company, not the Junior, so Vittorio's expectations were usually met. Even though I was the only woman and the youngest member, he did not single me out or give me special treatment. He treated me as one of the company and that suited me fine. I sought only to be a part of the whole. Regrettably, it was quickly evident that certain members were not so graciously inclusive. Like a middle-school lunchroom, there were stares, cold shoulders and seats made "unavailable" in the commissary. Mr. Fortis, the percussionist, an acerbic man, made it clear early on that he did not appreciate playing in an orchestra with a woman. "This is not some put-together ensemble," he said to Vittorio. "For centuries, we have held tightly to our traditions, and you dishonor them without a second thought by bringing in this young girl."

"How regrettable that you are so troubled, Mr. Fortis," Vittorio said. "Fortunately, you are not glued to your seat. As fine a percussionist as you are, I'm sure you could find another orchestra that does not dishonor you, as I am equally sure we could find another fine percussionist."

I wanted to stand and applaud as Mr. Fortis was put in his place, but I kept my control. Nonetheless, Mr. Fortis managed to exclude me from the Green Room — the performers lounge just beside the orchestra pit. He told me it was a dressing room and inappropriate for women. Vittorio told me not to fight that battle. Sometimes it is better to let a lion roar rather than to force him into a corner. Vittorio helped me to see these exclusionary tactics as minor obstacles to overcome. Bumps in the road. They were totally unfair, but I should think of myself as a trailblazer, a pathfinder. I would not be the first woman to fight such battles and I would not be the last.

As I was able to observe during my ten-day stint with Uncle Wilhelm and the Berlin Opera, an opera conductor's duties are much broader than a symphony conductor's. He must be continuously alert, supporting the singers and the orchestra as their needs dictate, balancing the sound level so that one does not dominate the other, and he must take care not to constrict a singer's artistry — her ability to color, decorate and embellish her vocal lines. That is why piano rehearsal time is so important for the conductor and the vocalists.

Opera demands equal vigilance from the orchestra. My father often told me that if Maestro Furtwängler was sick, the Philharmonic could perform the entire symphony without a conductor and no one would notice. Not so with an opera. A conductor must keep the orchestra and singers together, using hand movements, body movements and facial expressions meant for each. There are many times that the orchestra must wait for the action on the stage or the singer's interpretation. Each must learn from the other.

While my life and career in Bologna was ascending, Mama's was descending. She was trying to adjust but the contrast in lifestyles was overwhelming her. She missed my father. She missed her home, her city and her way of life. She either could not or would not make a connection with Bologna. I felt guilty when I left for rehearsals or on those few occasions when I went out with Franny and Natalia. My mother would just sit in the apartment. Sometimes she'd read, sometimes she'd listen to the radio, but most often she just sat and stared out the window. Once Berlin's most vivacious woman, she was now dispirited. On most days, she only left the apartment to shop for groceries or to take Mitzi for a walk.

My father wrote at least twice a week. Like me, he was busy with rehearsals, but he promised to come to Bologna during the Philharmonic's fall break. His letters were very chatty. Mama read them over and over and kept them by her nightstand. He told us what was going on with the Philharmonic, with our friends and, disturbingly, what was happening to life in Berlin. A new concentration camp had been opened in Buchenwald, near Weimar. "What irony," my father wrote, "that a political prison has been constructed in the birthplace of German constitutional democracy."

Buchenwald is the third concentration camp opened by the Nazis to imprison political opponents, intellectual dissidents and targeted racial groups. Now with Dachau and Sachsenhausen, they've made plenty of room for prisoners and it has become more dangerous than ever to speak out. We frequently hear about Jews being snatched off the street and taken to concentration camps for so-called interrogation. I am glad that my two loved ones are far away and safe. I learned that over a thousand Jews emigrated to Italy last year and even more are coming this year. Look for them. Make a connection.

Love, Papa

My mother immediately replied to his letters. She wrote glowingly about my progress with the company and about our life together in Bologna. She tried to be upbeat, but it was a thin disguise. Between the lines, I'm sure that Papa could easily see her melancholia. She wrote that we haven't met any German émigrés, that she hasn't been able to establish much of a social life, and most of all, she wished she could come home. "I cannot wait until October to see you" is the way she ended every letter.

Last week I finally decided to intercede. I wrote to my father and told him I was worried about Mama. Our little apartment, though fine for me, was too confining for her. I expressed concern that she was retreating into a deep depressive state. She had no interest in activities. In a city known for delicious food, she had little appetite. She would complain that there was no place to get a good brisket or schnitzel or spaetzle. She would complain that the cobblestone streets hurt her feet. "How does anyone wear high heels in this medieval town?" she'd say to me. She would complain that the students were so noisy she couldn't get a good night's sleep. I would try to cheer her up and point out the bright side of Bologna, but her complaints were only symptoms of her longing to be with her husband in her home. I urged Papa to visit, if only for a few days. Even a weekend. It would brighten her spirits immensely. Alternatively, if he couldn't come to Bologna, could I send Mama back home for a few days?

He answered me right away. He told me that the Philharmonic was hard at work every day preparing for opening night. He had talked to Uncle Wilhelm and mentioned that the separation was hard on Mama. But, he wrote,

I have wonderful news. Ever since Felix Weingartner left Vienna, Wilhelm has been its main conductor, spending much more time there. Wilhelm told me that he would like me to move to Vienna at the end of the spring season next June. I will be concertmaster of the Vienna Philharmonic! I will send for Mama and we will be together in Vienna. That should lift her spirits. Sadly, I cannot come to Bologna before the end of October. As to Mama coming home on the train, I absolutely forbid it. The trains are full of Nazis, SS and Brownshirts. You know how nervous she gets. What if she were confronted? I fear such an episode might push her over the edge. Berlin gets meaner and more dangerous every day. Most of her friends have moved away. This is no place for her. Please make sure that she stays in Bologna. I will see you both in October.

Love, Papa

Twenty-Eight

Pienza, August 2017

"I need to talk to Aunt Gabi," Liam said to Floria. "If I am to have the slightest chance of locating Carlo Vanucci, I'm going to need more information."

Floria shook her head. "She is not in very good spirits. She won't come out of her room. For three days now, I have brought in her meals. It is as though she has been wounded. When Lenzini cut Ada's vines, he cut out pieces of her heart."

"I need a starting place, Floria. Do you know anything about Vanucci? Were you here when the deed was delivered?"

Floria shook her head. "No, I've only been here since 2007. But I will try to talk to the signora and ask if she knows."

A few minutes later, Floria reappeared and led Catherine and Liam into Gabriella's room. Gabriella was reclining in her bed when they entered. She looked weakened, defeated. "How are you doing today, Aunt

Gabi?" Catherine asked.

She shrugged. "We can't stop them, you know. Lenzini and VinCo. They've already taken what they want. They've destroyed the soul of my vineyard."

"Aunt Gabi, it's not that bad," Liam said. "They didn't destroy your vineyards. They just took a few random cuttings. It was all for show. You have acres and acres of grapevines."

Gabriella wagged her finger. "No, no. Lenzini knew exactly what he was doing. It wasn't random, it wasn't for show and it wasn't about mold. He took from Ada's vines. Enough to make root stock."

"There's still so much left."

"You don't understand. Every year, I win awards for the wine produced from Ada's Vineyard. I told you it's the best in Tuscany. VinCo produces tens of thousands of bottles, but they don't win awards. Don't you see, that's why they want my vineyards. It's not about the inconvenience of farming around my little plot. It's about the awards. The prestige. It's about Ada's Vineyard. VinCo could never replicate that vineyard."

"They took small cuttings, Aunt Gabi. I don't know much about farming, but you have old vines deep in the Tuscan soil. Even if they could replicate Ada's vines, it would be decades. And Ada's Vineyard has that special location you told me about."

Gabriella smiled. "You learn quickly, young man."

"We'll do our very best to stop VinCo. It's not over yet, but I need your help. Who was Carlo Vanucci, and how do I get in touch with him?"

Gabriella shook her head. "I don't know. Truly."

"But he's the one who deeded this property to you. Surely, you must know who he is."

"I only met him the one time."

"And you've lived here . . ."

"Practically all my life."

"You lived on Carlo Vanucci's farm all your life?"

"I never thought so. I never thought it belonged to Mr. Vanucci. I didn't have any idea who Mr. Vannuci was. In 1995, a lawyer showed up with Mr. Vanucci and we all signed a deed. It was a total surprise, but the lawyer said that this was the way my family had purchased the land. He told me to record the deed and I would have absolute ownership."

"That's all he said?"

"He said we have to record the deed right away because Mr. Vanucci was very ill. The lawyer took it to Siena and had it recorded. That's all I knew until VinCo started pestering me."

"What was the lawyer's name?"

"My memory is foggy. I think it was Hernandez, or something very similar. He was Spanish and Italian. A very nice man. Are you reading Ada's story?"

"Yes, we are. Is it in the story?"

Gabi's breath was becoming labored. She shook her head. "Please, read the story. I don't want to talk anymore. I'm sorry."

TWENTY-NINE

Bologna, September 1937

A buzz of anticipation ran through the orchestra on the first day we rehearsed with the singers. Our opening night was just a week away. The sensational Italian soprano, Licia Albanese, was singing the role of Violetta Valéry, *Traviata*'s frail courtesan, and oh, how she looked the part. Young, slender, stunning. She had made her debut in Milan three years ago and took the Italian opera scene by storm. Everyone could see that Maestro Vittorio loved working with her.

Miss Albanese was born to sing *Traviata.* It's a three-act opera and Violetta is onstage almost the entire time. To carry off such a strenuous part and stay in character requires a strong, athletic woman and Miss Albanese fit the bill. As in other Verdi operas, the strings play a prominent role, almost like another singer on the stage. Even before the curtain rises on act one, two violins play a soft, slow, passionate prelude, setting the mood for the tragedy to come. Gradually the orchestra joins in and the curtain rises on a nineteenth-century high society party at Violetta's Paris salon. The party has been thrown to celebrate Violetta's reemergence on the social scene. She has been ill for a year and this is her big comeback. Ah, but don't be fooled, because she is not really better. Soon Alfredo arrives and professes his love. Violetta is struck by the fact that she could actually be in love with someone for the first time in her life. "É strano." "It is strange," she sings, "that perhaps he is the one."

The parallel was not lost on me. It made me think of Kurt. I hadn't seen him since we met in the Tiergarten on the night he warned me about Kleiner. Nor had he written, but I forgave him for that. I was sure he didn't have my Bologna address, and if he addressed a letter to my house in Berlin and if it was discovered by Kleiner, that would endanger Kurt and my family. Still, I thought about him often. I missed him, and I wondered if he still felt the same about me.

With only seven days left before opening night, Maestro Vittorio was under pressure to bring it all together and we were having trouble with the opening scene of act three. *Traviata*'s third act begins with a somber melody from the strings. They foretell of heartbreak. They set the mood — mournful

255

and despairing. As the curtain rises, Violetta is lying on her bed in the last hours of her life. She is attended by her maid, Anina. The room is dark but for a single candle. The first violin, in solo, plays a somber melody with great pathos. It must mimic her anguish. It must follow her as she struggles to rise from the bed and walk to the window in vain hopes of seeing Alfredo. It becomes a sad duet between Violetta and the first violinist. In falling couplets, the violinist draws out her longing and her frailty. Without raw emotion from the solo violin, the scene falls flat.

We hadn't put it together and Maestro Vittorio was not happy. We had gone over this final scene several times. Vittorio shook his head. He slapped his baton on the podium, once so hard he broke it. *"Quanto volte?"* he barked. "How many times must we go over the same passage?" He was frustrated that his first violinist, Rico Lassoni, could not get the mood or the tempo to his liking.

"Dammi emozione! Give me the emotion? I don't believe you, Rico. Make me believe you."

He glared at the violinist. Lassoni was shaking. *"Ancora una volta,"* Vittorio said sharply. "Once again."

The scene began, Miss Albanese rose off her couch and Lassoni played. The maestro shook his head violently and stopped the

scene. "No, no, no." She stood still on the stage and everyone was silent while Vittorio berated his first violinist.

"Ancora una volta, per favore," he said, and Lassoni played it yet again. Lassoni's bow shook so badly he could barely draw it. He was totally intimidated. I don't know how he played at all. Maestro Vittorio made a sour face and shook his head, but nevertheless motioned for Miss Albanese to continue with the scene.

Anina walks in and hands Violetta a letter. As she speaks the words in her weakened and breathy voice, the violin plays the background melody. It is sad and sweet, but it must be in tempo with Violetta's reading. It didn't go well. The timing was off. Maestro slammed his hand on the score. "Do you see what Verdi wrote on this page?" he yelled. Lassoni nodded his head. "Read it," Vittorio commanded with a reddened face. "Read it out loud for everyone to hear. Read how Giuseppe Verdi wants his music played."

Lassoni swallowed hard and in a shaky, nervous tone said, " *'Legge con voce bassa suono ma a tempo.'* "

"Esattamente," Vittorio said. " 'She speaks with a low voice but *a tempo.'* Is that what you are hearing when you play, Mr. Lassoni? Are we *a tempo*?"

257

He lowered his head and shook it slowly from side to side. "No, Maestro."

"No, Maestro, no Maestro," Vittorio mocked. "She is, but you are not." Then Vittorio turned and pointed at the second chair. "Mr. Ayers," he said, "From bar 620, please." Ayers, equally intimidated, picked up his violin and played the section. He was at least a beat behind Miss Albanese. Vittorio listened but his facial expressions did not improve. He halted the music with a wild wave of his arms. "Stop!"

Then he looked directly at me and tapped his baton. "Miss Baumgarten, if you please. From bar 620." I was not a first violinist. There was no way that he should have turned to me. But he did. Ayers turned around and handed me the sheet music. Vittorio nodded to Miss Albanese on the stage, who picked up the letter and started the scene again. I felt my stomach drop out of my body. I watched Maestro Vittorio as he gently lowered his hands to begin the music. In order for me to succeed, my instrument must radiate profound sorrow. I listened to Miss Albanese read the narration, I listened to her breaths, counting the rhythm, and I weaved the melody in as best I could. The scene continued. Only once, in a cautionary tone, did Maestro Vittorio repeat the score's notation, *"a tempo."* Miss Albanese sang the final notes, Violetta died

and the scene concluded. Maestro exhaled. He gave a little bow of his head to the orchestra and then to me. *"Perfetto,"* he said. Miss Albanese raised her eyebrows, nodded and smiled at me.

Maestro beckoned me with his fingers. "Miss Baumgarten, please change seats with Lassoni." I hesitated. Lassoni was the first chair. I was an eighteen-year-old girl. "Miss Baumgarten, are you asleep?" he asked with eyebrows raised. I quickly gathered up my things and moved into Lassoni's chair. In that moment, I became the Bologna State Opera Orchestra's first violinist. Me.

"Once again, everyone," Maestro said. "From the beginning. Act three."

As I left practice, I was justifiably concerned that other orchestra members, especially Lassoni and the string section, would resent me. I saw several of them gather around Vittorio and whisper. The afternoon had been horribly embarrassing for Lassoni. A temporary replacement, a woman no less, had just unseated the first-chair violin. Surprisingly, some were complimentary. Some commended me on my playing. Lassoni himself walked by and nodded. He didn't speak to me, his eyes were down, but he nodded in a complimentary way. I felt sorry for him. Ayers, with whom I was then to share a music stand, told me that he was happy he wasn't chosen to sit in the hot seat. Other members, however, shook their heads disapprovingly when I walked by, as though I should have declined to play when Maestro called on me.

I rushed back to the apartment. I couldn't wait to tell Mama. First chair! I called her name as soon as I walked in the door, but there was no response other than Mitzi's barking. I assumed Mama had gone to the store, but then I saw a note on the table.

My Dearest Ada,

I have taken the train back to Berlin. I am proud of you and your successes here in Bologna, but it is not for me. It is not my home. This is a young person's city. Perfect for you, Ada, but I don't fit in. I feel out of place and I miss your father terribly. I know that you will do just fine without me. You have made so many friends. I know there is danger back in Berlin, but I feel like I should be with your father. He has no one to take care of him. Perhaps your father and I will come and visit when there is a break in the Philharmonic schedule. Please don't be angry with me, but I need to be at home with my husband where I belong. Keep up with your practices. You are a star!

Love, Mama

I broke down. I blamed myself for being the reason that Mama had to leave her husband. Now she had to travel alone. I knew I shouldn't have been worried; she was a competent woman who could certainly travel by herself. But I was. My father warned me that the trains were full of Nazis. Anything could happen. I knew that the train would stop at the German border. Everyone would have to show their papers. Everyone was subject to questioning. Just the sight of a Nazi or a Brownshirt could send my mother over the edge. She saw Herbert Kleiner in every Nazi uniform. I wonder if she thought of that before she left.

I didn't know whether she had been planning this trip or whether it was a spur-of-the-moment decision. I knew she was depressed, but Bologna was such a warm city, I thought she'd get over it. I wondered if she had even told Papa she was coming home.

I decided to go to the telegraph office and send a wire to my father. Letters could take a week, and if Papa didn't know, he should be alerted that she was coming. He should meet her at the station. I hoped the telegram reached him before Mama's train arrived.

Two days later, I received a letter from my father. It was addressed to both my mother and me. It was full of the usual happenings at the Philharmonic and news of what was

261

going on in Berlin. Obviously, it was written before my mother arrived or before he received my telegram. I replied the same day, both to him and to Mama. I asked how she fared on the train trip home. I asked Mama how her garden had survived in her absence. I told Papa how I came to be elevated to first chair. I knew he would be proud when he read that part. I ended by telling them both that I hoped they would still come and visit me at the end of October.

I posted the letter and later in the day I received a telegram from my father. "Mother never arrived. When was she supposed to get here? When did she leave? What train did she take? Call me!"

I was stunned. I ran to the post office where I could make a telephone call. I called on three separate occasions without success. Finally, late that evening, I got through. He answered the phone. "Did Mama get home?" I asked frantically.

"No, she didn't. Which train did she take? When did she leave?"

There was panic in my voice. "Oh, Papa, I don't know which train she took. She left two days ago. I found a note saying she was going home. Where could she be? Should I come home?"

"No, she's not here and there's nothing you can do in Berlin. I will contact the railroad. There could have been an equipment failure or a delay on the line."

"Papa, when we traveled from Berlin to Bologna, Mama and I had to change trains in Munich. The station was chaotic. There were Nazis and SS officers checking everyone's papers. Returning to Germany, they will confront everyone and ask for papers. Something dreadful could have happened. She's so frightened of the SS. I should go to Munich right away. I'll ask if anyone saw her."

"Don't go yet. First, let me see what I can find out. Maybe in the change of trains there was a mixup. Maybe she got on the wrong train. I'll reach out to Wilhelm. He has connections everywhere. You stay in Italy and take care of your career. There is nothing waiting for you here in Berlin."

THIRTY

Pienza, August 2017

"I'm striking out," Liam said. "No one seems to know anything about a lawyer named Hernandez who supposedly practiced here twenty-two years ago."

"That's really disappointing," Catherine said. "There's got to be some record of him."

"I've tried the legal registers, bar association memberships, even the clerk of the court in Siena. No Hernandez."

"Maybe his name is not Hernandez, but some other Spanish name," Floria said. "Maybe the signora got the name wrong. She said her memory was foggy. He was Spanish and Italian."

"How many Spanish Italians can there be in this area?" Liam asked.

"There can be a lot," Floria said. "Spain once controlled this region. The office building in Pienza's square is named for the Borgia pope."

"I think I'll drive into Pienza and ask

around," Liam said. "Are you having any luck finding local counsel, Cat?"

Catherine shook her head. "I've spoken to six attorneys, and when I get to the part about VinCo and Lenzini, they all respectfully decline. They don't want to take him on. The policeman was probably right when he warned us about Lenzini. I'm afraid he wields influence in the Siena legal community."

"I don't understand," Floria said. "He's just a pompous little fat man. How can he frighten off so many other *avvocati*?"

"As we say in Chicago," Liam answered, "it's because the fix is in. No sense making enemies in a case you can't win."

"But the signora was able to hire two *avvocati;* Signor Giangorgi and Signor Santi. They agreed to take him on."

"And what did they do?" Liam said. "They folded up their tents. They took the signora's money, but they didn't contest the eviction. Santi was trying to make a deal with Gabi that gave the property to VinCo."

"You could be right," Catherine said. "The lawyers could have been paid off, but I don't know about the fix. We need someone who can tell us about Judge Riggioni. I have an appointment with another attorney in Siena later today. His English is poor. Floria is going to drive and be my interpreter. We have to keep on trying. We have no choice."

Liam grabbed the car keys. "I'm going into Pienza. I'll ask around. Maybe someone has heard of *Avvocato* Hernandez. Maybe I'll come across a lawyer who has the guts to take on Lenzini."

"Bring me some pastries from that little store on the square."

The narrow streets of Pienza's centuries-old city center were pedestrian only. Aside from the usual assortment of cafés, clothing stores and gift shops, there was a smattering of professional offices. Liam noticed a sign outside an office door which read, G. RO-MANO, SERVICI LEGALI. He shrugged and opened the door.

A young woman was seated behind a desk in the small reception room. Liam paused to appreciate the moment. He was in a charming medieval town in Tuscany, he had ambled down a cobblestone walkway adorned with plants and flowers, he had located a lawyer's office and the woman behind the reception desk was strikingly pretty. Not a bad day's work.

Liam guessed the woman was in her mid-to late twenties. She was dressed in a light blue summer shift. A floral silk scarf was knotted at the neckline. Her dark hair was pulled back and held in a tortoiseshell French barrette. She smiled, raised her eyebrows and said, *"Buongiorno, Signore. Come posso aiutarti?"*

Liam had no idea what she had said, but she said it delightfully. He scrunched his face.

"English?" she said. Liam nodded.

"How can I assist you?"

"I wonder if Mr. Romano might have a moment to spare for me?"

"*Mister* Romano?"

"The lawyer."

She smiled.

"Uh-oh," Liam said with a grimace. "I'm sorry. I take it you are G. Romano?"

"Are you disappointed?"

"Goodness, no!"

She stood and extended her hand. "Giulia."

"Liam Taggart. I'm embarrassed. Please forgive me."

A shake of her head brushed away the concern. "*Non è un problema.* How can I help you, Mr. Taggart?"

"Well, to tell the truth, I'm looking for a lawyer named Hernandez. Do you know him?"

She shook her head. Her smile was intoxicating. "No, I'm sorry. Does he practice in this province?"

"He did twenty-two years ago."

"I have only been practicing for three years. I do not know of him. Is there something else?"

"Well, now that you ask, what sort of practice do you have? Do you specialize in certain types of cases? I mean . . . what kind of lawyer are you? I mean, do you do real estate or litigation or . . . I'm usually not this clumsy."

She laughed. "This is a small town, Liam. I have a general practice. Family-oriented. Wills, trusts, real property sales, the occasional divorce. What do you need?"

"Before we go much further, we should clear any conflicts. Do you have any professional connection with VinCo?"

She shook her head. "Not at all. Wish I did. They have a lot of money. I believe that Lorenzo Lenzini does most of their work."

"I'm afraid that's true." Liam stopped and considered the next question. Why not? "Do you like him? Lenzini?"

Her answer was quick. "No. Not in the least."

"Great. We are in a jam and we need a lot of help."

"I think I have some idea. Have you come from America to help Signora Vincenzo?"

"Yes, how do you know that?"

"Word gets around. It's a small town."

"We are trying to stop Lenzini from evicting Gabriella Vincenzo. So far, we've been totally ineffective. We need someone who practices here to help us. There are issues concerning who owns the land — who has good title to the land. Lenzini has managed to get court orders ex parte, without anyone else present. In fact, Gabi has been held in default. Recently, Lenzini has been showing up at the property. I had a run-in with him. And then I had a run-in with the police. We have tried to be reasonable, but Lenzini is maniacal. My wife, Catherine, is an outstanding attorney in Chicago, but here in Pienza, she can't do much on her own. We need help."

"I understand."

"Well, how can I get you interested in helping us?"

Again, that dazzling smile. "I quote a fee. You agree to pay the fee. Isn't that how it works in America?"

"Yes, I believe it is."

"Where is your wife, Catherine, now?"

"She was going to Siena, but she'll be at Gabi's villa later on. We're staying there."

Giulia handed a business card to Liam. "I have an appointment in an hour. I will drive out to the villa at five o'clock."

"Fabulous."

Catherine returned to the villa at three. Liam was sitting on the veranda, his feet up, holding a bottle of beer. He had a smug look on his face.

"Well, I struck out today," Catherine said. "As soon as we said Lenzini, the lawyer backed off." She took the bottle from Liam's hand and took a drink. "What's with the big smile? Did you at least bring me pastries?"

"Better. Much better. I brought you a lawyer. Giulia Romano. She'll be here later this afternoon."

"Seriously? How did you get a lawyer?"

"Me Irish charm."

THIRTY-ONE

Bologna, September 1937

Though my mother's disappearance weighed heavily on my mind, I returned to rehearsal the next morning. As distraught as I was, there was nothing I could do at home, and if I didn't show up for rehearsal, I would lose my job. There were five *Traviata* performances, and we were getting ready to begin rehearsals of Rossini's *The Barber of Seville.* As we prepared to move from Verdi to Rossini, I wondered if Maestro Vittorio would put Mr. Lassoni back in his first chair. That question was answered as soon as I arrived at the Teatro. Maestro called me into his office.

"What I say to you, I say in private. Inside these walls only."

I nodded.

"Ada, I am impressed by your talent, your skills, your passion, your feel for the instrument. Wilhelm did not mislead me. You are at least as fine a violinist as any in my orchestra. You lack only experience, and that will come. But I cannot keep you in the first section."

My heart sank. I feared this was coming. I saw the men gathering around Vittorio when I was promoted. I knew they were leveling a grievance. Again, I nodded.

"It is political, Ada. Many were unhappy by what I did. They thought I shamed Lassoni, though that was not my intention. I sought only to give Miss Albanese the orchestral support she deserved in *Traviata*'s most emotional scene, but some of my members did not approve. They did not like replacing Lassoni with a new person, a young person."

"A female person?"

"I am glad you understand. But the replacement itself was a good thing, not only because of your skill but because competition makes for better artistry. Ada, your assignment here is temporary, only as long as Signor Fishman is on sabbatical. When you leave, I will once again have to rely on my senior members, the ones who have played for me throughout the years. Like Rico Lassoni."

I was sad, but he was right. I had no claim to first chair.

Maestro smiled. "When we begin *Barbiere,* you will please return to second section. And in the future, who knows? Competition is good. When I came in today, I saw Lassoni practicing *Barbiere* very intensely."

Rehearsals, performances and practices absorbed all my time, some days from eight thirty in the morning to eleven at night. Still, only half my mind was on my music. The other half was on my mother. Each night I returned to the apartment to see if there was a telegram waiting for me. In my most recent telephone call, Papa told me that there were no mechanical problems noted on the rail lines. "It is possible that Mama was taken off the train and detained for some reason. Uncle Wilhelm is using all his influence to find out what happened. He has even reached out to Joseph Goebbels. But don't be disheartened. There are no reports of her arrest or her death. She is simply missing."

Papa insisted on maintaining optimism. He made me promise to be upbeat. "We will only send out positive vibrations," he said. "No negative thoughts allowed. Perhaps Mama has fallen ill along the way and is recuperating in a clinic somewhere. Maybe Switzerland. I am checking the hospitals. Have faith. We must continue to have faith. It's all we have." He refused to believe something horrid had happened. I was not so confident. I cried for an hour after hanging up.

There was no performance on Monday and I was supposed to go out with Franny and Natalia that evening, but I didn't feel up to it. They knew about Mama and they knew I didn't want to go out of the apartment for any reason, except to rehearse or perform. I spent all my free time in the apartment practicing *Barbiere* and trying to stop thinking of tragic scenarios. Thank God I had my music. Otherwise, I would have gone mad. Half of me wanted to run to the station, get on a train, take it to Munich and go off searching for her.

At eight o'clock there was a knock on the door. It was Franny, Natalia and two other girls. "Come on," they said. "It's time for dinner. You need to get out." I protested, but they insisted. They said either I would walk or they would carry me.

It was a warm September night, the city was alive and I was with friends who cared about me. I tried to be upbeat, but my spirits were down. There were tears in my eyes that just wouldn't go away. I apologized to my friends, but they would have none of it. They continually drew me into conversations. I was sick at heart and they were spoon-feeding me the very best medicine they could — concern, warmth, friendship and love.

Natalia turned to me and said, "Thursday is Rosh Hashanah. Have you made plans to attend synagogue? Will you come with me?"

That was a surprise. I had forgotten she was Jewish and I had forgotten about the High Holy Days.

I shook my head. "I don't know. I'm sorry. I'm not thinking very clearly. Being here in Italy, it's easy to forget I'm Jewish. No one is pointing it out to me everywhere I go. In Germany, we are *Juden.* We are people to be avoided. Here in Italy, no one seems to care if you're Jewish. No signs tell you where you can or cannot go. No one asks if you're Jewish before you enter a restaurant. Everyone gets along. You're lucky, Nat. Italy hasn't seen the horrors of a regime that makes it a national policy to exclude Jews."

Natalia raised her eyebrows. "Just to the right of the Two Towers, behind the gelato store," she said, "what is the name of the street?"

I thought for a minute and finally said, "Via Inferno."

Natalia nodded. "That's right. It's called Hell Street. Do you know why?"

I shrugged. "No."

"The several blocks in that area were formerly known as Ghetto Ebraico, the Hebrew ghetto. In the middle of the sixteenth century, in an effort to combat so-called religious contamination, the Catholic church confiscated and burned copies of the Talmud throughout Italy on the charge of blasphemy. In 1555, Pope Paul IV ordered all Jews in the Papal States to sell their houses and move into a walled section of the city that would be locked at night."

"That was the Ghetto Ebraico?" I said.

Natalia nodded. "Most people agree the word *ghetto* comes from the Italian word *borghetto,* meaning 'small neighborhood.' Jews were forced into small neighborhoods."

"Jews were locked into a ghetto?"

"They could come and go during the day, but they had to be in at night. That arrangement lasted for about forty years. Then, in 1593, the Jews were totally expelled from all of the Papal States, except for Rome. Expelled. Had to leave the country. It wasn't until the nineteenth century that they wandered back, reestablished the synagogue and opened their businesses."

"I didn't know."

"So, you see, Italy has not always been as accommodating to Jews as you thought."

"But that took place hundreds of years ago. There are no restrictive laws in Italy today. In Germany, it's happening right now and getting worse by the day. You have to agree, it's much better for us in Italy."

Natalia slowly shook her head. She wasn't convinced. "Better today, but there is talk. I hear the rumors at the university. Mussolini

and the Fascist Grand Council are considering laws restricting Jewish life. At the moment, it's just talk, but we can never be
sure."

That shocked me. I hoped she was wrong.

"Again, come to High Holy Day services
with me," Natalia said. "We'll pray for your
mother."

I nodded. "I will. Thank you. Where do we
go?"

"In the Ghetto Ebraico, where else? There
is a new synagogue, built in 1928."

"Where did your family go before the
synagogue was built?"

"Oh, my family doesn't live here. They live
out in the country in a little town where nothing ever happens. It is far too quiet for me. I
have only been in Bologna for the last five
years working on my degrees. My wish is to
teach right here at the University of Bologna.
Someday maybe you will go with me when I
visit my parents."

"I'd love that. What town do they live in?"

"My family comes from a small town in
the Tuscany region. It is called Pienza."

THIRTY-TWO

Pienza, August 2017

A red Fiat pulled up to the villa at five o'clock, and Giulia Romano stepped out. "Lovely," she said as she took a moment to scan the landscape.

"Exactly my reaction," Catherine said, extending her hand. "I'm Catherine Lockhart and this is Floria, Signora Vincenzo's most able assistant. You've already met my husband. Thank you for driving out here tonight."

"It is my honor."

They strolled over to a table on the veranda and Floria didn't waste a moment. "We have to stop Lenzini," she said. "You can be sure he'll come back, and he'll dig and he'll cut and he'll drive my poor *padrona* to the grave. He's a monster. He must be stopped!"

Catherine patted her on the shoulder. "We're going to stop him, Floria." Turning to Giulia, she said, "Liam tells me that you already knew we were here to help Gabi."

"Yes. As I told him, Pienza is a small community. Everyone here knows that the signora has been fighting with Lenzini about her farm. There are no secrets in Pienza. Tell me what I can do for you."

"Ultimately, we want to reopen the case, retry the ownership of the property and prove it belongs to Gabi," Catherine said. "More urgently, we need to get before the judge and stop Lenzini from bringing his work crew out here. We need to vacate a court order Lenzini obtained that gives VinCo the right to conduct digging and testing on Gabi's land."

"Can I ask a question?" Liam said. "What do you know about Judge Riggioni?"

Giulia shrugged. "Not too much. He has a solid reputation. I've only had one matter before him. It was a border dispute. He read the file and ruled fairly; not all judges do that."

"Our friend in Chicago has suggested that he can be reached."

Giulia squinted. "Reached?"

"Improperly influenced. You know, on the take."

Giulia straightened up. She had a shocked look on her face. "And you want *me* to . . ."

"No, no, no. Just the opposite. Gabi's nephew is of the opinion that Lenzini may have reached the judge."

Giulia laughed. "Reached. Interesting. I suppose that is an opinion held by many who lose a case. Well, this is not Chicago and I do not think that Judge Riggioni is 'on the take,' as you say. Appellate courts in this province will review the decision quite carefully and reverse it if it is not correct. Paying a judge would not be money well spent, even if such a thing were possible."

"But Lenzini has been described as a man who wields influence. Lawyers are afraid to litigate against him."

"In some respects, that's true. He represents a client, VinCo, that has a lot of money and will spend it. Lenzini will use that money to litigate an opponent to death. He will file dozens of motions, engage in repetitive procedures, all to — how do you say — impoverish his opponent. He is aggressive, and the fees and costs of opposing him are high. But our time today is better spent discussing Gabriella's case and possible strategies, rather than worrying about Lenzini's influences, don't you think?"

Catherine smiled. "Well said." She took out her file and laid it on the table. "This is the most recent order, the one permitting VinCo to conduct digging and cutting. We would like to appear before Judge Riggioni as quickly as possible to vacate this order, or to stay it until September 10, the date for surrender of possession."

"I could file for an emergency hearing," Giulia said, "but what is the emergency?

What is the harm in taking soil samples or vine cuttings? Especially, since the judge has ruled that VinCo will have the property in a month."

"I will tell you," Gabi said forcefully, walking slowly out to the veranda, banging her cane along the way. "The cuttings may destroy my vines and limit production of the grapes. Digging in my fields will interfere with my farming operations. The manner in which I farm and harvest is confidential and proprietary. VinCo has cleverly chosen to cut my most valuable vines because they covet my success. I win awards with those vines. How does it hurt the great VinCo to wait a few weeks?" Giulia stood and bowed slightly. *"Piacere di conoscerti, Signora Vincenzo."*

"She has a point," Catherine said. "What is the harm to VinCo in waiting until possession date?"

"You will be asking Judge Riggioni to reverse an order he has already considered," Giulia said. "We must be mindful that Italian judges do not like to revisit their rulings. There must be a good reason, supported by evidence, perhaps something the judge may not have considered when he made his decision. In this case, Judge Riggioni has already ruled that VinCo owns the property. Preserving vines for Gabriella's future use or interfering with her farming operations are weak arguments, considering she will be gone in a few weeks anyway. We must first convince the judge that Gabi may *not* be gone in a month, that she has a valid argument that VinCo does not own the land. If Judge Riggioni thinks that the ownership will once again be an unresolved issue, then he might be more agreeable to staying his digging order."

"I totally agree, and I am impressed," Catherine said. "How many years did you say you've been practicing?"

Giulia smiled. "Long enough to learn some lessons the hard way."

Catherine took the two deeds out of the file. "The judge's ruling focused on these two deeds. When the judge reviewed the registry books, he found that Quercia's name is shown as the owner all the way back to 1980. Thus, a deed in 1995 from Vanucci would not have been valid. But he only considered the most recent book, not the previous book. We don't know how Quercia claims to be the owner."

Giulia nodded. "What is *Avvocato* Hernandez's involvement? That was Liam's initial question — did I know a lawyer named Hernandez."

"He was the lawyer who came with Mr. Vanucci in 1995," Gabi said. "We all signed the deed, and then he took it to the registrar for recording."

"No one seems to know him," Liam said.

"So, I guess the obvious question is, why

282

would Hernandez and Vanucci go through all this trouble if they couldn't give Gabi a good title?" Giulia said.

Catherine nodded. "Exactly. Gabi was not well represented against VinCo and Lenzini. We need help. Are you interested?"

Giulia smiled and said, "I will take the case. I'll start by reviewing the court records tomorrow. Hopefully, I will find an opening. Maybe something was overlooked. Meanwhile, we must find evidence. Judge Riggioni will not review this case again without evidence."

"What about the order permitting Lenzini to dig on the land?" Liam said. "We need to stop him."

"Gabi said she never had notice of the motion," Catherine added.

"I will check the file," Giulia said. "If she didn't receive notice, the judge may vacate the order. Would you like to help me draft the motion, Catherine?"

"I'd love to."

"We also need to fill out a request to see the older registry book, the one before 1980."

"Mr. Santi told us that he did that several weeks ago, but did not follow up. Liam and I filled out a request for the book a few days ago."

"Then it should already be in. Depending on what is in the book, we may need to establish proof in other ways as well. We also need to find out what we can about Vanucci and Hernandez."

THIRTY-THREE

Bologna, October 1937

It had been twelve days since my mother disappeared. Papa and I exchanged letters and occasionally talked on the phone, but there wasn't any news. We were assured that Uncle Wilhelm was using his connections in the German government, but no one seemed to have any information. She had just vanished. I blamed myself for not being there when she made the decision to leave. I could have talked her out of it. I should have spent more time with her, made her feel more welcome. Maybe I could have done more to bring her out of her depression. The simple fact was, if I had paid more attention to my mother, she wouldn't have felt so isolated.

I was sick at heart. I was losing hope that she was alive. Still, for my father's sake, I kept an upbeat attitude. Papa would say, "Only good thoughts, Ada. Only positive. We'll find her." And I would answer, "Of course, we will."

The BSO was now performing *The Barber of Seville* and starting to rehearse *Tosca*. I had returned to my seat in the second-violin section. Since it was clear to all that I was a temporary replacement and no longer usurping Signor Lassoni's first-chair privileges, the evil glares started to abate. After all, hadn't Maestro Vittorio put me in my place? Wasn't I back in second violin? Evil stares or not, playing with the professional orchestra was a dream come true for me and most of the members were kind.

Of course, my father did not come to Bologna in October as he had earlier planned. He was concerned that he might be out of the city when there was news about Mama. He needed to be at home or with the Philharmonic. Uncle Wilhelm was our best hope, but so far, he'd come up empty. The Philharmonic had traveled to Brussels for a series of concerts. The orchestra was staying at the Regent Hotel, and Papa gave me the telephone number to call if I heard anything at all.

I was preparing to go out to dinner with Franny and Natalia when I received a telegram: "Wilhelm found her! Call me at the Regent." The telegram sent chills through my body. Was she all right? Was she well? Where did he find her? Why didn't he give me more information? I ran all the way to the post office to make a phone call.

"Papa, tell me, is Mama all right?"

"She is. Wilhelm, God bless him, called everyone he knew in the Third Reich, and he knows plenty. He found out that she is in Munich at a detention center."

"At a detention center! What did she do?"

"I'm not really sure. The story I got was that Mama was running wildly through the Munich train station and screaming at the soldiers. They assumed she was mentally ill and took her to a detention center."

"Oh, Papa, I knew this would happen. I'm sure she got mixed up changing trains and wandered into the station. There must have been hundreds of soldiers in their green uniforms and SS in their black uniforms and Brownshirts everywhere. You know, Nazi officers scare her to death. She must have panicked."

"That's what they said. She was running through the station and an SS officer stopped her and asked to see her papers. Other officers came over and encircled her. Apparently, Mama lost it. She became hysterical. According to Wilhelm, she started screaming, 'Kleiner, Kleiner. Kleiner is after me.' "

"Where did they take her?"

"They took her to a holding facility some-where in Munich while they tried to figure out who Kleiner was. It was an unofficial detainment and they didn't register her name, so no one knew she was in custody. Finally, they took her to Wittelsbacher Palace. It is the Munich headquarters of the Gestapo and also a Gestapo prison. They put Mama in solitary confinement as a mental patient. They registered her name and that's how Heydrich found out and he told Wilhelm. He's the head of Reich Security, you know. Detention centers come under his authority."

"Reinhard Heydrich?"

"Yes, the same, the one who praised your solo. Thank God he found her. There's no telling what the Gestapo would have done to her, Ada. Heydrich recognized the Baumgarten name, called Wilhelm and told him she was there."

"And she's there now?"

"Yes," Papa said. "At Wittelsbacher Palace in Munich. There is a train out of Brussels tomorrow afternoon, and I'm going to Munich to get her. If I make my connections, I can get there by Tuesday."

"Tuesday? Papa, we can't leave her in a Gestapo prison in solitary confinement for another hour. I can get a train to Munich tonight."

"But you have your orchestra. Are you sure?"

"Papa, she's in a prison. Yes, I'm sure. I'm not going to leave her to be mistreated

in solitary confinement."

"Please be careful. Wilhelm has secured orders for her to be released, but we are still dealing with the Nazis. Nothing is ever certain. When I said I would pick her up, they told me to go to the administration office inside the front entrance and they would bring her out. I'll make sure they know you're coming instead of me."

That evening, I told Franny and Natalia the news. It was a relief she had been found. Learning that she had been imprisoned in Munich for almost two weeks was very disturbing. She had been detained for mental issues, not for crimes, so I hoped they had treated her fairly. Both of my friends offered to go with me, but they did not have visas to travel to Germany, and even if they did, I would not put them in danger. Since Uncle Wilhelm had arranged for Mama's release, I felt pretty comfortable going alone.

This whole Kleiner episode at the Munich train station had me shaken. I know that every Nazi was Kleiner to Mama, but what if she actually saw him? What if he was alerted? If there was anyone that Kleiner wanted more than my mother, it was me. What if he was assigned to Gestapo headquarters? For me to walk into a prison where Herbert Kleiner was working would be about the dumbest thing I could do. Still, I had no choice. I would have to go to Munich, get my mother and hope that Kleiner wasn't anywhere around.

The train from Bologna Centrale to Munich Hauptbahnhof took eight and a half hours, with stops in Verona, Bolzano, Innsbruck and at the German border at Kiefersfelden, where a number of soldiers and SS personnel boarded. With a train full of Nazis, conversations among the passengers immediately ceased or were conducted at a whisper. SS officers walked down the aisles checking passports, visas and papers. I fingered my magic locket. Keep me safe, magic locket. They stared at me, looked me up and down and then demanded my papers. When they were satisfied, they hmph'd and walked on.

The Munich station was a beehive of armed personnel. Wehrmacht soldiers, SS, Brownshirts, Gestapo and Munich police. It was all I could do to hold it together, and I could easily understand how my mother would have gone over the edge. Her anxiety about Nazis was the principal reason she had left Berlin in the first place.

I got into a taxi outside the Munich station and asked the driver to take me to Wittelsbacher Palace. He looked at me like I was crazy. "Do you know what that is?" he said.

"Yes. I'm on official business." My reply seemed to shake him up a bit.

The area around Wittelsbacher was patrolled, and other than official vehicles, no cars were permitted within a two-block radius. Formerly King Ludwig's palace, the imposing structure easily covered an entire city block. Now housing the Gestapo headquarters and prison, it was three stories of red brick with a gothic exterior. It had turrets on the four corners and two large stone lions guarded the entrance. As I approached, a young soldier no older than Kurt, with his rifle in his hands, stopped me and asked what I was doing.

"I am here to pick up a woman named Friede Baumgarten. She is to be released to me on orders from Maestro Wilhelm Furtwängler."

The guard chuckled and told me to go away; I had no business at Gestapo headquarters. "Nobody stops by and picks up any of the prisoners here, especially not on the orders of a music conductor," he said. "You don't want to be here. Go away."

"But Friede Baumgarten is detained in this facility, not for a crime but because of her confused mental state," I said. "Arrangements have been made for her release. I am here to pick her up. Please check with your superior officer."

Now he was losing patience and he started to wave his rifle around. I could see that he was a nervous young man, no more than eighteen. "You are mistaken," he said. "No one gets released from Wittelsbacher to a young girl. A prisoner would have to be released to someone in authority. Not you. You are most definitely mixed up. Now you must go."

I couldn't blame him for his logic. What was a young girl doing trying to pick up a prisoner at a Gestapo prison? I sure hoped my father had the story right. I would give it another shot.

"Friede Baumgarten's release was arranged and communicated to Maestro Furtwängler by Brigadeführer Heydrich himself."

The guard smiled and shook his head. "I don't think so." He waved his rifle at me. "Go!"

I was shaking like a leaf, but somehow I found the strength. "Please check with your office. Would I stand here and make up such a story? Go inside and check. If what I say is true, and you refuse, then you are disobeying an order from Reinhard Heydrich. Not a good career decision on your part."

The guard thought for a moment and then stepped inside. When he returned, he nodded. He asked to see my papers and looked them over carefully. "It seems your crazy story is right. She is being held in solitary confinement. But I am also told that Master Sergeant Kleiner has been notified and is on his way to pick her up himself. She apparently demanded to see him several times when she was arrested. He has since been contacted and has made arrangements to pick her up."

"She is to be released to *me*," I said. "Check your orders. The Brigadeführer's orders are clear. I am the one to pick her up. Ada Baumgarten."

"I don't want to be in the middle of this," he said, grimacing. "I don't want Master Sergeant Kleiner to say I didn't follow *his* orders. Why don't you wait for him? Then the two of you can straighten it out. I am told he is on his way." He started to walk away.

"Those are not your orders!" I yelled. "Your orders come from Brigadeführer Reinhard Heydrich. If I leave, I will have to tell Brigadeführer Heydrich that his direct orders were willfully disobeyed by a guard who would rather wait for orders from a sergeant."

He exhaled. "One way or another, I'm gonna get screwed," he said, under his breath. "Stay here. I will go and see about the prisoner."

I stood outside the entrance for thirty

minutes, nervously watching every person and every official car that approached the building. I desperately hoped that Mama would be released before Kleiner arrived. From time to time a black car would drive up and stop at the entrance, and uniformed soldiers would alight. I would turn the other way, hiding my face. Finally, the door opened, and the soldier brought Mama out.

The dress she wore, elegant when new, looked shabby, dirty and wrinkled. I assumed she had been in that dress since she was arrested. Mama had lost weight, and her beautiful hair, which I had seen her brush fifty times a day, was all knotted. She had a glazed look on her face, and at first I didn't think she recognized me, but then she started crying. And so did I.

"Mama, we are going to have to walk a few blocks to get out of this area. Are you able to walk?"

She nodded. "I'm sorry I left you. I . . . ."

"We can't stand and talk. We have to walk now, Mama. Before someone comes."

"Okay, Ada," she said weakly.

The weather was chilly. I took my coat off and wrapped it around her. I put her arm over my shoulder and held her by the waist and we started walking. Her gait was weak and unsteady. I had to hold her to keep her from stumbling. It was important to get us off Briennerstrasse as quickly as possible before Kleiner came, but I didn't want to tell her that.

Mama was suffering from malnourishment, and she had undoubtedly been mistreated, emotionally if not physically. She could walk with my help, but slowly, and we had to stop every few steps to rest. Finally, we were out of sight of Gestapo headquarters. It had been strenuous for her, and there was no telling when my mother had last eaten. I asked her, but she didn't remember. I took her to a café for coffee and scrambled eggs. Then I flagged a taxi to take us to the Munich station.

"Mama, I'm going to take you back home and everything is going to be all right, but first we have to get on the train at the Munich station. You're going to see soldiers again, Nazis in uniform. You'll see them in Munich and you'll also see them when we get to Berlin. Don't look at them, just look at me. Keep your eyes on me. I'll be with you every step of the way, and I will protect you. You have to believe in me. Nobody in a uniform is going to harm you. You have to hold it together. Can you do that?"

She bit her lip, swallowed and nodded her head.

"You can't scream, no matter what. You can squeeze my arm as hard as you want, but you can't scream. Do we have a deal?"

She nodded and brushed the tears from

her eyes. "I love you, Ada."

The taxi dropped us at the train station, but before we entered, Mama stopped me. "I don't want to go home, Ada," she said. "Please don't take me back to Berlin. I don't want to be in Germany anymore." She looked at me with plaintive eyes. "Would it be all right if I came back to Bologna and lived with you again? Please?"

I threw my arms around her. I could feel her bones. My words caught in my throat. "Oh Mama, that would make me so happy."

THIRTY-FOUR

Pienza, August 2017

Giulia called early in the morning. "I think I've found a procedural error," she said. "It appears that you were right, Catherine. Gabriella did not receive proper notice of VinCo's motion to conduct soil and plant testing."

"That's what Gabi said. She didn't receive notice at all. But I thought she had been held in default," Catherine said.

"That is incorrect. There has never been an order of default entered in this case. It's true that no one appeared for Gabi on the day of the hearing, but Judge Riggioni did not declare Gabi to be in default. Even though *Avvocato* Santi did not show up, his appearance is still on file as Gabi's attorney. He never withdrew it."

Catherine smiled. "I get it. Since Santi still represented her, Lenzini was obligated to serve Santi with a notice and a copy of his motion. Are we sure Santi didn't get notice?"

"The court file does not contain a copy of such a notice, which is required anytime a motion is filed. Also, I called Santi to confirm. He told me he never had notice of Lenzini's motion. If he had received notice, he would have called Gabriella."

"How soon can we get this before the judge?"

"I will drive to Siena today and file it. I will try to set the motion for Friday morning."

Judge Riggioni's courtroom was on the second floor of the large government complex where the province of Siena's civil litigation courts were located. Giulia had scheduled the motion for 10:00 a.m. Lenzini entered the courtroom and laid his papers on the table. He gave a slight tug to the sleeves of his seersucker suit and smugly shook his head at Catherine and Liam as if to say this foolish motion is bothersome and annoying.

The courtroom personnel rose when Judge Riggioni entered. He looked to be in his late fifties, slightly gray at the temples and narrow-shouldered in his judicial robe. He smiled at the attorneys as he placed a copy of Giulia's motion and the court file on his desk.

"Please explain the nature of your emergency, *Avvocata* Romano," the judge said. "Why must my ruling be reevaluated at an emergency hearing?"

"*Signor Presidente della corte,*" she said,

"with due respect, it is because it was entered without any notice to the defendant, Gabriella Vincenzo. As such, the order is voidable."

The judge peered over his reading glasses at Lenzini and said, "*Avvocato* Lenzini, did you provide notice before the motion was heard?"

"It wasn't necessary, *Signor Presidente*. She had been held in default."

The judge thumbed through the court file and shook his head. "I do not see an order of default."

"She abandoned her case when no one appeared at the trial. That is equivalent to a default. It isn't necessary to prepare a notice once a litigant abandons the case."

"*Avvocato* Santi is still of record as Signora Vincenzo's lawyer, is he not?"

"His name is on the file, but he did not show up on the date you set. They abandoned their defense."

The judge shook his head. "No. It is true they may have foregone their right to present evidence or to make an argument on the day I ruled, but that was essentially a decision to stand on their papers, not to abandon the case. There is no order of default and Signora Vincenzo is entitled to notice of any motion you present. Since you gave no notice, I vacate the order that allowed VinCo to enter the property for testing."

"But, Your Excellency, I will simply bring the motion again, this time with notice, and you will end up making the same ruling because the property belongs to VinCo and they are entitled to make testing to preserve the farm."

"If you please, *Signor Presidente,*" Giulia said, "it is presumptuous for *Avvocato* Lenzini to tell you what you will or will not do. Were the motion to be presented to you again, we would show that the testing is harmful to Signora Vincenzo's operations, which she is entitled to conduct every day until she is deprived of possession. Further, I am working on a motion to reopen the case. Because no one appeared, you did not hear both sides of the argument. The constitution provides that I may petition to reopen the case if I am in possession of newly discovered evidence that would change the outcome."

"And are you in possession of such evidence, Signorina Romano?"

"I am not prepared to discuss my evidence at this time, but I will do so shortly."

The judge nodded. "Well, you only have twenty-six days before Signora Vincenzo must relinquish possession. I would suggest you plan to make such a showing well before then. But I want to admonish you not to bring such a motion unless you have solid evidence. Not mere supposition." He looked at Lenzini. "In the meantime, I hereby vacate

300

my previous order allowing testing. Signor Lenzini, VinCo may not enter the property before the possession date. Court is adjourned."

"There is one more thing, *Signor Presidente,*" Giulia said. "*Avvocato* Lenzini and his workers came onto the property under the authority of the voidable order that you have just vacated. They took valuable vine cuttings from the property. In other words, they engaged in acts of pruning and harvesting. Prior to September 10, VinCo is not allowed to commence operations on the property. I request that you order Signor Lenzini and his client to return the valuable vine cuttings to Signora Vincenzo."

The judge nodded. "Agreed. So ordered."

"But, Your Honor, we are only testing for disease and mold," Lenzini said nervously. "What is the harm?"

"Exactly the point. What is the harm? In twenty-six days, you may do all the testing you like. Return the cuttings. We are adjourned."

On the way through the courthouse doors, Lenzini brushed hard against Liam.

"Well, excuse you, buddy," Liam said. "I guess you had a bad day today."

"You have won a minor skirmish — you have taken a hill but you cannot win the war. That's how this goes, Mr. Toughguy. What you do not realize is that you have taken on a powerful enemy."

"I've met tougher enemies than you."

"It is not me, Mr. Taggart. I am only a spokesman. It is my client. You have kicked a sleeping lion."

"Then I guess you're in for an uncomfortable time this afternoon. I'd hate to be in your shoes, having to report to your lion that you got out-lawyered."

"You are a fool. VinCo will stop at nothing to get what it wants. Signora Vincenzo should have taken my offer. Now they will obliterate her. She will have nothing." Lenzini shook his head and left the building.

"He just threatened Gabi," Catherine said.

"I don't think so. I think he warned us. I think he's afraid of his client and what his client might do. What's the chance that VinCo would try to harm Gabi or her property rather than lose it in a court battle?"

"Gabi thinks they covet her awards, her prize-winning wine," Catherine said.

Liam shook his head. "It's hard to believe that this is all about a blue ribbon. There's something more involved. I'm sure of it."

"Nice work today, Giulia," Catherine said on the walk back to the car.

"We still have a long way to go in a very short time. We need to find out why the deed came from Carlo Vanucci. Mr. Vanucci apparently believed he had good title, and there must be a reason for that."

"What about the property index books, the registry books? Won't they show a grantor-to-grantee progression? Wouldn't we find out how Quercia claims to be the owner? Might we see Vanucci's name?" Liam asked.

Giulia stopped at the curb. "Perhaps, but as yet we do not have the book and time is of the essence."

"Santi ordered it from storage and so did we."

"Then it should be there. Let's go to the Registrar of Titles. If it's not there, we'll ask for an expedited search for the book."

THIRTY-FIVE

Bologna, December 1937

There were consequences and changes as a result of my mother's imprisonment and release. For one, my father could breathe again. His worst fears had been assuaged. As to her rescue, he gave me far more credit than I merited. He saw me as heroic, which I did not deserve. After all, it was he and Uncle Wilhelm who found her and made the arrangements. Most importantly, Papa was now focused on getting himself out of Germany and moving us all to Vienna.

Mama, of course, had been traumatized. Every day was a quest to regain her equilibrium. For several days after our return, she didn't want to be left alone. She came to rehearsals and sat in the theater. She was quiet, and I could sense her struggle to calm her mind and move on.

As for Mama and me, we saw each other in a different light. We had evolved. We developed a deep appreciation for the respective strengths of character that each of us had demonstrated. Ironically, her tragedy brought us closer together. I respected the fact that Mama didn't want to talk about her confinement at Wittelsbacher, but little snippets would come out now and then, and I came to understand the terror of her ordeal and what a strong and determined woman she was.

Soon the holiday season arrived, and the timing could not have been better. Bologna became a magical city. The lights, the parades, the food and the holiday music filled the air with gaiety. No matter your religious beliefs, the pure joy of the season was sure to raise your spirits. It was true for me and it was true for Mama. Bologna was beginning to agree with her. We would often stop at a café or a bakery just to have an espresso and watch the bustle. No longer did she complain about the cobblestone streets or the noisy crowds. No longer did she make disparaging comparisons between life in Berlin and life in Bologna. She wanted no part of Berlin. Of course, she missed Papa, but the plans were for Papa to join the Vienna Philharmonic Orchestra next year and the two of them would settle in Vienna. Those thoughts carried her through many sad moments.

As for our daily life, Mama and I had developed a routine, a division of labor. I had my professional life and she assumed the responsibility of making our little apartment into a home. She was cooking meals on a regular basis and, even more important, she was eating them. She was a creative decorator and found ways to make our apartment deliciously warm and cozy. Above all, I saw the qualities in my mother that I had never appreciated before and I liked it a lot.

Papa wrote on a regular basis. We could expect at least one letter a week, sometimes more. They were upbeat and told us all about the happenings at the Philharmonic, but I could read between the lines. He was lonely too. I could tell he was counting the days until Vienna. Knowing that Mama would never come back to Berlin, he put the house on the market. Unfortunately, many Jewish homes were on the market as well, but ours was very nice and he hoped to find a buyer soon.

During the second week of December, Maestro Vittorio told me he needed to talk to me in private. He summoned me to his office. *Oh, no,* I thought. *This cannot be good. What did I do now?* He closed the door and motioned for me to sit down.

"You know, Ada, I gave you a golden opportunity here in Bologna. I was skeptical when Wilhelm sang your praises and told me how lucky I would be to have you in my orchestra. After all, you are young, inexperienced and, frankly, a woman. But I had a vacancy to fill. So, I took a chance on you, and you did not let me down. Ada, you are a gifted, talented woman and I am proud to have you in my orchestra."

I sat there waiting for the axe to fall. *Here it comes,* I thought. The next word will be "but."

"But," he sighed, "I cannot promote you or move you up in the orchestra, no matter how superior your talent. I cannot feature you in solo numbers as I did in *Traviata.* I was harshly criticized by several senior members for embarrassing Rico, even though your performance was magnificent."

Okay, I thought. *Where is this leading?*

"Ada, I feel it is my obligation to do something to further your career. I cannot let such a gifted artist pass through my life without doing whatever I can. Unfortunately, my hands are tied with my orchestra, but I have found an opportunity for you. Sister Maria Alicia is once again organizing her series of Christmas concerts at the Basilica. This is no small matter. She draws some of the finest musicians and singers in all of Italy for her series. Lina Cavalieri and Magda Olivero are the finest sopranos in Italy, and they are likely to perform in the series. I am certain that the great Beniamino

Gigli will return to perform again this year. Ada, she needs a top-notch violinist in her ensemble, and there isn't a violinist in Italy that wouldn't jump at the opportunity. I have recommended you."

I was floored. "Thank you. I don't know what to say."

Maestro smiled. "You are to meet with Sister Maria Alicia tomorrow night at six o'clock at the Basilica. She will fill you in on the selections and rehearsal times."

"Thank you so much."

"But," he said, raising his index finger, "this is a side job. You are not excused from your duties with the orchestra. If there is a conflict down the road, we'll deal with it at the appropriate time." He stood. "Let me know how the meeting goes."

I rushed home and gave the news to Mama. She was so excited, as happy as I'd seen her since we returned to Bologna. "We'll have a celebration dinner tonight," she said. "I've been working on my Bolognese cooking and I'm dying to try out a spinach lasagna. This is the perfect occasion." It was so heartening to see her in such good spirits. "Why don't you invite Franny and Natalia?" she said.

Then I remembered, I had already made plans with Natalia. She and her boyfriend were fixing me up with a friend of theirs and we were supposed to all go out together. I had totally forgotten and now Mama was making dinner. I couldn't disappoint my mother. I told her I would go and ask Franny and Natalia if they were available, but my real purpose was to run to Natalia's apartment and tell her I could not go out with them.

I was too late. Natalia and her boyfriend, Theo, were in her apartment having a glass of wine. Another fellow was sitting on the couch. "Ada, so glad you came early," Natalia said. "I didn't expect to see you so soon. Let me introduce you to Frederico."

Frederico was dark-haired and tall, at least six inches taller than me. He wore a tweed sport coat over a black T-shirt and very tight pants. He had a broad smile and a dimple on his chin. All in all, he was very good-looking. "Delighted to meet you, Ada," he said. "Can I pour you a glass of wine?"

"I'm glad to meet you as well, Frederico, but I have a problem. I'm sorry, but I'm going to have to cancel dinner tonight. This afternoon, I was offered a very special position. I'm going to play in the Christmas concert series at the Basilica."

"Wow," Natalia said. "That's wonderful, but the series is two weeks away."

"I know. When I got the offer, I ran home to tell Mama and she was so excited, she made a special dinner for us. I can't disappoint her."

Natalia nodded. She understood. Apparently, Frederico did not. He looked at me with an annoyed expression, shrugged his shoulders and started for the door. Then he turned around and said, "Theo, I could have gone out with Angela tonight. I passed up a good date for this. Next time you ask me to do you a favor and take out some poor girl who has no social life, remind me to say no thanks." And he left.

I looked at Natalia. "Poor girl? No social life? I was a favor? Seriously, Nat?"

"I didn't phrase it like that, Ada. I'm sorry. You know, you don't get out much, you haven't been dating anyone. You work hard and spend most of your time with your mother. We just thought maybe . . ."

"I happen to love my mother. You know what we've been through, Nat."

"Ada, you're taking this all the wrong way. I didn't say 'poor girl' or 'no social life.' I just mentioned that you weren't dating anyone. Maybe you were too busy to meet boys. Frederico was a jerk to say what he said."

That made me feel bad. Natalia was trying to be a good friend. "It's okay," I said. "I know you meant well."

"I really did. I was just trying to get you out of the house and into the Bologna social scene. I mean, you are a terrific girl — you should be dating someone. You don't have anyone. I thought I could fix you up."

I nodded. "I understand, but I do have someone. He's a guy I've known since I was eleven."

Natalia bit her lower lip and smiled. "I didn't know. You never mentioned him. Where is he?"

"He's in the army."

"The army? The German army? Your boyfriend is a Nazi?"

"It's complicated. He's really not a Nazi, but I guess he is. It's not at all what you think. He's just a soldier. He abhors the politics. Above all, he's very kind and he loves me." I shrugged. "It's complicated, but I really like him."

"When is the last time you heard from him?"

"It's been a while. But I know he still loves me. We have plans to get together when he gets out of the army. Now I have to get back to Mama. I'm sorry I screwed up your evening."

Natalia gave me a hug and said, "Don't worry. You didn't screw up anything. Frederico was a jerk anyway. You need to take care of your mama after what she's been through."

"Thanks, Nat. She's had a rough time and she misses my father. I'm really all she's got, at least until next June."

"What's happening next June?"

"My father is going to leave Berlin and join

the Vienna Philharmonic. Mama's going to join him there. A fresh start in a new place. Who knows, maybe I'll go with her."

Natalia grimaced and shook her head.

"What?" I said. "Why the look?"

"It's out of the frying pan and into the fire," she said with a shrug. "You won't find any greener grass in Austria."

"What's wrong with Austria? They don't have any racial laws. There are no Nazis. It's not Germany."

"No, it's not. I guess you're right," she said, but with a most unconvincing smile. She was hiding something. She knew something she didn't want to say.

"What do you know about Austria, Nat?"

"It doesn't matter. Things change almost every day. By June, it may be just fine."

"Come on, Nat."

"Ada, Austria may not be what you think it is. There is a strong Nazi influence and an unofficial group of Austrian Nazis. There are random bombings and frequent demonstrations that get violent. They're energized by Hitler and his radio speeches, and we believe they are funded by the SS. So far, the police have been able to control them, but it's not so peaceful in Vienna."

"It's not Berlin. There are no concentration camps, there are no Brownshirts, and there is no Reichstag passing anti-Jewish laws every week."

"That is true. You're right." Once again, she was unconvincing. "Listen, Ada," she said, "why don't you meet us for a drink at Cesare later, after your mama goes to bed? We'll talk about more pleasant things."

I nodded. "Sounds good."

The organizational meeting with Sister Maria Alicia took place at the concert venue, the Basilica di San Petronio, Bologna's oldest and most important church and one of the largest in the world. The fifteenth-century church sat in the center of the city facing the Piazza Maggiore. It was a giant structure, longer than an entire block, and divided into three naves and twenty-two chapels.

Sister had recruited a six-person ensemble to perform as instrumental backup to the choirs and soloists. It was a modified sextet: a violin, a cello, a double bass, a horn, a clarinet and a flute. We gathered in a semicircle while Sister laid out the plans for the 1937 series. As I looked around at our group, there were three women. Three out of six. How about that? Good for Sister.

She explained that the series would feature two a cappella nights where our ensemble would not be needed. The remaining four nights — two with the Christmas chorus and two with operatic stars — would involve our ensemble. Then Sister announced the stars. "We are privileged to have the great Magda Olivero on December 22 and the one and only Beniamino Gigli on December 23." A buzz of excitement ran through the group. Two of the greatest vocalists in the world.

Sister passed out the scores for the two nights with the Christmas chorus. "Please arrange for rehearsal times among yourselves. There will not be much time to practice with the chorus before the concert. I do not yet have the music for Signora Olivero or Signor Gigli. It is likely we will not see their selections or the scores until earlier on the day of performance."

With that, the meeting ended. I started out when one of the women, the cellist, stopped me. "You are Ada Baumgarten?" she said. I nodded. "And you are a member of the Bologna State Opera Orchestra?" she added.

"Right, the BSO. At least for this season," I said. "I'm filling in for a man on sabbatical."

"I was at the Teatro to hear you when you played the solos in *La Traviata.* I saved my lunch money to buy that ticket. Then I borrowed money from my friends so I could come back and hear you at the third performance. You were so beautiful. You know what I thought?"

I shook my head.

"I thought: Ada's a woman. That's what I thought. She's playing with a major opera orchestra, and someday I will play my cello in an orchestra, just like Ada. I hope you know that all of my friends think the same thing. You give us all hope. You are our hero."

She brought tears to my eyes. I didn't feel like anybody's hero. I just wanted to play my instrument, and I guess that's all she wanted to do too.

Gigli showed up for rehearsal a mere four hours before his concert, but we were given his music earlier in the day. Not much time to practice, but the music was familiar and the scores were simple. He was a little taller and chubbier than I had imagined from his photographs. He had the habit of leaning back when he sang, pushing his chest forward. At the time of the performance, he was forty-seven years old and in his prime. He was the undisputed successor to Enrico Caruso. He was often referred to as *Caruso Secondo.* He smiled a lot, and he had the cutest cheeks. I wanted to pinch them.

His concert had several arias that were Gigli standards and a few Christmas songs. He began with Puccini's "Nessun Dorma" and ended with "Adeste Fideles," but it was "Silent Night" that would become one of my fondest memories. At the rehearsal, he shocked me by insisting that it be sung with solo violin accompaniment. Just me and the great Beniamino Gigli. Stage center. And it was gorgeous. The large crowd gave us a standing ovation.

The Gigli concert was the finale to Sister Maria Alicia's Christmas series, which by all accounts was a roaring success. When the concert was over and the group of us were standing around sharing cookies and hot spiced wine, Mr. Gigli came over to talk to me.

"Very well done, Signorina Baumgarten. I understand your father is concertmaster for the Berlin Philharmonic." I smiled and nodded. "Mine was a shoemaker in Ricanati. And here we are playing together, and very well, I think. I do several benefit performances in Italy each year. Sometimes I have trouble finding the right musicians. May I call on you to accompany me one day in the future?"

Flabbergasted. That's what I was. "I would be honored," I said.

THIRTY-SIX

Pienza, August 2017

Catherine, Liam and Giulia decided to enjoy a tasty lunch on the Campo before going to the registry. Actually, the lunch was Liam's idea.

"There are differences, as I understand it, between deeds in Italy and deeds in the United States," Giulia said. "Here buyers and sellers will hire attorneys, *avvocati.* There will also be a notary public, the *notaio.* Their roles are different. *Avvocati* give advice about the transaction and the contract. They check out the title online or at the Registrar of Titles and conduct searches on the ownership of the property before a purchase contract is signed. A *notaio* is a public official who meets the parties for the first time at the closing to sign the deed. Then he registers the deed with the Registrar of Titles. Today he would file it online."

"The notary is supposed to check the

registry book, isn't that right?" Catherine asked.

"Correct. So we may assume that Vanucci had the *notaio* certify that he had the right to sign the deed and transfer ownership to Gabi."

"Since the book shows Quercia Company as the title owner at all times since 1980, then the notary must have based his decision on what was in the previous book, is that right?" Liam said.

"We hope so. Let's go take a look at it."

Giulia asked the clerk for the registry book covering Gabi's area. He was a tall, thin man with a mole on his right cheek. He brought out the current book. It was a large, cloth-bound volume with a number embossed on the cover. It was at least eighteen inches tall and five inches thick.

"I'd like to see the prior book as well," Giulia said. "The one before 1980." The clerk nodded and went back into the stacks. A few minutes later he returned empty-handed.

"I am sorry, but the prior book is in storage off premises."

"It was ordered," Catherine said. "A few days ago, I paid a twenty-euro fee. It was also ordered by *Avvocato* Santi."

The clerk shook his head. "I do not see any record of a cash fee being paid a few days ago. The book is not here."

318

"This is my receipt," Catherine said, tendering the paper. "Twenty euros."

The clerk looked at the receipt and shook his head. "I'm sorry, someone must have misplaced the order."

"We'd like to place an expedited request for this registry book," Giulia said.

The clerk nodded and made some notes. "There is the fee," he said.

Giulia took out her credit card and handed it to the clerk.

"Giulia, would you ask the clerk if the registrar keeps a record of credit card receipts? I paid cash, but Santi probably put it on his credit card. I think we might find out whether Mr. Santi actually ordered the registry and who took the order."

The clerk shrugged when he heard the question. "Of course," he said. "What date would it have been ordered?"

"About four or five weeks ago," Catherine said.

He stared at his computer screen for several minutes, shaking his head the whole time. "There is nothing. No one ordered the book. No fees were paid."

"The book was ordered twice, and there's no record of the orders?" Liam said.

"Sir, I do not see that the book was ordered by anyone, but I will take your order and call as soon as the book is retrieved."

"I hate to be a conspiracy theorist," Liam

said, "but it seems awfully strange that the registrar's office would keep losing request records."

Giulia handed her business card to the clerk and asked him to call her as soon as the book was delivered.

When they arrived back at the villa, Gabriella was anxious to know how successful they had been. "Our motion was granted," Catherine said. "Lenzini has no right to come here anymore. Not until September 10 anyway."

Gabriella was delighted. "That's wonderful news. Now all we have to do is stop Lenzini from taking my property in September."

Liam smiled. "Is that all?"

"Of course. Lenzini is my number one enemy."

"Not according to him, Aunt Gabi. He says that VinCo is the sleeping lion, the one who will stop at nothing to get your property."

"That's nothing new."

Liam shook his head. "I'm a little concerned by Lenzini's warning. He said VinCo would obliterate you and you would have nothing. That's probably a lot of rhetoric, but to me it sounds like a threat. Maybe he means to damage your vineyard, although I don't know how that would benefit VinCo."

"Well, maybe it would," Giulia said. "Without a vineyard, the case would go away. It might not pay for Gabriella to defend barren land. With no court case, VinCo wouldn't have to worry about people investigating missing registry books or phony titles."

"Assuming there is a threat, what is the most likely way of damaging Aunt Gabi's vineyards?"

"A fire," Floria said. "They happen all too frequently. The weather gets hot, things dry out, lightning hits or someone is careless with a match. Boom. The fire spreads quickly."

"Then we need to protect against it. Let's keep a vigilant eye and warn Franco."

Giulia's cell phone buzzed, and she read a text message. "Santi swears that he ordered the registry book and paid for the expedited service with his credit card. He has a receipt. He also has no explanation for why the book wouldn't be at the registrar's office."

"Is there a name on the receipt? Do the receipts disclose which clerk took the order?"

Giulia looked at her receipt and shrugged. "I don't see any names on it. It's just a credit card receipt from the Siena registrar's office."

Thirty-Seven

Bologna, March 1938

Despite all the progress Mama had made, her dark clouds returned on March 12, 1938, when German soldiers marched into Austria and took over the country without firing a single shot. Austria was swallowed up by Germany in the Anschluss. In a single moment, the country of Austria ceased to be. Even the name was erased. Vienna became a German city. Austria's regional districts became districts of the Reich. All of our plans to join Papa and move to Vienna were summarily canceled.

Immediately after the Anschluss, Nazi officials imposed their racial laws. Whatever applied in Germany, now applied in Austria. Any hope of improving our conditions by moving to Vienna vanished. Father's plans to join the Vienna Philharmonic as concertmaster were abandoned. Mother's hopes to join her husband in the fairy-tale city of Vienna were shattered.

Austria had two hundred thousand Jews and most of them lived in Vienna. As in Germany, many of them were professionals. They were teachers, doctors, lawyers, judges, scientists. All of them immediately lost their positions, not gradually as we had seen in Berlin, but instantly. Not only were they expelled from all cultural, educational and professional activities, they were subject to torture and public humiliation, as though abuse of Austrian Jews had become a Nazi sport. Fanatical Storm Troopers went on rampages of cruelty, grabbing Jewish men and women at random and forcing them to scrub the sidewalks, gutters and latrines. Jewish businesses were taken away and handed over to Aryans. Thousands were taken to detention centers.

News reports of the Anschluss and its aftermath were sketchy in Bologna, maybe because Mussolini was courting friendship with Hitler and vice versa. We learned the details through other sources. My father's daily letters told us what he had learned in Berlin, and Natalia was a wealth of information. She seemed to have information that no one else had. For example, she knew that Mussolini gave Hitler his approval for the Anschluss, even though four years earlier Mussolini had guaranteed Austria's independence. Natalia told us that Il Duce's change of heart was due to Hitler's promise not to invade the Tyrol region, which Italy had been occupying since the Treaty of Versailles. Most distressing was the fact that the Western European powers — England, France, Belgium — did absolutely nothing.

Mama was devastated. She had been counting on moving to Vienna. For the past few months, she had been furnishing a home in her mind. Now her future was up in the air. Vienna was just another German city with Storm Troopers, Gestapo and soldiers. To her, it meant that Kleiner was standing on every corner. She would stay in Italy. She wrote to Papa, telling him that life in Italy was comfortable. Together, they would find a home in Bologna, or maybe in the countryside.

Papa conceded that Vienna was now out of the question. He intended to rejoin Mama as soon as possible, but he wasn't sure that Italy was the best place for them. After all, he was a professional musician and he needed to find the right opportunity. Papa preferred the United States, which had several fine orchestras, and a recommendation from Uncle Wilhelm would ensure senior placement with a top American orchestra. He had spoken at length with Uncle Wilhelm, who said he would do everything he could, but he asked Papa to remain with the Philharmonic until the end of the fall 1938 season. Just eight more months. Uncle Wilhelm promised that he would guarantee Papa's salary and would find him a position with a prominent orchestra by January 1939. Papa agreed to stay.

Natalia and I were becoming very close friends, in part because she loved Mama's cooking. She was a frequent dinner guest. As always, she had inside information about world affairs and what Italy was doing and why. Deep down, I suspected that she was involved in some kind of underground resistance movement with other young people who opposed the Fascists. There was street talk that groups like those existed, especially in the university communities. But I was not about to broach the subject with her.

One night, as we were devouring a plate of wiener schnitzel, one of Mama's tried and true triumphs, Natalia said, "My mother is also a very good cook and I would like to repay your kindness. Do you have plans for Passover seder next month?"

We shook our heads. I hadn't even thought about Passover.

"Sounds lovely," Mama said. "Does she live here in Bologna?"

"No, in Pienza. It's a small town south of here. We'll take a train to Siena and a bus to Pienza."

Mama looked at me and I shrugged.

"Sounds like an adventure."

. While we were talking, there was a knock on the door. It was a delivery from the telegraph office. Mama gave the boy a tip, brought the telegram to the table and read it:

My darlings. I have found a man who wants to buy our house. We are negotiating. Sadly, it is far below our asking price, but it is urgent that we sell immediately. I am also going to try to sell as many household furnishings as I can. As soon as I complete the sale, I will immediately keep my promise to you.

All my love, Papa.

"Why is it so urgent to sell immediately and take a low price?" Mama said. "Your father is so impulsive. He was never good with money. I think I will send him a reply and tell him to wait. He has to stay through the fall anyway. Maybe someone will come along and pay more. And I don't want my precious treasures sold to some stranger. It took me years to gather those furnishings. They mean something to me. Selling in a hurry is foolish."

"What promise, Mrs. Baumgarten, if I may ask?" Natalia said.

"He's been promising to come visit us in Bologna. He was supposed to come in

October, but I fouled up those plans. I'm going to wire him and tell him not to sell."

"You might want to hold off on that telegram, Mrs. Baumgarten," Natalia said. "He's not being foolish. A law is presently under discussion in the Reichstag and will undoubtedly be enacted very soon. It will require all Jews to register their property with the Reich. I wonder how your husband learned this information."

"Wilhelm, no doubt."

Natalia was deep in thought. "Once that law is passed, it is only a matter of time until the Reich taxes your house or simply takes it away from you. Your husband is being wise to sell the house. It's the smart thing to do, but it's the second part of his telegram that worries me."

"You mean his promise to visit me? Is there something wrong with that?"

Natalia nodded. "Not the visit itself, but the fact that his decision to visit seems to be tied to the sale of your house. The law will affect all Jewish assets, not only real estate property but cash and personal property as well. If your husband plans to sell the house and bring the cash to Italy, that would be a direct violation of German law. I hope he's not thinking of doing that."

Natalia's warning shook up Mama. "What can I do? Should I send him a telegram and tell him not to take any money out of Germany?"

"No. The Gestapo routinely monitors international telegrams and telephone calls."

"That's how the Gestapo learned about Uncle Wilhelm's negotiations with the New York Philharmonic," I said. "But Papa's smart. That's why his telegram didn't say anything about money or even coming to Bologna. Natalia is right. We shouldn't contact him. We should trust that he knows what he's doing."

"But I don't want him to get caught," Mama said, her voice quivering. "I have to do something."

Natalia patted Mama on the arm. "He's doing what he thinks is best."

I couldn't imagine a scenario where taking funds out of Germany and bringing them to Italy could be done safely. I couldn't telegraph or phone him. I didn't even want to put it in a letter in case it was intercepted. I would just have to wait and pray. As March was about to end, we received another telegram from Papa.

My dearest Friede and Ada. I sold the house. Hallelujah! There was some squabbling at the end as the buyer tried to whittle down the price, but I held firm and he took it. I think his wife was the deciding factor. She loved the way you

328

decorated our house. She said she could move right in and wouldn't change a thing. I couldn't exclude any of your precious things, Friede, and for that I am sorry, but the offer was contingent on the furnishings. Given the circumstances here, in a few weeks I would not be able to sell the house at all. The Philharmonic has a two-day set in Munich on April 9 and April 10. Isn't that exciting!

Love, Papa

There would be no reason for any of us to get excited about the Philharmonic performing in Munich. They played there several times a year. The telegram could only mean that he would try to come to Bologna on April 11. Unless we were all wrong about his intent to smuggle money out of Germany, we had to prepare for him. I would go to the bank and rent a safe deposit box.

Mama was worried, but she understood. She trusted Papa's judgment. Nevertheless, it broke her heart that some other woman was moving into our house and taking possession of Mama's treasures, all the things she cherished. I was with her when she bought many of those things, and I can recall the joy we shared when she'd come across a find. Maybe it was a chair or a dish or a swatch of fabric. "Don't you just love this?" she'd say, and the piece would have a special place in our home. Now they all belonged to some other woman, who couldn't possibly appreciate them in the same way.

THIRTY-EIGHT

Bologna, April 1938

We were confident that Papa would arrive on April 11. The train from Munich by way of Verona, the one I took when I rescued Mama, was due to arrive at 2:00 p.m. Mama went to the market and placed beautiful spring flowers all around the apartment. She made a Bolognese sauce for dinner. She did her makeup and her hair and put on a pretty dress that she hadn't worn since she left Berlin. And then we waited.

The more the hours passed, the more anxious we became. Two o'clock came and went. Evening came and still no Papa. Mama paced like a tiger, back and forth across the room, stopping only to stare out the window. We started to believe that either something had gone wrong or he had decided not to come. Natalia stopped by to ask if we had heard anything, and Mama invited her to stay for dinner.

"Maybe we misread his letters," I said. "It

was our conclusion that he was coming, but all he said was that the orchestra had two dates in Munich."

Mama shook her head. "There's nothing exciting about playing in Munich. That was a coded message for us. Maybe the plans have changed. I pray to God that he didn't get caught."

Just before midnight, there was a knock on the door. There stood Papa with a suitcase in one hand and his violin case in the other.

"Jacob, Jacob, oh my God," Mama shrieked and wrapped her arms around him. She hadn't seen him in twelve months and the two of them stood in the doorway locked in each other's arms and crying their eyes out. The emotion of the moment wasn't lost on me either. I picked up his bag and violin and brought them into the room where Natalia sat smiling.

Mama finally released Papa and they entered the apartment. "Mmm. Something smells good," he said, and Mama smiled. Then it was my turn. "Where's my Ada!" he said, and I was once again in his arms. Lord, how I missed my papa.

He nodded to Natalia. "I am Jacob," he said, holding out his hand.

"I guessed as much," Natalia said with a chuckle. "Welcome to Bologna. I'm Natalia, the girl who comes here as often as she can to have dinner."

Nothing was said about the house or Papa's journey. Just a lot of talk about what we'd all been doing. I told him of my progress with the orchestra and my private talks with Maestro Vittorio.

"It's not easy for him to bring a woman into his orchestra," Papa said. "I'm sure he's catching his share of protests and grievances. Men do not want the door opened to women. There are only so many seats in an orchestra."

Papa was delighted when I told him that I played at the Christmas series. "You accompanied Beniamino Gigli?" he said. "I'm impressed. I hear he's very difficult, very hard to work with."

"Not at all," I said. "He was most complimentary. And he insisted I accompany him next year when he returns."

"I shouldn't be surprised. Nothing you accomplish should surprise me, and everything you do amazes me. I am so proud of you every day."

We sat at the table eating dinner and finally Mama said, "All right, Jacob, it's time to quit the small talk. Tell us about the house and what you've done over the last few days."

Papa furled his forehead and tipped his head in Natalia's direction.

"She's a good friend, Jacob. She can be trusted."

Papa grabbed his violin case and opened it. Inside were thousands of reichsmarks wrapped in newspaper. "Here is everything we own," he said. "We sold the house and all the furnishings."

"How could you possibly smuggle that money in your violin case?" I said. "They searched mine on the train."

Papa smiled one of his all-knowing smiles. "When the Philharmonic travels, all the instruments are packed, placed on a cart and loaded onto the train. No Nazi dares to search through the instrument cases of the mighty Berlin Philharmonic. As concertmaster, it was my job to supervise the baggage car where the instruments were placed. I made sure they were properly loaded and stayed with them until moments before departure. At the last minute, I grabbed my violin case, jumped off the Berlin train and boarded the train for Torino. From that point on, no one cared what was in my possession."

"Very brave," Natalia said.

"Where is your violin?" I asked.

Papa winked. "As fate would have it, there happened to be an empty violin case that Wilhelm was carrying, and he took it back to Berlin. Thank God, I got our money out before it had to be registered. I am told that there will be a mandatory order for all Jews to register assets in excess of five thousand reichsmarks. Apparently, the money will be earmarked for Göring's program called 'Safeguarding the German Economy.' "

"That is what I have heard as well," Natalia said. "I am told it will happen during the last week of April."

"How do you know — ?"

"Don't, Papa," I interrupted. "What she knows and how she knows is Natalia's personal business."

"That's all right, Ada," Natalia said. "We are among friends."

"Well, as I was saying," Papa continued, "I am happy to move my money to Italy, where it won't be taken from me and where Jews are not persecuted."

Natalia lowered her eyes and shook her head.

"What, Nat?" I said.

"I'm afraid that's a false sense of security. There are anti-Semitic forces at work here as well. Just like in Germany, it starts subtly, creeping into the newspapers. Last week, on April 9, *La Civiltà Cattolica,* the Jesuits' official journal, warned about the dangers of the 'Jewish problem' and cautioned against Jews and Catholics commingling. It also took a stance against the church accepting Jewish converts or condoning mixed marriages."

My father shrugged. "There's a big difference between a Catholic newspaper warning against mixed marriages and the Nazi racial laws."

"The Catholic newspaper wouldn't have printed it without encouragement from the anti-Semitic forces within the Fascist Party. Fascists are no friends of the Jews," Natalia said, "but you're right, the two regimes are not comparable. Jews are not arrested or abused here in Italy. We have no concentration camps. Jews are still prominent in all fields and in the educational community."

"It's true," Mama said, "we're safe here. Don't go back to Berlin, Jacob. Stay here."

"You know I can't move right now. I must keep my word to Wilhelm. I have to return to Berlin. It's only for eight months, just until the end of the year. I'm confident that Wilhelm will find us a position in America. If he can't, then we will live here."

Papa left on April 14 and the very next day, Mama, Natalia and I boarded the train bound for Siena. From there it was a bus ride to Pienza and a Passover seder with the Romitti family. Mama was wistful. A day and half with her husband was not nearly enough. She had begged him to stay longer, but he had to get back. The Philharmonic had a concert that he could not miss. It was a tearful send-off.

The bus ride through the Tuscan country-side was lovely. The Romittis lived in a two-story house on the outskirts of Pienza. The tiny city center was quaint and charming, with winding walkways and well-maintained historic buildings, like a miniature Bologna without the porticos. Mama seemed to like it. She commented that it was peaceful, warm and inviting. There were no universities with sixty-five thousand noisy students, no beeping horns from public transportation. Indeed, there wasn't a car to be seen.

Natalia's mother and Mama hit it off right away. Naomi Romitti had curly brown hair with touches of gray and a pleasant rosy face. I imagined that at a younger age she must have looked just like Natalia. She was hard at work in her kitchen, and Mama immediately asked if she had an extra apron.

Natalia's father, Nico, owned a shoe store in Pienza. He had large hands, broad shoulders and a warm smile. Her brother, Matteo, a few years older than Natalia, lived on a farm outside Montepulciano and ran the retail operation for a small winery. Matt and his wife, Lidia, and their two children came for the seder.

Natalia told me that her parents weren't overly observant, but they did celebrate the holidays and would attend Shabbat services every now and then in the tiny town of Pitigliano, an hour to the south. "There is a sizable Jewish community there and a fifteenth-century synagogue," Matt said. "In fact, it was settled hundreds of years ago by Jews escaping the edicts of the Vatican, and it became known as Piccola Gerusalemme, or 'Little Jerusalem.' " Nico said the Romittis were descendants of that community.

It seemed awkward to attend a seder without my father leading, but the Romittis' seder was nice. Matt brought an outstanding bottle of wine, and, mysteriously, Elijah's cup was emptied long before the seder was over. To my mother's delight, Naomi's brisket was tender and juicy, just like Grandma used to make. After dinner, we all took a walk through the town. Naomi and Mama gabbed the whole time, and I thought to myself, she's finally found a friend in Italy.

THIRTY-NINE

Pienza, August 2017

Catherine, Liam and Giulia returned to the registrar's office in Siena. It had been three days since they had placed the request for the pre-1980 registry book, and it was sure to be there by now. Giulia handed her receipt to a clerk at the counter whose name tag read JOSEPH. He smiled and said he would bring it right out. Fifteen minutes later he returned empty-handed and said, "I'm sorry, but it's not in the stacks. Perhaps it's still in storage off-premises at the archives."

"That's not good enough," Giulia said. "I paid for that book to be brought here on an expedited basis three days ago. And *Avvocato* Santi did the same thing a few weeks ago. That book should be here. We need that book for a lawsuit."

Joseph looked bewildered. "I'm very sorry," he said. "Someone must have misplaced your request. The registry archives are off-premises, but not too far. I will take my car and get the book myself at lunch. You have my word."

"Thank you," Giulia said. "Just to make sure, we want the book covering the Pienza section, prior to 1980."

"I understand," he said. "The one you want is Book 143. I'll bring it."

"Normally, this delay would make me unhappy," Liam said. "But there is a pepperoni pizza waiting for me on the Campo."

After lunch, they returned to the registrar's office to wait for the clerk. Two hours later, he walked in, empty-handed again and shaking his head. "It's not there. I looked everywhere. I even had two interns helping me. It's just not there."

"Is it possible that someone might have checked it out?" Catherine asked.

He shook his head. "That's not permitted."

"What about a situation where a judge would want to see it as evidence in a case? Maybe it's sitting in a courtroom?"

Again, Joseph shook his head. "One of us would take it over to the court, wait until the judge was done examining it, bring it back here and shelve it. These books do not circulate. They are valuable historic records of property transfers, especially in the older times. More recently, paper archives are being digitized, but not yet for this property."

"Without the official registry book, is there

any other way to prove who owned property at any given time?"

"Signore, I do not know. Maybe someone has a deed that is notarized."

"That's the problem," Catherine said. "There are two notarized deeds and they are conflicting. We need to know who owned the property before the deeds were issued."

The clerk shrugged. "Then we would have to find the book. It must be somewhere."

Liam stepped forward. "Joseph, may I ask, which clerk took the request to retrieve Book 143 when Mr. Santi ordered it last month? That wasn't you, was it?"

"No, Signore. I did not know it was missing until today." He looked at his computer terminal, typed a few keystrokes and said, "It was Fabio. He took the order and gave the receipt to *Avvocato* Santi."

"May we speak to Fabio, please?"

"*Mi dispiace.* He should be here, but he is out today."

"When was he last here?"

"Three days ago." The clerk pointed to Giulia's credit card receipt on the counter and tapped it with his finger. "On the bottom of your receipt, Signora, the initials FL. That stands for Fabio Lombardo. He took your order three days ago."

"Tall guy with a mole on his cheek?" Liam asked.

"*Si.*"

Liam looked at Catherine. "Dead fish."

"Excuse me?" the clerk said.

"One more thing," Liam said. "Is it possible to tell if a request was put in for Book 143 previously, before Mr. Santi — say, within the past year?"

The clerk nodded and consulted his computer screen. "*Si*. Three times it has been requested. Once by *Avvocato* Lenzini in October 2016, once by *Avvocato* Santi, almost four weeks ago and your request three days go. All of the times for Book 143 only."

"Who took the orders?"

"All three times it was Fabio Lombardo."

"I wonder what happened to my twenty euros," Liam said. "Can you give me Fabio's home address?"

"Oh, no, Signore. It is against the rules."

"We need Book 143 to show to a judge. Otherwise a very nice woman could be wrongfully evicted from her villa where she has lived her entire life."

The clerk nodded. "Strict rules prohibit me from revealing any personal information about our employees. It is even against the rules to tell you that his address is in the public telephone book for the Cassone section of Siena."

Liam nodded. "Thank you. If you come across the registry book, please let us know."

"*Certo.* Happy to help in any way I can."

■ ■ ■ ■

The listing for Fabio Lombardo led them to a small street in Cassone, on the east side of Siena. When they arrived at the small yellow frame house, they saw a car in the driveway and two newspapers on the front porch. Liam rang the bell and knocked on the door. There was no answer.

"Well, we have his phone number," Giulia said. "I'll call him later."

The mailbox adjacent to the front door was stuffed with mail. Liam shook his head. "Something's not right." He tried the door. It was unlocked. He entered.

"We shouldn't be doing this," Catherine said.

"Fabio? Fabio Lombardo?" Liam called, but there was no response.

"Let's go, he's obviously out of town," Catherine said.

Liam looked around the foyer and suddenly backed out. He put his hands over his nose and mouth. "Oh, Jesus. Call the police, Giulia. There's a dead body in here."

The police took statements from all three. Liam told them that they came looking for Fabio because they thought he might know something about a missing registry book, but Fabio was obviously dead when they arrived.

The police reported that he had been shot three times, once in his left temple, which would have been instantly fatal. The medical examiner estimated he had been dead for three days. Liam asked for permission to search the house for the missing registry book. That was denied.

"I am sorry, Signore, but this is now an active crime scene and nothing may be disturbed."

"If you come across his cell phone," Liam said, "please make note of who he talked to three days ago. I'd be interested in seeing whether there were calls with an attorney named Lorenzo Lenzini."

"Do you think Lenzini shot him?" Catherine said on the way back to Pienza.

"No, I don't," Liam said. "Not Lenzini. He wouldn't get his hands dirty. But he's involved, I'd bet the farm on it. Fabio initially took the order from Lenzini last October, about the time VinCo filed suit. Maybe something in the registry book showed that Quercia didn't get good title or that it wasn't listed as the owner at all in Book 143. It's possible that Lenzini talked Fabio into letting him take the book. A bribe would certainly not be out of the question. When Santi placed his order, Fabio knew he would be in trouble. He probably tried to get it back from Lenzini, but since Santi didn't follow up on his order, maybe Fabio thought the whole thing would go away. When Catherine, and then Giulia, placed the order, Fabio knew it wasn't going to go away and he must have panicked. My guess is he contacted Lenzini and demanded the return of the book. That was his fatal mistake."

"We need the book to prove our case." Catherine said. "Without that book, we can't prove that Gabi's deed was valid. Why don't you think Lenzini shot him?"

Liam shrugged and shook his head. "It's possible, but I doubt it. Lenzini's a worm, but I don't see him having the brass to shoot an innocent man in cold blood."

"Then who?"

"Lenzini told me that we had kicked a sleeping lion. He meant his client, VinCo."

FORTY

Bologna, May 1938

Hitler made a state visit to Italy in May 1938. It was a grand show of solidarity: the first time Hitler had come to Italy since the signing of the Axis agreement in 1936. His seven-day visit was a newsreel splash. He, Goebbels, Göring and a large Nazi entourage arrived by train at the brand-new railway station that Mussolini built solely for the occasion. Hitler's motorcade drove into Rome on the newly paved Via Adolf Hitler.

The papers reported that the two leaders stood on the balcony of the Palazzo Venezia where Hitler said to the screaming crowds below, "As führer and chancellor of the German Reich, I ask Benito Mussolini, Il Duce of this *Volk,* to which the world owes the great inventor and scholar Galileo Galilei, to accept this Zeiss telescope, complete with the entire equipment for an observatory, a present and as a symbol of reverence and friendship."

The photographers followed Hitler as he toured Rome, and on May 5 they traveled with him to Naples, where Mussolini proudly showed off his Italian navy, one of the largest fleets in the world. The next day in Rome, Hitler reviewed Italian troops passing before him, in *passo romano,* the Italian version of the German goose step. The newspapers were full of photos. There were newsreels in the theaters. Thousands lined the streets to see the German leader.

On May 9, Hitler traveled to Florence. And so did the Bologna State Opera. On short notice we were asked to perform Verdi's *Simon Boccanegra* in Florence's Teatro Comunale for the German and Italian delegations. Prior to the opera, the orchestra was requested to provide an afternoon concert in Florence's Piazza della Signoria.

The weather could not have been nicer for the afternoon event. Hitler and his delegation sat on a raised platform with Mussolini and his cabinet. We played Rossini overtures, including the fan favorite: the overture to *The Barber of Seville.* There was so much applause, we encored with *Guillaume Tell,* which Hitler especially liked. I could have sworn that as he stood clapping, he looked directly at me and recognized me.

That evening, Mussolini and Hitler watched *Simon Boccanegra* from Il Duce's box. Out of the corner of my eye, I saw the great Duce sleeping through most of the performance. He was known to be a cultural boor. Hitler, on the other hand, an aficionado of German opera, watched the performance intently. After the show, Hitler, Goebbels and Mussolini came down to compliment the singers and the orchestra. Hitler was all smiles. I wondered how much he'd smile if he knew that my father, concertmaster of his beloved Philharmonic, had just snuck out tens of thousands of reichsmarks before Göring could get his racist hands on them.

Once again, Hitler looked directly at me. Then he turned to Maestro Vittorio and said, through his interpreter, "The young lady, the violinist, I have heard her play before. I wonder if she might honor us with a few measures of Massenet's 'Meditation'?"

I was shocked. What a memory. He was referring to the Junior concert two years ago at the Winter Olympics. Vittorio beckoned me forward. Apparently, Hitler did not remember my name and would not make the connection to my father. I thought about refusing him, saying that I did not remember the score. But then, he asked, "What is your name, Fraulein?"

There was no way I wanted to solo for Hitler, nor did I want to give him my name, but I was flustered and afraid of being rude. He could have my father thrown into a concentration camp on a whim. "My name is Ada Baumgarten."

He said, "Please, a taste of the 'Meditation.'" It sounded more like a command than a request. I bowed and played the piece I knew so well. As I played, Hitler stood there with his eyes closed, conducting the piece with his index fingers. I finished, he bowed ever so slightly and said, "Well done, Fraulein Baumgarten." He did not shake my hand, but wouldn't that have been dandy newsreel footage? Hitler and his favorite Jew.

"You played for Hitler?" Natalia said.

"I did."

"Too bad you didn't have a bullet in that bow."

"It was creepy," I said. "Seeing the two of them laughing it up, taking in the opera, made my skin crawl."

"It's a very bad alliance, Ada. Mussolini idolizes Hitler and seeks his approval. He knows that Hitler is building the largest army in the world and starting to gobble up countries. Mussolini wants to be his partner. That's why he invited Hitler to review Italy's armed forces: to flex his muscles. You can be assured that he will move Italy closer to Germany in social policies as well. I know for a fact that discussions are taking place right now to limit the number of Jewish professors in the universities. Since the beginning of the year, they are down thirty percent."

"With Hitler it is a madness, a compulsion, but I didn't know that Mussolini hated Jews."

"Ha! The fat cow could care less. He is quoted as saying that the Jews have lived in Italy since the days of the kings of Rome and should be left undisturbed. Everyone knows that his mistress, the socialite Margherita Sarfatti, is an Italian Jew. Many of his supporters are Jewish socialites. But now, after seeing him suck up to Hitler, you can bet your last lira, it's only a matter of time until anti-Jewish measures are taken to appease *der führer* and court his support."

I hoped that Natalia was wrong, but she was right on the mark. That summer, the newspapers started running stories on the negative influence of Jews. They reported on the problems that Germany and Hungary had encountered with Jews and the measures they had taken to curb so-called Jewish financial abuses. On July 15, 1938, the *Giornale d'Italia* published a report entitled *Manifesto della Razza,* the Manifesto of Race, supposedly prepared by doctors, anthropologists, zoologists and other scientists to prove that Italians were descendants of the Aryan race — and Jews were not.

In August, Mama wrote to Papa to tell him what was going on. She told him about the newspaper slurs and the manifesto. She told him that Mussolini admires Hitler. She warned him that Italy would soon be another German colony. As far as she was concerned, it was time to leave. She begged him to take her to the United States. Her father and mother were living in New York. Maybe they could be sponsors. She wrote that it was only a matter of time until Storm Troopers were marching through the piazzas of Bologna.

Despite my efforts, I couldn't calm her down. We arranged for a telephone call with Papa. After telling Mama how wonderful it was to hear her voice, Papa reminded her that both he and I had contracts through the end of the year. We really couldn't leave before January. We could make plans, but we'd have to stay put through the end of the year.

"Things are moving too fast here in Italy," Mama said. "Natalia told me that racial laws are under discussion in the Fascist Grand Council. She knows things, Jacob. And Mussolini issued a press release on August 5 stating that restrictions on Jews were going to be enacted."

"But they haven't been enacted yet," he said. "It's not Germany. There are no anti-Jewish signs in restaurants in Bologna, no banners across roads leading into town, no students kicked out of Italian schools, no businesses refusing to sell to Jews. The Italian people do not hate Jews and in four and half months we can leave."

"Why does it matter what the Italian people think when their dictator can make it illegal to be a Jew?" Mama said.

"You're panicking, Friede."

"Maybe I have a right to. I've been in a Gestapo prison!"

"Please try to be patient, and at the end of the year we'll all move somewhere safe. Conditions in Bologna are so much better than here in Berlin."

"I think four months is too long," she said. And she was right. In the next four months, our entire world would turn upside down.

FORTY-ONE

Bologna, September 1938

On September 1, 1938, Italy announced the first of its racial laws. All Jews who had settled or obtained citizenship in Italy since 1919 were subject to expulsion and ordered to leave the country within six months. We were planning on leaving anyway, but the promulgation of that law set a deadline. Natalia had been right: the racial laws that had secretly been under discussion were now a reality. More laws would rapidly unfold over the next several weeks.

On September 2, 1938, all Jewish students, teachers and professors in Italian public schools were ordered to leave by October 16. An exception was made only for native-born Italian Jews who were enrolled in a course of study before the act. Natalia, doing her doctoral studies, was exempt and would not be expelled, but many of her friends would be gone in six weeks.

On September 15, we received a telegram from Papa. More terrible news. Grandpa had passed away in New York on August 15. The letter, which was delayed due to Papa's forwarding address, had been sent by the director of the Jewish Home for the Aged, where both Grandpa and Grandma were living. Grandpa had been experiencing chest pains and he died peacefully in his sleep. Memorial services were held on August 17 at Temple Chai. Regrettably, the director mentioned, Grandma was not doing well. She was suffering from senility. She was in poor health and seemed disoriented without her husband.

Mama's world was spinning out of control. The new Italian law required Mama and me to leave by March 1, and Mama refused to go back to Berlin. In order to emigrate to the United States, we had to have a sponsor or close family member there; our plan now depended on Papa getting a position with an American symphony orchestra, and that depended on Uncle Wilhelm. The neighboring countries of Hungary, Austria and Czechoslovakia were all under Nazi control.

Of course, we weren't the only ones looking for a new home. In 1938, Europe faced an emigration crisis: over a million European Jews were in the crosshairs of racial laws; over five hundred thousand were trying to emigrate. To address this problem, and at the urging of President Roosevelt, thirty-two countries came together for a conference in mid-July in the town of Evian-les-Bains, France. Hitler did not object at all. He stated that if other nations would be willing to accept "these criminals," he would put them at their disposal, "even on a luxury ship." Sadly, if each country had agreed to accept only 17,000 refugees, all those émigrés would have been saved. But after ten days of discussions, the conference ended without any meaningful solution.

We knew that unless Papa could get a position somewhere — the United States, Britain, France — Mama and I would have to return to Berlin in March. But on September 18, our situation brightened. Mussolini proclaimed that Jews who held Italian citizenship (like me and Mama) and possessed unquestionable civic merit in regard to the country could apply for an exemption from the harsh racial orders. The details of his proclamation were not immediately available. What was "civic merit in regard to the country"? Would my artistry and performances in the BSO qualify? And what about Mama? If I were granted an exemption, would that apply to my family as well? Natalia thought I qualified and we made an application.

I wired Papa to come for a visit, that

Mama wasn't doing very well. He needed to make time, no matter how difficult. He replied that he would come on October 10 for a long weekend. That lifted Mama's spirits a little and she started to make plans for his visit. He was her rock and he could always make her feel good. He could remain positive under the most trying circumstances. He could reassure her. But it was not to be.

Before October 10, Germany invalidated all Jewish passports. They were required to be surrendered to Reich offices and would be reissued only after a *J* had been stamped on them. The bureaucratic delays made travel in October impossible for him. Once again, Mama felt adrift and I did the best I could to comfort her.

On November 9, during rehearsal, I received a note from Natalia. "I need to talk to you and your mother. Very important. I will see you tonight."

When she arrived, she was frantic. "Can you contact your father in Berlin? Does he have a telephone?" she asked.

"I think so. We had one at the house, but he moved. I think he has the same number. And I have a number for Uncle Wilhelm. I can get hold of one of them. What's going on?"

"All hell's going to break loose in Germany

tomorrow. You need to warn your papa."

"What are you talking about? He's safe."

"No Jew is safe. My people have intercepted a directive from Reinhard Heydrich to all of his district commanders in the SA. There are going to be riots throughout Germany, all directed against Jewish businesses, synagogues and individuals. And that's going to happen tomorrow."

"Heydrich told them all to riot?"

"Not exactly. In his directive, he ordered his commanders not to endanger 'foreign Jews' or 'non-Jewish Germans' or their property, but he told them not to interfere when the rioters go after German Jews. When the rioters sack the synagogues, he ordered the SA to remove the archives and written records and deliver them to SA headquarters. It's all in his directive. You need to get word to your father. Tell him to stay in his house. Do not go on the streets."

"Why is this happening? And when are the riots supposed to occur?"

"Tomorrow, Ada! The Nazis are manufacturing a reason to ravage Jewish businesses and places of worship because of a shooting in Paris."

"In Paris?"

"Recently, Hitler ordered all Polish Jews to leave Germany. Since Poland has strict immigration quotas, they had nowhere to go. Right now, they're being kept in a camp.

A Polish Jew who lives in Paris found out that his parents were being held in a camp. He went to the German embassy to try to get them out. He got into a heated argument with the German diplomat and shot him. That's the spark. It's the excuse the SA needs for the riots — a Jew killed a German diplomat. The retaliations in Germany will be insane."

"We could go to the call center to make the call, but what can I say? If I tell him to stay inside the house, he'll ask why. I can hardly say that we know about Heydrich's secret directive. The Gestapo monitors long-distance calls. I can't warn him about a riot that hasn't yet occurred. Anything I say would connect my father or Uncle Wilhelm with the underground."

Natalia agreed. "You're right. We can't even send a telegram with that information. We'll just have to hope nothing bad happens to your father."

That night the riots began, and they continued throughout the next day. They called it *Kristallnacht* — the Night of the Broken Glass. Natalia had all the information correct. The rioters broke windows on thousands of Jewish stores and looted the property. They destroyed 267 synagogues, many of them burned to the ground. Jewish cemeteries were desecrated. Thirty thousand Jewish men were yanked off the streets by the SS and the Gestapo and taken to concentration camps.

Bologna newspapers reported the riots but said they were provoked by Jewish murderers. I needed to be sure my father was unharmed. I called his number for two hours, but there was no answer at his apartment. Then I tried calling Uncle Wilhelm. Finally, I got through to Zitla Furtwängler. I asked her if she had seen Papa. She told me that all rehearsals and performances were canceled. "I haven't been out of the house for two days," she said. "It's so dangerous on the streets. Wilhelm is at the Philharmonie. You might try him there."

After going through a few staff members, I heard the familiar voice, "Ada, my dear, how are you?"

"Worried, Uncle Wilhelm. Is my father with you?"

"Be glad you are not in Berlin, my child. This is dreadful. Shameful. Someone has opened the gates of hell."

"My father, Uncle Wilhelm. Is he there with you at the Philharmonie?"

"No. Rehearsals and performances have been canceled for at least two weeks. I haven't seen Jacob since Wednesday."

"I'm so worried about him. He doesn't answer his phone."

"He lives in an apartment in the Jewish section now, just off Oranienburger Strasse.

359

Unfortunately, that's where the riots are. They have sacked the New Synagogue. But if I don't hear from him, I'll go over there when things calm down a little and check up on him. I'll tell him to wire you."

"Thanks so much, Uncle Wilhelm."

"I hear wonderful things about you, Ada. Your father is busting his buttons."

"Thanks. Things are going well for me, but Italy is changing."

"So I hear. I'll look after your father. Don't worry. Tell your mother hello."

"Will do."

Two days later, we received a telegram from Uncle Wilhelm: "Stopped by the apartment. Jacob not at home. Neighbors say they haven't seen him. Will try to find out."

"I think I should go back to Berlin and find Papa," I said to Natalia and Mama.

Natalia shook her head. "Bad idea, Ada. What can you do that Furtwängler isn't already doing?"

"I don't know, but he's a very busy man. I could run messages for him, I could go places when he doesn't have the time."

"Germany canceled all Jewish passports," Mama said. "How will you get in and how will you get out?"

"I have an Italian passport. The border guards won't stop an Italian citizen."

"You have an Italian passport with a Jewish name. That might be worse."

"I feel like I have to take the chance. What if Papa's injured? What if Uncle Wilhelm finds out where he is, but he's unable to get to him?"

"And what if he was part of the tens of thousands of men who were arrested, detained and held in a camp?" Natalia said. "As much as we hope that didn't happen, it's the most likely scenario. Isn't Furtwängler with all his connections the best one to arrange for his release? Wasn't it Heydrich and Furtwängler who found out about your mother?"

"I agree," Mama said. "The danger to you far exceeds any chance you could rescue Papa. Let's leave it to Wilhelm for the time being. After all, he's Papa's best friend and a very powerful man."

As a consequence of the riots, which they blamed on the Jews, Germany enacted a series of extreme anti-Jewish laws, turning the vise even tighter. On November 12, the Reichstag enacted the Decree on the Elimination of the Jews from Economic Life. The law forbade any Jew from owning a store, carrying on a trade or selling goods or services of any kind. All Jewish-owned businesses were to be immediately transferred to Aryan owners. The next day all Jewish children were expelled from public schools. The next week Jewish movement was curtailed and Jews were prevented from entering theaters, cinemas and certain designated "Aryan zones." Of course, that meant there would be no Jewish attendance at the Philharmonie.

Mussolini, in a show of solidarity with his partner in the north, pushed through anti-Jewish laws of his own. Jewish children were not permitted to attend Italian public schools, marriage between Jews and non-Jews was prohibited and Jews were excluded from the army and certain professions. On November 17, a law directed all presumed members of the Jewish race to appear at the local municipal office and record their religious status. This census would then be available to governmental authorities.

"I'm not going to do it," Mama said. "How do they know if I'm Jewish? Maybe my religious status is that I no longer attend synagogue or believe in God anymore. Maybe I'm nothing."

"You had a Jewish mother and a Jewish father," Natalia said. "Under the law, you're a Jew no matter what you believe."

"We have to register, Mama; we already disclosed our religion when we immigrated last year. If they catch you breaking the law, they'll deport you back to Germany."

"January can't come soon enough for me," Mama said. "I hope and pray that Wilhelm

362

can find Papa, get him released and secure a position for us in America. It won't take two minutes for me to pack, that's for sure."

FORTY-TWO

Pienza, August 2017

"We have yet to develop any meaningful evidentiary support," Catherine said to Liam and Giulia. "We're nowhere near putting together a motion for a new trial. We need to do something to postpone the eviction, or at the very least get an extension. There are only eighteen days until VinCo gets possession, and you can bet that Lenzini will be here on the morning of September 10 with a police escort and a moving van."

"Postpone possession on what grounds?" Giulia asked. "As you say, we've uncovered no new evidence."

"What about the missing property book and the dead clerk?" Liam said. "Doesn't that create an inference that there's an effort to suppress evidence favorable to Gabi?"

"Suppressed evidence is not evidence. By definition, it's suppressed. The judge said he wants evidence."

"I have a feeling that there may be something in Fabio's house," Liam said. "What's the chance we can get in there and take a look?"

Giulia shook her head. "It's a crime scene investigation. Besides, what are we searching for? We don't even know."

"Can we ask the judge for permission to enter the premises?"

"For what?"

"To look for Registry Book 143," Catherine said. "Back home, we can get an order to view premises. We could say we have reason to believe that the decedent took the book and did not return it. The book will be the best evidence as to who owns Gabi's property."

Giulia shrugged. "I've never done that before, but maybe Judge Riggioni will give us a writ to explore Fabio's house and search for the book. It can't hurt to ask."

Liam nodded. "I agree. The judge never heard Gabi's side. Maybe he'll give us a little room to work. I know it's all supposition, but there's so much here that doesn't smell right. Gabi lives on the property all of her life. No one bothers her. No one tries to remove her until last year. Why?"

"We don't know."

"Okay, and how about this Vanucci character? He appears out of nowhere with a lawyer named Hernandez that no one can find and delivers a deed to Gabi. What's that all about?

And why in 1995?"

"That's not the only date that's mysterious," Catherine said. "VinCo has owned the surrounding property for years, and to hear Gabi tell it, they've wanted her little piece for a long time. Why does VinCo wait until 2015 to investigate who owns Gabi's parcel and then miraculously discovers the Quercia Company and a dead shareholder?"

"It would be nice if we could find Vanucci or Hernandez," Liam said. "Nobody in the Siena legal community knows an attorney named Hernandez."

"What about Bologna?" Catherine said. "Are those two different practice regions? Maybe Bologna lawyers would know Hernandez."

"Why Bologna?" Giulia asked.

"Just a hunch. I've been reading about Bologna."

Giulia nodded. "Could be. Lawyers in Bologna typically limit their practice to the Bologna city court. There might be some attorneys there who know Hernandez."

"I think we should take a ride up to Bologna."

"First things first," Giulia said. "Let's see if we can get an order allowing us into the house to search for evidence. I'll draw up an emergency motion."

"*Signor Presidente della corte,* I have two matters to bring before you this morning," Giulia said. "The first is a request for the issuance of an order giving the defendant access to the premises of Fabio Lombardo, a deceased clerk of the Registrar of Titles, to search for a certain registry book, number 143. We believe that book may contain evidence that Gabriella Vincenzo is the rightful owner of the property."

"Nonsense!" shouted Lenzini. "Pure nonsense brought up to obfuscate the clear meaning of your order declaring VinCo to be the absolute owner. This matter has been tried to its conclusion. The book does not exist, and if it did, it would confirm that my client is the rightful owner. I happen to know that *Avvocato* Santi requested the book over a month ago and was told it was missing."

"How do you know what he was told?" Liam interjected after Floria whispered the translation.

"Excuse me, Signore," Judge Riggioni said to Liam, "only the *avvocati* may address the court."

"Right," said Lenzini. "Not you, Mr. Toughguy."

"But he has a point," the judge said. "How do you know what Santi was told?"

Lenzini took a deep breath. "Simple. By deductive reasoning. He did not bring it to the court's attention. So he must have been told it was missing, or he saw it and it was

367

unhelpful."

"*Avvocato* Santi did not come to court at all," the judge said. "He and his client were inexplicably absent. What is your objection to allowing them to look for the book? I would think if they found the book, it might clear up a lot of mystery."

"Because the case is over. You have ruled. A judgment is a judgment. How much longer do we have to belabor the point?"

Judge Riggioni looked at Giulia and nodded. "I'll grant the motion. You may search Mr. Lombardo's premises for the book, but only in the presence of the police and under their supervision."

"Thank you, *Signor Presidente.*"

"What is your second matter, Signorina Romano?"

"I wish to postpone the date for possession."

"Of course, you do. Perhaps indefinitely, no?"

"Ultimately. But for now, I ask for time to gather evidence to show that Gabriella Vincenzo is the real owner, not VinCo. How odd is it that she has lived there for most of her seventy-eight years undisturbed? How odd is it that less than two years ago, VinCo suddenly appears with a deed from a deceased German citizen? Signora Vincenzo and Carlo Vanucci signed a deed to her property before a *notaio* twenty-two years ago. We are trying

368

to contact the notary and the seller, but we will need more time."

The judge shook his head. "I have been through this before. I saw the registry book that shows a German company as the title holder for all the years since 1980, as far back as the book goes. I'll give you the right to search for the older registry book, and if you come up with something, then I'll reconsider. That's all for today."

Liam stopped Lenzini on the way out of the courtroom. "We're getting closer. When we go to your buddy Fabio's house, do you suppose we'll find the book and your fingerprints all over it, Lorenzo?"

"You should have taken the money."

FORTY-THREE

Bologna, November 1938

It has been two weeks since *Kristallnacht* and not a word from Papa. I sent him two telegrams but received no answers. Mama and I have been on pins and needles. Finally, an odd telegram arrived from Uncle Wilhelm:

"Ada. Hope this finds you well as you rehearse for the Christmas season. Contacted by KK, who has found what we were looking for. I'm so pleased that you are coming to visit us for a guest performance. Zitla has our guest room waiting for you. See you tomorrow. Love, Uncle Wilhelm"

Mama, whose hopes were initially raised when the telegram was delivered, became angry. "What is that supposed to mean? You know, I think the old goat is losing his mind."

"No, Mama. I think it means he's located Papa. He wants me to come to Berlin immediately. To his house. He just can't say so in the telegram."

"Who is KK?"

Only one thought came to my mind: Kurt Koenig. I packed a bag, grabbed my Italian passport and my magic locket and headed to the train station. The first train would get me into Berlin at 10:00 p.m. I wired Uncle Wilhelm that I would meet him at the Philharmonie.

It was a frightening experience reentering Germany, now a total military state. As we crossed the border, I was stopped and examined by a young guard who compared my face to my passport several times before letting me pass. Twice on the train from Munich, SS officers asked to see my papers. *"Italienerin?"* one said.

I nodded. *"Ja."*

"Where are you headed, Fraulein?"

"Berlin."

"Are you visiting? What is the purpose of your visit?"

"I am to perform with the Berlin Philharmonic."

He looked up at the luggage shelf. "Where is your instrument?"

"Maestro Furtwängler has it. It has been repaired."

He thought for a minute, then nodded and moved on. The German train was a stark contrast to the Italian trains. There was little

371

or no conversation. No joy on anyone's face. All seriousness. If possible, Germany had become even colder and more impersonal than when I had left. I arrived at Berlin Hauptbahnhof precisely at 10:00 p.m. The station was filled with military and uniformed personnel. People walked quickly and looked straight head. I went directly to the Philharmonie.

Uncle Wilhelm met me in the empty lobby. There was no concert scheduled and the building was dark. "We've located your father, Ada. Sorry to be so circumspect in my telegram. Actually, it was your friend Corporal Koenig who found him, and he contacted me. I had given up hope. None of the people I knew had any idea where he was. It is impossible to imagine the chaos that has existed here for the past two weeks. Thirty thousand men were arrested. At random. Well, I shouldn't say random; they were Jews. It was madness. Until they are all processed, no one really knows who was arrested or where they were taken. Two days ago, Kurt came to see me here at the hall. He had been assigned to an office job in Berlin, creating a central data ledger of the arrestees at the camps. He came across your father's name and saw that he was detained at the Buchenwald camp."

"Did he say how my father was?"

"According to Kurt, he is not listed as

deceased or injured, and that's all he knew. As with all of the detainees, he is being interrogated. I don't know much more."

"I want to take him out of here. Out of Germany."

Uncle Wilhelm shook his head. "I can try to get him out of the camp, using whatever influence I still have with the hierarchy, but even then, he has a Jewish passport. In order for him to leave Germany, he must secure an exit visa. And he will have to pay a Reich flight tax based upon a percentage of his assets. I'm afraid it would be tens of thousands of reichsmarks."

"But he doesn't own . . ."

"I know what he did when he sold his house, Ada. I know he took the money to Friede. I told him at the time I thought it was foolish. The Gestapo also knows he sold the house. They track all property sales. They will want to know where the money is, and he certainly can't tell them he took it to Italy."

"What can we do?"

"I don't know. If it's possible, you will have to get the money and bring it back to Germany. Then, hopefully, when he's released, he can get an exit visa and pay his flight tax. I will get him a position in the United States. I have spoken to Serge Koussevitzky in Boston. He will guarantee him a position with the Boston Symphony

Orchestra whenever he gets there."

"Okay, I know where the money is and I can get it. How do I get my father out of Buchenwald?"

He shrugged. "That I don't know. Kurt said he will meet you here tomorrow morning at eight."

I spent the night in the darkened Philharmonie concert hall, sitting fifth row center, where I sat so many times before, watching my father. I drifted off, now and again, and the hall replayed my memories. I saw Papa sitting with the orchestra. First chair. A sweet symphony was playing. Maybe the Brahms Third. Whenever the strings reached a rest in the score, he'd look down at Mama and me and smile. Such a proud papa. Such a polished gentleman. Such a great artist. So many memories in that hall. I had even performed on that stage myself before Germany imploded.

I was sound asleep when Kurt woke me. At first, I thought it was a dream, but there he stood in his Wehrmacht uniform. Damn, it was good to see him, even under these circumstances. It felt like only yesterday that we were together. We kissed in the empty hall, a desperate kiss, the kind I could get lost in. Finally, I let go and took a deep breath.

"What do you know about Papa?"

"He's in the Buchenwald concentration camp. I came across his name when I was registering the men who were arrested during *Kristallnacht.* I've been temporarily assigned to SS headquarters to assist documenting the people detained during the riots. There were thousands of them. I don't know why the SS decided to arrest so many people, all at one time, all Jews. It created a statistical nightmare for us. Each and every name and address had to be written and entered into two different registers." He shrugged. "Germans and their statistical efficiency."

"Don't make light, Kurt."

"I'm sorry, I didn't mean it that way. When I saw your father's name, I immediately contacted Furtwängler because I knew he had deep connections. But even with all his political pull, he has been unable to get him released. We won't finish processing the names for weeks. Ada, Furtwängler tells me that the Gestapo knows your father sold his house. They contacted the buyer to find out exactly what was paid. Your father did not report the money as an asset. They have been asking him what he did with the money. It was supposed to be registered."

I swallowed hard. "It's in a Bologna bank, Kurt. He brought it to us to hold for him."

"He committed a serious crime, Ada, and lying to the Gestapo to cover it up will only make it worse." Kurt shook his head. "He can't fool them. No one can."

"I'll go get the money and bring it back."

Kurt shook his head. "It's too dangerous to bring money into the country. Especially thousands of reichsmarks. Weren't you searched on the train?"

I nodded.

"You'd get caught and the money would be confiscated. You'd end up jailed as well."

"Maybe. Maybe not. Maybe I could hide it like he did when he brought it to Bologna. We need to do something. Can I at least go to him?"

"No. He's in a concentration camp."

"What can we do?"

He leaned forward and spoke softly. "I have a plan and I've been working on it. When I spoke with Maestro Furtwängler, he told me he believes that if the money is returned to Berlin, he can use his political influence to get the charges dropped."

"He told me that too, but you said I can't bring the cash across the border."

"True, but banks can make transfers by wire. I have obtained the authority to take your father to the Ministry of Finance in Berlin to make a wire transfer from the Bologna bank to the ministry. Then we'll let Furtwängler work his magic. Let's hope that Furtwängler's influence is as strong as he thinks it is. If it works out, your father could be back playing with the orchestra as soon as he's back on his feet."

"What do you mean on his feet?"

"I'm sure he's had a rough time."

"I want to see him."

Kurt shook his head. "The plan is for me to drive to Buchenwald, pick up your father and drive him to the ministry where he'll authorize the wire transfer. You can drive with me, not to the camp, but part of the way. On the way down, we pass through Leipzig. I'll drop you off there and pick you up on the way back to Berlin. I'm going to go now and finalize the arrangements. I'll be back in a while."

I hugged him as tightly as I could. I didn't want to let him go.

Four hours later, Kurt returned. "It's all set. I'm going to bring him out tomorrow morning. It's a three-hour drive from Berlin. You'll ride with me. With any luck, he'll be back with the orchestra in a few days."

I was amazed. Kurt was a hero. My hero! I hadn't seen him in a couple of years. I didn't know if he ever thought about me or whether he still cared. Now he was sticking his neck out to save my father. "I can't believe you're doing this, Kurt. So much can go wrong and you'll be risking your future."

"Future? In what, the German army? You know me, Ada, I never wanted to be a soldier. All I ever wanted for my future was to sit next to you in an orchestra. Or anywhere else. Whenever I think about my future, whenever I dream about it, you're in it, sitting right next to me." He leaned over, brushed the hair back from my face, kissed me and said, "Someday, when this is all over, all this idiocy, I'll come and find you, no matter where you are. That will be my future. And it can be yours, if you'll have me."

Was that a proposal? It sure sounded like one to me. I threw my arms around his neck and gave him my answer.

Early the next morning, Kurt came by in a small military truck and we drove south out of Berlin. The route toward Leipzig reminded me of 1935 and the time Papa drove into the countryside to show me the anti-Jewish banners and the military buildup. The memories made me sad. Back then, my father was sitting next to me. Back then, I felt safe in his company. Back then, it was an eye-opener. Now, as Kurt drove south, I could see huge military installations where farm fields had been.

Kurt dropped me at a coffee shop in Leipzig and drove on to Buchenwald. I couldn't wait to see Papa. The last time I saw him was when he brought the money to Bologna for us to hide. He was so confident and courageous. He was taking care of his family. I thought he was taking a dangerous risk in carrying the money, but I knew he did it for us and I was so proud of him. He was planning on moving us far away to another country, and he knew he would need money to make a fresh start. Some countries required immigrants to show a means of support. He felt he might need that money to get into the U.S. You would never think of my father as the intrepid type, but what he did took a lot of courage.

I sat in the coffeehouse for two hours, nervously fidgeting and fingering my magic locket. Finally, I saw them pull into the parking lot. I knew Papa would be hungry, just like Mama was when I took her out of Wittelsbacher, and I took a sandwich in a carry-out bag and walked out to the truck.

Kurt had wrapped Papa in the long army coat. He teared up when he saw me, and we hugged for a long time. He had lost weight in the three weeks he was imprisoned, but it was his face and arms that shocked me. He had sores and bruises and dark circles around his eyes, and he was shaking. Not just shivering from the cold, but actually shaking, like his nerves and his muscles were out of sync. Kurt started the car and we drove north toward Berlin.

"Ada, I'm so happy to see you, but you

shouldn't have come," Papa said. "You must get out of Germany as soon as possible. Don't you see what's going on here?"

"Of course, I do. I am going back to Bologna as soon as I can arrange for your safety. Kurt and Uncle Wilhelm are working it all out. We're going to set things straight with the Gestapo. Then you'll rejoin the orchestra. It's Uncle Wilhelm's plan to get you a job in Boston and soon we'll all be together."

Papa shook his head. "Go home to Mama. Go back to Italy. They're never going to let me out of Germany. I can't leave the country."

"Yes you can, once they have the money. The ministry will receive the money, they'll release you from all charges and you'll go back to being concertmaster. Uncle Wilhelm has arranged it. He's very influential."

He shook his head from side to side. "It's not going to happen."

"Of course, it is."

"I'm not giving them the money, Ada."

"What do you mean, Papa? You have to. That's the only way to get you released. The bank will transfer it."

"First of all, the ministry can't transfer it, it's in a safe deposit box."

"Mama can take it out of the box and deposit it. It can easily be done."

"You don't understand, Ada. I'm not giving

up the money. That's our house money. It's all we've got. I'm not giving it to the Nazis. It's our savings, it's all our belongings, all the precious things that your mother acquired over the years. It's our whole life. That money belongs to Mama. It's there for her to buy a house and start a life."

"Papa, you're talking about property. She doesn't want precious items. She doesn't want a life without you. You and Mama will go to America and you'll earn money in Boston. The two of you can support yourselves and buy a new house."

"You're wrong. The Nazis will make promises to Wilhelm, but they won't keep them. They'll take my money and they'll keep me here. Maybe Wilhelm can protect me for a while, but I have committed a crime. That is what they screamed at me over and over at Buchenwald. I am a criminal. A Jew-criminal. I am an enemy of the Reich. I am only alive because they don't have my money yet. And they're not going to get it. It's for Mama."

"Please, Papa. You don't know how much she misses you. She's been so sad. She wants you and a new life in America. Not money."

"Ada, I'll never get to America. I am finished here. They told me they will never let me out of the camp. I have to accept that. I know that I will never see my Friede again, so I have to do the best I can for her.

That money is all we have. Without it, Mama won't be able to support herself and I won't let that happen to her."

"You've been through a terrible time and I can understand why you feel defeated. But we can make this work. Even without the money, we'll get by. I have a job. Remember what you told me, Papa: keep positive. Only positive thoughts."

When I said that, he burst into tears. "I only wish." Then he turned to Kurt. "Take me back to Buchenwald. Please turn the car around, Kurt. I have made my decision. I won't give them the money."

Kurt pulled the truck over to the side of the road and looked at me. "Drive, Kurt," I commanded. "Don't listen to him. He's delirious. Keep driving."

"No," Papa said. "I'm not delirious. I've never thought more clearly. Turn the truck around, Kurt. Even if you bring me to the ministry, I will refuse to transfer the money, and it will only get you into trouble. I won't give them our life savings no matter what they do to me. It is Friede's money. You're a good boy, Kurt, and I don't want to see you in trouble. Please, honor my wishes. Take me back to the camp."

"Papa, no," I cried. "That's crazy. You can't go back into a concentration camp. No one does that. You'll die."

"I understand."

I was rapidly losing it. "I don't want you to do that. I don't want you to die. Please, Papa. Mama would never agree with this decision. She would never choose the money."

He grabbed my wrists and squeezed hard. "You are never to tell Mama what I did. Promise me that you will not tell her about my decision. Or even that you saw me."

"Papa . . ."

"Promise me!" he said sternly.

At that moment I knew I had lost. "I promise."

Kurt turned the car around and started driving south. I was hysterical.

"Kurt, will you do one more favor for me, please?" Papa said.

"Anything, sir."

"After you take me to the camp, make sure Ada gets back to Wilhelm. Tell him he must protect her, get her on the train and get her safely out of Germany."

"Yes, sir. I will make sure as well."

We returned to the coffee shop in Leipzig. I hugged my papa so tightly. The greatest man I have ever known. I wouldn't let go. My heart was broken, but there was no changing his mind. He whispered in my ear, "Kurt's a good boy. I always liked him. Maybe someday, God will shine on you two. Now I'm going to give you a big kiss, and I want you to carry it to Bologna and give it to your mama. From me to her. Just don't tell her."

He gave me a kiss that had so much love I could feel it. I would deliver it to Mama on my return.

"And this one is for you," he said, and he kissed me again. I would carry that kiss for the rest of my life.

"Ada," he said, as I got out of the truck, "never forget for an instant that you have all the tools, all the ability and all the talent that God ever gave to a musician. Show the world what you've got. You are my Ada, my prodigy."

"I love you so much, Papa," I said.

I watched the truck pull away, then I took my magic locket and flung it as far as I could.

My return to Bologna was a blur. I reported to Mama that I was unsuccessful. As the days passed and we heard nothing further from Papa or Uncle Wilhelm, I stopped praying for a miracle and accepted his fate, just as he had. Ultimately, a package arrived from Berlin. There was a note from Uncle Wilhelm that read, "With deepest sorrow, I report that my beloved concertmaster died on December 6, 1938. He was the finest man I have ever known. Ada, I am sending you his violin. I am sure he would want you to have it."

FORTY-FOUR

Siena, August 2017

There was a chalk outline of Fabio's body on the bathroom floor. It was evident that the house had been searched thoroughly by the police. Doors and drawers were open. Cupboards were emptied. Even the bedding had been bundled.

"We have dusted for prints and photographed every inch of the house," the police officer said. "You may search, but I do not recall seeing a registry book here in the house. They are very large volumes. I would have inventoried it."

Catherine, Giulia and Liam searched in every conceivable place one might hide a book. The sun began to set, and Catherine looked at her watch. It had been two hours. She was ready to leave but Liam was tapping the walls and the floors listening for hollow sounds.

"Really?" Catherine said. "Do you think there are hidden staircases and revolving walls? Do you think that Colonel Mustard is hiding in the study with the candlestick? This is a twenty-year-old, run-of-the-mill subdivision house."

"No stone unturned," he said.

They left the house empty-handed and the police locked the front door. On the way out, Liam noticed a blue Toyota sitting by the curb. "That car has been sitting there the whole time," Liam said to Giulia. "There's a man in the front seat watching us. I'm going to talk to him. Would you come with me to translate?"

The driver lowered his window. Liam turned to Giulia. "Please ask him if he knew the man who lived in this house?"

"I speak English," he said with a strong accent. *"Un po."*

"Did you know Fabio Lombardo?"

The man swallowed hard and teared up. He nodded.

"Was he a friend of yours?"

Again, a sad nod.

"My name is Liam Taggart. This is *Avvocato* Giulia Romano. Would you mind talking to us for a minute?"

He eyed Liam suspiciously and said, *"Avvocato?* You with Lenzini?"

"Why do you ask? Are you a friend of Lorenzo Lenzini?"

"No. I curse him." He pretended to spit.

386

"Good. We do too. Lenzini is representing a company that is trying to evict our friend."

"VinCo?"

"Right."

"You are helping the old lady?"

"Yes, what do you know about the case?"

"Plenty. I am Berto."

"Can I buy you a cup of coffee, Berto? Or a cappuccino?"

He nodded and pointed forward. "La Dolce Pasticceria."

"I know where that is," Giulia said.

Sitting around a small table in the corner of the busy bakery, Berto quietly said, "We were friends, partners. Fabio, he always wants better for us. Like a bigger house. We don't need it, but Fabio, he's like that. One day last October, Lenzini comes into the registry. He orders up an old registry book. It's at the archives. When Fabio brings it, Lenzini looks at a certain page very, very closely. He shakes his head. Fabio says Lenzini doesn't like what he sees. Lenzini takes Fabio aside. 'How many euros to make this book disappear?' he says. Fabio, he is shocked. Disappear? He shakes his head. 'How about five thousand euros?' Lenzini says. Fabio shakes his head. 'I cannot destroy a public record.' Then Lenzini says, 'Ten thousand and you don't have to destroy it, just hide it. Someday much later, it can reappear.' Ten thousand is a lot of money to Fabio. I told him no. But he took the money. That night he brought the book home."

"What happened to the book?"

Berto shrugged. "It was in the closet under some sweaters. I know that a month ago — what's her name, the old woman?"

"Gabriella Vincenzo."

"*Si,* Gabriella. She has an *avvocato* who wants to see the same book. Fabio takes the order. Now he tells me he's in trouble. If he brings the book back, he has to return the money to Lenzini, which he doesn't have anymore. Not all of it."

"So he calls Lenzini?"

Berto nodded. "Lenzini tells Fabio to destroy the book. Fabio says he can't. Lenzini says to give *him* the book. Fabio says no. Lenzini tells Fabio to keep hiding it and he will give him another five thousand euros."

"And Fabio takes the money?"

Berto nodded. "He takes the money. The book stays under the sweaters. Here's the thing; Gabriella's *avvocato* never comes back to the registrar. He orders the book, but he never comes back to pick it up. Fabio is happy. He just got another five thousand for doing nothing."

"But *Avvocata* Romano orders the book last week?"

"*Si.* Fabio calls Lenzini and tells him he has to return the book now. Fabio's sorry, but he has no choice. There is shouting on the phone." Berto teared up, wiped his eyes with the back of his hand and said, "Fabio was not a bad man; he was just foolish."

"Where is the book now, Berto?"

Berto opened his hands and shrugged. "I don't know. Maybe the killer took it."

"Who is the killer?"

Berto hesitated. He pursed his lips. "Not Lenzini."

"How do you know?"

"He'd pay someone. That's his way."

"Well," Catherine said, "that's unfortunate. We sure could have used that book."

Berto looked at Catherine with raised eyebrows. "I saw the page. The one that Lenzini looked at when he was at the counter. Fabio showed it to me and he laughed."

"Why did he laugh?"

"Because he said VinCo doesn't own the property. Gabriella Vincenzo owns it. Fabio said Quercia never got a deed. Quercia never owned the property. It was owned by Carlo Vanucci."

"Quercia's name did not appear in the registry book?" Giulia asked.

"Oh no, I saw it. But Fabio said there should have been a deed from Vanucci to Quercia and there wasn't. Fabio said it looked like someone just put Quercia's name on the page in 1944 without a deed or any details."

"I don't suppose that Fabio made a copy of the page."

Berto shrugged. "Not that I know."

"But you saw the page with your own eyes, and the handwritten entries that Fabio pointed out to you?" Catherine said.

"*Si,* I saw the page."

"Would you come before the judge and tell him what you told us?"

"*Si.*"

Giulia took down his personal information and the meeting was over.

In the car, Giulia said, "That's a good story, but without the book, that's all it is. It's just the memory of what someone else told him. Berto doesn't know to his own knowledge if there was a deed or not. He just knows that Fabio told him there was no deed."

"Back in the U.S., we would call that hearsay. The testimony would probably be barred."

"It would be permitted here, but it is very weak. It's better than nothing, and so far, it's all we've got."

"I hate to keep saying back in America, but back in America, we build our cases brick by brick."

"Same here. And that's a brick. A little one."

Forty-Five

Bologna, December 1938

I spared her the details. I honored my promise to Papa and did not tell Mama the whole story. In that respect, Papa was right: she would not have come to grips with his decision to face death rather than give up their savings. I didn't tell her that I saw him or that he was ever outside the walls of Buchenwald, not even for the two hours. I only told her that Kurt discovered that he was held at Buchenwald and that everyone was trying to arrange for his release. She will never know that he chose to die so that she could live without worry. As noble an act as it was, as proud as she would have been, the guilt would have overwhelmed her. As always, Papa was right.

Mama was trying hard to keep her balance, but she was caught in a tailspin. The man she loved and admired had been taken from her and she wasn't there for him at the end. She wasn't there to tell him good-bye.

She wasn't even there to bury him. He had been her rock. All of her plans, all of her dreams, had burst like a child's balloon. Now there were no plans and there were no dreams. Now she was on her own in a strange land without a clue how to navigate the rest of her life.

She sat alone most of the time, staring at nothing. I would leave in the morning for rehearsal and return to find her in the same chair. I would beg her to go out, to come with me to a café. Sometimes she would go just to appease me, and we would end up sitting across from each other in silence. A handkerchief was frequently in her hand, and it was usually damp.

Previously, when she was depressed and frightened, she would accompany me to rehearsals and sit in the hall. Now, I couldn't coax her out of the house. She had lost interest in everything. When she did speak, it was to retell a memory of Papa. Did I remember when he took us to the lake? Did I remember when he would read to me on his lap? "He loved you so," she would say.

I was thoroughly ill-equipped to handle her depression or to provide the necessary support. To tell the truth, I was struggling with my own inadequacies. I should have brought him out. I should not have let him return to Buchenwald. I blamed myself. At one time, I sought out a psychologist at the university, who counseled me it would take time for each of us.

Late December arrived, and Bologna was again dressed in its Christmas best. Smiles were exchanged in the piazzas. Street vendors were selling hot chocolate, chestnuts and gingerbread. Bologna seemed energized, but Mama's spirits continued to be low and she felt out of place. Her frames of reference were missing. The ground on which she stood was unstable and she couldn't get a foothold.

The BSO was having its Christmas party, and I thought it might be a chance to get Mama out of the house and into a brighter atmosphere. She shook her head. "I can't," she said, "please don't ask me to do that. I couldn't face all those people. Go without me. I would just be a distraction."

I decided to take a stand. Something had to be done. "No, you wouldn't. You know everyone there, and they'd all be happy to see you. You can't stay in this room forever, Mama. It's not good for you and it's not good for me." I had no right to be self-centered, but it just came out of my mouth. Tears rolled down her cheeks. I was immediately sorry, but she waved me off. "You're right. It's not fair to you. Help me get myself together and I'll go with you."

"Are you sure?" I said.

She smiled. "You made your point. Don't make me change my mind."

The night of the party, I asked Franny and Natalia to come over and go with us. Mama was waffling. In the end, we practically had to drag her to the Teatro. It was nothing short of a kidnapping. We made sure she wore her nicest evening dress, and Franny did her hair and applied her makeup.

The BSO party — the singers, players, producers, directors and theater staff — was sparkling and festive. The food, the drinks and the conversations were carefree and lively. The evening was a great release for our hardworking opera company. In the midst of this gaiety, Mama was forced to wear a smile and interact with people at the party. It wasn't all that long ago that my mother was active in the Berlin social scene. She could be charming, elegant and fashionable. I just had to nudge her into that persona. Soon I could see vestiges of it returning, and it was a pleasure.

At one point, Maestro Vittorio came over, engaged Mama and me in conversation and then said, quite unexpectedly and with a twinkle in his eye, "Ada, we know that your contract with us will expire at the end of January, and that makes us all very sad. What would you say to an offer to stay on for an additional year?"

I looked at Mama. This time she had a genuine smile on her face. Almost giddy. "I would say I am honored, Maestro," I said. Mama clapped. It was so good to see her mood brighten. Maybe she could turn the corner. I wondered if Uncle Wilhelm had arranged the extension, but Vittorio said, "It appears that Signor Fishman will be leaving us. We'll be short a first violin. Ada, I need to tell you that the entire orchestra, almost every person, asked me if I would extend the offer to you."

I was dumbfounded. The orchestra that viewed me with a jaundiced eye for the first six months of my residence? That orchestra? Then I looked around the room and all the members were facing me and smiling. I was blushing so much my cheeks must have been purple. They all raised their glasses in a salute. I bowed to them and said, *"Grazie mille, miei cari amici."*

The party went well into the night, and although it was ten days before Christmas, the temperature was agreeably warm, and the outdoor cafés were alive. Mama and I stopped for a hot mulled wine with Franny and Natalia. Natalia mentioned that she was leaving in a couple of days to join her family in Pienza. Her mother was making a Chanukah dinner. "Her latkes are the best," she said. "Why don't you all come with me?"

"I'll come," Franny said, "but I don't know

395

what a latke is. Is it a cookie?"

Mama laughed. She actually laughed!

"You should come too, Mrs. Baumgarten," Natalia said. "My mother would love to have you, and I know that she welcomes your expert cooking advice."

Mama looked at me. "I don't know, I'm not really very good company these days."

"Nonsense," Natalia said. "My mother would love to have someone else in the kitchen. Lord knows, it's not me."

Mama looked at me. "Should we go?" she said.

"Absolutely, Mama. It would make me so happy."

I was booked for Sister Maria Alicia's Christmas series. I couldn't cancel even if I wanted to, which I didn't. Beniamino Gigli had asked for me personally. "You go with Franny and Nat," I said. "I'll join you when the series is over."

Mama hesitated and started to shake her head. This was a lot to ask of a woman who had been practically comatose for the past month. But Franny and Natalia were up to the task. "Oh, come on," Franny urged. "We'll all take the train and the bus. It'll be fun. We'll spend a week in the country, and we'll eat Mrs. Romitti's latke cookies!"

To my surprise, Mama agreed. "All right. I think it would be very nice," she said. "Ada, you have to join us as soon as your concert is over."

"It's a deal," I said. "But, Franny, they're potato pancakes, not cookies."

FORTY-SIX

Bologna, August 2017

"A classmate of mine practices with a large firm in Bologna," Giulia said. "She told me that Giuseppe Hernandez is still registered on the roll of active attorneys, and she gave me his address on Via Farini, two blocks from the Bologna courthouse. I tried calling him, but I keep getting a voice message."

"So we'll pay him a visit," Liam said.

"Exactly."

On the second floor of a small, three-story, cameo-colored building in central Bologna, an office door listed the names of six attorneys. One of them was Giuseppe Hernandez. An older woman was seated behind a reception desk. "Is Signor Hernandez in today?" Giulia asked.

The woman smiled and shook her head. "He doesn't come in very often. He's retired now, but he still keeps his licenses current as an *avvocato* and a *notaio*. Once in a while, someone will ask him to prepare a contract or notarize a purchase. These days you're more likely to catch him in his garden than at the courthouse." She wrote down his address, Giulia left her business card and they departed with a thank-you.

Hernandez's house was south of Bologna in hilly country, almost all the way to Madonna di San Luca. His home was tucked in a wooded grove of cedar and fir trees. True to the prediction, Hernandez was out behind his house tending his large vegetable garden. He wore a wide-brimmed straw hat. A white cotton shirt loosely covered his thin frame. He was bent over, pruning a bush, when he noticed their arrival. Peering over his glasses, he said, "Something I can help you with?"

"We're sorry to disturb you at home, Signor Hernandez, but your office gave us your address," Giulia said. "She said you wouldn't mind."

He raised his eyebrows. "Luisa said that?"

"Well, not those exact words."

He nodded his understanding. "So now you're here, what do you want?"

"A few minutes of your time, if you wouldn't mind."

Hernandez thought for a moment, shrugged and said, "Well, you've driven all this way on a hot day. Would you care for a glass of ice tea?"

"Thank you, you're very kind."

Hernandez served tea on his patio and set

out a plate of kumquats. "I picked these just this morning," he said. "They're delightfully sweet and juicy, not like what you'd find in the stores."

Catherine picked up a kumquat and closely examined it.

Hernandez laughed. "It won't bite you. It's the only citrus where you eat the skin and the pulp. In a kumquat, the skin is much sweeter than the pulp, but mine are sweet all the way through. Try it."

Catherine took a small bite of the rind. "It is sweet." He nodded and smiled. Then she bit though the fruit and made a puckery face.

"Sometimes the insides are a little tart, if you don't know what to expect," he said. "You have to get used to the taste. Now, why did you folks drive all the way out here?"

"In 1995, you notarized a deed from Carlo Vanucci to Gabriella Vincenzo."

As soon as Catherine uttered those words, Hernandez face turned serious. "And?"

"That deed has been challenged and ruled invalid in the Siena court."

Hernandez nodded. "The judge, did he rule it was out of the chain of title?"

"Yes. How did you know?"

He shrugged. "Because it was."

"Out of the chain? You notarized that deed," Giulia said forcefully. "A notary is responsible for researching the property records and verifying ownership. A notary stands behind the deed as a guarantor of its authenticity."

"What is it you want of me, Signorina Romano?"

"An explanation. The truth."

"I have just told you the truth. Now you may show yourselves out."

"Not so fast," Liam said. "We didn't drive all the way out here to be dismissed like schoolchildren. Gabriella Vincenzo is about to be evicted from her property, the property she's lived on all her life. She says it's her property and I believe her."

"I do too. I met her just that one day in June 1995. She seemed very honest."

"Why are you so flippant?" Catherine said. "As a notary, you can be held liable for negligently certifying title to property. Gabriella could sue you for the value of her property."

"Is that why you came out here, to threaten me with a civil suit? If so, you would be wasting your time. Now, please leave."

"Not until we get an explanation," Liam said. "I won't see this woman tossed out of her home."

"You *will* leave, all of you, because I will call the *polizia* if you don't. Now go!"

Catherine sensed that Liam was preparing for a standoff. She took his arm. "C'mon, Liam, there's nothing more we can do here."

As they turned to leave the garden, Liam

said to Giulia, "You're going to have to find this Vanucci guy, and when you do, I'll wring his neck."

"You'll do no such thing!" Hernandez called. "You leave Carlo's family alone. Do you hear me?"

Liam spun around. "Really? If you're threatening me, Signor Hernandez, you're wasting your time. Isn't that how it goes?"

Hernandez lowered his head and said, "Come back. Sit down."

When they reassembled, Hernandez said, "Carlo Vanucci was a close friend and like an uncle to me. My father and his father were partners in their law firm. Carlo's daughter is ill, and she knows nothing of this transaction. You leave her alone."

"What about Carlo?"

Hernandez shook his head. "He is dead for many years. He died two days after we signed the deed to Vincenzo."

Liam leaned forward. "Come on, Giuseppe, tell us about the deed. Tell us why Carlo would give Gabi a phony deed for property that he didn't own."

Hernandez shook his head. "It wasn't a phony deed. Carlo said his title was good. If Carlo said so, it was true. He was a man of his word."

"I want the whole story," Liam said.

"That is the whole story. Carlo showed up at my office in June 1995, dying of cancer.

He was weak and thin and could barely stand. Carlo said he was under an obligation to deed a farm near Pienza to Gabriella Vincenzo. I agreed to help him, but we had to follow the statutes. I know my legal obligations as a notary. We would have to go to Siena, to the registrar's office, I would have to check the property book and verify the ownership, and then we would go to Gabriella's, where we would all sign the deed. He said that was fine because he was the owner.

"When we got to the registrar's office and I looked at the book, I saw that the property was not in Carlo's name. I said, 'Carlo, you cannot deed this property, it is in someone else's name.' A corporation, as I recall."

"Quercia?"

Hernandez nodded. "Yes, that's it. Quercia Company. Carlo said, 'That's a mistake. I am the owner.' He was insistent. He said he got the property by a valid deed forty years earlier. He said there must be an error in the registry book. The book we were looking at didn't go back forty years. It only went back to 1980. We needed to see the prior book. Sometimes there are copying errors. It's not unheard of. The clerk said that the older book was off-premises, that he would have to order it and it would take a few days."

Hernandez stopped again as his words caught in his throat. "Carlo looked at me and put his hand on my shoulder. 'Giuseppe,' he said, 'I don't have a few days. It took every ounce of strength to get here today. I am in horrible pain. Please believe what I say. The book from the 1930s will show I have good title.'

"Like I said, I would do anything for Carlo, but to protect my license, both Carlo and Gabriella signed a waiver acknowledging that I could not confirm ownership in the registry book. I took the signed deed to Siena and placed it for recordation. My dear friend died two days later. End of story."

"I wonder why Gabriella never mentioned the waiver," Catherine said.

"Please don't bother Carlo's family," Hernandez said. "His children don't know anything."

"May we have copies of the documents in your file? There may be something that would help us."

"There is nothing in my file," Hernandez said tersely. "It has all been destroyed. I only keep records for seven years. There are no files for this matter. You should leave now."

"It seems like we're back to square one," Liam said in the car.

"With this testimony, do we have enough to ask the judge to postpone the eviction?" Catherine asked. "Maybe just to give us time to check out his story?"

Giulia shrugged. "I don't know. We really don't have any evidence to show that Quercia's deed is invalid. We still lack tangible evidence, but we could be getting closer."

"Yes, but can we get there before September 10? Maybe we should ask for an extension now."

"You're more experienced than I am," Giulia said. "What would you do back in Chicago?"

"I'd file a motion. What do we have to lose? We can offer to bring in Berto to testify to what he saw. Maybe he'll mention what Fabio said to him. We can bring in Hernandez, who will testify about Vanucci and that Vanucci was an honest man. And there is the matter of the missing registry book. Maybe there's enough mystery that the judge will give us a little time to finish the investigation."

"I find it very disturbing that Hernandez destroyed the file," Giulia added. "Most attorneys I know keep their real estate files in storage for many years. There's no need to destroy a file in seven years."

"And why would he want to destroy a signed waiver that protects him from a lawsuit?"

The group settled in around the dinner table with a mixture of hope and frustration. The day had produced hints but no solutions.

They felt sure they were close to a break in the case, finding that smoking gun; they just hadn't come across it yet. Floria had prepared ravioli and Liam was eagerly eyeing the meal. As they were passing the dish around, Liam's phone rang. "Signor Taggart, it is Lorenzo. I am standing at the end of your driveway. Can you come and talk to me? Alone?"

Liam raised his eyebrows. He pointed to his phone and mouthed, "Lenzini."

Catherine shrugged.

Liam looked at his plate of steaming ravioli. "Damn."

"What do you suppose he wants?" Catherine said.

"Maybe he wants to make a deal? I don't have a clue." Liam frowned. "All I know is that he's interrupting my ravioli dinner."

"Watch out, Liam. He's a snake."

Lenzini was leaning against his car when Liam approached.

"Thank you for talking to me," he said, and he extended his hand. "I am really not the bad person that Signora Vincenzo assumes. As they say in the American movies, I am only a mouthpiece."

"I've seen you in action. You're a prick. What is it you wish to talk about, Lorenzo?"

"I see in you a practical man, a man who has been around in many a heated controversies, but a man who keeps his head on straight. You must know the signora cannot win this case. VinCo will never allow it. Your young *avvocata,* Giulia Romano, is a child. She lacks the experience and credibility to convince the judge to overturn his rulings. I am sure you realize that —"

"Hold on, Lenzini. First of all, she's a damn good lawyer, and secondly, you aren't going to scare us off this case by —"

"No, no, no, no. You misunderstand me. I am not trying to scare you. Just the opposite. I am appealing to your practicality. The signora cannot win. You can't defeat VinCo with the testimony of an unemployed boyfriend and a broken-down old lawyer. You won't have the registry book. You won't have the contract. We've taken great care to close all the open doors. We're not amateurs, Liam."

"Where is this going?"

"I'm sure you know that VinCo has offered a generous settlement to the signora."

"Which she has rejected."

"Again, I know this. But I am talking to Liam, the practical man. There is a lot of money here. VinCo is a billion-dollar company. There is money for Signora Vincenzo, and there is also more money. What does Liam and his lovely wife need to make this trip worthwhile? Hmm?"

"What?"

"How would two hundred thousand euros sound?"

"You're offering me two hundred thousand euros?"

Lenzini shrugged. "That kind of money can go a long way for a hardworking private detective and his solo practitioner wife raising a young child. Maybe a new home? School expenses?"

"What about Gabriella?"

Lenzini smiled. "Now I can see you're thinking clearly. We could add another fifty thousand euros to her offer. Do we have an arrangement?"

"Is that how you took care of Santi and Giangiorgi?"

Again, a wide smile from Lenzini. "Much, much less, I assure you. What do you say, Liam? Can we end this today?"

Liam smiled and nodded. "Of course we can. You can drop your suit, leave Gabriella alone and get the hell off this driveway."

"Seriously, Liam. It's a lot of money. Go and talk to your wife."

Liam shook his head. "I can't believe you interrupted my dinner for this bullshit. You're a dirtbag, Lenzini. And you're trespassing. If you don't get off the land, I'm going to throw you off." Liam turned and started walking up the driveway.

"You're making a big mistake," Lenzini called. "VinCo will never let you win. They will stop at nothing to win this case. You're in way over your head."

"What did he want?" Catherine said.

"He wanted to pay us two hundred thousand euros to drop the case and he'll throw another fifty at Gabi."

"Bastard. I'm sure that's how he got rid of Santi and Giangiorgi."

Liam smiled. "They were cheaper."

"I still don't understand why this is so important to VinCo," Giulia said.

Liam shook his head. "Lenzini said something odd. He told me we couldn't win the case with an unemployed boyfriend and a broken-down old lawyer."

"That would be Berto and Hernandez."

"Right. And then he said we won't have the registry book and we won't have the contract. What is that all about?"

"Registry Book 143," Giulia said.

"I know. But what contract?"

Catherine shrugged. "Maybe he means the deed."

Liam shook his head. "Nah, I don't think so. We have the deed. He said the contract."

FORTY-SEVEN

Bologna, December 1938

As the year was drawing to a close, we had two more performances of Puccini's *Tosca*. In an effort to end with a bang, Maestro Vittorio was working us very hard. "Giacomo Puccini's family lived near mine in Lucca," Vittorio told us. "I met the great man when I was a boy. He loved fast cars, well-tailored clothes and his cigars." The orchestra laughed. "He even attended a performance of *Tosca* here at the Comunale in 1906. Before my time, of course. But here's the point: we need to stay true to his vision. We must respect his *verismo* style — his real-life characters, their passion, their violence and their romance. Puccini speaks directly to the heart, and we must convey his emotions to our patrons. He is the last in the chain of great Italian opera composers. Who knows if there will ever be another?"

Although *Tosca* takes place in Rome, in the year 1800, the subject matter seemed very timely and unsettling to me. It hit home. In fact, the entire story of *Tosca* frightened me a lot. It tells the story of Baron Scarpia, a ruthless chief of police, in command of a deadly force of malevolent guards. He imprisons and murders his opponents on a whim. To me, Scarpia is strikingly similar to Kleiner or Heydrich and his SS. The two lovers, Floria Tosca and Mario Cavaradossi (read here, Ada and Kurt) are Scarpia's targets and they don't stand a chance against his wickedness. It is hard for me to sit in the orchestra pit every day and watch the opera unfold. There are just too many parallels.

The opera's most heart-wrenching moments take place in the final scene. Scarpia has tortured Mario and sentenced him to death by firing squad. Moments before the execution is to be carried out, Mario bribes his jailer to give him a paper and pencil to write a farewell letter to Floria. He reminisces on the nights they had together and bemoans his fate. He will never see Floria again. His song, "E Lucevan le Stelle" ("And the Stars Were Shining"), is a tearful sonnet in homage to their star-crossed romance. The verse ends with:

My dream of love forever disappears.
The hour passes, and I die in desperation.
And never have I loved life so much.

411

And there's not a dry eye in the house. Mine included.

Playing in the BSO was a dream come true. So was playing in the Bologna Christmas concert series. It was a giant step in my career. This year, we received notice that Beniamino Gigli would be singing eight numbers: three opera arias, two Christmas songs and two Neapolitan songs, and his encore would be "Je Crois Entendre Encore," his signature aria from Bizet's *The Pearl Fishers.* He owned that aria. Our ensemble rehearsed the scores in anticipation.

The San Petronio Basilica was sold out for his performance. The giant structure was festively decorated with thousands of candles, wreaths and ribbons. Gigli's entrance was met with a standing ovation, which did not quiet for several minutes and not until he calmed them down with a gentle wave of his hands. He delivered his arias beautifully. Perfect in pitch and modulation, smooth as a glass of milk. Each number was met with roaring approval. The audience was in awe, as was our small ensemble.

When his last selection, "Gesu Bambino," had ended, he left the stage to thunderous applause and shouts of "Encore." We sat in our seats and waited for him to return, knowing he would come back to sing his *Pearl Fishers* aria.

After a few minutes, he returned to the stage, all smiles, nodding to the audience's adulation. He calmed the crowd until there was utter silence for his trademark, "Je Crois Entendre Encore." Then he nodded, and the cellist and I began the introduction in 6/8 time. The entire aria is sung in a high register, but when Gigli hit and held that high B, it was as effortless and as sweet as music gets. He bowed several times to a standing ovation and left the stage, but the applause would not stop. "Encore!" they shouted.

Gigli returned. He bowed appreciatively to his adoring fans, thanked them again for coming to the concert and walked off the stage, but the adoration would not stop. The crowd did not leave, and they continued to shout for more. Now we had a problem: we hadn't rehearsed any other songs. Finally, to roaring applause, Gigli came back onstage, turned to the ensemble with a smile and a shrug, and said, "I guess we better do another. Do we know 'E Lucevan le Stelle'?" The members shook their heads, all except for me. I had been working on *Tosca* for a month. "I can follow you," I said.

"I should have known," he replied with a smile. "Let's begin."

It was another crowning moment I shall

never forget. Gigli was widely recognized as the foremost *Tosca* tenor in the world. I wished my father had been there, but I held his violin and it played beautifully. In a way, I felt like Papa was guiding my fingers and laying the bow on the strings with a perfect touch. We finished, Gigli walked over to me, laced his fingers in mine and raised our hands up high. We bowed together.

Following the performance, at the post-concert party, Gigli took me aside. "I met your father once," he said, "when I sang in Berlin. He was a fine musician. I heard about his passing and I am so very sorry for you."

I thanked him and pointed to my instrument. "This is his violin," I said.

"You do it honor."

I wanted to say something in response, but my lips were quivering.

"Miss Baumgarten, next June I am performing *Rigoletto* at the Baths of Caracalla. Are you familiar with the venue?"

"Not really."

"It is the summer home for the Rome Opera. Anyway, I am also giving two solo concerts. I would like you to play in the ensemble for my two concerts. Are you available?"

"Oh, yes," I said. "Yes, I am."

"I shall contact you."

I was breathless. Gigli wanted *me* in his

ensemble. "I am humbled, Maestro. Thank you so much."

"Miss Baumgarten, your technique is exquisite. You should be proud, not humbled. I will see you in June."

Who's that walking on air? That would be me.

Two days later, I joined Mama, Franny and Natalia at the Romitti home in Pienza for a Chanukah dinner. Mama and Naomi had fried enough latkes to feed the Roman legions. The candles were lit, the prayers were said and dinner was served. Lots of food and laughter.

It was readily apparent that Mama and Naomi had formed a solid friendship. Each effusively complemented the other. Mama made great latkes, Naomi made wonderful brisket, this one sautéed delightful vegetables, that one made delicious soup, both of them created delicious cookies, and on and on. All accompanied by Matt's wine, a silky Montepulciano d'Abruzzo.

We were sitting in the living room, all of us too stuffed to move when Mama first floated the notion of life in Pienza. The oblique way in which she addressed the subject was very Friede-like. "It's so peaceful down here, don't you think, Ada? I sure enjoy the pace of life, the markets, the friendly neighbors and, of course, the Romittis."

I agreed.

"And the town is so charming," she added.

I agreed.

"We can't move to Vienna anymore. And now that Papa is gone, I'm afraid America is out. This might be a good alternative for us, don't you think?"

Naomi jumped right in. "Oh, what a wonderful idea."

No doubt, this had been expertly choreographed for my benefit. Pienza was too far for me to live and commute to Bologna. But for Mama? Why not? It was a great solution.

"We should look into it, Mama," I said, which brought a wide smile to her face. If life in Pienza could lift her spirits, I was all for it.

FORTY-EIGHT

Pienza, September 2017

Dinner on the terrace was abruptly interrupted by Franco running up and shouting, *"Signora! Signora! Fuoco!"*

Even Liam and Catherine knew he was shouting "Fire." Franco went on to say that he had seen two men piling brush on the south perimeter. He was sure they were coming back with gasoline as soon as night fell. Now, he said, he sees one of the men hiding among the VinCo vincs.

"Give me your shotgun, Aunt Gabi," Liam said, "and some rope and tell Franco to get the golf cart."

"I'll get it," Franco said.

Liam looked at him quizzically. "You speak English?"

Franco shook his head. "Maybe little."

"Call the police, Floria, and tell them to get out here. I'm going down there to stop them."

Franco drove the cart toward where he had

417

seen the brush piles, stopped two hundred yards short and they quietly made their way toward the area. Two men were standing at the brush pile, spreading gasoline on the sticks. Liam and Franco snuck up from behind.

"Tell these sons-of-bitches to freeze or I'll shoot them," Liam said to Franco, and Franco shouted the instructions. The two men turned to run, and Liam fired a shot over their heads. They dove to the ground.

"Tell them to stay down," Liam said to Franco. "Tell them I'm an American and we shoot arsonists."

The two men, who appeared to be unarmed and scared to death, did what they were told.

Liam took the rope and tied their hands behind their backs. "Who sent you here?" he asked. "Who told you to burn Gabriella's vineyard?"

No answer.

"Franco, tell them to answer me or the next shot is between their legs."

Franco relayed the message, and one of the men answered in Italian. Franco looked at Liam and shook his head. "He say, *'Non lo so.'* He doesn't know."

"Bullshit." Liam cocked the shotgun. The man on the ground started crying. *"Non lo so, Non lo so."*

Liam lifted him up and backed him into a

tree. "Who sent you?"

The lights of a police car interrupted Liam, and two officers got out. Liam recognized Foresta, the policeman who stopped him from attacking Lenzini in August. The other was older and stockier. Franco explained the situation, how he saw them setting up a brush fire, how they stopped them as they were pouring gasoline.

"I'll take it from here," Foresta said.

"Give me a minute. I'm just about to get some answers," Liam said.

He smiled. "Afraid not. We'll interrogate both of them back at the station. Evidence of arson is pretty clear."

"Here's the thing, Officer," Liam said. "If I can show that these men were hired by VinCo or its attorney, as I'm pretty sure they were, that would help us save Gabriella's farm."

He shrugged. "I'm sympathetic, but I can't let you do the interrogation. We'll talk to them back at the station. They're not going anywhere for a while. But this scenario you suggest, that VinCo is behind the attempted arson, is not logical. A brush fire like that could spread to many acres, including some of those vineyards owned by VinCo. Why would VinCo want to put its own vines in jeopardy?"

"The damage to VinCo may be a drop in the bucket of their acreage, but it might totally destroy Gabriella's farm."

419

"Does that make sense to you, Mr. Taggart? VinCo has won the court case. The judge has ruled that Gabriella must leave in nine days. The eviction order has already been placed in our office. Why would they want to burn the farm if they're going to have it in nine days?"

"There's a last-minute motion asking the judge to postpone the eviction. We filed it two days ago, and it's set for tomorrow. It's weak, but we're hopeful." Liam shook his head. "I know it's them. I don't know why they want to destroy the farm they're trying so hard to own, but I know it's them."

At the morning court call, the parties assembled before Judge Riggioni once again. "I have before me Gabriella Vincenzo's motion to stay the eviction and reopen the trial," he said. "I've read the motion, *Avvocata* Romano, do you have anything else to add?"

"Signor Presidente della corte," Giulia said, "I realize that you have entered judgment in this case, but you only heard one side of the case. We're only asking for a level playing field where everyone gets to tell their side of the story. Signora Vincenzo was not represented at the trial."

The judge held up his hand. "She *was* represented. *Avvocato* Santi was the attorney of record. Neither she nor her attorney chose to show up on the trial date to offer any evidence. That conduct usually speaks for itself. Normally, it means that there is no evidence to offer."

"As you say, that may normally be the case, but Gabriella's attorney urged her to give up, not to contest. We believe he may have been influenced to say that. I do not believe that Signora Vincenzo understood the consequences of failing to appear. It didn't mean that there was no evidence. In the one month that I have been her lawyer, and with the help of *Avvocata* Lockhart and *Investigatore* Liam Taggart, we have uncovered significant evidence and testimony that would show that things are not as clear as you were led to believe."

"Is that the evidence you refer to in your motion?"

"Yes. The single most important piece of evidence for your honor to consider would be Registry Book 143," Giulia continued. "But we have discovered that the book was stolen from the registrar by Fabio Lombardo, a clerk. We know that he illegally took the book after meeting with *Avvocato* Lenzini."

"We know no such thing!" Lenzini shouted. "It is true that I met with a clerk — I do not know his name — and I requested that he retrieve the book from the archives. And he did. And I saw the book. With my own eyes. That book, if it were here today, would prove that Quercia was lawfully in title for many,

many years. I saw it myself."

"I do not believe that for one minute," Giulia said. "We met with a person who actually saw the book in Fabio Lombardo's home and will testify that the book does not contain the notation of a deed from the owner to Quercia. He will also testify that Mr. Lombardo accepted money from Mr. Lenzini to hide the book."

"Outrageous!!" Lenzini shouted. "Where is this person? Where is the money, where is the book? This is a slanderous accusation. She comes into court without a shred of evidence, without a single witness, and accuses me of tampering with evidence? Bribing a clerk? This young girl has no concept of the ethical responsibilities of our profession. She should have her license taken away."

"I can and will produce the witness if your honor will reopen the proofs and allow testimony. I did not name the witness in my motion for fear that the same people who killed Fabio Lombardo and who tried to burn Signora Vincenzo's vineyard would seek to do the witness harm. It all points to the plaintiff, VinCo."

"Oh, please," Lenzini said with a sneer. "Even if this unnamed person came into court and testified as Signorina Romano says, why would his testimony be any more credible than mine? I am an officer of the court and I saw the book. I am sorry we do not have that book, but we must not jump to bizarre conclusions. I understand it has been misplaced, and that would not be the first time in Siena history that a book has been misshelved or lost in the archives. Perhaps if we had that book here today, Signorina Romano would see that she is wrong. It would certainly show your honor that this futile and untimely effort to interfere with VinCo's possession of its own land should be immediately dismissed."

The judge sat back. "Enough bickering. This is neither the time nor the place to argue about whose testimony would be more believable. Suffice it to say, there are many perplexing facts raised in *Avvocata* Romano's motion. I am bothered by the fact that the registry book is missing. But missing evidence is not the same as admissible evidence. I am also bothered by yesterday's attempt to burn Signora Vincenzo's fields. Does that have something to do with this case? Perhaps the perpetrators, who are now in custody, will provide information to the police. We should give them that opportunity. I am not going to vacate my judgment. The judgment will stand, at least for the time being. I do believe it would be fair to postpone the eviction and give *Avvocata* Romano a little time to prepare her evidence. And here, I use the word *evidence*. Not theory, not supposition, not conclusions to be drawn from mysteriously

423

missing books. *Evidence.* I will continue the possession order to September 30."

FORTY-NINE

Bologna, April 1939

The spring season had begun for us at the BSO, and once again we were hard at work. I remained in the second section, and I resigned myself that I would be there for the duration. I know Vittorio's decision was motivated by political pressure and not by the measure of my performance. Over the winter months, while the company was on hiatus, I found part-time work entertaining in a restaurant. Even afterward, when we weren't busy, I continued to appear and play popular musical numbers for Andrea's customers. It wasn't the "Meditation," but it was fun, and the money was good.

With Natalia's help and Maestro Vittorio's attestation, I applied for and received the governmental certificate of *Discriminati.* That certificate, rare and valuable, permitted me to continue to live in Italy and work as a professional musician despite the Italian racial laws. I was declared "exempt" because of my excellent service to the country as an indispensable member of the Bologna State Opera Company. It also extended the exemption to my mother.

Mama's outlook was improving every day. She corresponded with Naomi on a regular basis. I was so grateful that Natalia had introduced them. We joined the Romittis for Passover seder in March. *Pasqua Ebraica,* they called it. The celebration of *il matzo.* Mama stayed with Naomi for an extra week, and she was more anxious than ever to find a new home near Pienza and her good friend. If and when Mama did find a house, it was my intention to remain in Bologna, where I had become comfortable.

Although Italy had enacted racial laws, they were not rigorously enforced. As a result, many of us had developed a laissez-faire attitude. The laws were on the books, but they were haphazardly applied and didn't really interfere with my day-to-day activities. Natalia thought my attitude was a mistake. "The racial laws call for the confiscation of Jewish property, yet many of our brothers and sisters have not secured their assets. It is only a matter of time until Mussolini decides that it is time to enforce the forfeiture laws. You and your mother need to act promptly."

I asked her what she meant. "Your father brought his life savings here at a terrible cost," she said. "I believe that money is sitting at the bank in a safe deposit box, is that right?"

I nodded. "What am I supposed to do? I can't keep all that cash under my mattress."

"Your mother's looking for a house. Use the money. Put it to work."

"But then it would be subject to seizure."

Natalia smiled. "There are ways. Find a house and leave the forfeiture problem to me."

It turned out it wasn't so easy to find a house in Pienza. I wanted Mama to live in the city, near the Romittis, in a small, manageable house. Low maintenance. Mama and Naomi spent weeks looking for just the right house. The funny thing is, people seemed to stay put in Pienza. It was a stagnant real estate market. Families lived in their homes for generations.

Mama asked me to join her for a midweek house hunt. She and Naomi had found a real estate agent, and she was going to schedule several appointments. Mama felt confident we would find something. I talked Natalia into going with me. I always enjoyed her company, but shopping for a house with Mama and Naomi Romitti was a lot more than I could handle by myself.

Our real estate agent was Sylvia, a large jolly woman who wore colorful dresses and laughed in loud staccato bursts. We gave her our requirements, and she showed up with a clipboard of handwritten listings from several properties. "Do not despair," she said. "I'll find you a house because I am the best *agente immobiliare* in all of Tuscany!" That was followed up with a series of hoots.

The first house she showed us was a four-bedroom townhouse right in the middle of old Pienza, a few steps from the Duomo. The stone exterior was charming, and the beamed ceilings were in relatively good shape, but the stairs were steep, and I worried about Mama in the years to come. Anyway, the house wasn't available until the end of the summer, so we passed.

The next house was located north of Pienza, thirty minutes in Sylvia's car. It was a charming country house, with two terraces and a detached apartment. "Wouldn't that be perfect when you come to visit?" Mama said. "Yes," I answered, "but you don't have a car. It's a long way from Naomi on foot." We passed.

The next house was back in the city, but it really wasn't a house at all. It was an apartment, no bigger that the Bologna apartment. We passed again.

By late afternoon, we had seen six houses, we were all tired and Sylvia was out of options. We returned to the Romittis for a rest and a glass of wine. "I'll tell her to keep looking," Naomi said. "Something will turn up."

The next day, as we prepared to return to Bologna, Sylvia came by. "I know this isn't exactly what you specified," she said with a series of chuckles, "but I understand that a certain villa, *fantastico,* is available for the right price. It's not advertised, but I know the seller, Signor Partini, and I know he wants to sell." She smiled and patted herself on the chest. "That's why you hire *me*! I know everyone in Tuscany! You'll love this villa. It is *perfetto* — several French windows, stone fireplace, gorgeous veranda, very high ceilings and a spacious kitchen. Best of all, it sits on twenty-eight hectares of prime arable farm land, almost all of it planted with vines and olive trees. It's a working farm."

I started to shake my head. "How far is it from the city, Sylvia? Mama doesn't have a car."

"She doesn't need one. It's on the SP18 bus line. There is a bus stop practically at the end of the driveway, twenty minutes from Pienza!"

Mama was excited, but Natalia and I were both befuddled. "Mama, what are you going to do with a farm? You need a little bungalow in town. You cannot undertake the management and upkeep of a farm."

"And that's what is so *meraviglioso* about

429

this property," Sylvia said. "It comes with tenant farmers who have lived there for years. You will be an impresario, Signora Baumgarten. They will take care of the land and your villa. You will live like a duchess!"

"Really? I'd like to be a duchess, Ada." She nodded sharply. "I want to be a duchess."

"Mama," I sighed. "This is not for you."

"Who says? I want to take a look. Set it up, Sylvia."

Need I say more? Mama fell in love with the property. The villa was right out of a Tuscan fairy tale. The caretakers had farmed the land for generations. Their grandparents had worked for the church that once owned all the land in the section. It was only a few hundred meters to SP18 and the bus came by four times a day. The caretaker had a horse and wagon and frequently went into town. If Mama needed to go to Naomi's, he would take her and pick her up. The price was doable, and we would have sufficient reichsmarks left over.

"I'm going to name my villa," Mama said. "After all, I am now a duchess."

I laughed. "What are you going to name it, Duchess?"

"Villa Baumgarten, of course."

We set a date for the closing. In the interim, we would have to get a lawyer and a notary. The purchase would take place at the villa.

Natalia took me aside. "She can't call it Villa Baumgarten and she can't even own it," she said.

"I'm confused," I said. "We have the money."

"The Italian racial laws. They call for confiscation of Jewish property. Remember, I told you I could take care of the forfeiture problem. Many Jews I know, especially my freedom fighters, are putting their property in the names of others. They designate non-Jewish Italians to hold property for them. I am going to tell my father to do the same thing. Before Mussolini takes our house, we will sell it to a non-Jew. And by sell it, I mean, let him hold it in his name for our benefit."

That was the first time that Natalia have ever admitted to me that she was with the underground. That was a risky admission. Freedom fighters were considered rebels and were hunted by the Fascist police. It showed how much she trusted me.

"I'm not comfortable with some stranger owning my mother's house," I said.

"It's done all the time. It's all by contract. You convey the property to a non-Jewish nominee, and the nominee will hold it for you until you want it. There is an *avvocato* in Bologna who will prepare the papers," Natalia said. "He is a good man. His name is Hernando Hernandez. He will also arrange for the nominee, what Italians call a *designata*."

"Hernando Hernandez? Are you serious?"

She smiled and shrugged. "His family comes from Spain, years ago. He is helping many of my friends hide property before the Fascists take it."

"And he will provide this *designata* for Mama's property?"

"He will do it all."

On May 15, we all met at the property. The group included Signor Partini, the seller, Mama, Sylvia, Natalia, Naomi, Hernando Hernandez and a man named Carlo Vanucci, who would serve as the *designata.* Signor Vanucci was a close friend of Signor Hernandez, and he would be paid a fee to take title to the property as nominee. Mr. Hernandez wrote an agreement whereby Mr. Vanucci would hold title in his name for as long as Mama wished. Signor Vanucci would deed the property at any time on Mama's instructions. She need only ask. If Signor Vanucci were to die, or if Mama died, the agreement provided for further transfer rights.

The papers were signed, the money was paid and prosecco was poured in celebration. My mama, the Duchess Baumgarten, was now the owner of a villa with a twenty-eight-hectare vineyard! Matteo had a new camera and we all posed for pictures. There we were: Sylvia, her arm around Vanucci; Mama standing next to Naomi, her new best friend; and all of us with our glasses held high.

FIFTY

Pienza, September 2017

"That's it!" Liam said, his head on the pillow, Ada's manuscript in his hand.

"What?" Catherine mumbled. "What's it? It's not even eight o'clock."

"The nominee agreement. That's the contract. Aren't you reading Ada's story?"

"I am, but I'm only at the part where her father died."

"You need to read faster."

"Excuse me, but I've been pretty busy with legal work as well. I read but I take my time and digest the words."

"Well, digest this: Hernandez's father arranged to deed the property to Carlo Vanucci in 1939. Vanucci was a nominee for the benefit of Friede Baumgarten, Ada's mother. Jews were asking non-Jews to hold property for them so the Fascist government wouldn't confiscate it."

Catherine sat up. "And of course, there would have to be a nominee agreement."

434

"Exactly. There was a nominee agreement drawn up by Hernando Hernandez, I guess he was Giuseppe's father. It provided for inheritance rights."

"That's fabulous. If we get that agreement, it's enforceable against all subsequent owners. Liam, it's all true. Vanucci would have been the title holder in 1939, and he certainly didn't deed the property to Quercia. Quercia never legally came into title. Fabio was right. Someone put Quercia's name in the book. No wonder Gabi wanted us to read the story. The answers are in there. Maybe Gabi doesn't understand it."

"I don't think there's much that Gabi doesn't understand. I think it's pretty clear, Gabi can't talk about it. It's too painful for her. She wants us to deal with it."

Catherine leaned over, grabbed Liam and kissed him hard on the lips. "I'm so proud of you."

"Mmm. I like where this is going," Liam said. "Good morning to you too." He wrapped his arms around her and lifted her onto his chest.

"Maybe we should wait," she whispered. "This bed has squeaky springs."

"Gabi's a sound sleeper."

"We have to get to Bologna," Liam said, as they walked out to the veranda. "Hernandez may have the nominee agreement in his files.

I'm going to call Giulia."

"If he had the document, wouldn't he have shared it with us? Why wouldn't he tell us that Vanucci was a nominee?"

"I think I know why. Lenzini told me, 'You won't have the contract.' Now I'm sure he meant the nominee contract, and I wouldn't be surprised if Lenzini had it destroyed. Let's pay a visit to Hernandez and find out."

Catherine dialed Giulia's cell phone and left a message on her voice mail. "If she doesn't call me back, I think we should go ourselves, right after breakfast. Hernandez speaks English. Let's call him and make an appointment."

"No, I don't want to warn him. Let's just drive up there."

"It's a two-hour drive and he may not be there."

"He's there, I guarantee it. He's puttering around in his garden like the Godfather. If he's hiding something, and we call him, he'll disappear. I prefer to drive up there and surprise him in his garden. A classic Liam tactic."

"Okay, but no more kumquats."

Hernandez looked up from his pruning and said, "I told you everything I know. You wasted your time coming back here."

"Why didn't you tell us that Vanucci was a nominee?"

"What is the word you use — 'nominee'? I don't know that word. I told you Vanucci said he had to deed the land to Vincenzo, that it was his obligation."

"Don't know the word 'nominee'?" Liam said sarcastically. "Then how about *designata*? Don't play games with me, Giuseppe."

"Who do you think you are? You cannot barge into my garden and order me around. I don't have to tell you anything. Good-bye." He waved his arm in a dismissive fashion and bent down to continue his pruning.

"Forget it, Liam," Catherine said. "Judge Riggioni will give us a subpoena for Hernandez's client files, and then he'll force him to testify at the trial."

"I want his father," Liam said. "I want Hernando Hernandez's documents subpoenaed as well."

"My grandfather, not my father," Hernandez said. "Leave my family out of this."

"Where is the nominee agreement?" Liam said sternly.

"I never saw it."

"I don't believe you. Where are your grandfather's client files?"

"In my office. I have assumed the practice of my father and my grandfather. But you will not find the *designata* agreement in the file."

"Who did you give it to?"

Hernandez hesitated and then said, "I don't

know what you're talking about."

Catherine stepped forward. "Signor Hernandez, you said that you would do anything for Carlo Vanucci. Why wouldn't you honor his promise to Gabriella? Why would you sully his memory? He's being accused of giving Gabi a fraudulent deed. You know we're telling the truth. Why don't you produce the *designata* agreement?"

"Because I cannot. It no longer exists."

"But it did exist — you know that. What happened to it?"

Hernandez's face began to redden. "You must go. I have told you what I can."

"You have told us nothing," Liam said. "Who is putting pressure on you? Is it Lenzini?"

Hernandez winced.

"Okay, so it's Lenzini. We can get you protection."

"Protection in Italy? Now it is you who knows nothing."

"I know you're an honest man, Giuseppe," Catherine said. "Do the right thing."

He lowered his head. "I can't. I'm sorry. I know Carlo would want me to, but I won't put his family or my family in danger. You can drag me into court in Siena, but I will say the same thing. My files have been purged and I will not testify."

"You won't help us in any way?" Liam asked in final desperation.

Hernandez thought for a moment and then said, "You will find nothing in the files. Nothing. Subpoena all the files you like, you can even subpoena the billing files, but you will find nothing. Now you must leave!"

Liam looked at Catherine, smiled and nodded. "Thank you, Signor Hernandez. *Buongiorno y grazie.*"

Back in the car, Catherine said, "What was that smile all about?" Then in a mocking tone she said, *"Buongiorno y grazie."* She shrugged. "Really, Liam?"

"He gave it to us, Cat. They purged his client files but not the billing file. Have Giulia issue a subpoena for Hernando Hernandez's billing files for Friede Baumgarten and Carlo Vanucci. I'm sure you will see time billed for preparation of a *designata* agreement and a house closing in 1939. Whoever was threatening him only looked in the client files, not the office's billing files."

Catherine threw her arms around Liam's neck. "You're amazing!"

Liam raised his eyebrows. "There are no squeaky springs in this car, Cat."

"Oh my God, just drive."

Liam smiled. "We put it together brick by brick."

FIFTY-ONE

Bologna, September 1939

The BSO was performing Wagner's *Götterdämmerung* on September 1, the day the world exploded. It was as if we were hired to record the soundtrack. *Götterdämmerung,* Twilight of the Gods, is the story of the violent collapse of Valhalla, consumed in a massive fire, signaling the end of the old order. We were performing it on the stage in the Teatro, while on the world's stage a million Nazi troops were marching into Poland.

Hitler attacked Poland without warning, in a lightning strike they called "blitzkrieg." Britain and France declared war on Germany two days later. Russia entered the war two weeks later and moved into eastern Poland. Central Europe was on fire. And in Italy, everyone was looking to Mussolini. What was he going to do? Was he going to jump into the fray with his Axis partner? Was Italy going to declare war?

Days went by and Mussolini did nothing. The papers recorded the news from war correspondents in Poland, and everyone was glued to the radio, but the fighting could have been a million miles away. It was on the other side of the mountains in Central Europe. For Italians, it was someone else's war. They heard about it, they read about it and then they went about their business. For me, a German ex-pat, it hit home. It was exactly what my father warned me about.

I decided to visit Mama and make sure she was doing all right. A train to Siena and a bus ride to Pienza transported me from the bustling city into a pastoral dream world. Lush valleys, dark green mountains and hillside vineyards were all bursting into a rainbow of harvest colors. I got off the bus at Mama's property and walked up her long driveway to the villa.

Guido, the head caretaker, greeted me. "Ah, Ada, welcome back, but your mother is not at home," he said. "I took her into town to Signora Romitti. If you like, I can take you."

I set my bags down in the house, freshened up a little and accepted his gracious offer. The wagon ride into Pienza took only fifteen minutes. Mama didn't have a phone and I hadn't written that I would be coming — it was a spur-of-the-moment decision — so Mama was surprised to see me. I told

441

her I stopped by the villa.

"Did you love it? Do you like what I'm doing with it? Did you see the color of your bedroom? Did you see all the flowers I've been planting?"

I nodded. It warmed my heart to see her so enthusiastic. "I love what you've done. I can see you've brought your decorating expertise from Berlin to Pienza."

"Ada, I'm not just going to decorate. I'm going to learn how to manage a vineyard and grow grapes. There is a school in Siena that teaches viticulture. And Guido is going to train me as well. The duchess and her vineyards. What do you think?"

I was amazed. It was quite an undertaking but just what she needed. "I think that's wonderful," I said. "I didn't know you wanted to go back to school."

"Give your mother a little credit now and then, Miss Prodigy. I can learn too."

Naomi walked into the room and gave me a hug. "So you came to join us for Rosh Hashanah?"

Uh-oh, I thought. I hadn't been paying attention to the calendar and Natalia hadn't warned me. I didn't know it was time for the High Holy Days. They always seemed to sneak up on me. I smiled. "Is that today?"

Mama shot me an exasperated look. "No, my too-busy daughter. It's on the thirteenth."

I thought that smarty look was a little

unfair. My mother wasn't exactly the most observant person I knew. "I'll be here," I said. "I'll come with Natalia."

"I haven't heard from her in a while," Naomi said. "How is my daughter doing?"

Actually, I hadn't spoken with her since Hitler's invasion of Poland. I assumed that Natalia was involved in some way or another with underground organizations, planning or plotting or whatever they do, and I was worried about her. "She's fine," I lied.

I looked for Natalia when I returned to Bologna, but I didn't find her until shortly before I was to return to Pienza. I asked her where she'd been, but she waved me off.

"I promised your mother I'd bring you down for Rosh Hashanah," I said.

She winced. Natalia had forgotten about it as well, but she agreed, and we made plans to meet at the train.

"You look tired," I said when I saw her at Bologna Centrale.

"I haven't slept very much. I've been in Rome, off and on."

I was pretty certain that it had something to do with her network, but she didn't offer and I didn't ask. She napped the entire way from Bologna to Siena. When we did talk on the bus, it was hard not to discuss the war; it was practically the only subject on everyone's lips. As far as Natalia was concerned, Germany's attack of Poland was no surprise.

"Hitler threatened it on the radio every day," she said. "Anyone paying attention heard him scream about the oppressed German citizens in the Polish corridor. Just like he yelled before Austria and the Czech Sudeten mountains. He always talks about unifying the Germans when he wants to conquer free and independent countries. He's been building a huge military for years."

I knew about the military buildup since 1935 when Papa and I drove into the country. So did the rest of the world leaders, but they did nothing. What was so surprising was the ease with which Germany conquered Poland. It was over in a couple of weeks.

Great Britain and France had declared a state of war but had not attacked Germany or engaged in any military battles. According to Natalia, that was consistent with Britain's prime minister, Neville Chamberlain, and his conservative appeasement policies. With Germany in solid control of Poland, all the battles had ceased, although there were reports of clashes on the high seas between the British and German navies. All in all, even though a state of war had been declared, the battlefields were quiet.

Mama and I, along with all the Romittis, attended Rosh Hashanah services at the ancient *Sinagoga* in Pitigliano. It was an hour bus ride from Pienza and a lovely outing. We prayed where Jews had prayed four hundred years ago. It was the start of the New Year, the birthday of the world — *hayom harat olam* — ushering in the ten-day period of self-reflection and prayers for peace and forgiveness. No one wanted to talk about the war in Europe. Still, even the rabbi could not avoid leading us in prayers for the Polish people and the Jewish victims in Germany and the German-conquered territories.

We all hoped that this war, now involving Germany, England, France, Poland, Russia and Slovakia, would come to a quick cessation and not expand into another five-year period of world war. The fact that no military battles were waging was a promising sign. Through the fall, hopes were high that a resolution was possible.

Christmastime in Bologna was unaffected by the European state of war. My focus was on the Christmas concert series and my opportunity to play once more with Maestro Gigli. In that way, I was not much different from any other Bolognese. Shop owners opened their doors every morning. Students went to school. Life was pretty normal. Even

445

the racial laws of 1938, mostly ignored, had very little effect on daily life in Italy.

As always, the Christmas concerts were sold out. Maestro Gigli greeted me like an old friend. He told me that in June 1940, he would be performing at the Baths of Caracalla again. Could I find it in my schedule to join him? Could I ever! The previous June, I played with Gigli and the Rome Opera Orchestra at Caracalla. I also soloed with Mr. Gigli in two numbers. I don't know why he took such a liking to me — the Rome orchestra had many fine players — but I wasn't about to complain.

I made New Year's Eve plans with Franny, Natalia and Genia. We were going out to Cesare's for dinner and then to the Piazza Maggiore for the midnight music and fireworks display. Franny was now engaged to Michael and he arranged for three of his friends to come along. There were eight of us at Cesare's and the wine was flowing. The guys paired up with the girls, and my date turned out to be a nice fellow named Denys. He was a mathematics student from Greece.

Sitting around the table, we debated what was going to happen in the war. All of us had very strong opinions based upon very little information. "Italy's never getting into this mess," Michael said. "Mussolini's too smart. Let them all fight it out on the other side of the mountains."

Giorgio agreed. "Hitler and Churchill and Stalin, let them carve up Central Europe. It's got nothing to do with us."

But Natalia shook her head, as if to say naïveté is running rampant tonight. She smiled wistfully.

"What?" I said.

She shook her head. She didn't want to get pulled into the discussion, and I understood. She had real information, but she couldn't say where she got it. She did give us something to think about, though. "Italy has limited resources, especially where coal and oil are concerned," she said. "It comes to us by ship, either through the Suez Canal or through the Strait of Gibraltar. Since September, Britain has been blockading the shipments." She shrugged. "Sooner or later something's got to give."

Once the conversation changed subjects, it became a lot more lively. Fashion, food, music and pop personalities dominated the table talk. We finished dinner and walked over to the piazza. Denys was shy, but he reached for my hand and we walked together. He was taller than me, with tousled hair and an infectious smile. We embraced at midnight and kissed under the fireworks, but that's as far as I would let it go. I wasn't ready to get involved. It wasn't just loyalty to Kurt, who was a million miles away in the middle of a war. I was just reluctant to get entangled with someone who would interfere with my career.

The BSO had an ambitious spring travel schedule. We were performing Verdi's *Un Ballo in Maschera,* A Masked Ball, in three northern Italian cities during the annual Verdi celebration. I looked forward to playing in Modena, Parma and Ferrara, where I had never been before. The tour would begin in March. Then in June, I would once again return to Rome for the Gigli concert. In between, I would visit Mama as often as I could. I was going to be a busy traveler, and I didn't want a serious relationship creating scheduling conflicts and demands.

FIFTY-TWO

Bologna, June 1940

Natalia had predicted it and she was right. With the economy struggling and Italy's dependence on Germany for raw materials, it was only a matter of time. Mussolini declared war on France and Great Britain on June 10. Our hopes that the war would not widen and that peace would prevail were quickly shattered. For months, they called it the "phony war," because it was a war of economics only. There were no theaters of battle. No new invasions. No expeditionary forces sent from Britain or France.

Then in May, Hitler invaded the Netherlands and Belgium. Natalia said it was his way of preparing to invade France, and sure enough, on May 10, the German army crossed into France. Now it was June and Italy was in the war. Newspaper reports told us that the Italian army had crossed the Franco-Italian border and occupied a swath of land from Nice to Grenoble. According to Natalia, it was Mussolini's way of grabbing the spoils. "He wants a seat at the peace table," she said.

How did all that change life in Italy? Other than the occasional groups of uniformed Germans who happened to be passing through Bologna, not much that I could see. It was something to read about when you came home from work and before you went out for the evening. The fighting was far from our home. More than most, I had seen what the Nazis did to their victims, and I was terrified to see them wandering through my town or sitting at the opera. But they were transitory, and whatever brought them to Bologna took them away soon enough.

"In every country that Germany occupies, the Nazis enforce their nazification," Natalia said to us one evening around a café table. "Their hatred of Jews, their hatred of Gypsies, their hatred of disabled people, their hatred of non-Aryans or anyone different propels them to savage persecution. In occupied countries, Jews are forced to wear armbands or yellow stars, visibly separating them from the rest of the populace. They are horribly mistreated and to the greatest extent possible, excluded from society. Of course, I don't have to tell you that, Ada. You saw it for yourself."

For Jews in Italy, we were safer being

450

Hitler's friend than his enemy. That was the ironic truth. We did not fear German invasion or occupation. As Hitler's strongest ally, Italy was free to be Italy.

"What happens when Hitler decides that his good buddy Mussolini isn't tough enough on Jews or doesn't adhere to Nazi policies closely enough?" I said. "Then what, Nat? Does he send his troops south? Germany gets stronger every day. He conquers more of Europe every day. When does he hunger for Rome?"

That seemed to be a conversation killer. Everyone just took another sip of wine.

The Baths of Caracalla, built two thousand years ago, was a Roman feat of engineering providing heated water through aqueducts to large public baths. Only the ruins remain and serve as a picturesque backdrop to an open-air concert venue, which in its setting is second to none. The opera stage was constructed less than ten years ago over what would have been the steam room. Opera performances began here in 1937.

The Rome Opera was performing four nights of Pagliacci, starring Beniamino Gigli. On June 22, Gigli was scheduled for his annual solo concert, the one to which I was invited. The evening was warm. The sun did not set until almost nine o'clock. The

451

copper-colored towers of Terme di Caracalla surrounded us, and in the moment, one could imagine we would be performing for Julius Caesar and the Roman Senate. Gigli asked me to accompany him on his second encore, his trademark aria from *The Pearl Fishers.* It was always incredible to me how silent two thousand people could become when Maestro Gigli raised his palms and sang so softly. Even the birds stopped to listen. When it was over and I looked at the audience, standing and shouting, it was hard to believe I was anywhere but in music heaven.

After the concert, Maestro Gigli introduced me to Bernardino Molinari, the conductor of the Rome Opera and also the prestigious Rome Symphony Orchestra. It was a fortuitous introduction, one that would play a significant role in my life.

Maestro Molinari had kind words to say about my father, whom he had met several years ago when he guest-conducted in Berlin. Maestro Gigli made me promise to play for him next Christmas in Bologna and the following June in Caracalla. The entire two days I was in Rome, not a word was said about the war. The next morning, I took the train to Siena and the bus to Mama's house.

It was grand to see my mother, healthy and

strong, working in her vineyards. She had become so knowledgeable in such a short period of time. It had been little more than a year, but you'd have thought that this Berlin socialite had been born to the Tuscan countryside. In her wide-brimmed hat and with her white dress billowing in the wind, she took me into the vineyards to explain what she was doing. And that she had a surprise for me.

We walked to an area where the ground had been cleared for planting. "This section will be perfect for Sangiovese, Ada. There is a gentle lift to the slope at about four hundred meters. It faces southwest and will grab the sun all day long. Do you want to plant it with me?"

I hesitated. "Mama, I don't know what I'm doing. My fingers are only good for playing a violin. I'll watch you plant."

She would have none of it. "Nonsense. You'll help, and we'll name this little patch Ada's Vineyard."

FIFTY-THREE

Bologna, October 1940

Maestro Vittorio announced in mid-October that the BSO would once again travel to Florence to play for Hitler, who was coming to Florence to meet with Mussolini. In September, Italy, Germany and the Empire of Japan had signed a joint defense agreement called the Tripartite Pact. Now the German chancellor was coming to Florence for a high-level strategy meeting following the Italian army's failures on the Greek peninsula.

Although the war was still far from our borders, Italy had sent troops into France, North Africa and, most recently, Greece. From what Natalia had learned, the Greek incursion was a disaster and the Italian troops were in retreat. She was sure that was why Hitler demanded a face-to-face with Il Duce. While Hitler was in Florence, he was to be wined and dined and entertained. We were scheduled to play in his honor in the Piazza della Signoria on October 29.

Hitler did not come to Italy alone. This was a high-level wartime meeting with top military advisers from both countries. Reichsmarschall Hermann Göring, the second most powerful man in Germany and leader of the German armed forces, accompanied Hitler. For the entire week, Florence was inundated with SS and Wehrmacht soldiers. There must have been a thousand of them. Everywhere you went, you bumped into a German.

As I walked through the narrow streets of Florence, I shuddered. This was what life would be like if Hitler invaded Italy, and let there be no illusions, he could have Italy if he wanted. But there was this strange mutual affection between Der Führer and Il Duce. They were partners. They had negotiated and signed the Tripartite Pact. The uniformed Germans flooding the streets were here for a state visit, not to impose martial law or persecute Jews. Still, when we walked around, we could feel their eyes.

Hitler and Mussolini met all day on October 28. We were in the middle of setting up for our concert when we learned that Hitler had abruptly gone home. There were rumors that he became frustrated and enraged at Il Duce, lost his patience, stormed out and returned directly to Berlin. With

Hitler gone and the state visit terminated, the organizers canceled all plans for the outdoor celebration.

Our train back to Bologna did not leave until the next morning, so we had an afternoon and evening free to wander about in this most congenial city. Some of the orchestra members had friends or family in Florence. Others, like me, were on their own for a night out in the birthplace of the Renaissance. I was standing in the market, shopping for a leather coat, when someone tapped me on the shoulder. I spun around and looked directly into the blue eyes of Sergeant Kurt Koenig in full uniform.

"Oh my God! What are you doing here?" I said.

"I'm on the Reichsmarschall's detail," he said, with an impish smile, "but Göring ducked out with Hitler and returned to Berlin before they could make travel arrangements for the rest of us. Our unit pulls out tomorrow."

"Is that also Kleiner's detail?" I said, and a shiver went down my spine.

He shook his head. "No, no. I'm in a different unit now. I've been promoted, and I'm generally sent in with the administrative personnel. You know me, I'm a record-keeper. I don't even carry a handgun."

I knew the kinds of records Nazis kept: who were the Jews and what did they own.

Now I was hearing stories about Jews being forced to move into walled ghettoes. I had to ask: "What kind of records do you keep, Kurt?"

"It's all logistics, Ada. How many motorized vehicles we have in any given area. What is necessary to move food and equipment from one place to another. On an assignment like this, I keep track of personnel, how they get to and from Florence, where they are bivouacked, how much food is needed. I don't make decisions, I just keep the records."

"Well, I glad you're not keeping track of Jews."

"Come on, Ada, you know me better than that."

I did know him better than that. He went out on a limb to save my father. But he was standing before me in full Nazi regalia and it gave me the creeps. I loved him, but I wished he wasn't wearing that uniform. I wished he wasn't German at all.

"And you're not with Kleiner? What ever happened to him? Something bad, I hope."

Kurt shook his head. "No, he's climbing ladders. He's been promoted to second lieutenant. His unit generally follows the expeditionary forces and imposes Nazi policies on the occupied countries. He's an enforcer, a brutal man. They call him 'The Hammer.' I think he's in Paris now."

457

"So, you're here in Florence and your boss is gone. What are you doing today?"

"Nothing. Enjoying this fabulous city." He pointed to the right, to a long three-story white-and-gray building with hundreds of recessed, sculpted windows. "I was planning on visiting the Uffizi Gallery. Do you want to come with me?"

To some, it might have seemed odd that a uniformed Wehrmacht sergeant would be strolling through the world-famous art museum studying the paintings, but then Kurt had always been interested in art. And music. My Renaissance boyfriend. Maybe that's what attracted me to him, other than his dashing good looks. He was gentle, kind and cultured. Not exactly what you'd expect in a career Wehrmacht officer. I wished we were on a romantic getaway, just the two of us. I wished we weren't on opposite sides. I wished there was no damned war.

We strolled through the halls of the Uffizi, making small talk. He told me again how sorry he was about my father, but he thought Papa had made the right decision. "I doubt that Furtwängler could have saved him," he said. "Your papa was right. I admired him."

I shook my head. "It haunts me, Kurt. Every day. I could have stopped him. At that point in time, I was the strong one. I should have taken it into my hands. I was the one who should have made the decision. He

458

was beaten down, he was weak."

"Don't say that, Ada. Don't even think that. Your father was brave, he was strong. That was the most noble act I've ever seen. He knew what he was doing. If your father had transferred his money to the Gestapo, they wouldn't have honored their promise. They'd have put him right back into Buchenwald. He knew that. He stood up to them and sacrificed himself for his family. He made sure you and your mother were secure. Please don't ever let me hear you call him weak."

I started sobbing. Kurt took me in his arms and we walked into an alcove. "He was proud right up to the end," Kurt said to me in a whisper. "Proud of you and proud of what he was doing. All the way back to Buchenwald he raved about you. He loved his family and made a hard decision. He died with his honor and his legacy intact. I hope that if the time ever comes, I will have that kind of courage."

It took me a few minutes to regain my composure. Kurt stood by me. I took a deep breath and we continued with our walk. I asked him about his father. He shrugged. "He's deployed somewhere, maybe in Poland," he said. "We haven't had much to say to each other over the past few years."

It was so comfortable being with him. I didn't see the uniform, I saw only Kurt. It had been exactly two years since I'd last seen him, and given the circumstances, two years was a lifetime. We had each taken such different paths; we were such different people. But when he touched me, when he held me, we were the same. No time had passed.

Out of the blue, I asked him if he had a girlfriend. It just popped out of my mouth. I wanted to know. He wasn't expecting it. He was a little flustered.

"A girlfriend?" he said, bashfully. He thought for a minute. "A girlfriend? Nope, not since Junior. After Ada Baumgarten, they all seem very shallow." He shrugged his shoulders and smiled.

"Aww."

"Seriously, the girls I've met, the ones I've gone out with, they're fascinated by things that do not interest me at all. But then, I don't have much time for socializing. How about you, Ada?"

I smiled. "Same. Nobody since Junior. Nobody but Kurt."

Our walk had taken us up to Botticelli's *The Birth of Venus* and Kurt stopped. "Not to be missed," he said. We stood before the painting, and once again Kurt amazed me with his knowledge of the humanities. "Botticelli painted this masterpiece four hundred and fifty years ago," he said. "I've always wanted to see it in person."

I had to admit, it was a lovely painting. It was a picture of Venus with long blond hair, standing naked on a seashell. There were figures to her left and right. I was pretty sure Kurt knew all about it. "Tell me what it means," I said.

Kurt smiled. "The figures on the left, the ones in the air, they are Zephyr, god of the winds, and in his arms, Aura, goddess of the breeze. They have blown Venus from the sea where she was conceived. That's why Venus is standing on a seashell. Do you see how her hair is moved by the breeze? To her right is Hora, goddess of spring, who stands holding a cloak with May flowers, offering to cover Venus' nudity."

"It is magnificent," I said, "and Botticelli's Venus is simply gorgeous."

Kurt nodded. "She is the goddess of beauty. She is the inspiration for human love. Botticelli painted an alluring but shy Venus, which, it is said, he modeled after Simonetta Vespucci, mistress to the Medicis."

We stood for a few minutes. Kurt was entranced. The painting exuded pure sensuality, and the effect was not lost on either of us. I was totally entranced, not only with the painting but also with my boyfriend. All I wanted was to be alone with him. To my delight, he had the same feelings. Kurt took my hand and led me from the gallery. We walked straight to a small hotel and booked a room for the night. I had to pay for the room: they didn't take reichsmarks. I didn't mind.

Kurt was nervous and so was I. It took so long to get his complicated uniform off; it sent us both into laughter. I wanted it all to be perfect. And it was. It was a magical night and the morning broke much too soon. "Do we have to leave?" I said, lying in the crook of his arm. "Let's stay. We could live here in Florence. I'll play my violin in the restaurants. The money is surprisingly good. You could be an art professor."

He chuckled.

"Seriously, Kurt. I'm very happy right now. I don't have to go anywhere else. Ever."

"I wish we could."

"Then we can. No one has a right to tell us that we can't be together. Damn Hitler. Damn Germany. Let's run off together."

"Ada, I'm in the army. They shoot deserters. But I want you to hold that dream. This war won't last forever, and afterward we will make that dream come true. I promise."

I begged him to stay in touch, but he was nervous about sending mail to me. The discovery of our correspondence could condemn us both. We finally agreed that he could send a letter every once in a while, addressed to the Bologna State Opera ticket office, attn: Francesca. Franny would know what to do with it.

We parted at the train station without knowing how or when we'd see each other again. It was one of those scenes from a movie. I cried like a baby.

FIFTY-FOUR

Pienza, September 2017

Catherine was packing to go home for a long weekend. "My poor Ben, he won't even recognize me. I've been gone so long."

"You've talked to him, FaceTime'd him, Skype'd him, whatever. How many times can Carol plant him in front of a computer?"

"It's not the same. I want to hold him."

"You went back two weeks ago. I'm not saying you shouldn't go, but you should quit feeling so guilty. He's doing fine with Sarah and his aunt and his cousins."

"Don't you miss him?"

"Of course, I miss him. But I have confidence that my two-year-old will still recognize me when I finish this assignment. We still have work to do if we're going to save Gabi's farm."

"I can still hear the judge's words in my head," Catherine said. " 'Missing evidence is not the same as admissible evidence. *Evidence!* Not theory, not supposition, not conclusions to be drawn from mysteriously missing books. *Evidence!*' And as of this date, we don't have it, Liam."

"I think the judge is sympathetic," Giulia said. "Who wouldn't be? A big corporation picking on an elderly woman. But you're right, Catherine. We need physical evidence. If we only had something tangible in our hands to back up the testimony from Berto and Hernandez. It would supplement the inferences from the missing documents. That registry book must be somewhere."

"I think we need to face facts," Liam said. "We're not going to find the book. If it ever existed outside the registrar's office, it has long ago been incinerated. Fabio saw the page, Fabio was bribed to hide the book and Fabio is dead. Vanucci is dead and any nominee agreement that existed in Hernandez's files has long ago been shredded. Let's face it: Lenzini has covered his tracks."

Catherine crossed her arms on her chest. "So, you want to give up?"

"You know me better than that. We need to find evidence, and it's not where we've been looking. We need to expand our search parameters. Look elsewhere. I think we need to start with the Quercia Company. How does some German woman come to own an Italian wine company? How did Quercia come to be listed in the registry book for land once owned by Friede Baumgarten? What the

465

hell is the Quercia Company?"

"When you involved me in this case, I did a quick check on Quercia," Giulia said. "It was organized some seventy-five years ago. It had one shareholder."

"Gerda Fruman?"

"Actually, the shareholder was a German trust. The German court held that Gerda Fruman was the sole beneficiary of the trust. So, in essence, Fruman was the sole owner of Quercia."

"That's a lot of effort to disguise the real owner," Catherine said.

Liam pursed his lips and nodded. "You're right. It's damn confusing. On purpose. It's bigger than a person named Gerda Fruman. According to Franco, she never set foot on the property. Maybe we need to start in Germany. Giulia, do you know an attorney in Berlin?"

She shook her head.

"I bet Walter does," Catherine said. "He has a network of law firms he works with all over the world."

"Who is Walter?" Giulia asked.

Liam and Catherine laughed simultaneously. "The eminent Walter Jenkins, senior partner in the Chicago firm of Jenkins and Fairchild, Catherine's first boss," Liam said. "Jenkins fired Catherine eight years ago over the representation of a Holocaust survivor named Ben Solomon. He gave Cat an ultimatum: 'Withdraw from Solomon's case or you're fired.' Since my baby doesn't take crap from anybody, she walked right out the door."

Catherine shook her head. "We had a difference of opinion on whether we should continue to represent someone who offended Jenkins and Fairchild's elite clients. Walter felt that continuing to represent Ben was harmful to our practice. That's all it was. I chose to leave the firm."

"Good for you," Giulia said. "But why would Walter help us?"

"Bygones are bygones," Liam said. "A few years later, Cat and I bailed his firm out of a jam when one of his lawyers was involved in wire transfer fraud. A year after that, Jenkins personally represented Catherine in a contempt hearing when my hard-nosed wife wouldn't divulge a confidential conversation with her client and a judge was going to throw her into jail."

"And you think that Walter Jenkins might know an attorney in Berlin?"

"I'm sure that Jenkins and Fairchild has done business with German industries," Catherine said. "He would know someone."

"Of course I know a lawyer in Berlin," Walter said. "Gunther Strauss. He offices in that huge Sony building in the Potsdamer Platz. Why do you need him?"

"Liam and I are involved in a case in Italy.

It's a dispute over a vineyard in Tuscany."

"A vineyard in Tuscany? How do you get cases like that? Do you need co-counsel? I'm available."

"Thanks, but what we really need is to research our opponent, a corporation that appears as owner of record. We're challenging the ownership. It's an Italian corporation owned by a German trust."

"Sounds like somebody's hiding something. Well, Gunther's very well connected. He can get things done in Berlin, if you know what I mean. He'll help you out. He's a good guy. Tell him I said hello."

"Mr. Strauss, this is Catherine Lockhart. I used to be an associate at Jenkins and Fairchild."

"My sympathies, I've played golf with Walter."

"He said to send his regards. I'm working on a matter in Pienza, Italy, and I need your help."

"In Italy? Do you need me there personally?"

"No, I'm sorry. We need work done in Berlin."

"Oh, that's a shame. What kind of work do you need?"

"We represent a woman in a dispute over who owns a farm in the province of Siena. The registry book lists an Italian company as the owner. We believe the book is in error. We're challenging the corporation's claim to title. The company's name is the Quercia Company. The sole shareholder is supposedly a German family trust. We'd like to know as much about that trust as possible. We'd also like to research the sole beneficiary, Gerda Fruman, who died sometime in 2015."

"We can do that. Would you like me to bring the report to you personally?"

"That's not at all necessary."

"Maybe not for you, but Siena in September would do me a world of good."

"Ha. We'd love to have you, but the report is all we need."

The report was delivered to Giulia's office two days later. It read:

Dear Attorney Lockhart:
We are pleased to present the results of our research into the Quercia Company S.p.A. and its shareholders. Our research led us to a 2015 file in the Berlin probate court. When Gerda Fruman died, a deccdent's estate was opened by petition of VinCo S.p.A., an Italian corporation, alleged to be a creditor of Quercia Company. The information for this report is extracted from details we found in the probate file.

Quercia Company. Formed May 18,

1944, in Italy. The corporation was organized by Hermann Rugel, attorney-at-law, who practiced on Friedrichstrasse in Berlin. The single shareholder was a trust. Neither the trust agreement nor its records were found in the probate file. Apparently, Mr. Rugel knew how to hide ownership. According to the probate court records, the sole beneficiary of the trust was Elsa Fruman, Gerda's mother, an unmarried woman. We cannot determine whether or not the Quercia Company ever did business. No income tax return has ever been filed here or in Italy. However, annual corporate filings identify a parcel of farmland owned by the corporation in Siena Province. It doesn't appear from any records we can find that the company had an ongoing business. It is our opinion that the company was formed for the sole purpose of holding the land, perhaps as an investment for future sale. There are no other corporate records that we have been able to locate. Neither the probate file, nor any corporate filings disclose how Quercia Company acquired ownership of the farmland. The location of Mr. Rugel's office was a building on Friedrichstrasse that was destroyed during the Allied bombing in 1945. Mr. Rugel's death is recorded in 1947. If there were successors to his practice, it would have been in East Germany and there are no records that we can find.

Gerda Fruman. Born April 4, 1944, in Munich, Germany; died January 16, 2015, in Berlin. Her mother was Elsa Fruman, the original beneficiary of the trust. There is no father identified on the birth certificate, but it was not legally necessary to name the father. As far as we can tell, Gerda Fruman was never married and did not have any children. She lived in East Berlin until German unification in 1990. Tax records for the years 1992 through 2001 reflect she was a clerk in a medical office, earning a modest clerk's salary. As sole heir to Elsa Fruman, she would have inherited her mother's interest in Quercia Company upon Elsa's death in 1956, although there were no probate proceedings ever instituted for Elsa. The tax records do not reflect that Gerda received any money from farming operations. We think it is likely that Gerda never knew that her mother owned Quercia. Within two weeks after Gerda's death, a probate proceeding was opened by VinCo, which claimed to be a creditor of Quercia, in that VinCo allegedly provided maintenance for Quercia's vineyard during Gerda's life. VinCo offered to buy the property for the value of the maintenance it had provided. The court ruled that

Elsa's interest was inherited by Gerda and thus could be sold to VinCo. There were no other parties in the probate proceeding and no one was there to object. Having conveyed the property to VinCo, the probate case was closed.

We are pleased to be of service to you in this matter. Please allow us to provide any further services you deem necessary.

Yours truly,
Gunther Strauss

"Well, that's a whole lot of nothing," Giulia said to Catherine on speakerphone. "We don't know any more now than we knew before."

Liam held his finger up. "Not true. We know that the Quercia Company was formed by a German lawyer at the very same time that it first appeared in the registry book — 1944. We also know that great pains were taken to keep Elsa Fruman's identity hidden, first by a corporation and then by a trust agreement. If you were to check the corporation, you would only see that it was owned by a trust. We know that Elsa was a single mother with one child. Maybe she or her child didn't know anything about the vineyard. It makes me think that Elsa was a placeholder. The same with Gerda. Someone else was pulling the strings. Then suddenly, immediately after Gerda dies, VinCo petitions the court to buy her interest. Two weeks! How did VinCo know she died? How did VinCo, this large Italian company, know anything about Elsa or Gerda? The trust kept their identities hidden."

"And what is this nonsense about maintaining Gabi's property?" Catherine said. "From what I've read, Friede was taking care of the property. She was going to viticulture school. Franco and his family have been taking care of the property for the last fifty years. I bet if we asked Franco if VinCo ever maintained the property he'd say no."

"There's something else," Liam said. "In Ada's story, she wrote that Matteo had a new camera and took pictures when Friede bought the property, right?"

Catherine groaned. "I'm not that caught up, remember? I'm a few chapters behind you."

"Here's what she wrote: Matteo took pictures of the group holding glasses of prosecco to celebrate when Friede bought the property. Friede, Ada, Signor Partini, Hernandez and a real estate agent named Sylvia were all in the picture. What if the deed is visible?"

Catherine chuckled. "I love the way you think, but that is what you call a real long shot. What's the chance that a deed is readable in a photo taken in 1939? Matteo was Natalia's older brother. He would not be alive today, nor would Natalia. The purchase was eighty-eight years ago and both of them were in their twenties at the time."

"Natalia and her family lived in Pienza," Giulia said. "I could see if any members of her family are still in the area."

"You know what confounds me?" Liam said. "With all the efforts to hide the owner, and a secret trust agreement, how did VinCo know about Gerda Fruman? She's not listed anywhere. And how would VinCo know to open an estate just two weeks after her death? There's way too many coincidences."

"And we don't believe in coincidences."

"We do not."

"Something else that's hard to believe," Catherine said, "is that you're still two chapters ahead of me in Ada's story and that you stay up late at night reading it."

"You want something else that's hard to believe? Last night I heard the violin."

"I knew it! I knew it!"

FIFTY-FIVE

Bologna, December 1941

Another year had come and gone. I hadn't seen Kurt since Florence, but I did receive three letters. He took care not to identify me and his sentiments were expressed in general terms. He was doing well. German confidence was high. Kurt couldn't tell me where he was or what he was doing, but he hoped his assignments would bring him back to where we last met. As always, he said he thought about me all the time and hoped to see me soon. He ended every letter with a sweet reminiscence of our night in that special hotel.

I followed the war closely in the newspapers and on the radio. From the reports in the Italian newspapers, the Axis troops had conquered all of Central Europe and were on Moscow's doorstep. North Africa was under Axis domination. The Mediterranean was an Axis fishing pond. There was reason to believe that the war could be concluded within the next year.

For me, that was conflicting news. I hated the Nazis, but I feared for Kurt's safety. So I ended up praying for the collapse and total defeat of Germany and everything it stood for, with the exception of a certain sergeant who worked keeping records of motor vehicles in an administrative office.

Back in Bologna, the war was on everyone's lips and everyone thought they had the latest news. They were mostly wrong, but Natalia, on the few occasions I saw her, actually did have the latest information. She was the first one to tell me about Operation Barbarossa — Germany's invasion of the Soviet Union, which began on June 22. Within days we heard that Mussolini had also declared war on the Soviet Union.

Natalia had a contact at the Excelsior Hotel in Rome, a part of her underground organization. She told me about a meeting at the hotel between the Japanese foreign minister and Mussolini on December 3. From what she understood, Japan was urging Italy to declare war on the United States in accordance with the Tripartite Pact. Natalia and her contact thought the request was odd and out of place — until four days later, when Japan attacked Pearl Harbor.

Italy continued mobilizing its troops. We now had divisions fighting in Egypt and Libya. Italian submarines were patrolling the

Mediterranean and the Black Sea, and the Italian air force, the Regia Aeronautica Italiana, was supporting the Luftwaffe. Many of the men in our social group were leaving: the Italians were being conscripted, and the foreign students were returning to their home countries. Some came from the Slovakia, some from Croatia and some from Hungary.

The orchestra lost three members to the army, and a sign was posted announcing auditions for a bassoonist. Our travel dates had been curtailed, and although our performances at the Teatro continued, lead roles were often filled with stand-ins or members of the opera school.

The days of pretending that it was someone else's war were over. There was no more life as usual in Bologna. The economy was on a war footing. Many items were rationed or not available at all. Cosmetics were in short supply. Forget about nylons. Automotive supplies, like rubber tires and gasoline, were impossibly scarce. Abandoned cars were seen along the highways.

We would frequently encounter injured or maimed boys returning from North Africa, from cities I didn't recognize, like Tobruk, Benghazi and El Agheila. They would tell of fierce fighting and the German commander General Erwin Rommel, the man they called the Desert Fox. But they would also tell about the strong opposition from the British, Australian and Canadian forces.

Maestro Gigli sent a letter to Sister Mary Alicia, informing her that he would not be appearing at the 1941 Christmas concert. In the envelope was a separate letter to me. "Although I regret not appearing in Bologna, it is still my intent to perform at Caracalla in June, and I would be pleased if you would attend as you have in the past," he wrote. I replied that I would be honored.

The Christmas concert went on, but without any star soloists and only for one night. Though the city was gaily lit for the season, festivities were reserved. We were more fortunate than Central European states. The battles were far from our borders. There were no bombing raids, no reason to have blackouts or to run to air-raid shelters.

Because we had fewer performance dates, and thus fewer rehearsal dates, I was able to spend more time with my mother. Traveling into Tuscany still remained an idyllic delight. Mama was totally absorbed in her farming and her vineyards and she looked marvelous. She was oblivious to the war.

It was so peaceful at the villa. I spent my days practicing and learning new pieces. Mama would ask me to sit on the veranda and play melodies while she worked in her flower gardens. On those occasions, it was hard to fathom that a war was going on all around us. It was also hard to conceive that our Jewish brethren were being corralled into ghettoes and forced into slave labor. In those days, the wolf was far from our door.

As December was drawing to a close, we were visited by a neighbor, one who owned the vineyards directly to the east. She told us that it was the custom among some of the landowners to celebrate New Year's Eve together and this year she was hosting. Since we had never come before, she wondered if the two of us would like to attend.

Mama was thrilled. She hadn't met any of her neighbors, and it was an opportunity to make new friends. "You will meet families that own the farms all around you in every direction," the woman said. "Bring something good to eat and a bottle of your estate wine." Mama promised to bring a pie. I offered to bring the music.

The hosting villa was very similar to Mama's house. Perhaps all these houses were built for tenant farmers when the church owned the land. There were six different families at the party. They all knew one another and were happy to welcome Mama into the group. Everyone brought a bottle of their own estate wine, specially wrapped for the occasion. They were all farmers just like Mama, and everyone lived within a few kilometers. Naturally, the dominant topic of discussion was this year's crop and all the nuances that went along with bringing it in.

FIFTY-SIX

Bologna, June 1942

I was preparing to leave for Rome, to perform in my annual June concert with the Rome Opera Orchestra and Beniamino Gigli, when Natalia knocked on my door. I hadn't seen her very much over the previous six months. Natalia confided to me that she and her compatriots were busy trying to find homes for Jewish refugees flowing in from Italian-occupied territories like Croatia and eastern France.

"I've been traveling," she said to me, "and I'm exhausted, but I have a situation, and if you're willing, you can help. I've been to Rome too often lately, and I think I'm arousing suspicion at the Excelsior Hotel. Tomaso is the head of catering and one of our best resources. He comes into contact with key military and political officials all the time. I need to get a message to him right away."

"And you're telling me this because I'm going to Rome in two days?"

"Exactly. We can get you a room at the Excelsior. You wouldn't arouse any suspicion because you're a famous artist performing at Caracalla."

"I've never stayed at the Excelsior. It's way over my budget."

"We'll cover it."

It made me a little nervous, but it was kind of exciting. "What would I have to do?"

"Just check into the Excelsior, find Tomaso and hand him an envelope."

"Maybe this is a dumb question, but how do I find Tomaso?"

"He works in catering, Ada. Be resourceful."

I was willing, but I must have looked tentative, because she said, "Ada, this is really an important time for us in Italy. Just last month, the Americans started providing assistance to the British in North Africa. The Germans are overextended, and the Italian army is in shambles. Soon the tide will turn. Italians don't give a damn about the Nazis or their war. Our country doesn't really support Mussolini — I hear it everywhere I go. You get that sense too, don't you, Ada? When the time comes, we must be ready here on the home front."

I boarded the train for Rome, just a three-hour ride, but it seemed to take forever. I had the envelope in my violin case underneath my music. The conductor came by and took my ticket without a second glance. This certainly wasn't a German train. It all seemed calm enough until a group of uniformed German soldiers boarded the train in Florence. Lately, it wasn't uncommon to see German soldiers in their green uniforms or even the occasional SS officer in a black or gray uniform. As the war progressed, their presence increased. After all, they were our allies. The soldiers walked through the car looking for seats. One of them tapped me on the shoulder and motioned to the empty seat beside me. I nodded and slid over.

"Good morning, Fraulein," he said in German. "I see you are a musician."

I shook my head. *"No sprechen Deutsche,"* I said as clumsily as I could.

"Italienerin?"

I nodded.

"Buongiorno," he said in a heavy German accent, but with a big smile. He pointed to my violin case. *"Violino?"*

I nodded.

"Suonare canzone?" he said with a wide grin, and his eyebrows lifted. He wanted me to play a song.

No way was I going to open my violin case and expose Natalia's envelope. I shook my head. He chuckled. He asked me again and

I shook my head again. He started to reach for my violin case and I grabbed it, stood up and walked to another car. He didn't follow.

Roma Termini, the central train station, was always crowded and bustling, but now there were more uniformed men than ever, both Italian and German. I hustled through the station and caught a bus to Via Vittorio Veneto and the Excelsior Hotel, the grandest hotel in Rome, the definition of elegance. I was not used to this level of opulence. The expansive lobby was a beehive of men in suits, men in uniforms and well-dressed women. All of them seemed to have a purpose to their walk or a clandestine reason for the seat they occupied. I looked around the lobby trying to imagine who among them were spies. Maybe all of them. Me included.

I approached the desk to check in and the concierge said, "Welcome to the Excelsior, Signorina Baumgarten, we are honored to have you. Please allow us to arrange car service to your rehearsal today and your concert tomorrow night."

I was shocked. "Well, thank you," I said. "How did you know?"

"It is my business to know." He snapped his fingers and a uniformed bellman appeared who took my bag. The concierge gave my room key to the bellman and gestured for me to follow him. "Enjoy your stay," the concierge said. "Please let me know if I can do anything to make your stay more pleasant."

My room was on the third floor. The porter set my bag down and stood there waiting for a tip. I didn't know how much to give him. *A spy would know,* I thought. I reached into my purse and gave him twenty lire. He twisted his lips, spun around and shut the door behind him. I guess that wasn't enough. What did you get me into, Nat?

I needed to get rid of Natalia's envelope as soon as I could. I walked around the lobby looking for a sign that said "Catering." I looked at the hotel's phone directory, and I saw the number for catering, but I thought it was a bad idea to call and ask for Tomaso. I was also afraid to ask the concierge. What business would a visiting musician have with the catering department? For all I knew, the concierge was an informant for the Italian police or the secret service or, heaven forbid, the Gestapo.

Then I got a very amateur idea. I wandered out to the lobby entrance where the bellmen were handling luggage. I picked out one young fellow who looked innocent enough and I said, "My sister is looking for a job. Do you know if the catering department is hiring?"

He shrugged. "How would I know? I don't

work in the catering department."

"Could you tell me how to get to the catering director?"

He shook his head. "All applications for jobs are taken by the personnel department on the second floor."

I smiled nicely and said, "I think I'd do better if I went straight to the director, don't you?"

He put a big grin on his face. "Oh, your *sister,* is it? I get it." He pointed to his brain. "Pretty clever of you, I must say. Take the stairs to the basement level, go all the way to the right and ask for Tomaso."

Tomaso was a large man with a close-cropped beard. "Natalia asked me to see you," I said.

"Natalia? Who's Natalia? That doesn't mean anything to me."

"Is there another Tomaso in the catering department?" I said.

He got a disgusted look on his face. "Jesus Christ, the people they send. Come with me." He grabbed my arm and pulled me through the doorway.

When we were in the corridor, he said, "We don't use names. It gets people killed."

"Sorry. I'm not a professional messenger. I play the violin."

"Do you have something for me, Miss Violin Player?"

I handed him the envelope.

"Good work," he said. "Next time just order room service. I'll know who placed the order. Don't come looking for me. Now go."

I returned to the stairway and walked up to the lobby level. When I opened the door and walked across the lobby, I could have sworn the concierge was looking at me. I was a very nervous spy.

My telephone rang at 2:00 p.m. It was the concierge. *"Buon pomeriggio, Signorina Baumgarten.* Your car is downstairs to take you to your rehearsal."

A large, black Mercedes was sitting at the curb, and a uniformed driver stood by the open door. I could get used to this. I slid into the backseat where Maestro Gigli was already seated and smiling at me. "Are we ready for a lovely concert?" he said. Then he added, "Tomorrow, right after the intermission and before I am to return to the stage, I would like an instrumental. Something rousing, full of life, to get the crowd excited and ready for the second half of the concert. I think it should be you. Do you have such a piece?"

I had been working on Pablo de Sarasate's *Zigeunerweisen,* the Bohemian airs — a real showstopper for violin and orchestra. I had studied it as an exercise for solo violin. It was a very tough piece, but I was getting good at it. "What about the *Zigeuner-*

weisen?" I said.

"That's wonderful, just what I had in mind. I will ask Bernardino to add the piece. I'm sure the orchestra has it in their vast repertoire."

Then it hit me and I gulped. A solo at Caracalla? The Roman Baths? Me on the stage with the Rome Opera Orchestra? In a ridiculously hard piece? My first inclination was to back out, respectfully decline, suggest that someone else should play it. But then I thought about my father, the last words he would ever say to me: "Never forget for an instant that you have all the tools, all the ability and all the talent that God ever gave to a musician. Show the world what you've got. You are my Ada, my prodigy."

"I would be honored," I said, "and grateful for your confidence."

That afternoon, Maestro Molinari told the orchestra that they were adding *Zigeunerweisen* to the program. His first violinist almost had a heart attack until Molinari said, "Miss Baumgarten will solo."

The night of the concert, it was warm and clear. A million stars shone over the pines and Roman ruins. This event was one of the summer highlights of the Roman music scene, and I was to solo! After the intermission, when it was time for the second half of Gigli's concert, I walked out to enthusiastic applause.

Molinari smiled at me, winked and quietly said, "Good luck, young lady." I didn't need luck. It was one of those days. I felt it in my bones. Everything was working.

The piece starts with a bold orchestral intro. The eight-minute composition consists of four sections played without pause. The second section is technically challenging but with room for improvisation. The third has sweet, familiar Gypsy melodies and opportunities for a violinist to show off her passion and emotion. The fourth section is lively, an all-out race to the end — *allegro molto vivace* — with extremely rapid fingering, difficult runs and a left-hand *pizzicato.* I was loving it. I might have made a few mistakes along the way, but I don't think anyone noticed. I finished in a flourish and bowed.

"Brava, Signorina," Molinari said as he smiled down at me. Then he tipped his head toward the audience. When I looked, they were all on their feet and cheering.

The next morning, a copy of the daily newspaper was delivered to my room with a red rose. The paper was folded on page twelve to show the headline: "Gigli and Baumgarten Shine at Caracalla."

489

FIFTY-SEVEN

Bologna, February 1943

Once again, tragedy had entered my life. My beloved conductor and the music director of the Bologna State Opera, Maestro Stefano Vittorio, had died. At rehearsal yesterday, he looked tired and disoriented. He stumbled while at the podium and shook his head as if to clear some cobwebs. When he started conducting again, he was out of sync, not at all in touch with the music. He was waving his arms erratically, almost flailing. We all looked at one another, knowing something was terribly wrong. We could see that he was struggling to hang on, to focus his mind, to bring it back to the present, to his orchestra, to the Teatro, but he was losing his hold. The here and now was leaving him. He tipped to the side and grabbed at the podium. Lassoni jumped up to help as the great man fell. He never regained consciousness.

"He died conducting Puccini," I said to

Natalia later that evening. "A massive heart attack, they said. He never suffered, not for a minute. Right up to the end he was doing what he was made to do. I suppose if God had given him the opportunity, he'd have scripted it that way. I will miss him very much. He was a father figure to me."

"What will become of the orchestra?" she said.

I shrugged. "Who knows. Because of the war, our season was cut down to a few weeks anyway. Now I understand that the balance of the season will be canceled."

"That is such a shame. What will you do?"

"I think I'll go stay with Mama for a while. Do you want to go down to Pienza with me?"

"Maybe I'll join you for Passover in April, but right now I have a lot going on. We're actually supporting the authorities in Italian-occupied France. They're standing up to the Nazi demands for Jewish deportation. The Italian governor in Lyons canceled an order to deport two hundred Jews to Auschwitz. The Italian military commander in Croatia did the same thing. So far, the authorities are stalling. They don't want to cooperate."

"What are we going to do, Nat? It's only going to get worse. How long can we hold out against the Nazis? How long will Italians be able to resist the Nazi demands for Jewish bodies? You know Mussolini, he's weak. He'll cave in and we won't stand a chance."

"Don't talk like that. We're going to do what we can until the world defeats Hitler. And it will. We hear from the Italian troops outside Stalingrad that the German army has suffered a major defeat. Millions killed. The Allied forces have turned the tide in Africa and they're getting closer to Italy every day. You have to have faith, Ada. You have to resist. We have no other choice."

Springtime on Mama's farm was as peaceful as could be. Everything born anew. Even the vines I helped her plant in the little patch of land she called Ada's Vineyard were showing little buds and flourishing. The rest of the world did not exist. Nature's rebirth defied the Nazis. It defied World War II with colors and tastes and fragrances. It seemed to say, "We are eternal. We will be here long after you and your bombs are gone."

"Will you be staying here now?" Mama asked.

"Just for a little while. The BSO is closed, but I need to earn money. I'll try to get dates in the Bologna restaurants. I'll make enough to get by until something opens up. Unless Gigli cancels, I'll go back to Rome in June."

It was heartwarming to see how well Mama was managing her farm. She had contracted with a winery to produce small batches of her wine, and to give my mother

her due, the wine was pretty damn good. The night before I returned to Bologna, Mama held a dinner party. She invited the Romittis and several of her neighbors. Mama even had a gentleman friend for dinner, a stocky man with a bushy gray moustache. His name was Enzo, and he was Pienza's chief of police.

"Mama, you didn't tell me you were seeing someone," I said to her in the kitchen.

"Well, I'm not exactly *seeing* him. I met him one evening when I was waiting for the bus. It was raining and he gave me a ride. It's nothing, really. We just enjoy each other's company, and he happens to like my Bolognese cooking."

The way to a man's heart. Mama's food was delicious, and the wine was out of this world. Each of her neighbors brought a bottle to the dinner. Would I be unfairly biased if I said Mama's wine was the best? It was.

Bologna seemed to be on edge when I returned. Rumors abounded that Hitler's Russian campaign was a disaster, and wounded Italian soldiers were straggling back with tales of massive defeat. The Axis had also failed to hold North Africa. Patton and Montgomery were in Tunisia, and from there it was a quick jump to Sicily. Hitler and Mussolini were now girding for an Allied attack from the south. Germany was sending reinforcements into Italy and their presence was more visible. I was getting ready to return to Rome for the June concert when Natalia paid me another visit. I knew she would. She had another envelope for me to deliver to Tomaso.

"Welcome back, Signorina Baumgarten," the concierge said when I arrived at the Excelsior. He snapped his fingers and a porter led me to my room on the third floor. There were fresh flowers and a box of chocolates on the table, along with a hand-written note from the hotel president telling me that I was an honored guest. When I had settled in, I called room service and ordered a pot of tea and a scone. I had a job to do and I wanted to get it over as soon as possible.

I waited for ten minutes, sitting on the bed with the envelope in my hand. Finally, there was a knock on the door. I opened it to see a young lady with a cart. *"Servizio in camera, Signora."*

She wheeled the cart into the room, set the tea and pastry on the table and said, "Will there be anything else?" I didn't know how to respond. Tomaso should have been the one to bring the cart, or at least he should have sent someone with instructions to ask for the envelope. I couldn't just give it to some woman. I thanked her and gave her a tip. She left without another word. I decided to try later.

It was raining, and our rehearsal was held indoors. Gigli and I were driven to the Teatro Reale dell'Opera, where we were met by Maestro Molinari, who took me aside. "I am so very sad to hear of Stefano's passing," he said. "He was a visionary. Stefano was a force in northern Italy. I hear now that your season has been canceled. They will have to find a new director."

I nodded, and a tear rolled down my cheek.

"Have you made arrangements with another orchestra?" he said.

I shook my head. "There is nothing for me. There are no openings for women."

"In these times, during war years, one must be flexible," he said quietly. "If the demands of presenting music at the highest level means filling a vacancy with a talented woman, it should be done."

"I wish the music world saw it that way," I said.

"Some of us do."

I was shocked. "Do you know of such a vacancy?"

He nodded. "We are doing *Lucia*. Rehearsals start on July 1."

I shook his hand like it was a water pump. "Thank you so much, Maestro. I hope I will never disappoint you."

That evening, after the rehearsal, I returned to the hotel and once again ordered room service. Once again, no Tomaso. This time the cart was delivered by a young man. What is a spy supposed to do? I handed a tip to the man and casually asked, "Does Tomaso still work in the catering department?" I knew the minute I asked that it was a mistake.

He shook his head. "I'm new. I've only been here for three months. I don't know anyone named Tomaso. What is his last name?"

I waved it off. "Never mind, it's not important."

"I will ask for you, Signora. I'll see if someone knows Tomaso."

"No, please don't bother. It's not important really. Let's just forget it."

He smiled, nodded and left.

The concert at Caracalla was a success. Another great review in *Il Messaggero:* "Stars Beneath the Stars." Maestro Molinari introduced me to several of the orchestra members. He told them I would be filling the vacancy beginning in July. They had all heard me play and were pleased to have me on board for the fall season. All in all, it was great to be in the right place at the right time, or so I thought.

When I checked out of the Excelsior, the concierge said to me, "I understand you were looking for Tomaso Reggio. Regretfully, he left here last year. Is there something I can help you with?"

I hoped I didn't look nervous. I tried to brush it off. "No," I said, "I was just asking for a friend. Someone in Bologna who asked me to say hello. Nothing really."

The concierge smiled. I thought I saw him give a slight nod to a man reading a newspaper in a lobby chair, but then I decided it was just my nerves.

FIFTY-EIGHT

Pienza, September 2017

Catherine returned to the villa, a little tired from the flight, but with plenty of pictures of Ben. "He is having a great time with his cousins," she said. "My sister told me he's been an angel. Liam, he didn't miss me for a minute. I don't even think he knew I was gone." She made a pouty face.

"Maybe that's because we Skype with him every other day. What about Ada's story — did you finish it on the plane?"

Catherine shook her head. "I think I'm caught up with you, but I fell asleep on the plane. The last thing I read was Vittorio's death."

"Did you read the part where Ada's mother had dinner with her neighbors?"

"Yes. That was the second time she mentioned it. The first time was New Year's Eve. What is so important about . . . ? Wait a minute — Friede had neighbors all around her!"

Liam smiled and nodded. "And none of them were VinCo."

"Liam, we've been focusing on the wrong company."

"Exactly what I've been thinking. VinCo owns all the vineyards surrounding Gabi, as far as the eye can see. It would have had to purchase them piece by piece from Friede's neighbors."

"Or . . ."

"Right. It may fit into a pattern. Maybe VinCo's name just appeared in 1944, like Quercia. Maybe there are no deeds. We need to see the registry books."

"If Lenzini hasn't destroyed them."

"The clerk, Joseph, he seemed to be an honest fellow. Let's go talk to him."

Catherine, Liam and Giulia returned to the registrar's office and asked for Joseph. "We would like to see the registry books for the properties surrounding Gabriella Vincenzo's land, please," Giulia said. She pointed to the sections on the plat of survey hanging on the registrar's wall.

The clerk nodded and filled out request cards. "All of that land is owned by VinCo. The tracts appear in three separate volumes."

He left for a short time, brought out three books and laid them on the counter. When he opened the books to the appropriate pages, they all read "VinCo S.p.A." Joseph shrugged. "Just like Quercia, VinCo is listed as the owner for the entire time the books have been in service, since 1980."

"As we suspected. We'll need to see the earlier books," Giulia said.

Joseph nodded. "I'll order them and call you as soon as they come in. And Mr. Taggart, I'll take care of them. They won't disappear. Don't worry."

"Giulia, I think it's time we took a look at VinCo S.p.A.," Liam said. "I mean the corporate status. What can we find out about it? When was it formed? Who were the incorporators? Who are the shareholders? What do they say in their annual report?"

"I'll start this afternoon. It shouldn't take too long," Giulia said.

"Have you been able to find out anything about Natalia's family, the Romittis?"

"There is a family named Romitti listed at the same address in Pienza. I went there yesterday, but nobody was home. I'll try later. In the meantime, I consulted Aurora, the oldest person I know in Pienza. You can always find her in the Duomo; she goes to church every day. She remembers the Romitti family from her childhood. She was able to point out the house. She recalled that they were Jewish and thought they may have been arrested when the Nazis came. Some years later, one of the children moved in and started a family. She thinks that the grand-children live there now. That's about all she knew."

"I'd also like you to find out what you can about a real estate agent named Sylvia," Liam said.

"Do you have a last name?"

"No. The only thing I can tell you is that she was a little heavy and had a staccato laugh. She's the one who found Gabi's property in 1939. I know it's a long shot."

"Maybe not as long as you think. There aren't that many real estate offices in Pienza, and I'm pretty sure there were even fewer in 1939," Giulia said. "Maybe there are records. I'll look."

"And you, Mr. Man-in-Charge, what are you going to do?" Catherine said.

"I'm going to call Gunther Strauss. I have a feeling there's something more we should be looking at in Berlin, and Gunther's the man to do it."

FIFTY-NINE

Bologna, June 1943

Rehearsals for *Lucia* were set to begin on July 1 and I had barely two weeks to move my belongings. I found an apartment in Rome, between the Campo de' Fiore and the Piazza Navona. If Mama thought my Bologna apartment was small, she should have seen the thimble I rented when I stayed in the Eternal City.

Natalia stopped by when I was cleaning out my Bologna apartment. It was a bittersweet experience, and we were both sad. I had lived in Bologna for six years. I had experienced tremendous artistic growth. I had forged a number of close relationships. I had grown to love the city and all its charm. But I had seen the devil rise. I had seen the world go to war. I had suffered tragic personal losses. And now my beloved conductor was dead.

"Now it is onto the next chapter," Natalia said. "To new heights, to perform on the stage in Rome, the first woman to sit in the Rome Opera Orchestra. I'm so proud of you."

"Thanks, Nat. But I'm a lousy spy. I failed to give the envelope to Tomaso."

Natalia nodded. "That was my fault. I found out too late that Tomaso had been discovered and arrested. I'm glad you didn't go looking for him."

"The concierge said he was terminated."

"The concierge? You didn't ask him about Tomaso, did you?"

"Sort of. Was that a mistake?"

Natalia drew air through her clenched teeth. "Maybe. We don't trust him. My advice: don't stay there again."

"I thought I saw him nod to a man in the lobby."

"The Excelsior lobby is a den of spies. You never know who is working for who. I won't ask you to go there again."

"Will you come and visit me in Rome? I can get you tickets to *Lucia.*"

"I definitely will, and I'll bring Franny. Oh, I almost forgot. Franny said to give this letter to you."

She handed a letter addressed to the Bologna State Opera, attn: Francesca. I knew it was from Kurt. I ripped it open.

My dear friend,
I saw the review in *Il Messaggero.* Another

triumph! I miss you and think about Florence all the time. Damn this war! But here is the good news: massive troop movements are going south. I will be staying in Rome with the seventh division. I will find you.

Love,
Kurt

"Is that a letter from your German boyfriend, the one in the army, the one you say is not a Nazi but he is?"

"I know. I'm sleeping with the enemy. He's kind and he's sweet. He tells me he's not a Nazi. All German boys were conscripted into the army, just like here in Italy. He didn't have a choice. He's a clerk. He works in an office keeping track of motor vehicles. He doesn't arrest anybody, he doesn't shoot anybody. But then he says that massive troop movements into Italy is good news. I don't know. I don't know how to reconcile it."

"I'm sorry. As you can understand, I have no sympathy for Germans in uniform."

"All uniformed Germans aren't the same. Kurt is sweet. There are exceptions."

She grabbed my forearms and looked straight into my eyes. "Be careful, Ada. Even the best people get compromised. I've seen it. Rome is going to be flooded with Nazis now that they've lost North Africa.

504

Everyone expects the Allies to land in Italy this summer. The Germans will make a stand at Rome. It will be in the center of the battlefield. Don't trust anyone, especially not a German in uniform."

I understood her. She was sincere and concerned for me. I nodded. "I'll be careful."

I gave Natalia my new address and told her I hoped to see her from time to time, whether in Rome or in Pienza.

SIXTY

Rome, July 1943

The Teatro Reale dell'Opera was a magnificent structure. The concert hall had four tiers of boxes and a balcony. The interior was beautifully decorated with colors, molding and stuccowork. But the most impressive feature was the giant chandelier that hung in the middle of the hall. It was nineteen feet in diameter and had twenty-seven thousand crystal drops. The orchestra pit was just below and in front of the stage. The venue was far more imposing than Bologna and, in many ways, reminded me of the Philharmonie.

Did I feel out of place? Did I feel like I was the only woman in an all-male industry? Did I feel like all eyes were on me? Yes, I did, but no one said a word. Everyone was polite. We were all professionals and this was our business. Besides, there was a war going on and they were happy to have me.

Maestro Molinari was a thin man, elegantly dressed in dark suits, often double-breasted. His movements were elegant as well. He had a delicate touch and could accomplish much with a minimum of movement. He was keenly focused on his soloists and would cue them subtly at just the right times.

We practiced late every night. Afterward, I would either go home or head to the Campo and join the crowd in the cafés. It was a delightful routine in the summer months. One night, on my way back to the apartment, I saw Kurt standing with two other soldiers under a streetlamp. I started to walk in his direction, but he shook his head sternly from side to side. I resumed walking home, aware after a while that Kurt was tailing me from a distance.

We closed the door and I was once again in his arms. In this crazy war, circumstances kept putting us together. Now we were both assigned to Rome. "Can you stay here tonight?" I said.

He shook his head. "I have to check in. When my shift is done, I can go out, but I have to be back in the barracks at night."

"Barracks? What barracks are there in Rome?"

He smiled. "We're in a girl's school dormitory."

"Girls!"

"School's not in session, Ada."

"How long will you be stationed in Rome?"

"That's a good question. British and American troops have landed in Sicily. We've sent troops and materiel south, but the Allies are formidable opponents. The Italian general, Alfredo Guzzoni, is the supreme commander of the Axis forces in Sicily, but back at headquarters they laugh at him. They have no confidence in him. Ada, I don't think we're going to be able to stop the Allies from landing on the mainland. That puts you right in the middle. It's only a matter of time before this area will be a battlefield. I think you should leave Rome and stay with your mother. It won't be safe here."

"Then you should leave too. You'll end up getting killed."

"I'll get killed if I desert, that's for sure. But you should go."

I shook my head. "I made a commitment. Maestro Molinari gave me a precious opportunity. He chose a woman to play in his orchestra. I'm the only one in the world! How would it look if I were the deserter?"

He nodded. He understood. We decided not to waste any more time talking. There were much better things for us to do.

Gaetano Donizetti's *Lucia di Lammermoor* is a rousing, violent opera with sword fights, duels and stabbings. It is punctuated with powerful percussion from tympani, bass

508

drums and tubular bells. Thus, it was not immediately unsettling when huge thunder-blasts were heard during the July 19 performance.

But Maestro Molinari was startled. The score did not call for thunderous bass. The Teatro shook to its very foundation and in a few moments, it was obvious to all that something outside the building was rattling the crystals on the chandelier.

Six hundred and ninety Allied planes dropped 9,125 bombs on the San Lorenzo train yards and steel factories that night. Those sites were a stone's throw from the Teatro. When they realized what was happening, the patrons screamed and dashed for the exits. Remarkably, the building survived intact. The remaining concerts in July were canceled.

Six days later, Mussolini was arrested by the Fascist Grand Council. The papers reported his arrest during the evening hours of July 24–25. The council voted to transfer Mussolini's powers to King Victor Emmanuel. Later that day, the king transferred the powers of the prime minister to General Pietro Badoglio. It was the beginning of the end and everyone could see it. Especially Hitler.

SIXTY-ONE

Pienza, September 2017

Giulia received a call from Joseph at the Registrar of Titles. He was holding the three books we ordered from the archives. We made arrangements to view them in the afternoon. Meanwhile, Giulia had made an appointment with Alfredo Romitti, Matteo's grandson. He had a photo album that contained pictures taken by his grandfather. The Pienza home had been in the Romitti family all these years.

Alfredo was a strong, barrel-chested, wide-shouldered, black-haired man with an open-collared shirt. Pictures revealed that he was a spitting image of his grandfather. He invited Catherine, Liam and Giulia into his Pienza home, the same one Friede and Ada had visited so many years ago. They sat on the couch and enjoyed a glass of cool lemonade.

"My grandfather had a new Nikon camera in the 1930s. When my wife and I moved in here there were pictures all over the house. She made me put most of them into boxes.

There are pictures of my great-grandmother Naomi and my great-aunt Natalia. I remember when I was young, my grandfather would tell stories about the old days, when he ran a winery in Montepulciano."

Catherine said, "It was our thought that if we could find pictures of your great-grandmother and her friend Friede Baumgarten, it might help us in our effort to save Gabriella's land."

He nodded. "This is my great-grandmother Naomi Romitti," he said. "I did not know her. She died during the war. In late 1944, the Nazis came through and grabbed every Jew they could find. Many of them were hiding in small towns. The Jews they found were arrested and sent north. Or they just shot them. There are horror stories about small towns totally annihilated by SS troops. My great-grandmother Naomi and my great-grandfather Nico were both arrested and sent to the detention campo at Fossoli and from there, we presume, to Auschwitz."

"I'm so sorry," Catherine said.

Alfredo nodded and pointed to a picture. "This is my great-aunt Natalia. I never knew her either. I was told she was a *partigiana*. She fought with the partisans during the war. I don't know what happened to her. Here is a picture of Naomi and her friend, I think it could be Signora Baumgarten. There are several pictures of the two of them laughing and cooking."

At last Alfredo came to a group photo. "This might be what you're looking for," he said. "That is Naomi, her friend, my aunt Natalia and four other people I don't know. They are sitting at a table with flutes of prosecco raised in celebration. There are papers on the table. Maybe that was the day Gabriella's property was purchased."

"Alfredo, we have to leave now. We have an appointment at the registrar's office. May we borrow this picture?" Catherine asked.

"Of course. You may have it."

"Liam, let's get this picture enlarged. We may be able to read some of the words on those papers."

At the registrar's office, Joseph brought three volumes out to the counter. He picked up the first one and turned the pages until he came to the tracts owned by VinCo. "These two tracts appear to have been purchased from two different families. The registry book shows that they were deeded from the families to VinCo on May 21, 1944."

"Would the registrar have a copy of the deeds?" Catherine asked.

"No. There were no copies made in those days. The *notaio* would show the deed to the clerk, who would write down the pertinent information."

Joseph picked up the second book. "There

were four tracts sold to VinCo. All of them were recorded on May 21, 1944. The same as the first book," he said.

The third book was the same story. All of the tracts were sold and the deeds recorded from the individual families to VinCo on May 21, 1944.

"So, as I understand it," Liam said, "VinCo became the owner of all the land it now possesses on May 21, 1944, right?"

"Yes. You are correct."

"Just to make sure, other than what is noted in the registry books, there is no proof that any of these people ever really signed a deed to VinCo in 1944, right?"

"The book is the proof."

"That's what I thought. Can we have a copy made of those pages, please?"

"Certainly."

"Very suspicious, don't you think?" Liam said on the drive back to the villa. "All those lots were supposedly purchased on May 21, 1944, which just happens to be three days after Quercia Company was formed."

"Suspicious? Coincidental? Stinks like a dead fish? Say what you will, it still isn't proof that any of those transactions weren't valid. It's not *evidence* and it won't carry the day with Judge Riggioni," Catherine said. "VinCo could have arranged to buy all the properties and close the sales on the same day. I've been involved in mass real estate closings where several units are purchased on the same day at the same time with the same closing officer. It's not uncommon. We still don't have any proof that VinCo, or even Quercia, *illegally* came into title. We're missing the smoking gun."

"Would you like to hear another stinky coincidence?" Giulia said.

Liam and Catherine nodded.

"I did some research on VinCo, as you asked. VinCo was organized on May 18, 1944, the very same day as Quercia, probably for the purpose of purchasing all the vineyards three days later. The sole shareholder was also a trust. The beneficiary of the trust is not disclosed. The name of the trust is Wolfsangel. And it's a German trust."

"Exactly the same way Quercia was organized," Liam said.

"Exactly."

"It's time to go see Gunther."

Sixty-Two

Rome, September 1943

On September 8, 1943, Italy's General Badoglio formally surrendered to the Allies and signed an armistice. Italy was no longer at war. It had capitulated, which was what most Italians had wanted all along. There had recently been massive worker strikes in Milan and Turin, and there was general discontent about the scarcity of fungible goods. Coal and oil were in short supply, and reports from the south revealed that the Italian army was in disarray.

There were celebrations in many quarters of the city, but they were short-lived and brutally extinguished when the German army drove into Rome two days later. In a matter of hours, the Nazis enveloped and occupied the city. The Gestapo was now in control. They set up headquarters with the SS on the Via Tasso, which soon became the city's most frightening address. German trucks patrolled the streets with loudspeakers blaring. Random abuse and persecution began immediately.

The Allied bombs continued to rain down on the outskirts of the city and on the industrial areas. The buzzing sounds of airplane propellers, the whining whistle of falling bombs and the thunder of their explosions shook me to the core. Whether by tacit agreement or respect for the antiquities or because of the pleas of the pope, Rome's city center was not bombed. Thus, it was Maestro Molinari's decision to resume the performance schedule.

Kurt and I had made plans to meet after rehearsal. The café was across the Tiber. I stopped briefly at my apartment to drop off my instrument. My route to Trastevere, over the Garibaldi Bridge, took me through the Jewish quarter. I saw uniformed Germans everywhere. Jewish families cowered, held their children and quickly went inside. It brought to mind the Brownshirts marching through the streets of Berlin. I saw my grandfather broken and beaten. I saw my father with cuts and bruises. I understood why my mother screamed "Kleiner."

I had taken this route many times before. The Jewish quarter was charming. Italian Jews had no reason to cower. There was no fear of brutality on the streets. But now the Nazis were here. Abject wickedness had descended upon the Eternal City. Should we expect all of the Nazi Nuremburg Laws to be imposed? Would Rome become another Berlin? Or Vienna? Or Warsaw?

Kurt was seated when I arrived, and two glasses of wine had already been set on the table. He rose to pull out my chair. It should have been a romantic late September evening, but I wasn't feeling it. I looked at him: handsome, strong, comfortable and confident in his military uniform. It was all wrong. I had just come from the Jewish quarter where men wearing his uniform were tormenting innocent families. As much as I loved him, it turned my stomach to be in the presence of a Wehrmacht officer.

"Do you have to wear your uniform when we go out?"

"I have to wear it at all times, Ada, you know that."

We finished our dinner with very little conversation. Kurt could sense that I was in a dark mood, and he suggested we take a walk. He reached for me, but I didn't want to hold his hand. How could I walk by the Jewish quarter hand in hand with a Nazi? We crossed the bridge and turned toward the Coliseum. He tried to make small talk to lighten the mood, but the more we walked, the more uncomfortable I became. What was I doing walking with a Nazi?

Our path took us by the Palazzo Venezia where Mussolini had stood on his balcony to address his cheering followers. "Duce, Duce!" they yelled. How could so many have been so clueless? The Roman Forum was across the street. We stood at the railing looking down at the ancient ruins of the Roman Empire.

"Do you see the analogy?" I said. "It couldn't be more graphic. The rise and fall of the Roman Empire? The mighty Third Reich? How long before the Nazi empire collapses as all oppressors must? It can't be soon enough for me."

"Please, Ada, we're just taking a walk."

I pointed to my right, toward the Jewish quarter. "Do you know what's over there, Kurt?"

He nodded solemnly.

"Of course you do, we just passed it," I said sarcastically. "That's the Jewish community that your noble leaders want to extinguish. It's only been there for two thousand years. The world's oldest continuous Jewish community. Do you know what the Gestapo did last week?"

Again, he nodded solemnly. He knew, but he didn't want to get into it with me.

"The Gestapo came in and demanded a ransom of one hundred and ten pounds of gold as the price of protecting the Ghetto. Protecting! From whom, you might ask? Why, from the Gestapo, of course! One hundred ten *pounds of gold,* Kurt. People sold everything they had to meet that demand."

We walked a little farther and came upon the Arch of Titus. Then I completely lost it. "Do you see what's carved into this arch?" I said, almost shouting. "It's a memorial tribute to the Roman conquerors of the Jews in Palestine. Do you see the menorah stolen from the Temple in Jerusalem? Do you see the golden trumpet, the procession of slaves? Is that what you are fighting for?"

Kurt stopped me abruptly. "That's enough, Ada. You know those are not my beliefs. You know that's not me."

"Do I? You're a Nazi. Nazis are putting Jews into camps and killing them. How can you wear their uniform?"

"I wear the uniform because I was conscripted. You know I don't agree with those policies."

I shook my head. "I don't know anything."

He reached for me. "Ada, come on."

"Don't touch me, Kurt. I can't do this anymore. I'm sorry, but I don't want to see you again. I have to go."

"Ada, wait."

I turned and ran as fast as I could back to my apartment, where I lay on my bed and cried for the rest of the night. My heart was breaking, but I was sure I had made the right decision.

Two weeks later, Kurt appeared at my apartment. He knocked on the door. I told him to go away. He said he would, but he had something he had to tell me first. I let him in.

"Kleiner is in Rome," he said. "I thought you should know. The Gestapo and the SS have established a headquarters and he's working there."

I nodded. "Thanks. I'll try to stay out of his way."

"No, you need to get out of Rome. Now! Go to your mother's and stay out of sight."

"I can't, Kurt, I told you. I made a commitment to the Rome Opera. To Maestro Molinari. I'm not leaving."

"Please, Ada. You have to leave, and I'll tell you why. Berlin sent Waffen-SS Colonel Hollman to Rome. He's here for one purpose: to round up all the Jews in Rome and send them north. Do you understand? They're going to clear the Jews out of Rome. He's at Via Tasso right now with Lieutenant Kleiner. If you stay, you will be arrested with the rest of them, put on a train and sent north. No matter what you now think of me, Ada, I have always loved you. I will always love you. I'm begging you, please go."

I was stunned. "All the Jews in Rome?"

Kurt nodded. "Ten thousand is their estimate."

"When is this supposed to happen?"

"Next week. The date is uncertain due to ongoing negotiations with the Vatican. The High Command wants to make sure there won't be a Vatican protest."

"I can't leave until next week. I can't leave Molinari without notice. We have three concerts before the fall break. I have to play. Maybe I'll leave then."

He shook his head, sighed and left.

A Sunday matinee performance of Mozart's *The Magic Flute* is normally played before an audience of families. Children love the characters, especially the silly Papageno, a bird catcher who is dressed up in a funny-looking feather costume. Sometimes we have to stop the music and let Papageno take a bow to the applause and laughter of the children. This Sunday, however, the Teatro was packed with uniformed Nazis. Some of them chuckled. Maybe they saw *The Magic Flute* in Germany when they were young. But there were no children present.

When I returned to my apartment, Kurt was waiting for me. "Ada," he said, "Listen to me. I can't tell you how urgent it is . . ."

"I know. You want me to leave Rome. But I have one more performance to do. I told Maestro Molinari that I would be leaving when the opera concluded its fall season.

521

He is very understanding. He sees the situation just the same as you and me. I have to play tomorrow night and then I'll make arrangements to go."

"No, Ada, you don't see the situation. The SS and the Gestapo are bringing hundreds of people into the office on Via Tasso. Right now. They're interrogating everyone who might have information on the whereabouts of Jews. They're also seeking information about the resistance. This morning they brought in the staff from the Excelsior. They questioned the concierge for over an hour. You stayed there, didn't you?"

"Did they bring in Tomaso?"

"Who is Tomaso?"

"He worked in the Excelsior catering department. I passed him a secret envelope from Natalia."

"Oh, Jesus. Did anyone else know that you gave him an envelope?"

"No one else saw the envelope, but the second time I was supposed to make a delivery, Tomaso didn't show up. I asked a staff member about him. The concierge knew I asked about him."

Kurt took me by the arm. "Grab a bag of clothes and we'll go right now. I don't know whether the concierge identified you, but let's not take the chance. They could be coming right now. Let's get to the train, and I'll go with you."

"You'll go with me? You mean you'll leave the army?"

He nodded. "I'll do anything to make sure you're safe."

"You'd be a deserter, Kurt. They would jail you or worse. I can't let you do that."

"It's not your decision, it's mine. Get your things."

I didn't expect to hear this. I had misjudged Kurt. He was going to give it all up for me. "I'm sorry," I said. My words were catching in my throat. "I'm sorry I doubted you. I'm sorry for the things I said."

He shook his head. "No, you were right to say what you said. I am the one who should be sorry. I am the one who marches blindly, the one who serves the Reich. No more. Please come with me. Let me take you to safety. Let's follow that dream that we have."

"I love you, Kurt, and we will follow it, but I can't go yet. I have to play tomorrow night. I will not have Molinari say that the only woman he ever hired walked out on a performance. We'll go after the concert."

Kurt sighed. "I understand. I'll meet you at the Termini. We'll take the midnight train north."

SIXTY-THREE

Rome, October 1943

Monday, October 18, 1943, was the company's last performance of the fall season. I would leave directly from the opera house. I had packed my bag and closed up my apartment. I would waste no time getting out of Rome. The performance would end at eleven and the Termini was only three blocks from the Teatro. Kurt and I planned to take the midnight train to Siena. He was buying the tickets and would meet me on the platform. I was glad he was coming with me. Truth be told, I was scared to death.

The thought of arresting ten thousand Jews and transporting them north to one of the German concentration camps was unthinkable, inconceivable, but I knew it was true. Hitler intended to make all Europe *Judenfrei.* He was intent on destroying an entire race of humans. The concept was so depraved as to make it absurd. Hitler was a madman, but what was even more incomprehensible were the legions of mindless followers who supported him. Thank God, Kurt was not one of them.

I had no right to think of this horrific roundup in personal terms. The thought of so many innocent people being victimized was catastrophic, but I couldn't help but think what it had done to me and my career. It made me furious. I had worked so hard to get where I was — the first woman member of a major orchestra. I had good reason to believe that Maestro Molinari would have kept me on permanently. It was unfair that I had to leave. Maestro was very kind and even encouraging when I told him I had to leave. He told me, "When this is all over, you come back and see me." It was not a promise, but it was a strong possibility.

In many ways, it was a relief to be escaping the city and going home. It was like taking a deep breath. It would be peaceful at the villa. It was another world. It would be good to see Mama. I hadn't been there in a year. I often wondered how things were going on her farm and in her social life. With the chief of police, no less. She wasn't much of a letter writer, so we would have a lot of catching up to do.

The walk from my apartment to the Teatro was daunting. I saw a number of canvas-covered trucks headed off to the right and entering the Jewish quarter. Shouts blasted from the loudspeakers in German. *"Raus,"* I heard over and over. *"Sich anstellen."* Line up. I picked up my pace and arrived at the Teatro, my suitcase in one hand and my violin case in the other. As before, the hall was full of uniformed men and their women guests. No children in attendance to laugh at Papageno. In three hours, I would be out of here.

The opera went well and many of the people did laugh at the dialogue. They were having a jolly good time, while out in the streets innocent people were being grabbed and put into trucks. Twice during the performance, we heard bomb blasts in the distance and the audience gasped. The time seemed to drag. I was anxious to leave. Finally, the curtain fell, and the applause ended. It was time for me to leave Rome.

I said good-bye to Maestro Molinari. "Be well," he said. "Come see me when the war is over."

I grabbed my suitcase and violin and rushed out the front door only to be stopped dead in my tracks. Right before me, in his black SS uniform, stood Lieutenant Herbert Kleiner, his arms crossed, a pompous smile on his face. Two SS officers stood to his side.

"So, Fraulein Baumgarten, we meet again. How fortuitous. Did you think your efforts to subvert my career had all been forgotten?

Your insolence, the way you insulted me in front of the general? Well, now you see it did not work. Here I am, in the flesh, a lieutenant, in wonderful spirits, and now in charge of carrying out the führer's directive to rid this lovely city of Jewish garbage. By the way, the Excelsior's concierge sends his felicitations. Would you care for room service?"

I knew that if I opened my mouth and responded to him in any way, I would be struck down. I stood awaiting my fate, wishing I had listened to Kurt and left town last week.

He glared at me with Satan's eyes. "Nothing to say this time, Fraulein?" He nodded to his companions. "Take her."

They grabbed me by the arms and shoved me into the back of a truck. They drove in the direction of the Vatican and onto the grounds of the Collegio Militare, a military prep school. They pushed me into a large gymnasium where hundreds of other people were already imprisoned. Maybe thousands, it was hard to tell. There were people in the gymnasium, in the lunchroom and in the auditorium. I heard a guard say that it was the "holding pen for *Judenaktion*." Most of the people had a suitcase or a pillowcase stuffed with clothes. Many were crying. Some were pleading. Some made futile demands for answers. Some showed signs of injuries. Perhaps they had resisted. Some were sick. All were frightened. But the guards were stoic and impervious.

There wasn't much I could do but sit on the floor and wait for whatever the Germans had in mind. I sat there with my suitcase and my violin and watched. Many of the families huddled in little enclaves, their arms around one another. Parents were comforting their children and telling them that everything would be all right. But the children knew better. The parents could not hide their own fear; it was palpable and hard to disguise.

A little girl caught my eye. She was wandering from group to group. No one seemed to know her. She couldn't have been more than three or four. She had golden blond hair, with long curls tied in ribbons. Her dress was white with a pink embroidered hem, but it had been soiled and dirtied. Her pretty little Mary Jane shoes had heart designs. Tears were rolling down her cheeks, but no one was comforting her. She seemed totally lost. I gestured for her to come to me.

She walked slowly and tentatively, her eyes down. She stopped a few feet away, unsure what I wanted.

"Come here, sweetheart," I said. "Are you looking for someone? Can I help you find your family?"

My words did not register. I tried again. It seemed as though she didn't know or couldn't hear what I was saying. Her lower lip quivered. I smiled, knelt down, reached my arms out and beckoned her forward. Finally, she came to me. I gently placed my arms around her and drew her to my chest. She put her arms around my neck and quietly cried.

A tall, thin man walked over and nodded. "Is this your daughter?" I said.

"No," he said with a compassionate smile. "She is alone."

"What about her parents?"

The man closed his eyes and shook his head. He mouthed, "They didn't make it."

"Who's been caring for her?"

He shrugged. "I don't think anyone."

"What is your name?" I said to the girl.

"She doesn't understand Italian," the man said. "I believe she came with the refugees from the French region. But I don't speak French."

"Parles-tu français?" I said to the top of her curly head. She looked up with her big blue eyes and nodded.

"Je m'appelle Ada," I said. *"Quel est ton nom, ma chère?"*

In a tiny voice, she said, "Gabrielle."

SIXTY-FOUR

Rome, October 1943

Morning came at Collegio Militare and no changes had been made to our confinement. From time to time throughout the night, more people were brought in. We were allowed a single bathroom break, under supervision, one at a time. It took hours. There were two fountains in the gym, and we were allowed to drink as needed. No food had been supplied. Gabrielle had slept on my lap all night. Now that it was morning and people were up and about, she wouldn't leave my side.

When I went to get a drink, Gabrielle clung to my skirt. When I went to the bathroom, Gabrielle came along. If we walked from one side of the room to the other, we walked together, my arm around her.

Sometime in the afternoon they brought out bread, one piece per person. Some of the people asked questions. "Why have we been brought here? Where are we going?

How long are we staying here?" But none of the guards would give an answer. Maybe they didn't know.

"Where do you live?" I asked Gabrielle, using the simple French words I had learned in high school.

"In a white house near the mountain."

"Do you know the name of the town?"

She shook her head.

"Is it Grenoble?"

She nodded.

"It's very pretty there, isn't it?"

She raised her eyebrows, nodded and smiled.

"What are the names of your mother and father?" That was the wrong question to ask. She broke down in tears and buried her head on my chest. There was no telling what she had seen. I wouldn't ask that question again. I patted her on the back. I told her it was okay, I would take care of her. Everything would be okay.

"Will you stay with me?" she asked, and I said I would.

"You won't leave me?"

"No, I will not leave you," I said.

"Promise?"

"I promise."

I slept a few hours with my back against the wall and little Gabrielle on my lap.

I estimated it was about 10:00 p.m. the next

day. More people had been brought in. We were all tired and hungry and the conditions were onerous. Then I saw him. Kurt walked into the room in full uniform. He had a document in his hand. He strode purposefully across the room looking at the faces of the detainees. Finally, he saw me and nodded. He approached a guard and showed him the paper. "I am to bring the woman with the violin to Via Tasso for questioning. Here are my orders." For the first time, I noticed that Kurt was wearing a pistol.

The guard read the order and nodded. Kurt walked over to me and took me by the elbow. "Come with me, Fraulein," he said brusquely. "It's time for some answers."

Gabrielle's eyes were wide with fright. Her little body shook. She stood behind me and clutched my skirt.

"I have to bring the child," I whispered to him.

"Ada, that's impossible," Kurt said. "The order states you are to come with me to SS Headquarters. You can bring your luggage, but not her."

"I will not leave without the child," I said quietly.

"Ada, be reasonable. She's not covered by the order," he whispered. "I can't get her out of here."

"I'm sorry," I said. "Then I will have to stay. I made a promise."

"Ada!"

"At some point, people have to stand up for what's right. I'm not going."

"Listen to me. I have a car outside. I'm risking my neck to get you out of here and drive you north."

"And I love you for that, but I'm not going to leave without this child."

He snorted through his nose. "Damn, Ada. You are the most stubborn woman I've ever known! All right. Hand me the child."

I lifted Gabrielle and tried to hand her to Kurt, but she wouldn't let go of me.

"Tell her it's just until we get outside," he said.

"Gabrielle," I said in French, "just for a minute. Kurt is my friend and he's going to carry you outside. He's very strong and you're such a big girl. And I'm coming with you."

She nodded. Kurt took her and started for the doorway. The guard came over and Kurt said, "She'll give us the information or she'll never see her child again."

The guard smiled. "*Ja,* clever."

Yes, it was clever, I thought, and I followed him out.

He had a black sedan waiting in the school parking lot. We got in and drove off, Kurt in the driver's seat, Gabrielle and I in the backseat.

"Where did you get this car?" I said.

"I told you, I work in administration. I'm a recordkeeper in charge of motorized vehicles."

"And they gave you this car to drive?"

"They don't know that yet."

We pulled out of Rome and headed north.

"If you can get us to Pienza, I can get you to Mama's."

I can only imagine what my mother thought when a large black Nazi sedan pulled into her driveway in the middle of the night. No one rushed out to greet us. We got out of the car and walked into the villa. "Mama?" I called.

She poked her head out of the door to her bedroom. "Who is that with you?"

"It's me, Mrs. Baumgarten. Kurt Koenig."

"In a Nazi uniform?"

"Yes, ma'am. With a Nazi car that just rescued your daughter."

"And the child?"

"Her name is Gabrielle, Mama, and she's very hungry," I said.

Mama smiled, took Gabrielle by the hand and led her to the kitchen. "We can take care of that problem. Do you like spaghetti, little one?"

"French, Mama. She speaks French."

Mama gave me the eye. "Spaghetti is spaghetti. It's universal." She looked down at Gabrielle and said, "Spaghetti?"

Gabrielle smiled widely and nodded.

"Ada, you'll have to fill me in, this is a lot to digest."

Kurt had burned his bridges, but they were bridges he no longer sought to cross. He had stolen a car and deserted from the army. It was likely that both of us had made the Most Wanted list. Wherever we went, we would have to keep a low profile. We told Mama that under no circumstances should she ever tell her friends that we were staying with her. If her friends, or her police chief, wanted to visit, she was to let us know so we could hide in the cellar.

I felt it was important that Mama understood her own criminal liability if she chose to give us shelter, and we talked about it very seriously. If we were discovered, we would all be subjected to imprisonment or worse. She could be charged as an accomplice. We offered to move on and hide somewhere in the Tuscan hills. I could contact Natalia in Bologna. She and her partisan group were finding places for people to hide. She would help us if I asked. Mama would have none of it. We would stay with her at her home, and what better place to hide? Like many Italians, she was sure that the Allies would come marching up the peninsula any day.

But she did take warnings seriously. "Ada,

if Natalia's right and they're rounding up all the Jews, then I'm at risk the same as you," she said, "but we're way out here in the country. Do you really think the Nazis are going to search every farmhouse in Italy? If they do, then we don't have a choice, and I hope the Americans hurry up."

"Kurt, what are we going to do with the car?" I asked. "We can't leave it in the driveway."

"I'll drive it somewhere and ditch it. Somewhere far away, maybe up near Florence. I'll leave tonight. It's dark and the roads are empty."

SIXTY-FIVE

Berlin, September 2017

Gunther Strauss' office was located in the Sony Center, an architectural jewel built by Helmut Jahn at the Potsdamer Platz. A huge indoor-outdoor plaza, covered by a glass canopy, lay between the high-rise office buildings, movie theaters, apartments, restaurants and museums. Gunther met Liam in the reception area and led him back to his twelfth-floor office. He had a spectacular view of the Tiergarten.

"Initially, we were only focusing on Quercia Company, the putative owner of Gabi's property," Liam said. "Catherine and I have learned that all of the parcels surrounding Gabi's farm were owned by separate farmers before the war. Individual families. They would come over to Gabi's house for dinner."

"The land wasn't all owned by VinCo?"

"No, sir. It wasn't even owned by a single landowner. They were all separate parcels with separate owners. Giulia researched VinCo and discovered that it was formed the same day that Quercia was formed. We had the registrar pull the older books, and there it was — VinCo is shown buying all the surrounding parcels of property from the individual owners on a single day in 1944."

Gunther nodded. "And you're going to tell me that the owner of VinCo is a secret German trust."

"Yes, I am. The name of the trust, as shown in the Italian corporate records, is the Wolfsangel Trust of 1944."

Gunther's expression turned serious. "Wolfsangel?"

"Right. Does that mean something? Is that a German expression?"

"I'll say — an illegal one. The public use of that phrase is against the law. The German Criminal Code forbids use of Nazi symbols to identify a group or to support an ideology, like a swastika or an iron cross. During the Nazi era, the *Wolfsangel* was a runic emblem used by the Waffen-SS. Now it's outlawed."

"Well, it sure wasn't outlawed in 1944."

"Hell, no. The SS used it throughout the war."

"Gunther, did you ever find out the name of the trust that owned Quercia?"

"No, we didn't see it in the probate court documents. We just figured it was called the Fruman Trust."

"Maybe it wasn't identified by name because it's another outlawed symbol."

"That's a good point. Use or display of banned symbols and emblems could subject the user to arrest and a jail term of three years."

Liam shook his head. "Isn't that something? Here in Germany, it's against the law to use or display Nazi symbols, but back in the U.S., punks march through Charlottesville and Skokie in full Nazi uniforms with swastika armbands yelling Jewish slurs."

"That wouldn't be permitted here. They'd all be arrested and face jail terms."

"And these American neo-Nazis even give the Hitler salute as they march."

"That salute is banned here as well. You'd go to jail. Why does the United States permit it?"

Liam shrugged. "Freedom of speech."

"Well, we have freedom of speech too, but not for Nazis, hate groups or Holocaust deniers."

Liam nodded. "How do we find out the name of Quercia's trust?"

Gunther shook his head. "I suppose you could get a court order, if you had a reason. How did you find out that VinCo's trust was the Wolfsangel Trust?"

Liam slapped his forehead. "Giulia! It was contained in the Italian corporate records. I bet she could find out Quercia's the same

539

way." Liam took out his cell phone and called. "Giulia, how hard was it to find out the name of VinCo's trust?"

"Not hard at all. The names of corporate shareholders have to be publicly disclosed. I was able to find it online."

"Remember you told me that Quercia's sole shareholder was a trust? Could you get the name of that trust?"

"Sure, give me a few minutes and I'll call you."

Gunther stood. "Have you had lunch, Liam?"

Liam shook his head. "Nothing since breakfast."

"Let's go downstairs. There's a terrific Italian restaurant in the building."

"Italian? Seriously?"

"Liam," Giulia said on speakerphone, "Quercia Company was formed in May 1944 with the same organizational structure as VinCo. The German trust that owned all of Quercia's shares was called the Totenkopf Trust."

"Holy shit," Gunther said. "Quercia is a Nazi organization."

"Giulia," Liam said, "were there any individuals named in the papers? Do we know who the beneficiary of the Totenkopf Trust is or was?"

"No, that is not disclosed."

"One more thing, Giulia," Gunther said.

"The name Quercia. That doesn't mean anything to me. Does it mean anything to you?"

"Yes, of course. It's Italian for oak or oak tree or oak leaf."

"Thank you, Giulia."

"What does all this mean, Gunther?" Liam said.

"They're all SS signs. *Totenkopf* is the death's head, the skull and crossbones used by the Storm Troopers and the Schutzstaffel — the SS. Oak leaves were worn by the SS. *Wolfsangel* was a runic sign used by the SS. Whoever formed these corporations was using SS symbols. If we can show that the Nazis seized that property in 1944, or forced people to sell it to them, you may very well have just won your case. I've worked on restitution cases in Germany and Austria, but not in Italy. Tell your wife and Giulia to research Italian law on the restitution of wartime property seizures. I'm sure that Italy's law would be similar."

"So you think it's likely that property was seized from farmers by members of the SS during 1944?"

"From the names, I would say it's very likely, but you'll need more than that. You need to show that the individuals behind the scenes of these companies were members of the Nazi Party, the SS or profiteers operating under the auspices of the Third Reich. We have to find out who formed and operated these companies."

"How do we do that?"

"I have a friend in the prosecutor's office. I'm going to lean on him to get a subpoena out for the records of these two trusts. My guess is the records are located at the same law firm that handled the Fruman estate."

Sixty-Six

Pienza, March 1944

By the time the vineyards and the flowers were budding, we had been on Mama's farm for four and a half months. During that time, neither Kurt nor I had ventured off the property, but we did have visitors. The first was Enzo, Mama's friend and the town's chief of police. When we arrived, we told Mama not to have visitors or let anyone know we were staying at the villa. But we had an immediate problem; we arrived without any extra clothes and all Kurt had was his uniform. Mama could go into Pienza and buy women's clothes for me without arousing suspicion. She could even buy dresses for Gabrielle because several of her friends and neighbors had children. But Kurt? That was another story. Questions would be asked. Why would a fifty-eight-year-old widow be buying a man's wardrobe?

So Mama picked up the phone, called the

police department and asked for Enzo. Bear in mind, Pienza was a small town. Mama and Enzo were seeing each other, and everyone knew it. It didn't take long to figure out that she and the chief were more than casual companions. I thought they were cute together. Papa had died almost five years ago, and it was heartwarming to know that Mama had found a new relationship. When she called him on the phone, I could have sworn she was talking to Papa.

"Enzo," she said in that firm direct manner of hers (some would call it bossy), "I need you to buy two pairs of men's trousers and a few shirts. And some underwear. And socks. Maybe a pair of shoes." Pause. "I'll tell you when you get here." Pause. "About the same as you, my dear, but a lot thinner." Pause. "And Enzo, do not tell anyone you are buying these for me."

That night, he arrived for dinner in his police car. He took out a big bag and brought it into the house. "All right, Friede, what's going on?"

She called Kurt and me into the kitchen. "This is what's going on."

He bowed and kissed my hand. "Ada, so nice to see you again. Your mother does not stop talking about you. Maybe you will play for me one day?"

I smiled. "It would be my pleasure."

Enzo looked at Kurt. He was dressed in

544

his army trousers and a T-shirt.

"This is Kurt Koenig," Mama said. "He and Ada have been friends since they were children. My Jacob used to drive him to and from orchestra practice. Yes, he is a German officer, but he saved Ada's life. The clothes are for him." Mama went on to tell him about our escape from the Collegio Militare. Mama is a nonstop talker, but the entire time she was telling the story, it was obvious that Enzo already knew about it.

"We received a bulletin about Sergeant Koenig," Enzo finally said. "It's posted on the board in the station. He is accused of stealing a Wehrmacht vehicle. He is also accused of desertion and treason, but those are outside our jurisdiction."

I was shocked. I was immediately sorry that we had come to the villa and that we had involved Mama. But I was wrong. Enzo loved my mother and he hated the Nazis. "What did you do with the car?" he asked.

Kurt shrugged. "It is enjoying a beautiful view of Firenze from the Piazzale Michelangelo. No one saw me leave it there. It was the middle of the night."

Enzo nodded. "We are a small police department. I have three officers on my staff, and they do not patrol out here unless they are called. You are probably safe here, but you would be well advised to stay out of Pienza."

545

Kurt and I both thanked him. "Who is this little angel?" he asked when Gabi walked into the kitchen wearing one of the new dresses that Mama had bought for her.

"That is Gabrielle and she is my daughter," I said.

Enzo bent low from the waist and kissed the top of Gabi's head. "Hello to you, pretty Gabriella."

Gabi looked at me quizzically. "It's Gabrielle."

I smiled. "You're in the Tuscan countryside. Out here, they would say Gabriella."

Mama could cook, and Enzo could eat. They were a perfect combination. And they both loved their wine. Mama's vines were mature, she was managing her vineyard expertly and her estate wine was out of this world. By the end of the meal, we had drained two bottles. Enzo stood, patted his stomach and said, "I'd better get going." He gave Mama a kiss, headed for the door and said, "I hope I don't give myself a ticket for driving under the influence." You had to like Enzo.

Our next visitors were the Romittis, who came in December to celebrate Chanukah. Mama had seen Naomi in town and confided that we were hiding at the villa. Naomi told us that Natalia was in hiding as well, somewhere in the mountains of Chianti. Her partisan group was being pursued by the Fascists and the Nazis.

The Romittis brought a doll for Gabi, and Naomi brought her famous latkes. I could see the light go on in Gabi's eyes when we gathered around the menorah. She was reconnecting with happy memories of her life in Grenoble. She helped us light the candles and I played a few Chanukah songs. Here we were — Germans, Italians and a little French darling — and we were all bound together by the traditions of our forebears. Jews in the diaspora, all different and all the same. And like our forebears, our Chanukah celebration had to be clandestine. Jews were being snatched off the streets by Nazi patrols and sent north to prison camps. We had also heard rumors that Jews were being shot, sometimes in large groups.

Generally, winter days on the farm were peaceful. The weather was chilly but with an occasional warm, sunny day. I practiced every day, sometimes on the veranda if the weather was nice, but most often in the living room with its high ceilings and its glorious acoustics. I played for Mama and Gabi and sometimes for Enzo. He loved the old Neapolitan melodies and he would supply the vocals. I nearly wet my pants when he got up to dance the tarantella. Those nights were special and for a moment we could forget that a war was waging three hours to the south.

Sadly, I could not get Kurt to play. I told Gabi that he was an excellent player as a teenager, but Kurt did not want to pick up the instrument. He finally revealed that his father told him that a violin was for weak, effeminate little boys, not German soldiers. He put Kurt's violin on the floor and smashed it with his foot. The dark memories were too upsetting for Kurt, and he declined whenever I suggested that he play.

Gabi, on the other hand, showed an interest. I was playing Papa's violin, but I had left my violin with Mama months ago. I decided to teach Gabi. It wasn't as easy as I thought. I was not my father with his endless patience, and Gabi was not me. Still, she began to learn the scales and a few simple melodies, ones that didn't strain her small fingers.

Gabi was a much better student when it came to baking lessons. Mama had an eager helper. Gabi spent hours learning the delicacies of baking challah, cookies, pies and cakes. Of all the things she had to do in a day — all the chores we had assigned to her, the books we wanted her to read and her violin practice — Gabi made time to sit with Mama in the kitchen, and that was Mama's delight.

For Kurt and me, it was a time to build on the strange bonds that had held us together for so many years. We embraced the opportunity to develop deep and mutual understandings. Our roots were so very different, and yet we saw the world with the same eyes. Kurt was a kind man and great with Gabi. She would sit on his lap while he told her stories of gingerbread houses and flying ships.

Late in the evening, Kurt and I would sit together. Our time was unpressured. There were no uncertainties about when or if we'd see each other again. A night by the fire with nothing more than intimate conversation was completely satisfying, without the urgency to make something bigger and better happen. We would be there the next morning, waking up in each other's arms.

We took walks through the vineyards, down the rows of trellises, enjoying the present and planning for the future — what we would do when this was all over, where we would live, how we would raise our family. And our family always included Gabrielle.

Gabi was a joy. Pure magical energy. Watching Gabi run through the gardens chasing ducks made us forget the horrific state of affairs that brought us together. Just four months ago she had closed herself in a shell. Now, like a tulip, she was opening up to the world. Her spontaneity, formerly repressed by unspeakable tragedy, was returning. Like a normal four-year-old girl, she exuded happiness. And it was infectious.

Natalia surprised us in early February. It was the middle of the night and we were sound asleep when we heard someone trying the front doorknob. Kurt jumped out of bed, told me to stay back, grabbed his pistol and headed for the door. There stood Natalia and she was a mess. Her clothes were torn and dirty, her hair was disheveled and tied with a scarf and she had dark circles under her eyes.

"They broke into our camp," she said. "We all scattered. They fired at us, but most of us were able to make it into the woods."

"Who broke into your camp?" Kurt asked.

Natalia shook her head. "I don't know if it was the Fascists or the Nazis. Probably Nazis, but in the end, what's the difference?"

"Did they follow you here?"

"No. Our camp was more than twenty miles away. I didn't know where to go. I can't return to Pienza. There are Nazis searching for Jews in the city and in cities throughout Tuscany. A squad of Nazis ravaged through Pitigliano last week, the place we went for Rosh Hashanah. They arrested the entire community, put them in a truck and took them north to a prison camp. I hope you don't mind that I came here. I warned my mother and father to get out of town, that the Nazis were coming, and I hope they went to Matt's."

We brewed a pot of tea and sat in the kitchen. Natalia took a sip, leaned back and closed her eyes. "I'm sorry, but I haven't slept in two days."

"We have a room for you," I said. "You can stay here. We're safe here."

"No Jew is safe. I thank you for your offer, but I have to rejoin my unit. The partisans are growing, Ada. There are tens of thousands of us now. Women too, you'd be so proud. There are thousands of women in the partisan fighting units. We move from sector to sector, sleeping in abandoned farms and farmhouses. We move equipment by horse and donkey and wagons. We derail their trains, set fire to their storehouses, and we kill them, Ada, we shoot them from the forests."

As we were talking, Gabi walked into the room. She was in her nighty, barefoot and rubbing her eyes.

"What is this?" Natalia said. "Who is this darling little girl?" She picked up Gabi and held her on her lap. "What is your name, sweetheart?"

"Gabrielle."

"My God, Ada, this child is precious.

551

Where did she come from?"

"Grenoble. I'm sure you heard about the roundup in Rome. She was swept up with the rest of us. We were being held in a detention center in Rome. We were all about to be shipped north when Kurt rescued us."

Natalia looked at Kurt with her mouth open. "You? You are the one who walked into the Collegio, took two of the prisoners, stole a car and drove away? That was you? You are Ada's German boyfriend?"

"Guilty."

"Bravo! You are legendary. All of my people know about you. You're a hero to us."

"The Nazis know about us too," I said.

"You're not kidding. They've posted notices. There's a monetary reward." She brushed Gabi's hair with her fingertips. "What a sweetie. What about her parents?"

I shook my head. "Don't ask, Nat, it upsets her. She's probably witnessed things that no little girl should ever see. She's blocked those memories and that's a good thing. Anyway, she's mine now, and I'm going to make sure she's loved and cared for."

"I'm so proud of you, Ada. I've always been in awe of what you've done."

"Me? Nat, you and your partisans are the real heroes. Why don't you bed down for the night? You're welcome to stay here as long as you want."

She leaned over and gave me a kiss. "Thank you, Ada, but I'll be gone in the morning. If you see my parents, tell them to be very careful, stay at Matt's and stay out of Pienza. And you do the same. Kurt, keep your gun loaded and by your side."

Sixty-Seven

Pienza, April 1944

Nazi patrols were searching all of Tuscany for Jews. Despite the fear of being discovered, Mama and Naomi were determined to keep Passover. It was agreed that we would have the celebration at our house, not at Matteo's. They had a car and we did not. We ended up with a full house: Naomi and Nico Romano, Matt, his wife and three children, Gabi, Mama and Enzo, Kurt and me.

Mama made a brisket and Naomi brought vegetables. Mama and Gabi spent most of the day making a flourless chocolate cake. The Passover service was short and sweet. I played the traditional songs, and the delight of the evening was watching the children hunt for the hidden matzo, the afikomen.

Enzo said that he heard the Allies were on the outskirts of Rome. "The Nazis are packing up their offices and heading north," he said. "It won't be too much longer until Italy is liberated."

"That's what Passover is all about," Mama said. We raised our wineglasses and toasted liberation. "Next year in Jerusalem and this year in a liberated and free Italy."

No sooner had she uttered those words than we saw the lights of a car pull down the drive and park in the front. Enzo rose from his seat. "Stay here. I'll see who it is. It could be one of my men." Kurt slipped into the back room, out of sight.

Enzo opened the door and a German corporal and two adjutants pushed their way into the room. "What is it you want here?" Enzo said.

"Just get out of the way, old man," the corporal said. Then to his companions, "Look at this. A Jewish ritual dinner! The informants were right. All you people are to come with us."

"I am the chief of police here, and this house is under my jurisdiction," Enzo said. "I am the senior law enforcement official in Pienza. Now I direct you to leave."

"Old man, you better get on your horse and ride away. We're taking these people to Fossoli. Those are my orders that come from SS headquarters." He moved quickly to the table and grabbed Mama by the arm.

Enzo rushed at him, "Let her go. You will not touch her," he said. One of the Nazis swung his rifle stock and knocked Enzo to the floor. Mama shrieked.

Right at that moment, Kurt walked through the door and into the room in full uniform, his hat square upon his head, his pistol in his belt. "Nice work, Corporal. I'll take it from here."

"We didn't know you were coming here, sir. We were instructed to come directly to this house, take all the occupants into custody and transport them to Fossoli for resettlement."

"Who do you think gave those orders, Corporal? They came from my office at the Via Tasso, direct from Lieutenant Kleiner. Now you can leave, I have this all under control. Two trucks are on their way here for the transport."

"But sir, I . . . I just saw Lieutenant Kleiner. He didn't say anything about you."

Kurt became angry. "Then maybe you didn't listen. Now turn around and walk out of here before I put all three of you on report! That's an order!" Kurt snapped his heel and shot his arm out. "Heil Hitler!"

The corporal swallowed hard and nodded to his companions. "Heil Hitler," he said. They turned and left the house.

Mama bent down to care for Enzo. "He's hurt," she cried.

"I'll be okay," Enzo said, "but all of you have to get out of here right now. They'll come back."

Matteo and his parents left to drive back to his home near Montepulciano. "We should be safe out in the country."

"We could go to Bologna," I said.

"That's not a bad idea," Enzo said. "You should all get as far from here as soon as possible. I will drive you to Bologna, but we must leave immediately."

I quickly packed a bag for Gabi and me, Mama packed a small suitcase, Kurt bundled up his spare clothes and we all piled into Enzo's police car. He had almost cleared the end of the driveway when our path was blocked by an oncoming car and a truck.

"Damn, they're back," Kurt said. "I'll handle this." He got out of the car with swagger, striding confidently toward the vehicles, every bit the quintessential Nazi officer. He raised his arm in a Hitler salute, and yelled, "Back those vehicles up. Out of the way now! We're in a hurry!"

Several men alighted from the vehicles, weapons drawn. And then I saw him. Kleiner.

"*Raus!* Everyone out of the car!" Kleiner yelled, pointing at us. *"Macht schnell!"*

We huddled in a group in the middle of the dirt driveway. I grabbed Gabi, turned her head into my skirt and held her tightly. Whatever was going to happen, she was not going to see it. Enzo stood in front of Mama.

"Well, well, look what we have here," Kleiner said, smiling at his comrades. "We hit the jackpot tonight, gentlemen. The deserter and his bitch. Look around. These criminals are living on land fit for a German emperor and they are nothing but Jewish trash. Now I will finally achieve my just reconciliation. The bitch that had me demoted is now in my custody. Isn't it marvelous how debts always get repaid?"

He pulled his gun from his holster, cocked the trigger and walked straight at me, wearing a sick smile from ear to ear. I tensed my muscles and hugged Gabi close to me, expecting the worst. All at once, Kurt flew at him from the side, knocking him to the ground. Kurt's fists flew and the two wrestled in the dirt. Suddenly, Kleiner's gun went off and Kleiner screamed. Kurt scrambled to his feet, was grabbed and pulled away, two men holding his arms.

Kleiner was lifted off the ground. His leg was bleeding and he was swearing furiously. "Someone tie me a tourniquet," he screamed at an adjutant, "and get me to a doctor."

Two of his soldiers lifted him and started to take him to the car when Kleiner shouted, "Wait!" He pointed at Kurt. "I want that son of a bitch. He's a filthy deserter. Shoot him.

Shoot him now!"

The Germans looked at each other, hesitating. "He's an officer," one of them said.

"They're right, Kleiner," Kurt said. "I am an officer in the Wehrmacht. I am entitled to a court-martial. These men may only be privates, but they know that they would have to answer for shooting an officer in the field."

"Bring him over here," Kleiner said.

"No," I cried. "Please don't. Kleiner can't be trusted. He'll shoot him."

Kleiner looked sternly at the soldiers. "I said bring him over here and hold him. That's an order."

The two SS privates dragged Kurt over to Kleiner. Kurt held his head high and smiled. "You're bleeding out, Kleiner," Kurt said. "End of the road for you. You only have minutes left. I'm proud to have ended the reign of such a brutal monster. Say good night, Hammer."

Kleiner pulled his pistol from his belt, pointed it at Kurt and pulled the trigger. Kurt twisted to the side and slumped to the ground. Kleiner reached over him and fired three more rounds into Kurt's lifeless body. A scream erupted from the bottom of my soul.

"Good night to you too, traitor," Kleiner said. As his soldiers picked him up to carry him to the truck, he pointed at Enzo who stood shielding Mama. "Shoot him," he said.

"Lieutenant," the private said, "We were told to arrest these people and take them to Fossoli. We were not told to execute anyone."

"That's an order! The old man is a criminal policeman and an enemy of the Reich. Shoot him and take the rest of them to Fossoli."

Two of the soldiers grabbed Enzo, took him to the side of the road and executed him. Mama wailed and collapsed in my arms.

As the soldiers carried Kleiner to the truck, he lost consciousness.

SIXTY-EIGHT

Pienza, September 2017

Printouts of court decisions sat on the table, the result of Catherine and Giulia's research into property seized by the Nazis during the war. "This is encouraging," Catherine said. "Italian law holds that seized property must be restored to the original owner if there is proof it was taken by the Nazis. If we can show that Quercia was a front for a Nazi land grab, then Gunther is right, the property cannot belong to Quercia or VinCo."

"What was the basis for those decisions?" Liam asked.

"There's a strong legal and factual basis," Giulia said. "Italy unconditionally surrendered in September 1943 and Germany immediately occupied most of Italy and set up a puppet Fascist government. During 1943 and 1944, the Nazi command ordered all Italian Jews to be deported to Nazi concentration camps. Their property was to be seized and forfeited. Many thousands of Jews were transported.

"After the war, in 1947, Italy signed the Treaty of Peace, which dissolved the puppet government, guaranteed individual liberties and provided restoration of property seized by the Nazis. That's the first legal basis. In 2009, Italy was one of forty-six countries that signed the Terezin Declaration, which provided for restitution of land wrongfully seized by Nazis, Fascists or their collaborators. That land was to be returned to the people who owned it before the seizure."

"That means the property must be restored to Friede Baumgarten or her heirs," Catherine said.

"Only if we can show it was seized by Nazis," Liam said.

"Based on the date — 1944 — and the SS names and symbols, there's a pretty good chance. That's what Gunther is working on," Catherine said. "He's trying to learn who owned or controlled Quercia."

"Wouldn't all this apply to VinCo as well?" Liam said. "They acquired all their properties in 1944."

"It would be the same. If Gunther can show that VinCo was owned or operated by Nazis when it acquired all that land, then VinCo's title can be voided as well. They'd lose their whole operation. The land would have to be returned to the heirs of the previous owners."

"VinCo's a billion-dollar corporation. If it's

owned and operated by former Nazis, it's no wonder that they would take extreme measures to protect their investment."

"Like destroying the registry books."

"Like threatening Hernandez and murdering Fabio Lombardo. It all makes sense," Catherine said.

"Gunther should be able to get some answers for us. The German court has issued subpoenas for copies of the original trust instruments. The owners' names would be disclosed in the agreements. Gunther said they have been served. It shouldn't be much longer."

Liam had a large white envelope. He opened it and took out an 11 by 15 picture of the closing celebration. "This is Matteo's picture. It shows Friede, Vanucci, Naomi, Hernandez's grandfather and the real estate agent. As you can see, there is a document sitting on the table. I assume it's the decd, but it's in Italian."

"It is a deed," Giulia said, "but I can't read very much of it. It's covered by a shadow. I can't read the names or see thc signatures."

"It's still valuable," Catherine said. "Hernandez can identify Vanucci in the picture. He's standing there with Friede. The picture was certainly taken a long time ago. Hernandez's billing records should be able to show that a deed was prepared at that time."

"And a *designata* agreement."

"Right. It's still not a copy of the deed, but we're getting close."

Sixty-Nine

Fossoli di Carpi, April 1944

The canvas-covered truck drove through the night on its way to the Fossoli detention camp, twelve miles north of Modena. We made two stops and picked up two more Jewish families, eleven in all. We sat on wooden benches, and I felt every bump and pothole in my backbone. I held Gabi on my lap, my arms around her tightly. The evening's scenario kept looping through my mind. Where had we made our mistakes? What should I have done? It was hard not to think that the entire situation was my fault. Didn't Natalia warn me? Hadn't we been fugitives on the run? After all, weren't we the ones that brought Kleiner to Mama's?

Before my intrusion, Mama's life was peaceful. She had her farm, her friends and Enzo. I was pretty sure she could have survived the war without my interference. I brought the legions of hell. It was me, and at this moment, I couldn't have felt worse. I should have saved my father and I didn't. Now I had brought these tragedies on my mother.

I had even condemned Kurt. I lost the one love of my life, the boy I'd been crazy about since we were teenagers in the Junior. The boy who never forgot about me. The boy who came back to rescue me and promised to spend the rest of his life with me. The vision of him lying twisted on the ground was burned into my memory. No matter what the future held for me, there would never be another Kurt.

We sat there dazed, semiconscious, as though we had been punched in the head too many times. Mama intermittently broke into sobs, her hands covering her face. She had lost her husband to the Nazis five years ago, and now her lover was shot to death trying to protect her. How could a woman possibly deal with that?

Gabi had retreated within herself. She stared straight into nothingness. Over the past few months, she had come out of her shell only to see the world betray her again and force her quickly back inside. I cradled her and rocked her back and forth, but she was in a state of emotional shock. I felt worse for her than for any one of us. Mama and I were adults. What sense could a four-year-old make of this sequence of horrors?

Fossoli had been an Italian prisoner-of-war camp, established two years earlier to hold Allied officers captured by the Italian army. Now it was a Nazi transit camp. Jews were being taken into custody all over Italy and thrown into camps like Fossoli, only to await transport to one of the Nazi concentration camps in Poland, Slovakia or Germany.

There were rows of wooden barracks for us to sleep on. Bare minimum amounts of food and water were parceled out. Bewildered Jews sat with suitcases, waiting for transport to an unknown and uncertain destination. Most were anxious to go, to get out of the Fossoli prison camp and reach a final destination that they were told would be a Jewish resettlement camp. They wouldn't be so anxious if they knew what Natalia had told me. As it was, there was nothing to do but sit and wait, and regret the fact that we were caught up in the sweep.

Mama and I tried to talk to Gabi. We would tell a story, sing a song and talk about the happy life we would have when we arrived at our new home. We hoped there would be lots of children and places to play. Above all, we assured Gabi that we would never leave her. I intended to keep that promise. I would fight like hell to keep her with me.

On the second night, Mama came over to

my bunk, after Gabi had gone to sleep. "She's a little angel," Mama said. "It's funny how such strange circumstances bring people together. She was lucky to have found you that night in Rome."

I wanted to say, Lucky? Was Gabi lucky? Were any of us lucky? How can you describe anything that's happened as lucky? But I didn't. I marveled that my mother could find positive thoughts. I hugged her and said, "Oh, Mama, I'm so sorry I brought all this on you."

She would have none of it. "No, honey, the Nazis brought it. All your life you have only brought me joy."

"But if I had stayed away, if I had gone into hiding with Natalia and her group . . ."

"Don't say that. If the decision had been mine to begin with, I would have insisted that you come home. The last few months have been precious to me. You brought me a darling granddaughter. The days were sweet. These last few months we were a family again. I wouldn't trade those months for anything."

It was during the third day that a guard came in with a clipboard and started reading names. "If your name is called, you are to come with me. Bring your suitcase, only one per person. You are to write your name and address on the side with the white paint. Keep your belongings with you. You will then move to the entrance of the camp to board the train. Soon you will arrive at the Jewish resettlement camp. You will be met there and told what to do."

Our names were called, and we painted our luggage. Mama and Gabi's address was the farm in Pienza. Since we were only given the right to take a single bag, I painted BAUMGARTEN, PHILHARMONIE on my father's violin case. We boarded with several hundred other people into a long train of boxcars.

Mama, Gabi and I were in a car with twenty-six others. The train started with a jolt and rolled slowly north and into the mountains. The journey was long, uncomfortable and chilly. I wrapped Gabi in my coat and we sat huddled with Mama. There was no food, no water and no bathroom facilities. There was an empty pail left for us that filled quickly.

Finally, many hours later, the train dragged to a stop at Auschwitz-Birkenau. The doors slid open suddenly, jolting our senses. Bright sunlight blinded us. Guards were shouting orders, vicious dogs were barking and children were wailing. There was a rancid, smoky stench in the air and the foul odor made me sick to my stomach. We were told to leave our baggage trackside, that it would be brought to us later, but I was not about to leave my father's violin. I didn't trust them to return it to me. I decided to carry it under my coat.

We stepped down from the car and moved slowly in a line, one side for the women and one side for the men. Mama and I walked with Gabi. As we approached the end of the tracks, I could see that SS officers were doing a quick evaluation and separating the women into two lines, one to the left and one to the right. The great majority of women, including all the older women, injured women and all the children, were being sent to the left. It looked like the younger and stronger women were being sent to the right. From what Natalia had told me, it didn't take much imagination to figure out why.

As the three of us were inching forward in the line, a uniformed guard came up to me, eyed me up and down, and said, "What are you holding under your coat?"

I took out the violin case. He looked at it and laughed. "You won't be playing the violin where you're going." He took the case from me and walked away.

Sometime later when we reached the front of the line, an SS officer looked us over, pointed at Mama and Gabi and said *"Links,"* to the left. To me he said, "You go that way, *Rechts,* to the right."

Gabi was clinging to my skirt. I shook my head. "I'm not leaving my mother or my daughter."

He shrugged and smiled. "Suit yourself. You made a bad choice. *Links.*" He pointed to the left. "Go, all three of you."

We joined the line with the other women shuffling slowly toward a cement building. There were hundreds in the line and it took a long time to move forward. As we neared the building, the SS guard who took my violin came up with another guard and asked the three of us to step out of the line. "Which of you is Baumgarten?"

"All of us," I said.

"Is this your case?" he said to me. I nodded. "You are to follow me."

The three of us started to walk, but the officer said, "Not you two, only her."

"That is my mother and my daughter. I will not leave them," I said.

He shook his head. "It is not your decision to make. You are to come with me; they are to continue in the line."

I grabbed Gabrielle and put my arms around her. "No," I said. "I will not leave her."

The officer said, "You are being foolish. We contacted the Philharmonie, spoke to Herr Furtwängler. Dr. Goebbels called us shortly thereafter. You are fortunate. Your skills are needed elsewhere. But only you."

"I don't want to be spared if it means leaving my mother and daughter. You can drag me, but I will not perform."

"Let them go," the other guard said. "If she wants to stay, let her stay. It won't be our fault."

"But we've been given an order. She is not to be sent into that building."

The two of them stood there arguing about whether I should live or die until an SS captain walked over. "This woman has a death wish," the guard said. "I say let her die."

The SS captain shook his head. "It's not our call. She has been ordered to Theresienstadt. The order comes from Dr. Goebbels and I'm not about to disobey the order."

"I understand, sir, but she says she won't go without her mother and her daughter."

"Children are allowed at Theresienstadt. She can keep the child." They nodded and turned back to me. "You may take your daughter."

Again, I shook my head. "No. My mother comes as well."

"She's not going, and you don't tell us what to do," the captain said. "Either you and your daughter come with me or I will deliver you to Theresienstadt in chains and your daughter will go with your mother into the camp. Make up your mind."

Mama grabbed my arm. "Ada, you must

take Gabi and go with them. I will not let Gabi die because of some foolish notion that you can save me. You can't. You and I both know why we are standing in this line and where this line is going. I can accept it if that's what God has in store for me. But you and Gabi have been given a chance. You must go."

I knew she was right. But how could I watch her walk to her death while I walked away? How could I make such a choice? I wouldn't do it.

"No, Mama. I can't. If Goebbels wants me to perform, he has to take us all."

"No, Fraulein," the SS captain said. "It's not going to happen like that. Either you and your daughter come with me, or I will handcuff you, put you in the car and leave your daughter here."

Mama leaned over, threw her arms around me and hugged me as strongly as she could. She kissed me and said, "Go. Take Gabi. Don't worry about me, I will soon be with my Jacob. This is my decision, not yours. I love you, Ada." Then she pushed me back as hard as she could, turned and ran quickly to the front of the line. I watched her disappear into the building.

I stood there in shock, tears running down my face. I felt too weak to stand. My heart was broken. My mother and my father, ripped from me by the Nazis and I did nothing to stop them. Why was I still alive? I had no right to be alive. I couldn't move and I didn't care. Then this little girl tugged at my skirt and said in her innocent little way, "Where is Grandma going?"

Her voice was a slap in my face and brought me to my senses. I dared not show my despair to Gabi. "To a settlement area, honey, where she can be with other grandmas," I said. "She'll be fine."

"This way," the captain said to me. Gabi and I followed him away from the lines and into a red brick building.

We sat on a long bench in the administration offices waiting for a truck to take us on another two-hour drive to the Theresienstadt concentration camp in northern Czechoslovakia. The SS captain told me that Furtwängler first requested that I be returned to the Philharmonic to rejoin the orchestra, but the request was denied by Goebbels.

"He told us that musicians are needed at Theresienstadt to play in the camp orchestra this spring," the captain said. "I am told there is an important project. It seems you have a reputation as an artist and a soloist, Fraulein Baumgarten. Dr. Goebbels directed that you be sent there immediately."

SEVENTY

Theresienstadt Concentration Camp, May 1944
It was late afternoon when Gabi and I arrived at Theresienstadt. Thick brick walls topped with barbed wire surrounded the large camp. The entrance to the camp was through an arched gate. ARBEIT MACHT FREI was painted above the arch, the same as I had seen at Auschwitz-Birkenau, but that's where the resemblances stopped. From what I could see of the Auschwitz-Birkenau camp, the prisoners were dressed in gray-and-white-striped prison uniforms and prison caps, and they shuffled about with their backs bent and their heads lowered. In Theresienstadt, inmates wore civilian clothes and some of them were neatly dressed. The buildings had been freshly painted. And I saw gardens! Vegetable gardens tended by residents. In the middle of the camp there were large parks with green grass and children's playground equipment.

Spring flowers bloomed along the walkways and in the parks. The flowers looked healthy and robust, but the people did not. They were thin and pasty-looking. The grounds were clean. There were signs: this way to the library, this way to the coffee shop. And most noticeably, there was no shouting, no barking dogs and no foul stench.

Gabi and I were met at the entrance by a man who introduced himself as Rabbi Murmelstein, a member of the Council of Jewish Elders. "Welcome to Terezín," he said, using the Czech word for the town. "This is a very busy time for us, as you can see. I will show you to your residence, and tomorrow you will meet our esteemed music director, Rafael Schächter."

As we walked along the sidewalks, I saw stores — bakery shops, tailor shops, shoe stores. It reminded me of the Hackescher Markt area in Berlin. Here in Theresienstadt, there were no people walking in formation as I had seen at Auschwitz. There were no SS guards with rifles prodding prisoners. "Is this what they mean by a Jewish resettlement town?" I said. "It's nice."

He looked at me solemnly and shook his head. "Make no mistake, Fraulein Baumgarten," he said quietly, "you are in a prison. It was formerly a Czech military fort and now it is a Nazi concentration camp. You have been brought here because you are a famous musician and because we are expecting visitors later this month. There are to be concerts, and you will fill a need. Hitler and Goebbels want the world to know that famous musicians choose to live at Theresienstadt. Come with me. I will assist you in settling into your barracks, and then tomorrow morning you will report to Maestro Schächter. Where are your suitcases?"

"I have only my violin."

"I will see that the two of you get clothing."

The barracks were long brick buildings, some of them two stories, some three stories. Many of them were freshly painted in a mustard color. Gabi and I were assigned two wooden bunks.

We decided to take a walk before dinner, but before we could go outside, I had to sew yellow stars on our clothes. Within limits, we were free to roam the camp, but we could not go out without the identifying Star of David. At dinner, we lined up to get a serving of potato and some bland soup. That night, as she would every night in Theresienstadt, Gabi slept with me in my bunk. In the morning, I was led to the performance hall, where I met Maestro Schächter.

"I heard that you were coming and I am delighted you are here," he said. "I regret I never had the privilege of seeing you perform. I met your father once, but only briefly." He looked down at my dress where Gabi was hiding. "This is your child?"

I nodded. "She is now."

"There are children's activities," he said. "I could arrange for her to be with other children during rehearsals. They draw, they paint, they do beautiful art."

"If it's all the same, I'd ask that she be allowed to sit here in the hall for the first few days. She's had a rough time."

Schächter nodded. "Very well, but you should understand, they've all had a rough time. Goebbels' staff insists that we add the 'Meditation' to our repertoire. I am told that you have soloed the piece all over Europe."

"Goebbels and Hitler heard me play the piece in Florence. I do know it well."

"Well, let me tell you how we work. We have a limited amount of sheet music. Most of it we play from memory. This is the music we are working on at the present, and we will add the 'Meditation.' We are rehearsing three symphonies, but our principal piece is the Verdi *Requiem.* Do you know it?"

I was shocked. The *Requiem* was an extremely difficult piece for orchestra and chorus. A large chorus. We performed it two years ago in Bologna. Even the consummate professionals and experienced principal singers needed months of practice before the work was ready. How could a put-together bunch of prisoners in a concentration camp hope to produce that work?

"I do know the *Requiem,*" I said. "I can't believe you're going to take that on here in a concentration camp."

"I brought the scores with me when I came a couple years ago. We have been practicing for many months in the basement of a barracks. It's cold and damp and dark, but our singers are inspired. We had a larger chorus; once it was one hundred and twenty, but many were transported last fall. Now there are sixty in the chorus. I think you will be pleasantly surprised at their proficiency. Everyone knows his or her part from memory. We have performed it several times for the residents. We are going to perform it later this month for the Nazis and their guests."

As we were talking, a tall man with white hair walked into the room. I thought I recognized him, but this man was very thin, almost bony. He looked at me, squinted his eyes and said, "Is that Jacob's little pip-squeak? Is it you, Ada? It's me, Aaron Spak."

I smiled and hugged him. "It's so nice to see you again, Herr Spak."

"Aaron. Just Aaron. I'd love to hear about your career. Have a tea with me after rehearsal."

The piece we were rehearsing was Haydn's Symphony no. 101 in D Major, "The Clock" symphony, which we had played in the Junior. It was clean, honest, formal and upbeat, like Haydn himself. In the second movement, which gives the piece its name, the violins play a delightful, lilting melody while the bassoons and plucking cellos create a background tick-tock rhythm. Out of the corner of my eye, I could see that Gabi was enjoying it, keeping time to the music with a little head and shoulder movement.

Afterward, we met Aaron in the barracks for a cup of tea. I could see that the leaves were well used. "How is your father?" he asked. "Is he all right?"

My eyes glassed over. Aaron didn't know. I shook my head.

"Oh, I'm sorry," Aaron said. "I thought he had emigrated. I always loved and respected Jacob."

"He was captured during Kristallnacht and died in the Buchenwald prison."

"I'm so sorry." He lowered his head and slowly moved it from side to side. "So, so many of us."

"What can you tell me about Theresienstadt?" I said. "I mean, if one has to be confined in a prison, it seems like this is a pretty good place to be."

"Oh no, it's a hoax, Ada. They're putting on a show. The International Red Cross is coming here in three weeks to make an inspection. Hitler and Goebbels want to fool the world and make believe they treat us well. A few months ago, they started sprucing up this camp. Before that it was filthy, barren and vermin-infested. No grass, just mud. This was a camp designed for six thousand residents, and last summer there were almost sixty thousand packed in. Starting last fall they began sending people away in transports. They say that they are sending people to the east, to new resettlement camps, but a few of us have learned that 'east' is really Poland and Auschwitz. We do not share that knowledge with the rest of the residents for obvious reasons. It is always better to have hope.

"Over the past several months, the SS has begun beautifying the camp. They call it Operation Embellishment. They have painted, they have planted, they have built fake shops and fake bakeries. Did you see the clothes in the window of the dress shop? They were taken from our residents' suitcases and displayed like they were for sale. They even made a pretend bank.

"You were sent here for your music skills. Everyone works. Some work in the orchestra and the art workshops. Others work in the coal mines, sew uniforms, manufacture coffins and maintain the grounds. There is no torture or mass murder here. Which is not to say that there haven't been executions. But it is not Auschwitz."

"I saw children in the streets," I said. "There are parks. There are flowers. It fooled me."

Aaron nodded. "For the time being. The Nazis boast that Theresienstadt is a 'spa town,' a place where elderly Jews can live safely. They have actually taken money from elderly Jews so that they could retire here. It's all a lie."

"And the beautification is all because of the Red Cross? Because of an inspection?"

"Yes, because of the inspection. The world accuses Hitler of creating a network of death camps where he is sending Europe's Jewish population, and of course it's true. You've seen it. Your father died at Buchenwald and you were there at Auschwitz. But Hitler denies it. He says there is no proof. And to show he is right, he is permitting the Red Cross to visit Theresienstadt. Don't you see? You were selected and brought here from Auschwitz because you are a well-known musician. Instead of killing you, they are using you, and all of us, to paint a false picture. Look world, this is really how Hitler treats the Jews."

"I don't understand. Why would Hitler give a damn what the world thinks? He never has before."

"I can only pass along what I hear. Last

October four hundred and fifty Jews were seized in Denmark. They were sent here to Theresienstadt because it has always been a transit camp, a place where people are collected before being sent to other concentration camps — labor camps or death camps. The king of Denmark was informed that the Danish prisoners were ultimately going to be sent to a death camp or a slave labor camp. He demanded an inspection by the Danish Red Cross. He was joined by Sweden's King Gustav. So Hitler and Goebbels seized upon the opportunity to create a grand deception. They will show the world how well Germany treats the Jewish captives."

I shook my head. "The Nazis have already occupied Denmark and captured its Jews, and Sweden is neutral. It doesn't make sense to me."

"Sweden took in eight thousand Danish Jews, almost all of the Jews in Denmark. The four hundred and fifty that were left were the ones that were captured and sent here. Denmark is demanding fair treatment for its Jews, and Sweden is joining with them. Germany does not want to alienate Sweden, which is the Wehrmacht's major source of iron ore. So Hitler decided to fool them. The head physician of Denmark's Ministry of Health, two Swedish inspectors and the International Red Cross are coming

583

here on June 23, and they will see a lovely little Jewish town that Hitler has built."

"And the orchestra is going to play a concert for them?"

"Not just for them. We'll also play for the residents of Theresienstadt, and that's the grand Nazi deception. Attending concerts, going to the theater, playing soccer — that is the wonderful life in the spa retirement town of Theresienstadt. At least that's what they're going to show the Red Cross."

"He's going to get away with it, isn't he? He's going to fool the world and we're going to help him."

"I'm afraid that's true. It's a setup and you've been conscripted. But you'd rather be here with your daughter than in Auschwitz, wouldn't you? After June 23, it's anybody's guess what happens to us all."

SEVENTY-ONE

Theresienstadt Concentration Camp, June 1944
We were doing our best to adjust to life in Theresienstadt. Of course, Aaron was right. They could dress it up, but it was still a prison. We were given minimal portions of food without regard to nourishment. Prisoners were subjected to forced labor for long hours each day. My only job was playing the violin, which gave me the opportunity to be with Gabi most of the time.

Gabi was attending art classes with other children and had actually made a few friends. She had yet to tell me anything about her parents or her life before I met her at the Collegio. I respected her right to lock those memories away and I suspected they would never come out. In the same way, we did not discuss Mama or what happened at the farm. The memories of my life over the past ten years — the deterioration of the Berlin Jewish community, my papa's death, Kurt's murder, Mama's sacrifice, all the tragedies that I witnessed — I tried to lock them away, but they came out at night to haunt me. I woke up shaking. It scared Gabi, but there wasn't much I could do about it.

Theresienstadt's SS commandant was Karl Rahm, but he was rarely seen. Aaron told me he was a drunk. The SS left the day-to-day operations of the camp to the Council of Jewish Elders, subject to SS oversight. The SS would dictate how many inmates were to be transported and the council would fill the order. The council distributed the meager supplies of food and drink. It allowed for a form of commerce in a stifled setting. It established a synagogue and oversaw the practice of Judaism.

Other than rehearsal times, I had abundant free time, and Gabi and I were allowed to wander around the camp. Paper, writing supplies and art supplies were always available. That is when I decided to write this memoir.

As the date for the Red Cross inspection neared, tension in the camp increased. So did the presence of SS guards. Commandant Rahm was seen more frequently. The path that the Red Cross inspectors were to take through the camp was carefully mapped out. Resident carpenters made finishing touches to structures along the path. Draperies were sewn and hung in the windows. Furniture pieces were strategically placed. A bandshell was erected in the middle of the park. A group of jazz musicians who called themselves the Ghetto Swingers were directed to play there several times a day.

A week before the inspections, the SS suddenly decided that the camp was too crowded. They wanted the inspectors to see healthy, happy people in roomy living quarters. Rahm ordered the council to provide the names of 7,500 inmates to be immediately transported to Auschwitz. Aaron told me that all sick, disabled or senile persons and all orphans were required to be on the list. Orphans! I immediately sat down with Gabrielle.

"Listen to me, Gabi. You are my daughter." She nodded, unsure what I was doing. "If anyone ever asks you, I am your mother, understand?"

"Why would someone ask me?"

"It doesn't matter. They might. You are my daughter. I am your mother. What is your name?"

"Gabrielle."

"Gabrielle what? What is your family name?"

Her lips tightened, and she did not speak.

"Tell me your family name, Gabi."

Her jaw quivered.

I held her shoulders. "Your last name is Baumgarten! Say it, Gabi! Baumgarten."

"Baumgarten."

"What is your name?"

"Gabrielle."

"Your whole name?" I was frightening her, but it had to be done.

"Gabrielle Baumgarten."

"Again. What is your whole name?"

"Gabrielle Baumgarten."

She cried and I hugged her.

As it happened, the council did take a census of each barracks before filling the deportation list, and they did ask each child his or her name. Every single child. All women with children were told to gather in the public square. Rabbi Murmelstein stood with an SS officer and a clipboard. "We know that many of you came here with your own children. We do not want to separate mothers from their natural children. But the high command has ordered us to identify orphans. We are told they will be sent to a children's camp. This order is not the decision of your council, nor is it our preference, but it has been ordered by SS Commandant Rahm and we are obliged to obey. If you have graciously taken in an orphaned child, please identify yourself."

Only a few parents identified an orphaned child. I did not. I would never allow Gabi to be taken from me. The SS officer suspected that many of us were lying. He ordered Rabbi Murmelstein to walk among us and ask questions. When he came to Gabi and me, he stopped. Gabi had blond hair, mine was dark. She was fair with rosy cheeks. She looked nothing like me.

He stared at me, like he knew my secret. He bent down until his head was even with Gabi's. "What is your name, little girl?" he said.

Gabi clutched my skirt. "Gabrielle Baumgarten."

He stood, looked me in the eyes and slowly shook his head.

"She goes, I go," I whispered to him.

He thought for a moment, nodded and moved on.

Later that day, 7,500 residents were told to pack a bag, write their name on the side and walk in line to the Theresienstadt train station. Each person was given a typed identification number. After the deportation, as Rahm had intended, there was more room in the barracks, and living spaces were reallocated.

Verdi's *Requiem* is a two-hour oratorio with orchestra and a good-size choir. Rehearsals for that strenuous work began to run longer and longer. The singers had been practicing for months in damp, dark, cold basements and they sang by rote. They had committed their parts to memory! I was overwhelmed by their technical and artistic perfection. It was as fine as I had ever heard. There was something special taking place. These men and women were dedicated vocalists to be sure, but they were impelled by a greater force, a statement of the liberation of their souls. They were prisoners in body only. Unable to resist by physical force, their artistry was a solid demonstration of spiritual resistance.

I didn't understand at first why Maestro Schächter chose to perform a Catholic mass in Latin for a Jewish concentration camp. But as we rehearsed it became clear. It was the content of the Requiem. There was a message in the libretto, words that no Jew would dare say to a Nazi commander. These very words were going to be sung right into the Nazis' faces in front of the Red Cross inspectors.

"How great will be the judge when he
    comes to examine!"
"All that is hidden shall appear, nothing
    shall be unavenged."
"Day of wrath, day of wrath, when the
    wicked shall be judged!"
"When the heavens and earth are
    trembling."

Schächter is brilliant. The Nazis will boast how the inmates presented the Requiem for them and for the Red Cross without having a clue what the Latin words meant. The Nazis will clap for a performance that mocks them. Brilliant.

As the date approached, Maestro Schächter made the decision to perform the work solely with piano accompaniment. It was impossible to have orchestra members playing from memory without sheet music and coordinate with the chorus in so difficult a production. An outstanding pianist, Alice Herz Sommer, whose family had played with Gustav Mahler, would provide the instrumental accompaniment on the piano. I needed to be a part of this performance and I asked Maestro Schächter if I could be given the job of turning Miss Sommer's pages.

The morning of June 23, the camp was clean and bright. Everyone was told to dress in their best clothes and fix their hair. The shelves in the phony bakery shop were loaded with bread and pastries. Women were prominently placed around the camp preparing fresh vegetables for dinner. People had been told to smile and sing. They even staged a soccer game and placed hundreds of cheering residents on the sidelines.

The inspectors walked through the camp nodding, pointing and smiling. SS guards chaperoned them. No prisoner dared come up to tell the truth. They entered the concert hall and took their seats. There they sat with dozens of SS in full uniform ready to experience the *Requiem*. At the appropriate time, the chorus filed in, followed by Maestro Schächter.

Maestro Schächter had done a masterful job in preparing the chorus for such a long and serious piece. They were as accomplished as any I'd heard. In truth, Rafael Schächter was a genius. It was obvious that the prisoners of Theresienstadt took great pride in what they had accomplished, and their triumph was felt by every resident in the camp. The Nazis had stolen their liberty, taken their belongings, enslaved them in concentration camps, but in the end, they had not deprived them of their artistry, their talents and their souls. They did not quell the music. It will forever be remembered that Theresienstadt was a tribute, not to Hitler's scheming mind but to the resilience and soul of the Jewish inmates.

I looked around the room. Commandant Rahm, SS camp guards, Nazi officers and the Red Cross inspectors were all silent. The uniformed Nazis sat at tables, smugly smoking cigarettes. They could have been watching paint dry. They were clay soldiers, incapable of emotion.

As far as the International Red Cross inspection was concerned, the hoax was a success. The inspectors gave glowing reports about the camp and how well-treated the residents were. It was so successful that Goebbels decided to send a film crew to Theresienstadt to make a propaganda movie. It was initially to be called *The Führer Gives a Village to the Jews,* but the name was later changed to *Theresienstadt: A Documentary Film of the Jewish Resettlement.*

Although some deportations resumed after the Red Cross visit, many in the orchestra and chorus remained exempt to make the film. The actual filming took place between September 1 and September 12. The orchestra sat for several sessions. The Ghetto Swingers played before "happy" actors and actresses in the park. Children were shown playing on the swings and eating bread slathered with butter. When the filming was complete and the film crew had departed, Theresienstadt returned to its true purpose — a bare-bones transit camp established to collect Jews and send them off to death camps and labor camps.

In the fall of 1944, the war was coming closer to Theresienstadt. With the Allies closing in, the Nazis stepped up the pace of deportations. In the fall months, 18,400 men, women and children were deported. Their names were chosen by Rabbi Murmelstein, the last remaining council elder. On October 17, 1944, the great Rafael Schächter and many of the chorus members were packed into boxcars and sent east to Auschwitz.

For whatever reason, Gabi and I remained off the lists. Perhaps it was because of my initial assignment, though I will never know. As year-end approached and the population of the camp decreased, it was only a matter of time until everyone would be sent to another camp. Theresienstadt was scheduled to be closed.

On February 4, 1945, Rabbi Murmelstein came to see me. We walked outside into the square and talked privately.

"Tomorrow a train will leave. It will not go east to Auschwitz but will travel south to Switzerland. Himmler and Kaltenbrunner have agreed to free twelve hundred Terezín inmates in exchange for five million Swiss francs deposited into escrow by world Jewish organizations. The money has been raised and deposited in Switzerland."

The rabbi handed a small piece of paper to me. On it was typed S174. "Show this to the guards at the gate and they will let you on the train. May God bless you, Ada."

I looked at the paper. It only had one number.

"What about my daughter?"

"We know that Gabrielle is not your daughter. I have no extra passes. Someone will take care of her here in the camp. I'm sorry." He stood and left the building.

There was only one thing I could do. I called Gabrielle over to me and whispered to her, "Gabi, let's go pack our bag. Tomorrow there will be a wonderful trip. Freedom awaits. No more Theresienstadt. No more concentration camp. Tomorrow you will see the beautiful mountains of Switzerland. Just like you saw in Grenoble."

Gabi was thrilled. She had a smile from ear to ear. She was bouncing on her feet. Neither one of us could sleep that night.

It is a cold February morning in Theresienstadt and the Switzerland group is assembling in the square. Gabi is bundled up in her warmest clothes. She has her little bag and some of the pictures she has painted. She is excited about going to Switzerland. The last thing I will do is hide my memoir in her duffel bag and kiss my sweet daughter good-bye.

My dear Gabi, you are all I have in the world. You are the sole remaining member of our family. That is why I have written this story in such detail, so you will know everything about the woman who loves you so, about your grandma, my papa and your extended new family. It will be just like I am there to tell you bedtime stories for the rest of your life. Read this story and I will always be there with you. I will never leave you.

All my love forever,
Mama

SEVENTY-TWO

Pienza, September 2017

"That's it?" Liam said with tears in his eyes. "Cat, please tell me I'm missing some pages."

Catherine shook her head. "I thought the same thing when I came to the end, but Floria told me that she sent us the entire manuscript."

"She didn't finish. How could she leave us hanging like that?"

"She did finish, Liam. She wrote the manuscript during her time in Theresienstadt. She wrote it so that Gabi would know everything about her adopted mother and her extended family. She finished her story, put it in Gabi's bag and put Gabi on the train."

"So Gabi went on to freedom in place of Ada. It makes me so sad for both of them."

"Ada sacrificed her life to save Gabi. Isn't that what a mother would do?"

"That might have been the end of the story in Theresienstadt, but it's obviously not the end of the story. Gabi is here. What happened next? What happened in Switzerland? How did Gabi end up here on the farm?"

"I guess you'll have to get that information from Gabi."

Liam shook his head. "Not a chance. It's all locked up. Just like Ada said, she locked away those memories."

"At least we know who Gabi is and why she is here. We know our client better and can more effectively represent her interests. That's why she wanted us to read the manuscript. But we have a court date in two days, and unless Gunther has found some new information, we're in trouble."

"He told us to call him at noon. The subpoenas were returnable this morning."

"Let's head over to Giulia's and make the call."

"Gunther, you have Liam, Catherine and Giulia here on the phone. Please tell us you found something."

"A treasure trove, my friends. The subpoenas were returned this morning along with all of the corporate and trust information. Additionally, I assigned two young associates to research the principals and they did a terrific job. Where do you want me to start?"

"Let's start with Gabriella's property, the one supposedly owned by Quercia Company."

"Quercia was formed on May 18, 1944. It

is an Italian corporation with a single share-holder, the Totenkopf Trust. That name ought to be enough to alert your judge that the property was seized by a Nazi-owned entity, but we've got more. We know that the sole beneficiary of the Totenkopf Trust was initially Elsa Fruman, and I have had my staff research her. She was a socialite during the thirties and forties. A very good-looking woman. There are pictures of her in the *Völkischer Beobachter* newspaper at various social functions. Oftentimes, she can be seen arm-in-arm with a uniformed Nazi."

"Don't tell me," Liam said, "one of the Nazis was Herbert Kleiner."

"Obersturmführer Herbert Kleiner. The very same."

"But I thought he died. He was shot to death by Kurt Koenig."

"No, he wasn't. He was shot, but he survived. Although Kleiner was married to Marta Kleiner, records show that Herbert and Elsa Fruman rented an apartment together in Berlin. Records also show that Gerda Fruman was born to Elsa in 1947."

"The birth certificate doesn't have the name of her father," Catherine said.

"Well, can you blame him? He was married to Marta Kleiner and already had two boys. Gerda's birth certificate doesn't name Kleiner, nor does she share his name for obvious reasons, but the certificate lists Elsa's address in Berlin. It's Kleiner's apartment."

"So, in 1944 Kleiner arrests Friede, Ada and Gabi, and sends them off to a concentration camp. He knows they will never return, and he transfers their property to his mistress."

"Right. Except he doesn't really transfer it. He has no deed. He just puts the name in the registry book."

"Marvelous. Great job, Gunther!"

"Now on to VinCo. VinCo was also formed on May 18, 1944, by Hermann Rugel, the same Berlin attorney, an attorney known to be a ranking party member. Same organizational structure. Italian corporation, German trust and German beneficiary. The Wolfsangel Trust had three beneficiaries. Want to guess?"

"Herbert Kleiner and his two boys."

"Right, you are. Herbert is long dead, but his sons are still alive. They still own and operate the company. They are very wealthy and very private. I would not doubt for a moment that they were still connected with the neo-Nazi network."

"There's one problem here," Giulia said. "The registry books show that the individual farmers deeded their properties to VinCo in 1944."

"Well, we don't know if the signatures are genuine, and Kleiner could have forced the farmers to sign their names, but what we do know is that four of those farmers were arrested by Kleiner in May 1944 and sent off to detention camps. German records were kept of the arrests and disposition of detainees."

"Ada didn't write that Friede's neighbors were Jewish," Catherine said.

"It wouldn't matter. The Nazis were arresting partisans, collaborators and enablers and sending them to camps as well."

"Now we see why VinCo fought so hard to own Gabriella's property," Catherine said. "When Gerda died without children, her property might have been claimed by some cousins or distant relatives. There could have been a court fight over who had a rightful claim to Quercia. Undoubtedly the lawyers would have done their research and discovered that the property had been seized. All of this history would have come out."

"If Quercia was found to have been a Nazi front, then wouldn't VinCo have been next?" Liam said.

"Exactly. VinCo couldn't take the chance of being discovered. It's a billion-dollar company. They had to keep the seizures hidden. While Fruman was still alive, the Kleiners let the property stand in her name. That may have been Herbert's wishes. But on her death, they couldn't let some strangers start to investigate the titles."

"Gunther, we can't thank you enough,"

Catherine said. "Would you please scan and e-mail all of the documents to Giulia? We need to prepare an emergency motion, and I want to attach all of the evidence for the judge to review before we appear. Would you please make certified copies of all the relevant documents, including the pictures, and overnight them to us? We only have two days to present our emergency motion."

"I'll do better than that. I'll e-mail all the documents to you right now and I'll bring the originals to you personally and testify to their authenticity."

"Oh, that's very generous, but you don't have to do that," Catherine said.

"You never know what the judge will require, and besides, I love Siena in the fall."

When they ended the call, Catherine and Giulia smiled at each other. "We know what we have to do now. Let's get all this information into an emergency motion, attach everything that Gunther sends to us and set this matter for immediate hearing."

Seventy-Three

Siena, September 2017

Judge Riggioni's courtroom was buzzing. Catherine and Giulia sat at the counsel table to the judge's left. Lenzini leaned back in a chair at the counsel table to the right and smiled smugly. Gabriella, Floria and Liam sat in the first row with Gunther Strauss.

The courtroom was called to order and Judge Riggioni entered. "We are here this morning on Signora Vincenzo's motion to reopen the proofs and vacate my previous order awarding possession to VinCo. I have read the motion and all the attached exhibits, including those certified by German counsel, Gunther Strauss, who is present in my court today. Thank you for bringing them, Herr Strauss, and welcome to Siena. Are the parties ready to proceed?"

Giulia stood. "The petitioner, Gabriella Vincenzo, is ready, *Signor Presidente.*"

"The respondent VinCo is *not* ready," Lenzini said, leaning back in his seat at the table.

"This so-called emergency motion, defective on its face, has taken me by complete surprise. To use an American expression, I'm being sandbagged."

"Really?" the judge said. "Which part of this motion sandbags you, *Avvocato* Lenzini? What information is in the motion that you didn't know before today? Did you know when VinCo was formed? Do you know who your clients are? Are you familiar with the Kleiner family?"

"Yes, yes, yes, of course."

The judge spread his hands. "Then how are you surprised?"

"I need time. Lots of time. I didn't expect to argue these issues in this court."

"No doubt. I guess you didn't expect the missing registry book to be an issue, or the murdered registrar clerk, or the lack of a deed from Signor Partini to be raised as an issue, but here they are. Perhaps the fundamental issue we consider here today is whether the Vincenzo property may have been seized by Nazis, Fascists or their collaborators. Is that also an issue you didn't expect to address?"

"That is correct, I did not expect to address any of those issues."

"Hmm. It is unfortunate for your client that Signora Vincenzo has hired more persistent attorneys this time around. I have read the motion and the attachments, and I deem those issues to be material and ripe for consideration. *Avvocato* Lenzini, there is a difference between not expecting to argue an issue and not being given an opportunity to produce evidence. Do you agree?"

"Yes, absolutely. Of course, I do. That's the point."

The judge smiled. "The latter would be unfair, wouldn't it? I mean if I ordered you to proceed to trial without giving you an opportunity to produce evidence that you have, that would be unfair to you, wouldn't it?"

"Yes, exactly."

"But, that's just what happened to Signora Vincenzo two months ago, isn't it?"

"No, that's different. Her attorneys didn't come to court."

"And isn't that strange as well? It seems that her previous attorneys, for some unexplained reason, lost interest in the case and ignored the very evidence that has been presented to me today. Do you suppose they were somehow induced to ignore all that evidence? Do you suppose there was unethical persuasion?"

"Well, I wouldn't know."

"Tell me, *Avvocato* Lenzini, if I give you more time, what evidence can you produce to counter the assertion that VinCo never obtained a deed in 1944 from the previous owner, Signor Partini?"

"None, there is no deed to be found."

"I see. What evidence could you produce to

show that the property was lawfully purchased by Herbert Kleiner's mistress in 1944?"

"I will not have that."

"Do you intend to offer evidence that Herbert Kleiner was not a Nazi Obersturmführer in May 1944, the date your client allegedly obtained title?"

"No. I concede he was a Nazi officer."

"As regards the picture of Carlo Vanucci and Friede Baumgarten, and the portion of a deed that sits on the table, do you concede that Vanucci was a *designata* by agreement?"

"I do not concede, but I will not have any evidence to disprove it."

"Very well. Is there any other evidence that you can produce if we gave you more time? Otherwise, I think we should proceed today."

"Not so fast, Your Honor. We have evidence that will show that Gabriella Vincenzo is not entitled to own the property. According to the petitioner's statement of the facts, Carlo Vanucci was a *designata* for the benefit of Friede Baumgarten, a Jew who wanted to hide her ownership."

The judge wrinkled his forehead. "Is there something wrong with a Jewish person using a *designata* agreement? I think that was done quite often during World War II."

"That is not my point. The nominee agreement was for the benefit of Friede Baumgarten, *not* Gabriella Vincenzo. Therefore, the

deed from Vanucci to Vincenzo would not conform to the *designata* agreement and would be void."

The judge rested his chin on his hand. "Let's suppose you are right. If the deed from Vanucci to Vincenzo was void because it was not contemplated by the agreement, that still would not vest ownership in Quercia, would it? I mean, how does that argument benefit your client?"

Lenzini sneered and pointed at Gabi. "Maybe it would, maybe it wouldn't, but she's not going to get the property either!"

"Oh, I see the wisdom of your position. It's personal. If you can't win, at least make sure your opponent suffers, am I right?"

Lenzini shrugged. "If we can't have it, she doesn't get it either."

"*Avvocato* Lenzini, when there is a nominee agreement and the principal dies, don't her rights pass on to her heirs? Here, Friede Baumgarten was the equitable owner. Why wouldn't Signora Vincenzo have inherited the right to own the property?"

"That's the whole point," Lenzini said, once again glaring at Gabriella. "She is not an heir. I happen to know she was born in France in 1939. I can do research too."

Gabi began to shake with rage. She started to rise from her seat when Liam tapped her on the arm. "Let the lawyers handle it."

"I can speak for myself," Gabriella said, rising to her feet. "I am the daughter of Ada Baumgarten, the granddaughter of Friede Baumgarten."

Liam hung his head. Just because Ada said that Gabi was her daughter didn't make it so.

Gabriella continued. "I was adopted. Friede was my grandmother. Here is my driver's license. It reads Gabrielle Baumgarten Vincenzo."

"Anyone can put a middle name on a driver's license," Lenzini said.

"Where did the adoption take place, Signora?" the judge asked.

"Well, I was ten years old, but I think it was here in Siena."

Catherine looked at Liam. She was grimacing as well. Gabi's statement could not be true. Friede died in 1944. Ada died in 1945. Gabi could not have been adopted when she was ten years old in 1949.

"I will recess the court for fifteen minutes. *Avvocata* Romano, would you take the signora down to the Siena clerk's office and bring me a stamped adoption certificate for Gabriella Baumgarten?"

"Gabrielle, Your Honor."

The judge nodded. "Gabrielle Baumgarten."

During the recess, Catherine said, "What do you know about this, Floria?"

"Honestly, Catherine, I know nothing. The signora never speaks of her childhood or her relationship to Ada. I have heard her refer to Ada as Mama, but only in passing, from time to time, and only indirectly. Today in court is the first time I ever heard her say she was adopted. I've never read Ada's story. It is written in German and I don't read German. I had it translated into English at the signora's instructions and I sent it to you right before you came."

Giulia and Gabi returned to the court holding a document. "Adoption certificate, Your Honor. Dated September 6, 1949."

The judge examined the document and smiled. "Gabrielle Baumgarten. She is indeed an heir. Anything else, *Avvocato* Lenzini?"

"No," he said with a sour expression. He turned, began to put his papers into his briefcase and reach for his coat when the judge said, "Just a minute, *Avvocato* Lenzini. We're not finished here. Please have a seat." Then to his courtroom deputy, he said, "Would you send for the prosecutor, please?"

"The prosecutor? I have done nothing wrong."

The judge shrugged. "Well, that remains to be seen. First, let's resolve the case at hand. It is my judgment that Friede Baumgarten was the principal of the *designata* agreement and the equitable owner of her farmland. The deed from Carlo Vanucci, from the nominee to the principal's granddaughter, was valid and would have vested ownership. Quercia's claim to title could never be valid because it was subject to seizure by a Nazi officer in pursuance of an illegal act. Accordingly, the court holds that Gabriella Baumgarten Vincenzo is the legal owner.

"Now onto VinCo. It appears that VinCo, a company owned and operated by a Nazi officer and his children, acquired its properties by unlawful seizures in 1944. That needs to be rectified. The Terezín Declaration requires restitution of seized real property. Therefore, your client, VinCo, must return all of its properties to the parties that owned them in 1944."

"Your honor, VinCo's property is worth many, many millions of euros."

"That will be just recompense for the survivors, won't it?"

Lenzini laughed sardonically. "Good luck to the prosecutor. How is he going to find nine families from eighty years ago? They probably all died in concentration camps. The prosecutor is going to have an impossible job."

"And you're going to help him, *Avvocato* Lenzini. You are going to use your clients' files and their cooperation in locating the heirs of each of the parties whose property was seized. If you can't find the original families or their heirs, the Terezín Declaration instructs us to declare the property as 'heirless.' In such cases, the lands are to be

610

sold and the money given to Holocaust survivors or used for commemoration of destroyed communities."

"But, Your Honor . . ."

"And you will perform these services free of charge."

"What? Hold on, Your Honor, I am not the guilty party. I have only been a lawyer serving my clients."

"You have knowingly advocated on behalf of a Nazi organization in violation of the Terezín Declaration and Italian law. You admitted in open court today that you knew who your clients were and that they obtained the properties during the Nazi occupation. And then there is the matter of the murder of Fabio Lombardo, the missing registry book and the possible corruption of Signora Vincenzo's previous attorneys."

"But, Your Honor, you have no evidence that I had anything to do with Signor Lombardo, the registry book or any bribes."

"That is why I have sent for the prosecutor. Eventually your guilt or innocence will be determined. In the meantime, you are to suspend your practice of law and immediately place yourself at the disposal of the prosecutor's office to cooperate in any way you can. The extent of your cooperation may be a factor at your sentencing. You are not to leave the jurisdiction without my permission. You will turn in your passport this afternoon."

Then, turning to Gabi, he said, "Signora Vincenzo, the court has found that you own your property free and clear. This case is dismissed. Good luck to you."

SEVENTY-FOUR

Pienza, September 2017

The case was over, Gabi's land was secured and Catherine and Liam were making plans to return to Chicago. Gabi prepared a special bon voyage feast. "Pasta bolognese. A recipe taught to me by Grandma Friede, may she rest in peace," she said proudly.

Giulia, Gunther, Catherine, Liam, Gabi and Floria took their seats around the dinner table. Gabi said, "Floria, please go to the cellar and bring up two bottles from Ada's Vineyard."

"The blue-ribbon winners?"

"Yes, the ones titled 'Meditation 1997.' "

Midway through dinner, Gabi set her fork down. "I suppose you're looking for an explanation," she said. "You have a right to ask why I didn't tell you the story myself, why I forced you to find the truth in my mother's narrative."

Liam nodded. "Well, it would have been nice."

"I know. I'm sorry. The fear of losing this farm, so dear to my family, had placed me in a dark corner. I had been through two lawyers who told me I had no right to the land. Lenzini seemed to be in total control, and I was about to lose my family's farm. It meant so much to my mother and my grandmother that I just couldn't face losing it. As Mama used to say, I went back into my turtle shell. I was emotionally paralyzed. You were my last hope, but in truth, I didn't think we'd win. I would have told you the story, but I couldn't. I knew you'd learn the history from my mother, and if the answers were there, you'd find them."

"The answers were there, Gabi."

"I'm so glad you got to know Ada. I want you to encourage Tony to read the story as well. He's the next in line to inherit these vineyards, you know."

"I'm sure he'll care for them just as lovingly as you have."

Gabi smiled. "He'd better! Floria and Franco will stay on to make sure he does."

"So, finish the story," Liam said. "Obviously Ada lived. What happened after you boarded the train?"

"Well, I'm afraid I made quite a scene at the Theresienstadt railroad station. My mother didn't tell me that I was going to get on the train alone. I had a paper in my hand with a number on it. Mama didn't have a paper. She kissed me good-bye and told me that she couldn't go right away. She would come later and find me in Switzerland. I was only five, but I could see right through that story. I became hysterical. 'You lied to me!' I screamed. 'You said you would never leave me. You lied!'

" 'I'm only leaving for a little while,' she said. 'We only have one train ticket and that one is for you. The other passengers will take care of you and make sure you get to a children's home in Switzerland. I will come later.'

" 'No, you won't; no, you won't,' I said. 'It's just like my other mother. You promised. You promised. You said you would never leave me.'

"She hugged me. We were both in tears. 'Please get on the train, Gabi,' she pleaded. 'Please don't let that train leave without you.'

"But I wouldn't. I grabbed her skirt and held on to it as tightly as I could. I said, 'I don't want this ticket, I don't want to go to Switzerland. I don't want to go anywhere without you. I want to stay with you.'

"While we were arguing, a man stepped down off the train. 'I have a ticket and I can't use it,' he said. 'I need to stay here with my wife. She's sick and she needs me. Here, you take my ticket. You need it.'

"Mother asked him if he was sure, and he said he was. With tears in her eyes, she took the ticket, gave the man a hug and the two of us boarded the train. It took us directly into Switzerland. Mother found a job playing her violin in a restaurant. We stayed in Zurich until 1946. Then we made our way back to Italy and moved onto the farm. Just the two of us."

"So, in 1946 you and Ada moved back and took over the farming operations?"

Gabi nodded. "We did. We had help, of course. Guido and his family were there the whole time, and the vineyards were well cared for. I went to school in Pienza and then went on to get my viticulture degree at the university in Siena. We managed the farm together, Mama and me. That is why the fields have done so well.

"I married Angelo Vincenzo in 1964. He was Tony's uncle, his father's brother. Mama, Angelo and I all lived here on the farm. Angelo was happy to take a hand in farm management, because he had an accounting background. Those were happy days." Gabi paused and took a breath.

"Mama became ill in 1998, just after her eightieth birthday. Her disease took her six months later. Angelo died in 2005. Now there's just Floria and me."

"That's a wonderful story, Gabi," Catherine said. "And all those years, you never heard anything from VinCo or the Frumans or the Kleiners? Nobody wanted your land?"

616

"Not until last October."

Liam turned to Gunther. "Whatever happened to Obersturmführer Kleiner? I hope he got what was coming to him."

"Eventually, he did," Gunther said. "I was curious as well, and I asked my young associates to dig up what they could. As we know from Ada's story, Kleiner was in charge of the roundup and deportation of Jews from Rome. He sent two thousand Jews to their death. Kleiner was also the person who demanded that the Jewish community pay fifty kilos of gold. After Rome fell to the Allies, Kleiner moved into SS headquarters in northern Italy and was active in rounding up Jews from the smaller towns. He bears responsibility for the massacre of three hundred and thirty-five Jews and partisans in the Ardeatine caves.

"After the war, Kleiner was sought as a war criminal, but he escaped through the SS network into Greece. He used his stolen wealth to set up an estate on one of the Greek islands and from there he managed his VinCo property with his sons. He was discovered in 1951, and just before his arrest, he escaped again, this time to the south of France. The Nazi hunters caught up with him in 1954, and he was extradited to Italy for trial before a military tribunal. He was sentenced to life imprisonment, and he died in prison in 1958."

"What happened to Elsa Fruman?"

Gunther shook his head. "We don't know what happened to Elsa, but it is likely that Kleiner considered the Quercia property as a gift to her and his daughter, Gerda. I'm sure that his sons kept track of the Frumans, and when Gerda died, they knew they had to acquire Gabi's property to keep the world from finding out that all these properties were seized. The Berlin probate case lasted almost a year, an administrator's deed was issued to VinCo and the case was sent to Lenzini in October 2016."

"Enough talk of the Kleiners," Gabi said. "We are celebrating tonight! Floria, let's fill our glasses and raise a toast to my nephew, Tony, who found these wonderful people."

"To Tony! *Saluti.*"

"I have a question," Liam said. "Did you ever learn anything about the man who gave your mother his train ticket?"

Gabi nodded. "We didn't know him. When we arrived in Zurich, one of the passengers told us that the man had been on the Jewish Council and had served the community well. But his wife wasn't sick. She had died months earlier. He saw our dilemma and was just a good man who wanted us to have his ticket."

"Whatever happened to the Romittis?"

"Mama spent years looking for Natalia and her family. She finally learned that Natalia's partisan unit had been taken in 1945. Naomi

618

and Nico, despite Natalia's warnings, returned to their home in Pienza and were caught in a sweep. Records from Yad Vashem confirm that they perished at Auschwitz."

After dinner, Gabi rose from the table, left the room and returned with a violin case. On the side, in white paint, was the legend: BAUMGARTEN, PHILHARMONIE. "This was Grandfather Jacob's violin, the one my mother played after he died. It has been played at the Philharmonie, the Bologna State Opera, the Baths of Caracalla, the Rome Opera, the concert hall at Theresienstadt, the restaurants of Zurich and of course, in this very house." She opened the case.

"May I?" Catherine said, and Gabi nodded.

Catherine gently lifted the violin from its case. "It's beautiful. It's like touching a holy object. Do you play it as well?" she asked.

Gabi shook her head. "This violin would know if someone else was playing it. My mother taught me to play, but I am not in her class. I play her other violin, the one she played before her father died." She smiled. "Sometimes I play in the middle of the night. I pretend she's sitting with me, telling me to practice my scales."

"After you returned to the farm, did Ada ever play professionally again?"

Gabi smiled. "I know what you're asking. It was always her dream to be a permanent member of a major orchestra. The first woman. And she was, for a brief time, in Rome. But I guess dreams change. Sometimes you get new dreams. She was offered the opportunity to rejoin the Rome Opera Orchestra in 1946 and she turned it down. We had been through a lot and she wanted to stay on the farm. Also, she had bitter memories of Rome and wouldn't have been comfortable living there. Maybe she wanted mother-daughter time. She did make several guest solo appearances. She even played with Gigli on two more occasions. He died in 1955. I think she played as much as she wanted. I never sensed that she was unfulfilled. That would be out of character for my mother."

"She was a remarkable woman, Gabi."

"Everything you read about her, all of the wonderful qualities she had, the ones you learned about because you read her memoir, please know that they are all true. She was an angel. I have something else to show you, my prized possession"

She left for a moment and returned with a leather portfolio. "This is the original memoir. It is in my mother's handwriting, the one she wrote while we were in Theresienstadt. I found it in my bag when we arrived in Zurich. I've kept this memoir right next to my bed for all these years. As my mother intended, they are my bedtime stories."

Catherine nodded. "She will never leave you."

ABOUT THE AUTHOR

Ronald H. Balson is a Chicago trial attorney, an educator, and writer. His practice has taken him to several international venues. He is also the author of *Karolina's Twins, Saving Sophie,* and the international bestseller *Once We Were Brothers.*

The employees of Thorndike Press hope you have enjoyed this Large Print book. All our Thorndike, Wheeler, and Kennebec Large Print titles are designed for easy reading, and all our books are made to last. Other Thorndike Press Large Print books are available at your library, through selected bookstores, or directly from us.

For information about titles, please call:
  (800) 223-1244

or visit our website at:
  gale.com/thorndike

To share your comments, please write:
  Publisher
  Thorndike Press
  10 Water St., Suite 310
  Waterville, ME 04901